WILL YOU
KEEP ME
TOMORROW?

Steven Irwin Fine

CENTRAL PARK SOUTH PUBLISHING

Publisher: Central Park South Publishing
www.centralparksouthpublishing.com

Fiction

Cover Design: L1 Graphics
Book layout: Victor Marcos

ISBN:
978-1-7370777-3-2 (pbk)
978-1-7370777-6-3 (hbk)

Contents

Part One

PART ONE

Chapter One

The worn-out tires skidded on the wet slippery road as the old faithful Holden that had seen better days pulled off the highway and slowly stopped by the side of the road. The engine sputtered and died. Exhausted and tired, the seventeen-year-old Kingswood just peated out.

The driver's door opened, and the hinges let out a rustic screech that filled the cold night air. A hand reached out to grab the handle, and Sophie stumbled out, holding on tight to the door for support.

"No, No—not now! Come on, please don't give up on us. Please!"

She looked around. The long road was deserted. Not a vehicle in sight. Fear gripped her as she wildly spun around, hoping against hope that a car would appear from nowhere. Tears welled up in her eyes. A cry came from inside the car. She leaned into the front passenger seat and awkwardly pulled out an old shabby-looking wicker bassinet. She had found it a few weeks earlier in a dumpster at the back of an alleyway with an assortment of household garbage. It was far from ideal, but it was the best she could do under the circumstances.

"Ssh," she cooed, trying to calm the infant. She opened the back passenger door and placed the bassinet on the back seat. She tried to soothe the baby by placing her palm on her chest and abdomen, gently rubbing her. She was wet and hungry.

Sophie began to shake and tremble uncontrollably. It wasn't because of the cold night but half-an-hour earlier, upstairs in her dingy studio apartment, she had added another bruise and hit to her vein.

The baby cried even louder. Helpless and confused, Sophie shut the passenger door and crawled behind the steering wheel. She closed her eyes and pleaded under her breath, and turned the ignition.

The engine fluttered and sputtered. Sophie felt a bit like the starter motor, overworked and old.

She turned the key again, and miraculously, the car kicked into life, spluttering.

Her shaking hand found the windscreen wipers by mistake but finally found the switch for the lights. She floored the clutch and stuck the gear into second instead of first. She failed to check the mirrors before the vehicle lurched back onto the empty highway, jerking, squeaking, creaking, and rattling.

The baby was crying softly; she desperately needed changing and feeding.

The radio had died a long time ago, so Sophie started to talk to herself out loud for the company and perhaps for the baby as well.

"I should have gone to America, but I came to Australia instead. I remember seeing the Sydney Opera House for the first time on TV. It was like Mother Mary's temple bursting into the sky. Then someone told me about the Grand Prix and the Australian Open Tennis, which attracted tourists from all over the world. All the rich, influential people from everywhere. Then the International Surfing competition. The Food and Wine exhibitions. It sounded so much fun and the cuddly cute koala bears. You'd love those. People flock from all over to be here, but what have I achieved? Nothing. It's already 1988, and I have been here nearly two years, and… nothing." Sophie stuttered as she spoke, trying to hold back the galling reality.

Amazingly, the baby had stopped crying and was listening to every word.

Gripping the wheel, Sophie took a deep breath and cleared her dry throat.

"There was no work in Moscow. Jobs had dried up, and nothing. I took a risk and came here to find work, even though it was illegal. Then I saw it was impossible with no paperwork. So, I had to seek out men. I needed food, shelter, and money. And where has it got me? Nowhere, just stuck in a vicious cycle. I haven't seen much of this country, not a wild koala bear or kangaroo. Yes, I saw them in a zoo, but that's it! God, I feel I'm trapped in a zoo too. I see low-class customers and my pimp visiting me in my cage."

Her anxiety subsided a little as she spoke, and the baby remained attentive, so she continued.

"First, Frankie gave me drugs for free. He said this was the country where men loved their women just as much as their BBQs and beer. He got me hooked; then they were no longer free—evil bastard! I needed him for money, for my drugs, and now I am tired, bitter, and have you. What am I going to do? Enough! I have had enough of him—his cheap aftershave, his crooked teeth and crooked wig, and his '70s synthetic fashion style. His whole outfit would look better on a scarecrow and far more effective in a cornfield," she spat, finally unraveling and letting loose.

"The day I was late, I knew straight away I was pregnant. I am ashamed to say I have no idea who your father is. There were so many possibilities..." Sophie tailed off.

"Malishka, my little girl. You grew in my stomach, and I tried to hide you, but Frankie noticed and beat me. Abort—have the baby? I went back and forth. I even thought I could come clean at some point."

Sophie looked out the windscreen up at the night sky ahead. It was a clear winter's night with a few clouds and a full moon. The old Holden was still the only vehicle on the road. She continued driving in silence for a while. There was no noise from the back seat; the baby must have fallen asleep. Sophie retreated into her thoughts until the self-pity and remorse bubbled over, and she started talking to herself again.

"A backstreet doctor — if he was even a doctor — delivered you. Luckily, my neighbor is overseas at the moment and left his keys with me. All his keys, including his car keys. It's thanks to him we have a ride tonight. Do you know why he left his keys with me?" Sophie asked, glancing in the mirror at her sleeping daughter.

"You know why? Because I also did favors for him and, besides...."

Sophie had been driving haphazardly for nearly an hour and well out of Footscray, heading East. She passed Blackburn, going through areas that she had never been to before. After an hour-and-a-half, she found herself following a sign to Sassafras.

She just wanted to drive. She wanted to clear her mind. She had no plan.

Now and again, a car flicked its lights or hooted as the old jalopy swayed from side to side as she tried to stay focused and in her lane.

Her eyes were bloodshot, and her head was pounding as the initial high from the drug wore off. The baby started crying again, and it was hard to think, let alone concentrate.

The road inclined, and she put the car in third gear to climb the hill. The baby's cries increased in volume. Her head felt like a coconut split in two. She couldn't take it anymore. She had to get away from the incessant screaming. She pulled off the road, stopping on the deserted hill.

The car light's beam lit up the tall trees, standing like wooden giants reaching for the black sky, and still, the baby cried with hunger.

She climbed out of the car, unsteady on her feet, highly agitated and disorientated. She turned to the rear door and swung it open. She clumsily dragged the tiny bassinet from the backseat and carried it to the other side of the old Holden. She placed it on the ground next to the wild ferns, surrounded by weeds and bushes. Sophie's mouth quivered as she took one last sorrowful look at her daughter and got back in the car, leaving little Malishka alone in the dark on the side of the road in the middle of nowhere.

She could hear the baby screaming. She probably knew she had been abandoned by her mother. Her screams pierced the icy cold temperature, and somewhere in the dark, an owl shrieked, which made Malishka's cries spill over into hysteria.

What she did not know was that somewhere off in the distance, a hungry fox out on his midnight hunt heard the now constant cries. Inquisitive, the animal sniffed the air, and the predator picked up the new interesting smell and began trotting towards its menu just as the moon disappeared behind the clouds.

Chapter Two

Chester Jones replaced the receiver with a self-satisfied smile on his face. He made a fist with his right hand, "Yes… yes… yes!" he celebrated quietly by himself, eyeing the exclusive bottle of scotch on his desk. It was one of the rarest bottles in the world—a Glenfiddich Janet Sheed Roberts Reserve. He picked it up, admiring the 1955 bottle anticipating the smooth taste, envisioning the comfort it would bring.

His reverie was interrupted by the cleaning lady appearing at his office door. "Is everything in order, Mr. Jones?"

Chester was impressed. She cleaned several floors of the office tower, and even though she did not know him personally, she must have seen his picture on his large jarrah mahogany desk. It had been taken at Chester's golf club and was inscribed: *To Chester Jones in appreciation of your humanity.*

"Certainly! It could not be better," he smiled happily.

"Good, sir. I have finished for the day. Have a pleasant evening," she said, turning around to leave.

"Oh, I certainly will."

Impulsively, he asked the woman her name, buoyed by his good mood.

"Maggie," she replied.

"Maggie, will you be cooking dinner for your family tonight?" he inquired.

She paused for a few seconds, caught off guard by his sudden pleasantries, and then said, "Sir? I have some pizzas in the freezer that I will heat up for everyone. Why do you ask?"

Chester reached into his suit jacket pocket and produced his wallet. "Why don't you take them out for a surprise dinner tonight? My treat," he said, fishing out a bill and offering her the money.

"But why, Mr. Jones?" she asked, her eyes widening when she saw it was a one-hundred-dollar note.

"I am celebrating and feel like sharing, Maggie. Here, come on, take it now. I need to leave soon, too as my wife is waiting for me." He stretched out his hand; there were two, not one, hundred-dollar bills.

"Thank you, Mr. Jones—wow! Thank you for being so generous, sir!" she gaped in disbelief. Her face was as red as an overripe tomato, and she hurried away in amazement at her sudden luck. In less than a minute, she had just earned two and a half days' salary.

Chester grinned. It felt good to bring a smile to someone's face and see their overt surprise. He wanted to shout out again but decided not to.

His sudden generosity was from the multi-million dollar deal he had had just secured—a massive equipment order from the head of one of the leading mining groups purchasing dozens of Caterpillar bulldozers, graders, crushers, excavators, dump trucks, and crawlers. The deal had taken months and months to negotiate, and Chester had used all his savvy acumen to navigate and cajole. His charming, persuasive salesman techniques had finally landed his catch. As CEO of Infinite Mining Equipment, or IME, as it was known, he was emerging as one of the front runners in the mining industry. He had steadily built the company's profile over the years and methodically placed trade articles in the various business page sections of national newspapers and international mining magazines.

Chester had paid nearly one hundred thousand dollars for the bottle of scotch on his desk, one of only fifteen in existence to commemorate the late granddaughter of Glenfiddich's founder William Grant. It was worth a lot more now, and Chester decided to give it to the mining magnate who lived in the Dandenong region. He had already told him he was going to stop by later that night with a gift, a very special one.

Chester's office was located on Collins Street near the famous ANZ building—one of Melbourne's historical landmarks designed by renowned architect William Wardell in the late 1880s, a majestic concept for revival the Gothic vision by banker Sir George Verdon.

He locked his office and took the elevator down to the parking garage underneath the building. His brand-new jet-black Audi S-Seven was waiting for him in his assigned parking space. He had taken delivery of this sleek beauty only a week ago, and, with the deal in his pocket, he felt like a king. He glanced at his exclusive Swiss Patek Philippe watch, which was almost the same value as his Audi S-Seven, and climbed in. He hit the speed dial button on the console. After a few rings, his wife answered.

"Hi, sweetie, how is my gorgeous wife tonight?"

"My, someone sounds like they are in a good mood — something happen that I should know about?"

The pitch of his voice was a giveaway. "I'll tell you the good news when I get home. All I can say is put some Cristal on ice," he teased. "I will be home in an hour or so; I have to stop by a client first. Love you, bye for now."

After many years of marriage, Megan was used to her husband's cryptic messages and, although intrigued, didn't push him. He had already hung up before she could say goodbye.

Most likely, she was now on her way to the kitchen to pick out the champagne to chill. Or if he would finally take her to Fiji as promised, work always gets in the way.

Chester sat in the driver's seat, admiring the latest technology and taking in the luxury leather surroundings. He had carefully placed his expensive gift on the passenger floor and put the car in reverse. His mind turned to the new deal and the logistics required to deliver such a major contract.

Chester was still an attractive man in his mid-50s. Over six feet tall, he had managed to maintain his weight and remain fit and healthy despite long hours and pressures from work. He had once boasted thick black hair that was now more grey than black; his salt and pepper mustache was the only thing that betrayed his age.

He pulled out of the garage onto Collins Street and crossed over the city's historic Yarra River. It was rush hour and already dark. It was the middle of winter, and the city was bustling with crowds of people scurrying to catch trams and trains for their ride home. A lively metropolitan city, Melbourne was home to nearly three million people and a number of bars and restaurants were filling up with customers ready to celebrate the end of the week and kick off their weekend in style.

Chester weaved his way through the busy Friday night traffic, and soon he passed the famous Chadstone Shopping Centre with all its sprawling fashion designer stores and its high-end retailers before joining Route 22 and heading towards the suburban town of Ferntree Gully. The Audi hugged the road, and Chester put his foot on the gas as the traffic thinned out, and he left the electric city vibe behind.

He knew he was crazy to make such a long drive so late in the dark, far from home, but he wanted to surprise his client and show his deep appreciation for his contribution to securing such a rich deal for the company. He thought about how his client would react to his generous gift and focused on how the visit would go.

Forty minutes later, Chester found himself driving through the old picturesque community of Ferntree Gully, but the darkness prevented him from admiring the popular tourist hiking trails and parks. Ferntree Gully was part of the Dandenong Ranges National Park, where the

Kokoda Memorial Trail attracts visitors from all over the world to take the *1000 steps* to honor the WWII vets. He only remembered it was the home of the celebrated cricketer Shane Warne, who captained the Australian cricket team to many victories.

But Chester had other things on his mind. Lost in thought and enjoying the solitude, the drive out to Sassafras was the perfect excuse to test the new car's suspension. Alone in the dark on the empty winding road, he was immersed in the euphoria of his new toy.

"Not far now," he thought when he saw the sign for Sassafras and turned onto Route 26.

He glanced at his Swiss timepiece. In about 15 minutes, he would be in the tiny scenic town nestled in the Dandenong Ranges. It was one of Megan's favorite trips. She adored *Miss Marple's Tearoom,* and so did he. It was a wonderful homage to the memory of Agatha Christie's notably fictional character and offered the best English Ploughman's lunches and afternoon Devonshire teas. Set in a purpose-built Tudor-style home, the restaurant was decked out with many Miss Marple memorabilia and trinkets adorning the walls, and the effect was completed with waitresses dressed in the old fashion black and white uniforms from the 50s.

Route 26 was deserted, which was just as well. Now, Chester really had the opportunity to test his new car and see how it handled the steep hills and corners. He wound down the windows and let the cold night air in as he accelerated.

"Now let's see what you've got" he grinned.

His Audi boasted a four-liter twin-turbo V8 engine, and it swallowed the Dandenong steep hills in almost silence. Chester was fifty-five years old, but tonight he felt like a teenager behind the wheel.

A few minutes before reaching Sassafras and while cruising up the hill on the Mount Dandenong Tourist Road, the vehicle's headlights captured a fleeting glimpse of something that caught his eye that was odd.

He continued for a few hundred metres more before he decided to turn around and investigate. He had no idea why but something made him curious, whatever it was looked out of place.

When he neared the strange-shaped object, he saw a layby up ahead, managed to do a U-turn, and pulled up behind. In the car lights, he saw a fox scurrying for safety and disappearing into the dark undergrowth. It almost looked irritable and disappointed.

He put the car into park mode and left the engine purring. He cautiously approached the dark object.

He nearly broke the world high jump record when he heard the desperate cry. His heart beat loudly as he gathered his senses and covered his mouth in total disbelief.

He peered into the basket, and in the shadows of the car lights, he saw a tiny baby, pale and nearly blue from the freezing cold.

The temperature was dropping rapidly, and it would be close to freezing during the night. Chester already felt the chill on his cheeks and nose the moment he had stepped out of the Audi.

He saw a soft dirty toy that looked like it had been a cute fluffy little koala when it was new.

His heart was thumping; his throat felt dry, and the palms of his hands were damp like the Dandenong dew.

The baby cried again. It's cry horse from the exposure, and God knows how long it had been there. The little one looked at him with desperate, lonely, empty eyes. Chester guessed it could not be more than a few weeks old. Gently, he touched the child and could feel it was sopping wet.

Shocked, he looked around nervously as though expecting to see whoever had done this horrible deed. No one was in sight. His mind was racing. He was confused and perplexed that any human being could dump a baby on the side of the road like this.

He started shaking; his teeth chattered from the cold and shock, and it sounded like a machine gun going off in the distance. He had to get the baby to the nearest hospital or police station so they could launch an immediate investigation and get the urgent medical treatment the infant obviously needed.

A few cars occasionally passed by while he considered what to do, but they ignored Chester's Audi on the side of the road.

As Chester was looking around amongst the overgrown ferns looking for clues, a vehicle pulled up alongside Chester's car.

"You all right there, buddy?" a deep voice shouted from within the vehicle.

Chester, nervous about revealing his find to a stranger, had to think fast. "Yeah," Chester waved, "All good, just taking a leak."

"No worries, man," the concerned driver said and drove off.

As soon as the road was empty and no headlights were in view, Chester picked up the bassinet gently and carried it to his car. He opened up the passenger door and placed the wet and smelly baby on the seat. He quickly removed his cashmere coat and covered the freezing little one. He shut the door and jumped behind the wheel. He found another place to turn around and floored the accelerator towards the police station he had noticed on the way.

Chester's head was spinning, but he had one clear thought: get the baby to safety.

The baby whimpered, it was obviously very weak, and the overpowering cocktail smell of urine, fecal matter, and vomit permeated the brand-new interior.

"Hush, little one, hush, ssh...ssh...ssh," Chester tried to soothe and placate the infant while trying to keep the terror he felt out of his voice. He glanced at the speedometer. He was doing 95mph in a 65mph speed limit zone and immediately tapped the brakes up and down as he saw the bright blue sign of the police station appear a few hundred metres ahead on the left.

Slowing down, he turned his indicator on but then something happened. In an instant, he turned it off and increased his speed again, and headed straight for home. He nervously glanced in his rear-view mirror to see if, by some chance, a police car might be behind him or if anyone was following.

He had suddenly realized what this could mean to him and Megan.

The foundling had gone quiet, and Chester was worried. He looked over to see if the baby was still alive. It wasn't moving. He turned up the volume of a song playing on FM. The baby didn't stir. He cranked the volume even louder and louder until it was deafening. Suddenly the baby began to cry again, and he turned the volume down. Its tiny rough voice was pitiful. The poor thing was dehydrated. Its mouth so dry, that it had no more saliva.

Chester hit the speed dial button and called his brother.

"Lance… Lance, listen," he said as soon as his brother answered.

"What's the matter? You sound nervous. Are you all right?"

"You wouldn't believe it. I've got a baby. I just found an abandoned baby on the roadside in the Dandenong ranges. Just be at my place in twenty minutes and bring your medical kit. The little thing is cold, wet and…" he had to pause, "I think slipping away."

Chester hung up before Lance could ask any questions and rerouted his journey to Toorak.

Then he called the mining magnate. He apologized profusely and told him he had a puncture and because it was late, he needed to return home. He would see him in the near future and would hang on to the special gift until then. The mining tycoon was completely understanding.

Chapter Three

Sophie had been driving aimlessly for over two hours; she was lost, both geographically and psychologically. Although still stoned, she was a tad more in control of her driving, but her reflexes were dull, and she was confused.

It had started to rain. She fumbled and activated the indicator by mistake instead of the wipers. Then she figured it out but failed to switch off the indicator.

She was completely turned around and was now heading south away from Melbourne. The fading lights of the city resembled a shard on the horizon, and then they disappeared as she drove further and further away. What she had done in the Dandenong rankled her. She knew it was wrong, but she had no choice. She has no one to turn to. No family. No friends. No resources.. She decided to keep driving, no matter how long it took, just to escape what she felt, even if it took the entire night.

The jalopy took her onto Princes Highway, and it continued to drizzle; she passed the waterfront tourist town of Geelong without knowing and headed southwest. She found herself just managing to keep the car from going over the edge of a steep cliff as she neared the Great Ocean Road. All the lights looked the same; the signposts meant nothing to her; she was so out of her element as she arrived in the artistic coastal little town of Lorne. She pushed on. The B100 road took her near the Cumberland River, and as the Kingswood came across the beach, it finally spluttered, backfired, jerked, and the engine died. This time for good.

Sophie tried a few times ,but there was no spark… nada… zilch. She looked at the fuel gauge—empty! She got out and, just like with her baby, walked away, abandoning the Holden by the side of the road. Dazed and groggy, she found herself stumbling towards the beach. The moon was full, and when it appeared from behind the clouds, its brightness glowed across the water, shimmering, inviting. She was shivering, this time from the cold. Her cotton floral dress underneath her denim jacket was no match for the bitter weather. The wet drizzle was starting to seep through her clothes, and she walked with purpose onto the beach, clutching a small plastic bag in one hand and stumbling every now and then.

The rain was gaining momentum and was coming down in sheets. The moon slipped behind a cloud, and she failed to see the log that had washed ashore until she tripped and fell face down into the wet sand. Her knee seared in pain, and she looked down at the nasty gash. It probably required medical attention, but her brain was so numb with pain there was no room to comprehend anything else. Blood oozed out and trickled down her leg.

She sat there on the damp beach looking around, but all she could see were grey shadows. She hesitated, then she opened the small plastic bag with her shaking hands and swallowed at least two dozen strong sleeping tablets, shoving them in her mouth as if they were a handful of peanuts. She stood up and hobbled towards the water.

Her feet felt the icy cold water through her flimsy sneakers as soon as she stepped into ocean bay, but it didn't stop her. She carried on, wading in, ignoring the waves coming to shore. Her teeth chattering a-mile-a-minute, but again it didn't stop her. When her feet could no longer touch the bottom, a strong current swept her deeper and deeper into the vast ocean. The moon danced behind a dark cloud, and the sea became black.

Her head bobbed up for a few seconds.

"Sssorry, Malishka. Sorry. You didn't deserve it. You did nothing wrong. I dumped you, and now it is my turn. Goodbye, my little one, goodbye Australia" were the few words she managed to utter.

She swallowed water, and when her head bobbed up for the last time, she gurgled a stentorian choke, gasping and coughing until there was nothing.

Chester pulled into the driveway of his home and felt a rush of appreciation for his baby brother. Lance had never been interested in the cutthroat world of big business — Chester's world — choosing general practice as a career, but while not always approving of his big brother, he could always be relied upon in a crisis.

By the time Chester had opened his car door, Megan and Lance were standing on the porch under the light. Bonzo, their six-month-old Kelpie pup, came bounding out into the driveway to greet him, jumping up and licking him with excitement. The pup was a recent gift to his wife to fill the void of their childless marriage. Normally it was a joy to be greeted with such exuberance, but the boisterous pup prevented Chester from getting out of his car. "Down, boy," he tried to calm him, rubbing his head and pushing him away at the same time.

"What's going on?" Lance asked over the yelping.

Chester leaned into the car and pulled out the dirty bassinet wrinkling his nose from a new whiff that filled the air. There was not a sound from the basket.

"Darling," he said, looking at his wife. "Lance, thank God you're made it."

Megan and Lance stared at Chester, holding the basket.

"What happened?" they both asked simultaneously.

"Chester, for God's sake, what is going on? Who is the baby?" Megan demanded in shock and surprise.

"Let's talk inside," Lance barked like a regimental sergeant major as he looked into the bassinet and saw the urgency.

Chester followed them into the warm house carrying the baby, shivering from the cold without his coat.

Bonzo, curious and inquisitive, trotted next to them, eager to be part of the rescue crew as he kept a close eye on the new arrival.

"Megan, quickly, go get towels, soap, and hot water—and turn the heating up," Lance instructed, taking charge.

"But..."

"No buts, go now!"

She obeyed.

Then Lance turned to Chester.

"Chester, what the hell is happening? Where did you find this poor baby?" he demanded, peering over his glasses and scratching his neck.

Megan hurried back with the towels and carried a bowl of hot water and soap.

The baby's face was now flushed, the skin dry. It had started to cry from the temperature change.

"For God's sake, it's crying without tears. This means it's totally dehydrated." Lance noted and removed all the baby's clothing while Megan handed him the towels. She ran back to the kitchen to get a plastic trash bag to put the soiled garments in.

"It is a little girl," Megan whispered. "Wow, look—she has one blue eye and one brown," she exclaimed, pointing at the baby's eyes.

"She can't be more than a few days old," Lance observed. "Her tummy is bloated, and this is a bad sign of severe dehydration. Shit! Look at her skin; there is no elasticity." Lance turned to his older brother and said, "Call an ambulance now, and no fucking buts."

This was the first time in her life that Megan had heard her brother-in-law swear.

Ignoring Chester and Megan, Lance checked the little one's blood pressure, which was extremely low. He was grim. He immediately mixed a concoction of sodium chloride, filtered water, sodium bicarbonate, glucose, and something else in a baby bottle he had brought in his medic bag.

He shook it vigorously and placed it in the baby girl's mouth.

The foundling sucked slowly, then faster, and soon she finished the bottle. He cradled her and burped her while he prepared another one.

Afterward, he listened to the little one's heart. The baby was now much warmer and clean and dry. "This little one has got fight in her. A normal baby would have been dead by now. She's a little tiger." Lance was now breathing a little easier.

"It is not common, the two different colored eyes," Lance commented. "It is known as heterochromia iridis, rare but nothing to worry about. Did you call the paramedics yet?"

Megan picked up the phone and was about to call 911 when Chester grabbed her wrist. "No, not yet," he ordered.

"What the hell are you talking about?" Lance interjected. "She needs to be hospitalized—and now! We can't play around—this is serious, Chester."

His brother looked at him steadily and spoke in a voice that Lance had never heard before from his usually so in-control brother. It was a pleading tone.

"Lance, please, Megan and I have always wanted children, but it's never happened for us, despite the In Vitro treatments, the medications, and all the tests imaginable. And now they say we're too old to adopt," Chester paused and gulped.

"Damn it; we are a loving, stable couple with more money than we could ever wish for. Today I closed the largest deal of my career worth millions," he looked lovingly at the baby. "And now, this poor little girl turns up. She needs parents. We want a child." Chester's eyes had tears in them, "Why can't she be our daughter?" he pleaded.

When Megan saw this, she started to quietly weep. Her inability to have children with the man she loved had always been a great sorrow, making her fear for her sanity at times, but until now, she had not realized that Chester also felt such deep sorrow. Her husband, who was always in control of everything, had not been able to control thi, up until now ... perhaps, there was still a chance for them to be parents.

"Chester, for heaven's sake, you know nothing about this child," Lance protested, interrupting Megan's thoughts and bringing her abruptly back to reality. "Even if someone did abandon her, she could still have family somewhere who want her. You can't just take a baby because you want one," Lance pointed out, his voice rising. "Besides, how will you suddenly explain a daughter showing up out of the blue?"

Chester knew by that last question Lance was weakening.

"We will take care of her," he said quickly, having thought about this since calling Lance. "'We'll watch the news on TV, and if no one reports her as missing, she will be our daughter, today, tomorrow, and forever. We'll tell people we adopted her privately. We won't have to say anything more than that."

Megan tried to hide her smile.

Chester looked at his wife and brother and then added, "Not a word to anyone. This will just be between the three of us. Our secret. If no one wants her, then why not? If she doesn't have a family, we can be her family. All we have to do is wait and see and then we'll know."

It was hard for Lance to fight his brother's reasoning and logic. He knew how much he and his sister-in-law desperately wanted a family.

"Lance, I want you to instruct us on every little detail about her care and nourishment so she can become healthy and strong as soon as possible. We need to know what type of milk, and what else we need to do, and what we must not do. We need you and can't do this without your support."

Lance was silent for a few seconds. He was weighing up what Chester was asking him to do professionally. He knew it was wrong, and it would ruin his career. He would be struck off as a GP. But on the other hand, he felt pity for his brother and Megan. He knew they would make good parents, and this baby had been left to die, even if no one knew the circumstances. The room went silent. Even the baby was quiet, and Bonzo looked up with sad soppy eyes. Lance glanced at the expectant parents, "You have my word — on one condition."

Chester and Megan held their breath.

"If no one claims this child and you raise her, you do not ever tell her how you came to find her. No child wants to know that they had been thrown out like garbage."

The tension in the room evaporated ,and both Megan and Chester suddenly looked years younger and heaved a sigh of relief.

"What shall we call her?" Megan tearfully said with excitement. "She has no name."

"Well, I found her in the bush amongst the ferns and red eucalyptus trees." Chester pondered. "Let's call her Fern."

Megan's eyes glowed, "Hello, Fern Jones. Welcome home, Fern Jones, I'm your mamma," she whispered, cradling her in her arms.

Chapter Four

S enior Detective Inspector Bruce Nash was taking a large bite out of his breakfast sandwich and catching up on paperwork when he received the call from a patrol officer. A fisherman had seen something shocking on the shoreline just a couple of kilometers from Lorne; a torso had washed up on the beach.

'Thanks, constable; where exactly did you say?"

"Outside Lorne on the Apollo Bay Road at the beach by the Cumberland River."

"OK, that's about seven kilometers or so from Lorne?"

"Copy that, sir; you will see a police vehicle parked by the road. A couple of our guys are already there."

"On my way, constable."

Bruce Nash had spent many years in the Australian military. He had a great interest in crime, so when he resigned from the army as a Captain, he followed his passion and joined the police force.

When he arrived on the scene, there were two police officers from Lorne talking with the fisherman, who had discovered the body, along with a number of inquisitive and hungry seagulls. When he approached the torso, a crab scurried away, and a small cloud of blowflies hovered like miniature drones over their booty.

"Sir," the senior officer on the scene addressed Detective Inspector Nash. His tag said his name was Brady. "Looks like a shark attack. The M.E. is on his way and will be here any minute."

Nash studied the body, muttering aloud. The officers did not know if he was talking to them or himself.

"There's a dark birthmark on the remaining leg near the ankle," Nash pointed out. "The eyes are very unusual—one blue and one brown."

"Sir?" Brady interrupted Nash's thoughts. "I need to show you something," Brady said. "Follow me," he beckoned to Nash while he placed the other officer to watch over the corpse.

"One second, constable," Nash said, suddenly noticing that the fisherman was nowhere in sight, "Where is the fisherman who found the body? He was here a minute ago."

"I released him, sir. He is in a state of shock, and besides I have all his details."

"All right then, what is it you wish to show me?" Nash asked as he looked around, surveying the area.

"This way, sir, just over there."

They walked at most a hundred metres to a large piece of driftwood and Officer Brady pointed out what appeared to be a small piece of skin and flesh on a broken tip and possibly blood.

Within minutes the forensic officer arrived on the scene with an assistant accompanied by the coroner's van. The area was immediately cornered off.

"Hello, Bruce,'" Doctor Max Blumenthal boomed as he approached the crime scene.

"Good to see you again, Max," Nash responded, and they shook hands.

"Look at the eyes, Max."

Max twisted his mouth from side to side, "Yes, indeed. Interesting… heterochromia iris. It can be hereditary, you know. It is more common in animals like dogs and cats. Australian Shepherds and Dalmatians are well known for it."

Dr. Blumenthal spent a couple of intense hours documenting every detail of the body and its location and measuring and taking copious notes of the distance and location in relation to the driftwood. He took hundreds of photographs before calling the paramedics to remove the body.

The entire log was also removed, and the jagged piece of wood with the tissue and flesh evidence was bagged and tagged for further examination.

An abandoned old Holden with an empty gas tank was also examined, fingerprinted, and searched from top to toe for any kind of evidence that would identify the body of the young woman lying on the beach.

"Max, let me know what the findings are as soon as you can. It looks like she must have gashed herself on the log before drowning, which would have attracted the shark. It is strange; if that is the case ,how come she washed back to the same area," Nash said, shaking his head trying to figure it out. "Anyway, warm regards to your lovely wife."

"Thanks, Bruce, and to yours too. We will talk soon." With that, Max walked back up the beach with his medical case and disappeared to his car that was parked above the rocks and out of sight of the public eye.

Nash stayed behind and continued to comb the area for any other last-minute clues that might have been missed. The heavy rain the night before had washed away a lot of potential evidence. Turning up blank, he instructed the two officers to remove the crime tape. He also instructed for the old Holden to be taken away by a tow-truck for further investigation.

Within a couple of hours, the sun was shining, the beach was clear, the crabs had disappeared, and life was back to normal. Even the gulls were soon resuming their standard flight over the waves and scanning the golden beach for food.

Nash sat in his office looking at his calendar. He was looking at two more years before it was *adios, sayonara,* and his well-deserved retirement. He had been on the job for 30 years and was looking forward to a well-earned rest.

He started to type up his report while looking at his notebook.

Partial body found on Apollo Bay Beach by local fisherman. No report of anyone missing in the area—female—one blue eye, one brown. Shark attack, birthmark on the remaining leg, left leg, and near the ankle, one arm missing and a hand.

Nash ran the license plate of the Holden. The car belonged to Michael Derian, an Australian citizen who had immigrated to Melbourne from Armenia. The car had not been reported stolen. Customs and border patrol confirmed the owner was abroad. Nash paused for a moment and sipped his coffee. He started to add some more notes to his report when his phone rang.

"Bruce, it's Max. We haven't finished the autopsy ,but I thought you would like to know what we have found so far. It's important."

"Shoot, Max, I'm listening."

"The woman was suffering from postpartum bleeding."

"Post what? You mean she's just had a baby?"

"Yes, Bruce, postpartum bleeding or lochia means she would have given birth in the last few days. It is a natural discharge, and it means there is a baby somewhere out there missing its mother. He or she could be dead or alive," Max said with some urgency. "Also, the poor soul was a drug addict. We found a high level of barbiturates in her blood. She overdosed and must have taken her own life. The bite marks are from a great white shark and possibly some other smaller fish. The shark didn't kill her, though, she drowned. She would have almost certainly been half-dead before she put a foot in the water."

Nash listened while scratching the back of his head, "Thank you, doc, thank you, it may just make my investigation easier." He scratched his head again in deep thought.

"Postpartum bleeding, postpartum," Nash rubbed his face. He now had another problem on his hands—a missing newborn. He muttered to himself as he scribbled a few more words into his notebook before picking up the phone to his supervisor.

Lance left the Jones residence in the early hours of the following morning.

Megan and Chester had hardly slept in between checking on baby Fern throughout the night.

Chester turned his cell phone off and took the day off. He deserved the break. At 6 am, his ears were glued to the radio listening to the local news, but there was no report of a lost or abandoned baby.

At 7 am, Megan and Chester were in the kitchen watching the morning show on TV and scanning for any news alert.

The presenter reported zero about a lost baby. The top news was about the latest political rivalry campaign, a scandalous doping case in the AFL league, and an unidentified body that had been washed up on the Lorne coastline, apparently the victim of a shark attack. There was an appeal to the public to contact the police if anyone knew anything about a missing young woman in her late 'teens, or earlier twenties.

Chester and his wife checked up on the infant every few minutes; the little one was still fast asleep.

They ate their breakfast in the kitchen, each lost in their own thoughts while they kept the television tuned to the news channel.

After she finished her toast, Megan got up and said, "I am going to get dressed and head to the stores. We will need to buy the essentials at least, like diapers and baby formula. I won't be long because I know she will be hungry as soon as she wakes up."

Once her car left the driveway, Chester called his brother to find out when he would be visiting again.

"Within the hour," he told him. "I listened to the news, and nothing has been reported."

"Yes, we know. We have been up since six and heard nothing too. I'll see you soon."

Chester heard Fern crying. He went to check on her. She was hungry but seemed to calm down as soon as she saw her new dad. It was as if she knew her suffering was over. He could smell she needed changing, but it didn't scare him off.

"Hush, hush, and good morning, my little girl." He picked her up. "Hello, my Fern, my little angel. You have special eyes—you are so gorgeous," he cooed with delight. His voice was soft and loving and would have surprised his business associates had they heard him.

"You're okay; you're okay, you are safe now," he whispered. Fern stopped crying; she looked deeply into Chester's eyes.

Chester carried her in his arms while he fetched the bottle Lance had prepared the night before to be given to her as soon as she woke.

Holding her gently and supporting her tiny head, he walked to his study with Bonzo trotting behind assisting.

She hungrily drank the mixture and then promptly burped.

When Megan returned home, Chester carried the baby into the hall, and they both greeted her with a big smile.

Megan was so full of joy as she came in and leaned in to kiss both her husband and baby Fern on their foreheads.

"How is she? I hope I haven't been too long. I got a little carried away as I realize we need more than just diapers and formula. I picked up a whole bunch of baby items like blankets, pillows, and toys. I also ordered a cot, which they will deliver later. I paid extra for same-day delivery, so they will drop off a changing table, rocking chair, and stroller. I also got a ton of disposable diapers," Megan said, excitably turning towards the car to unload.

"Ahh, talking about diapers, Fern needs changing. Here, you take her," Chester offered. "I'll bring the stuff in." Changing babies was not something Chester was familiar with, but neither was Megan, although he didn't give it a second thought as he passed Fern to Megan.

She grabbed a packet of disposables and headed for the bedroom to change Fern on their bed.

Shortly afterward, Lance arrived and was greeted enthusiastically.

"Let's have tea,'" Megan invited.

"I could do with a cup, but first, I want to examine Fern," Lance said with more than a pinch of concern.

"Should we be worried?" Chester asked.

"We do not know her history. We know nothing about her and nor who her mother was—she could have been an alcoholic or even a drug addict or both." Megan looked wildly at her husband, concern written all over her face.

Lance took out his stethoscope and listened to the baby's heart and lungs. He then checked her blood pressure and her temperature.

"Is she healthy?" Megan asked anxiously.

"So far, all seems to be in order, but I need to run some tests."

"For what?" Chester and Megan asked again in unison.

"If the mother was an addict of some sort, the drugs or alcohol or both would have passed through the placenta. She must be monitored closely for any changes or spikes in temperature, her sleeping pattern, or any odd behavior because if her mother was an addict, then baby Fern here could be suffering from neonatal abstinence syndrome," Lance said solemnly. "Which, in a nutshell, means she too could be an addict."

"Oh my God," Megan gasped, somewhat shaken.

"I want her fed with a high-calorie formula if this is true. I've brought plenty for you. It should last you a week or more," Lance reassured them.

The intercom at the gate buzzed, and they jumped with surprise. Megan grinned, realizing it was just the delivery truck arriving with all the baby furniture.

Chester took Fern and left Megan to attend to the driver who had brought along his assistant. They were young, fit men, who obviously spent plenty of time in the gym and had the biceps to prove it.

"Where would you like me to put everything, ma'am?"

"I will show you. There's a twenty dollars tip in it for you if you would kindly put the cot together for us. It shouldn't take you long."

"Sure, ma'am," and he followed Megan upstairs while turning his baseball cap around, so it faced the front.

Chester ,with Fern, and Lance disappeared into the living room, where they sat down and waited for Megan.

"I can see you have attached to the baby already, Chester," Lance remarked.

Chester kissed Fern on the cheek and smiled, "Yes, Lance, she is definitely ours. I love the smell of a new baby; it's intoxicating. Isn't she gorgeous? I love her eyes and the fact that I found her. Our family is now complete. You know, she would have died out there otherwise. We're giving her a second chance. We are giving her a new life, and you are also part of this miracle."

Lance smiled. He couldn't disagree with his brother, and he happily noticed Fern's skin was returning to her natural color.

"Lance, I see such intelligence in those eyes. It is almost uncanny,' Chester grinned boyishly with pride, looking at his baby daughter.

They heard Megan come downstairs with the delivery drivers and exchange pleasantries. Before sauntering to his truck, the senior guy turned his cap back to the front again while blocking the sun from his face with his huge hand.

The front door closed, and Megan came into the room.

"How is our baby, Lance?" Megan asked.

"She seems fine but still needs special care and supervision. We are not in the all-clear yet," Lance said seriously, his tone returning to his professional demeanor.

"Let me get that tea, I promised," Megan said cheerfully, heading for the kitchen.

As soon as she was out of earshot, Lance addressed the reality at hand. "Chester, you do realize her mother or father may come forward, or some other relative approach the police? It would then become complicated. Questions will be asked about why you didn't come forward yourself."

Chester paused. "That is my worry, Lance. Leave it be for now." Ever the risk-taker said, "We'll cross that bridge when and if it shows up." He then turned smiling to his beaming wife, who had returned with a tray of tea and cookies for everyone.

Later Lance departed, promising daily visits.

Chapter Five

Detective Inspector Bruce Nash replaced the receiver of his office phone. He had just spoken to customs and passport control at Melbourne International Airport and requested the return flight details of Mr. Michael Derian, the registered owner of the old Holden. He had also instructed them to hold Mr. Derian when he did eventually return to Australia.

Nash had received confirmation that Derian was currently in the Republic of Armenia and, as far as Australia was concerned, he had no criminal record whatsoever.

He headed towards the coffee machine and poured himself his fourth of the day. He returned to his desk and pulled out his Rolodex. He flipped through the numbers and eventually found what he was looking for. He punched in the digits and rearranged some papers on his desk. He took a sip of coffee and cleared his throat while the phone rang. After a few rings, a lady's voice answered, "Melbourne Police."

"Detective Inspector Nash here; put me through to Detective Hughes, please."

"Putting you through, Inspector."

"Detective Hughes here."

"Ashley, it's Bruce Nash." The two men had been friends since Nash agreed to mentor Ashley when he first joined the force. Hughes was half Nash's age, but the two got on like brothers.

"Hello, Bruce. How are you, and what news have you got?"

"Did you hear about the fisherman's find near Lorne a few days ago?"

"Yes, poor girl. The Jane Doe case. What do you have in mind, Bruce?"

"I'd appreciate it if you could keep an eye on things. Let me know if anything crops up on your end. A guy we're interested in, Michael Derian, the owner of the abandoned vehicle, lives in your neck of the woods. Be great if you could do some background checks—talk to his landlord, neighbors, and friends so we can get a better picture of this guy. I have been in touch with customs and border control and waiting to hear when he is expected home. He will be flying back from Zvartnos International Airport at some point in the next few weeks. I will email you all the details."

"Of course, Bruce. We will look into it and keep you in the loop if we find anything."

"Thanks, Ashley—I owe you one."

Chester and Megan had enjoyed a pleasant evening fussing over their new baby daughter and, after dinner, had put Fern down in her cot for the night. Chester opened up a nice bottle of red wine from the Barossa Valle,y and they settled in to watch TV and wait for the eight o'clock news to come on.

When the signature tune started, Chester turned the volume up to hear the anchor read the headlines ...

"It has been the coldest weather on record; snow has forced the closure of Hume Highway between Melbourne and Sydney for the first time in thirty years—the political campaign is heating up, and in other news; a little girl is lost ...."

"Chester, oh no," Megan gaped in fear.

"Ssh, listen, ssh," Chester waved his hand, jumped to his feet, and looked with dismay at his wife.

"Come on, get on with it," Megan demanded, staring hard at the presenter as if she could hear her.

After several nerve-racking minutes and a couple of commercial breaks, the presenter finally got to the missing child segment that had kept them transfixed to the screen, "And finally in other news, the little lost girl who was playing in the park has been reunited with her parents. She had been missing since this morning, and it appears she had walked to her friend's house several blocks away." She smiled into the camera, "All's well that ends well. And now here is Johnny with the weather, our intrepid meteorologist."

Megan stood up, and the two hugged. Fern was still theirs.

Michael Derian's plane landed at Melbourne International airport, and it was not long before he was in line at passport control.

He waited patiently, along with everyone else. It had been a long flight, but he was in no hurry. He knew he still had to wait for his luggage at baggage claim and nonchalantly stepped up to the red line—he was next.

The customs officer waved him forward, and he handed him his passport, happy and relaxed. In an hour or two, he would be home.

"Good afternoon," he said pleasantly.

"Your passport, sir."

Derian placed his passport on the counter.

"Where were you in Armenia, Mr. Derian?"

"With family in the capital, in Yerevan."

"Hope you had a pleasant time, Mr. Derian? Wait one moment, please?"

"Is there a problem, officer?" he asked, surprised.

"Just a few seconds, sir," the officer replied, and then she signaled to another officer at the back. He approached, and they exchanged a few words.

The other officer approached Derian without a word while his passport was stamped.

"Mr. Derian, can you please come with me, sir?"

"What for? What seems to be the problem, officer? I have nothing to declare." Derian was confused. He looked around and took a deep breath as the next passenger was being called forward for passport inspection.

He was taken to an office close by. It was sparse except for a table and a few chairs—two of which were occupied by two official looking men in suits.

"Mr. Derian for you, gentlemen."

Bruce Nash and Ashley Hughes stood up and showed Derian their identifications.

"This is Detective Ashley Hughes, and I am Detective Inspector Bruce Nash," the elder officer said and briefly waited for a response while this information sunk in.

None was forthcoming.

"Please have a seat, Mr. Derian," Detective Hughes waved his hand.

"I don't understand what is going on," Derian protested.

Nash stared at Derian. "Do you own a car, Mr. Derian? An old brown Kingswood Holden? Derian nodded, bewildered. "Do you know where it is?"

Derian looked up in surprise. "In my garage at home—why?"

"Two weeks and three days ago, your car was found abandoned on the Great Ocean Road, near Lorne."

"I don't understand—how did it get there?"

"We also discovered the grim remains of a half-eaten body by a shark washed up on the beach in the same vicinity."

"What! Oh my God." Derian was sickened and visibly shaken.

"The deceased's fingerprints were all over your car—on the doors, the steering wheel ,and the back seat as well. Does anyone else drive your car ,Mr. Derian?"

"No. No. This makes no sense whatsoever. Do you know who it was?" Derian asked, clearly upset.

"We matched the prints to a young woman named Sophia Semenov. Do you know her, Mr. Derian?"

"Sophie! Jesus Christ!" He was trembling, obviously very upset.

Detective Ashley Hughes never took his eyes off Derian as he spoke, "What is your relationship with Ms. Semenov?"

"She is, …eh was my neighbor. Are you sure it was Sophie?" he looked up uneasy.

"Since you weren't around, we got a warrant and searched your apartment. Your landlord confirmed it is Sophie. He identified her from the picture we showed him, and he was the one that told us you were abroad. How well did you know her?"

Derian rubbed his face, still trying to take in the news. "Detective, did she have one blue eye and one brown eye?"

Nash nodded.

"Poor Sophie, poor girl," Derian said, shaking his head in a shocked tone.

"What exactly was your relationship with her, Mr. Derian?" Nash leaned on the table, looking directly at him.

"We were neighbors, that is all," he stated. "I know she saw men, but she had a good nature."

"Really?" Hughes chimed in for the first time. "She was a whore and a drug addict, wasn't she?" he said incredulously.

"That doesn't make her a bad person," Derian shot back. "She was a lost soul but was always pleasant. She might have been down on her luck, but she was surviving the best way she knew. God, it's hot here. Okay, if I remove my jacket?" He stood up to take off his coat, and then he suddenly jumped up and realized, "What about the baby?"

"So, you know about the baby?" Nash enquired. "Do you know what happened?"

"She was due when I left for my vacation. She originally considered an abortion when she first learned she was pregnant and then decided against it."

"Do you know where the baby might be now, Mr. Derian?' Hughes interjected sharply while his eyes darted between Derian and Nash.

"No, of course not."

"Did you sleep with her?" Hughes fired back.

Nash interrupted. His years on the job told him how important it was to keep subjects calm ,so they had a better chance of gaining more information. Insulting him would only shut him down. A baby's life depended on this interview.

"Derian, she was working illegally in Australia. Were you aware of that?"

"Uh huh—no."

"Did you have sex with her?" Hughes fired again while removing his glasses and fixing Derian with a stare.

"I... I... I," he cleared his throat. "Once, only once, and that was nearly two years ago," he nervously admitted.

"What do you do for a living, Mr. Derian?" Nash deflected the subject again.

"I'm a handyman, an independent contractor. I specialize in woodwork for my customers."

"Do you know if Sophie had any family here or abroad?" Hughes asked in a quieter tone taking Nash's lead.

"Not that I know of. Her father died years back; I only know what Sophie told me. Her mother disowned her the day she left for Australia. She was alone in this country."

"Can you think of anyone she might have gone to for help and given birth?"

"No—I never met any of her friends, if she had any," he stared at the floor. The sadness of a wasted life and unfulfilled dreams emanated from the room.

"All right, Mr. Derian," Nash broke the desolation. "Apologies for delaying you a bit. You can go now, but if you hear anything or remember anything… we need to find the baby. Take my card. My number is on it. Call me anytime," he offered his hand. "We may be in touch again." Hughes stood there silently and looked on.

"What about my car? I need it for work."

"I'm afraid Sophie ran it to the ground. The motor ceased. It is being held at the police yard and, as soon as we have finished with it, you are welcome to collect it. Leave your number with us, and the station will call you to make arrangements. It will need to be towed." Nash made a note of Derian's number in his notebook.

Derian walked out of the office, clutching his small, well-worn bag, toward the baggage claim area. His face was red from frustration, surprise, and shock. It was hard to believe that Sophie was dead. She was good company when he was lonely. He had not lied about the sex with her; it was only once, and that was way before Sophie fell pregnant.

Nash and Hughes left the office.

"I believe him. I don't think he is lying, Ashley."

"I'm with you on this one, Bruce."

"I'll be in touch, Ash. I'll contact the Russian embassy to see if they have any records on file that can help locate her family. Check with immigration and see what documents they have that might tell us more about Sophia Semenov. Also, have another chat with the building manager and get Vice to track down her pimp."

"You've got it, boss," Ashley acknowledged, heading towards the parking garage.

"We need to find that baby and quick!"

Chapter Six

C hester's phone rang. He looked at the screen. The call was from Lance. "Chester, as I suspected, the baby is addicted. The laboratory confirmed this. But don't panic. This little girlie is tough."

"Does she have to be hospitalized?"

"I can treat her at your residence, but if the response is slow, I will have to admit her."

"That's a relief, Lance. When will you be popping over?"

"Later today. I'll let Megan know."

"Give me a few minutes before you call her as I prefer to break the news to her myself."

"All right, Chester, see you later."

Chester took a deep breath while walking to the window of his office. He looked out of the soundproof window and called Megan.

Megan was rocking Fern in her arms, talking to her softly, gently, and in between humming softly.

Tiny Fern gazed up at her new mommy, and then she cried out. It was a loud, sharp, piercing cry that lasted only a few seconds.

Megan moved towards the ringing phone. She hit the speaker button while she still held Fern in her arms.

"Hello, Fern is well… but a bit restless. Something is worrying her. One moment she is happy and content, and the next, she screams and sobs for a short while."

"I know."

"What do you mean, you know?"

"Lance just phoned me. He confirmed little Fern is suffering from withdrawal."

"Oh my God, oh no."

"Don't worry, darling. In Lance's exact words, she is a toughie and only slightly addicted to her mother's drugs. He said he can treat her at home, so relax."

"I hope so," Megan said anxiously. "How will he treat her?"

"We will find out later when Lance comes over. I must go now; the office phone is ringing—bye for now."

Chester's office phone had not rung, but he didn't want to get caught up in a long conversation with his wife on the subject. He preferred to wait until his brother was around to allay any fears Megan might bring up. Anyway, he did have a number of calls to follow up on the major equipment order in the works. It involved collaborating with several countries to coordinate the delivery of the machinery.

Chester took care of his calls and actioned his urgent emails.

From his desk, he looked towards the window and saw that it was raining.

It was late afternoon, so, before the traffic went from bad to worse, he locked his office door and took the elevator to the parking garage.

In the car on the way home, he played his favorite music—the nutcracker suite by Tchaikovsky with the volume turned up. He tapped the wheel with his fingers and bobbed his head in tune with the beat as he headed home.

Detective Ashley Hughes parked his car away from the streetlights in Footscray. He killed the engine and watched a couple of hookers for the third night in a row. A new girl had joined them tonight and, after twenty minutes, some guy approached them. He was slim, draped in a vintage coat, which blew in the wind like a poorly erected tent. His shoes seemed too long for his feet, and one hand pressed down on his head. Ashley Hughes could see that he was holding on to his wig to stop it from blowing away.

This was his man, the pimp. The Armenian who knew the dead girl had given him the description. Sophie had told him his name was Frankie, and he always wore a cheap wig.

Ashley slowly climbed out of the car, closing the door quietly so as not to alert him of his presence. He approached from an angle and, within less than a minute, was almost next to the three hookers and this weasel of a man.

"What do the girls charge?"

The shifty-eyed pimp looked at Detective Hughes in surprise, "Can't you see I am busy, dude? Gimme a minute. I'll see what I can do."

"Frankie, we need the business," one of the girls protested.

"Yeah, you're right." Frankie turned to look at Detective Hughes, and they stepped out of earshot from the ladies.

"How much, Frankie?" Hughes asked again.

"Depends… what you want and how much you got."

"I've got this for you!" Hughes took out his police ID and showed it to him.

He whipped out his cuffs and cuffed Frankie before he knew what was happening.

"What the fuck! What have I done?"

"Sophia Semenov is dead. I am arresting you on suspicion of murder. You were the last to see her alive," he hissed into his ear.

"What? What! You've got this all wrong, dude," Frankie protested, genuinely shocked.

"I've got you on pimping and pandering charges as well as peddling drugs for starters. This way, scumbag."

Detective Hughes gripped the pimp's coat at the shoulder and escorted him to his car with a glint of self-satisfaction in his eyes.

Frankie comically kept a hand on his ersatz wig despite the handcuffs while cursing under his breath like a spendthrift reading his latest credit card statement.

"Fuck man!" the pimp swore incessantly.

"Now, stay in the car and shut your mouth. I will be back in a short while," Hughes said as he crossed the road back to the ladies of the night. He turned, hit the remote to his car, and locked the pimp inside.

Hughes beckoned to the girls to approach him.

One of the prostitutes self-consciously held her dress down, protecting it from the gusts of wind, while the other one teasingly let the wind reveal her cute pink panties with little red hearts for Ashley to enjoy.

"We want no trouble, officer," she coyly said.

Ignoring her, Hughes asked, "Did either of you know Sophie?"

"I know her but not well," the hooker with the pink panties answered.

"What can you tell me about her?"

"I think she is from Russia, yeah, she came from Russia. . Keeps herself to herself when she isn't with a customer. Haven't seen her for a while now. Oh, my God, has something happened to Sophie?" The news finally registered and the girls looked at each other for support.

"Did that creep in the car beat her or any of you?"

"No," pink panties replied.

"No, he only comes three times or so a month when he collects his cut," the more reserved girl replied.

"What about drugs? Do you buy any from him?"

They shook their heads without a word and Ashley Hughes knew they were lying; even if they did not use, their reaction told him they knew Frankie was selling drugs.

"If you hear or find anything out about Sophie or if you wish to contact me, here's my card." Hughes gave each of them a card. He then turned around and crossed the street back to his car.

"See ya," one of them said.

"Is Sophie alright?" pink panties called out.

"She isn't coming back," Hughes shouted back as he reached his car.

Chester arrived home, and Bonzo bounded towards him as he parked his Audi.

He saw Lance's car coming up the driveway behind him and immediately opened the gates with his remote.

His brother pulled up next to Chester, who stood waiting.

They shook hands. They had remained formal ever since they were young.

"Lance, any further news with the stool test and any other results?" Chester asked impatiently.

"Let's go inside, and I will tell you everything together with Megan."

They walked into the entrance hall, and Megan greeted them.

"Where's Fern?" Chester asked.

"She is sleeping upstairs. Don't worry. If she wakes up, I will hear her," Megan said confidently as she indicated the baby monitor in her hand.

They followed her into the lounge.

"Little Fern is suffering from neonatal abstinence syndrome," Lance told them. "It is a concern, but this is not as serious as it could be. I think she has only a mild case, so her odds look good."

"Elaborate, please. Treatment, what do we do, Lance?" Chester asked.

"The tests show she has been exposed to several drugs like heroin, codeine, cocaine, and methadone. One of Australia's top medical professors believes that these symptoms are also caused by the fetus being continually exposed to smoking weed. Symptoms include mood changes, fever, and high-pitched crying."

Chester interrupted Lance, "That's just what Megan said to me a short while ago."

"Let me finish," Lance held up his hand. "Shakes and shivers, excessive sucking on her bottle are common with addicted babies. As I have said before, Fern is strong. I will increase her feeding formula to a high-calorie one. She must be fed more often but in smaller amounts. Also, she must have plenty of attention and rest. Keep her away from bright artificial lights and noise. If she does not settle in a few days, we will have to feed her a concoction of drugs with her milk but a low dose. Then we will wean her off the drugs."

" I am so worried," Megan said.

"Of course, understandable. I will visit again tomorrow. Do not hesitate to call anytime. I am here for you both too. Before I go, I want to see her."

They all went to Fern's room. She was sound asleep. Lance tiptoed in and took a peek in the crib. He put his finger on his lips to indicate she was asleep. He then gestured with his hand for them to follow him out.

"Her color looks better, and her breathing is good, but time will tell," Lance commented. The brothers shook hands, and then Megan escorted Lance to the door.

"What would we do without you, Lance?" Megan said with appreciation while Chester nodded his gratitude too.

Chapter Seven

Frankie, the pimp, sat in the bare interrogation room with the one-way mirror.

"Frank Perreira, nice record," Detective Ashley Hughes, sitting opposite him, sneered. "Reads like a bad Santa list. Your wrap-sheet is as long as a fireman's ladder: four previous convictions of drug peddling, five counts of theft including fraud for credit cards. Not to mention several traffic offenses and an assault charge for punching one of your ladies."

Frankie said nothing, staring at Detective Hughes.

"When was the last time you last saw Sophia Semenov?"

He shrugged, completely indifferent to the insults being hurled at him.

"Why were you peddling her, eh? Didn't you know, she was pregnant?"

Again, no response.

"I need to know everything." Hughes slammed his hand down hard on the table and made Frankie jump.

"I've got the patience of a hungry hyena. You're going down for a long time, so I'll know where to find you. Is that fucking clear enough for you?"

"Ok—okay, I sold her drugs once; that's all I know."

"Not so tough now, eh? You know what, Frankie swanky, I just had a look at your new home where you'll be until your trial. It's the luxury model," Hughes sardonically grinned. "Six by six, cold and draughty, and your roommate is the size of a gorilla, and he loves his pad. He doesn't have another home, so has nowhere to go. He is very friendly," Hughes smirked, "makes all his cellmates his house boy!"

"All right, all right dude! I sold her a bit of ice and crack from time to time, that's all. Then the stupid bitch goes and gets pregnant," Frankie said, irritated.

"It's Detective! Now, where's the baby?" Hughes looked at him hard.

"I don't know, and I don't care," Frankie glared back. "The bitch disappeared months ago. She was worthless to me at that point. Completely useless."

"You still made your money off of her, you arse-hole! I have a witness who says you sold her drugs every week—every fuckin' week! I am going to make sure you go down for a long time. You'll need at least five calendars or more to hang on your cell wall."

The pimp looked at Ashley, stunned; the silence in the room was deafening.

"OK, I... I will help; I'll tell ya everything you want to know. I'll tell you where I get the drugs, everything, I will tell ya."

"Guard!' Hughes shouted, and a uniformed officer entered the room.

"Yes, sir."

"Take him away and read him the riot act. If there is one thing I hate, it's a drug peddler. They are lower than shark shit," Hughes growled in a cranky voice.

"Everything, I'll tell ya everything!" Frankie repeated.

"You had better. I told your new cellie about your wonderful wig here," Ashley toyed with his suspect, picking up a couple of strands with his fingers, "And, do you know what his reply was?"

"What the fuck!" Frankie screeched, trying to duck the insult. "It ain't no one's business." He looked worried. Ashley was getting to him.

Hughes continued to tease, "He said he would rip it off and polish his shoes with it." He laughed, enjoying the humiliation. "He loves shiny shoes. He always keeps his shoes shiny, shiny like a fuckin' mirror." Ashley leaned in closer for greater effect, "And, I'll tell you something else—it's drafty as hell, and there is no insulation against the cold winter nights. It blows like hell at times, and if he does not rip your wig off, the winter wind sure as fuck will," he grinned with delight.

That evening Fern cried and screamed, and her face turned a sickly yellow. It was heartbreaking, but Megan and Chester never left her side. While one watched over her, the other slept in the rocking chair next to the cot. The feeds were more often, and the love immeasurable.

Both were sleep deprived, like most new parents, but this was obviously different and more demanding. The next day Chester stayed at home again and took the day off. He was determined to chip in and take on his share of the duties for the newest member of his family.

Megan was relieved and grateful. She was exhausted. The lack of sleep was bearable, but the screaming and crying waswere unnerving and painful to hear. She knew poor little Fern was in extreme discomfort going through the withdrawals.

While Megan rested and caught up on her sleep during the morning, Chester took charge. He prepared Fern's bottles and rocked and held her in his arms. Cooing and reassuring her, that she was safe and things would get better soon. He fed and changed her when she needed it and burped her after each feed. He never put her down, only held her even tighter, letting her know he would never abandon her.

At 2 pm, Megan woke up and they ate a light snack together before Chester handed her over to Megan. He went to his study to make a few calls before he took a much-needed nap himself.

He flicked through his address book and picked up the phone.

"Hello, Danny, it's Chester Jones. How are you—well, I hope?"

"Chester! Good to hear from you—what's up?"

"Something has cropped up, and I need a favor but not over the phone. Can we meet tomorrow mid-morning, my office, say between 10 am and 11 am?"

"Sure—that works! Look forward to seeing you after all this time."

Chester made more calls to his warehouse manager and emailed the distribution companies that were handling the shipping orders. Everything seemed to be in order and going smoothly. He was in a buoyant mood; the mining equipment and vehicles were on schedule for delivery.

That evening Chester and Megan sat in front of the fire together in their sitting room, watching the news. Fern had finally calmed down, probably from exhaustion, and was resting quietly in her brand-new bassinet next to her parents. Fern whimpered and fussed every so often, but the gentle rocking back and forth seemed to comfort her. There was no concern from the news that night so they adjourned to the kitchen for dinner. Megan had made her late mother's Irish Stew recipe that was perfect for the winter weather.

"Ahh," Chester beamed. "This is what I always dreamed about; a family dinner. What could be better—a beautiful wife, a gorgeous baby, a delicious meal, and a loyal pup," he said, looking down at Bonzo under the table.

Megan teared up and affectionately reached out her hand and squeezed Chester's. Her gratitude was beyond words.

Danny had secured a table in the corner of the sandwich bar. It was one of those obscure places that was only really known to locals. It was very non-descript and easily missed unless you were looking for the place. Danny had arrived early to scout out the best place to sit so he would go unnoticed by any regulars stopping by. He had grabbed a black coffee and sat there wondering what had caused Chester to reach out after all this time. He learned from his past dealings with him that he was a powerful, ambitious man and willing to pay top dollar when he needed something.

Danny was somewhat of an enigma. He kept himself to himself and led a very solitary life. Few had met him face to face, and he only took on clients through referrals. His job depended on it, and he couldn't afford to take risks with unknown clients without a thorough background check. His reputation as a high-class forger was rumored to be one of the best in the world, and he was not afraid to charge accordingly.

He sipped his coffee and remembered how he first met Chester. His company needed specialized permits to explore the undeveloped landscape around the historical town of Bourke on the Darling River in New South Wales. It was nearly a decade ago, and Danny had produced all the necessary paperwork in two-and-a-half days, all twenty pages, which had been a record for him in those days. He pondered what Chester was working on now.

Danny looked at his watch. It was time to meet Chester.

He walked up to the cashier, smiled at the lady, paid, and was soon walking on the sidewalk up towards Chester's office on Collins Street.

He took the elevator to the sixth floor. The shiny brass plate Infinite Mining Equipment confirmed he was at the right place.

He knocked and peered around the door, which was ajar.

"Danny, come in, come in," Chester was standing in the reception area and came forward to shake his hand. "How you keeping, Danny?"

"I'm good, I'm good, and you?"

"Also, just busy and longing for the day when I can play golf more than once a week. Come, let's go to my office so we can talk. Can I get you a coffee?" Chester asked as they walked down to his office.

"Sure, if you are having one, I could do with a second cup."

"Still drinking long blacks, Danny?"

Danny chuckled, "You have a good memory, Chester."

The office was quiet. It was Saturday, and they were alone. The coffee grinder sounded like an automatic drill bouncing off the walls of the empty office and then hissed and spat loudly while it brewed.

"That machine would be more at home in a busy restaurant," Danny commented, making small talk before the real reason for his visit was explained. "Looks kind of industrial, Chester," he questioned.

"You know it does the job, and besides I work it overtime, so believe me, I never want it to break down."

Chester handed him his coffee.

"So, what can I do or try to do for you today, Chester?"

"You remember the papers you helped me out with all those years ago for the Bourke development? I wondered if you are still in the same business," Chester cautiously enquired.

"Of course! Never been busier. What can I do to help?"

"Ahh, this one is not so complicated, I believe. It should be a walk in the park for someone as experienced as you. And, hopefully, easy to turn around quickly?"

Chester poured himself a second cup.

"I need a birth certificate," he said, looking directly at Danny.

"Uh-huh, I can certainly help with that, but it is a lot more involved than you think. Who is it for?"

Chester removed an envelope from his desk drawer and handed it to Danny.

"Here are copies of my birth certificate and my wife Megan's. We recently adopted a little baby girl. Her name is Fern Anne Jones, born August 12, 1988."

Danny nodded immediately, understanding the confidentiality and, judging by Chester's demeanor, this was not open for discussion. He cleared his throat, "I will need to create a registration number and duplicate the Coat of Arms shield with the kangaroo and emu signature. I will also need a copy of your marriage certificate," he looked at Chester intently.

He put the papers back in the envelope.

"When did you say you needed this?"

"Yesterday," Chester responded in all seriousness.

Danny gulped the last of his coffee, licked his lips, and stood up. He shook Chester's hand and said, "Don't worry, I'll take care of this for you. You're in good hands, Chester."

"What's this going to set me back, Danny?"

"10K for this one. It will be just like the original," he grinned. He turned towards the door, "I'll see myself out. Have a good weekend, and give my regards to your wife and congratulations!"

A few days later, Danny delivered the *new* birth certificate to Chester's office. It was impeccable.

Megan hung up the phone. She was so happy she almost danced a jig. Lance had confirmed that finally, Fern was out of danger and free of her dependency on the drugs. All her tests had come back, and she was in good health.

She picked up the phone and called her husband, "Chester, Chester!"

"Hi, sweetie; I can hear the excitement in your voice. Tell me."

"Chester, you were right; Fern is a fighter. She's made it. She is out of the woods! I just spoke to Lance; she really is strong and resilient— just like her dad!" she laughed.

Frankie, the mirthless pimp, was sentenced to four years in prison for theft and drug peddling. The Detectives could find anything to support any evidence that he had anything to do with Sophia Semenov's death.

Her neighbor Michael Derian was a free man, and no charges were filed against him. It was determined that Sophie had taken his car without his permission, and he was punished enough by the financial burden to replace his beloved Holden.

In time, Detective Ashley Hughes was promoted and transferred across the country to Western Australia, the largest state in the country. It made his parents happy to have their son back living and working in their hometown of Perth, which was also home to some of the largest mining corporations and blue-chip companies.

Detective Inspector Bruce Nash had no joy with the Russian Embassy. There was no record of Sophia Semenov on file, and her family history fizzled out into nothing. No documents could be found, despite vigorous inquiries and searches, so no one could determine if anyone was looking for her. And, if they were, it was impossible to know. It still haunted Nash greatly to think that a baby was possibly still out there. Even if it hadn't survived, the baby at least deserved a proper burial.

His retirement was fast approaching. Nash began to look forward to lazier days away from the denizens of society. He and his wife started to search the outskirts of Melbourne and seek the solitude of nature near the forest, where the wildlife would give them peace and quiet. They eventually settled on a rural area in the Dandenong Mountain Ranges.

Chapter Eight

Skipper Todd was patrolling and checking the shark nets in the bay near Lennox Head in New South Wales.

It was just after sunrise. The sky was blue, with a touch of pink and orange hue and wispy clouds scattered overhead. The waters were calm and the morning sea air invigorating. He looked over his shoulder while he steered the small motorboat and glanced at the shoreline and back. Up ahead, he noticed a shadow-like object.

He opened the throttle, gaining speed until he was almost on top of it before he realized a massive shark was caught in the nets.

He turned the helm hard over and pulled the throttle to neutral, and drifted near the monstrous shark. It was a great white, and he estimated it to be an easy twelve to fifteen feet long.

It must have died recently as the Skipper saw no fresh wounds or blood present. There were no signs that other fish had been nibbling, so he knew it had happened in the last few hours.

He radioed his find to the scientific research station and told them to send a boat with the hoist. While he waited, he tied and secured a chain around the shark. He looked at his watch. It would take them at least an hour or so to arrive. He was hungry and wished he had brought something to eat.

He made a note in his log book of the exact location where he found the shark and tied a bright orange color buoy to the net so the crew could find it easily and repair the net's damage. He then started his engines, and pulled away slowly, heading for the harbor while curious and hungry seagulls circled above.

It was a beautiful rainbow-shaped cake with all the rainbow colors and a large pink candle in the middle to celebrate little Fern's very first birthday. Megan and Chester were full of smiles and love. Uncle Lance was there too, and Fern smiled and giggled in her highchair every time Chester tickled her tiny toes. She gazed at them with her adoring different colored eyes—one blue and one brown—soaking up the attention and loving every minute.

Chester was enjoying a fine scotch and admired his wife. She was still sexy in her tight black slacks and a pretty green and blue top. She still maintained a youthful figure for someone in her mid-forties, he thought.

"Here ,darling, take the matches," Megan said.

"Thank you, my angel. Look what Daddy is going to do, Fern. I am going to light your first candle. You are one today," he beamed.

Chester lit the candle, and the three of them clapped and sang happy birthday. Fern giggled and smiled and clapped too.

"Now, you must blow out the candle like this," Megan said, and she picked Fern out of her chair and lowered her closer to the small flame. She demonstrated by blowing a few puffs so her daughter could copy her.

"Just look at my baby girl; how clever she is!" Chester said with parental pride.

Lance started to count, "One, two, and three...."

Megan blew the candle out, and baby Fern continued with her contribution by puffing little bursts of air out of her tiny mouth.

"Lance, can I get you another drink?"

"Just a drop more wine will do, Chester; thank you."

"Megan, can I pour you a little one as well?'"

"Yes, darling, just a half glass."

Megan put Fern back into her highchair and gave her a small piece of cake.

"I would like to propose a toast," Chester said, raising his glass.

"To our little pot of gold who was in such a terrible state. I thank God every day for her rapid recovery, for allowing her to be our daughter, to cherish, to love, and to see that she has everything she needs and anything she wants. To commemorate her first birthday, this week, I opened a bank account in her name."

Chester was becoming unusually emotional as he spoke. "Thank you, Fern, for giving Megan, your mom, and me a new life, a life we never knew before. Last but not least, a very big thank you to you, Uncle Lance, for saving this beautiful girl's life."

"Hear, hear," Lance said, and there was tumultuous applause as they clinked glasses and hugged one another.

Inspector Bruce Nash froze in his chair as he caught the news on television.

A great white shark measuring nearly fifteen feet had been caught in the nets at Lennox Head in New South Wales. A human finger and a gold ring had been found in the shark's gut when it was dissected.

Nash quickly found the phone number of the local police station there and called.

"Sergeant Burberry speaking," the voice at the other end answered.

"Detective Inspector Nash here from Melbourne; put me through to your station commander immediately, please."

"Yes, sir, putting you through."

The phone rang once before he heard "Superintendent Wiley."

"Superintendent, Detective Inspector Nash here phoning from Melbourne. I just caught the news about the Great White you found and the discovery of a human finger and a ring in its gut."

"Yes, what can I do for you, Detective Inspector Nash?"

"Some months back I was called to view the remains of a corpse that had washed up on a beach on the Great Ocean Road here in Victoria. It had been mauled by a Great White. We finally managed to identify the body as that of a Russian girl, Sophia Semenov."

"Hold on; I'm holding a plastic bag now with the ring as we talk. It's been cleaned by the lab and there's an inscription on the inside. Hang on, it looks like a number 8 and an S, no, no, the word looks like *Softy*. Hang on, no, it is *Sophie*, I'm pretty sure, it says *Sophie*. Give me your address, and I'll overnight it to you."

Nash was speechless for a moment.

"Nash, you still there? Seems like your poor lady was shark bait, and that bugger swam over a thousand kilometers to our neck of the woods. Christ!"

Nash was too stunned to comment.

Chester and Megan decided to take Fern away for a weekend and rented a picturesque cottage in Halls Gap in Grampians National Park. It was one of their favorite getaway places. They loved the landscape and the majestic mountain ranges. They loved reveling in the vistas and the awe-inspiring iconic MacKenzie Falls.

Chester kept the fireplace burning as it was bitterly cold outside. Amazingly, a gorgeous butterfly was braving the weather outside playing hide and seek with the flowers on the window sill. Fern was fascinated and giggled with delight at her new discovery.

In the late afternoon, Chester bundled up and prepared a BBQ despite the chill in the air. While he waited for the grill to heat up, a large mob of kangaroos, about 30 of them, gunned at full speed across the fields in front of the chalet. They watched with fascination as they all cleared the five-foot fence surrounding the property with such ease.

After enjoying the delicious ribs and sausages and all the trimmings, Megan put Fern to bed. Chester poured Megan another glass of Penfolds Grange red wine that he had brought along to celebrate their first family mini-vacation. It had been nearly a year since he had been intimate with his wife, and she deserved some pampering after he had been so preoccupied with his work.

They made love on the thick-piled carpet in front of the fireplace, caressing one another, kissing until they both climaxed. Chester moaned a sigh of pleasure, and Megan's heavy breathing soon subsided.

"Oh, Chester, I've missed this. We need to do this more often," Megan whispered with pleasure. "It always seems work; deals come first, and then your golf and AFL."

"You're right, I get so involved, and I've forgotten my priorities," Chester murmured, kissing Megan's shoulder. "Fern has changed all that, and I agree we need to get away more often. I promise from now on, we will plan more family breaks."

Monday morning, Chester loaded his Audi with their weekend belongings. They each had their own bag. Chester had a large canvas bag, Megan a valise with printed cities of the world all over it, and Fern had a small pink Gucci one.

The drive back home took them just under four hours.

Early Tuesday morning, Chester went to fetch Bonzo from the kennel. The dog's tail flicked like a whip. He was so happy to see his *dad*.

Megan waited inside by the window with Fern. "Look, there's Daddy with Bonzo," she happily pointed as he got out of the car. Fern bounced in Megan's arms and clapped at seeing her pup again.

Bonzo bounded in as soon as Megan opened the front door. His little body wiggling in delight. He went to greet Megan, and she lowered Fern onto the floor, and he immediately started licking her face and hands at being reunited. Fern giggled and laughed.

Megan greeted Chester with a kiss and said, "I meant to ask you how much money did you put into Fern's account?"

"Couple of grand — to be exact two-hundred and fifty-thousand dollars," he responded casually.

"Wow, isn't that a bit much?" Megan replied with a serious look.

"Darling, we are currently worth about eighty-five million dollars, and that does not include the new deal I just completed. Our net worth will be over a hundred million, in addition to all our properties and other values," Chester smiled and hugged his wife. "When I clock out one day, and hopefully that is not for a very long time, you and Fern will be very well provided for and won't know what to do with all your money. You will be swimming in it." He laughed.

Megan was both shocked and comforted. She had no idea of the vastness of Chester's estate.

Chapter Nine

Inspector Bruce Nash was going through his mail and saw that a small padded envelope from Lennox Head had arrived. The superintendent wasted no time, he thought.

Nash opened the envelope. He paused for a few seconds and then took the ring out, holding it in the palm of his hand as if feeling the weight. He then held it towards the light and fumbled for his reading glasses. It clearly had Sophie's name engraved on the inside.

His mind flashed back to the scene on the beach, the poor woman's eyes, one brown and one blue, the flies, the crabs, the missing limbs. He shook his head and quickly replaced the ring in the envelope and chucked it into a drawer.

He glanced down at the calendar. It was now only weeks until his retirement.

Then he phoned Steadfast, the main real estate agent in the Dandenong, and spoke with Morgan Carlson and told her exactly what he wanted. Just a small, modest house amongst tall trees that would attract the birds, somewhere near Sassafras and Olinda. It needed to be off the main tourist road and somewhat secluded.

She said she had a few properties and was sure one would fit his needs. He made arrangements to view the properties that Saturday.

That weekend Bruce and his wife Merle drove out to Dandenong. They had been married for over 25 years, and he had loved her from the day they had met. She was a country girl from Queensland so moving to a rural area was perfect for her.

Morgan greeted them warmly when they met her at her offices. She had a couple of properties for them to view.

One house stood out amongst the rest for Bruce and his wife. It was set back from the main road and was situated in the middle of the property, surrounded by tall Mountain Ash trees, which were about at least a hundred feet from the property. This gave them the privacy they were looking for.

The property had been on the market for a while, and they were able to negotiate a great deal.

Their current property was already on the market, an, within a few weeks, they had an offer from a buyer. They would be able to move to Dandenong as soon as Nash's retirement was official.

Merle was extremely happy and relieved. She would no longer have to worry about her husband being on the job.

Once they had moved, Bruce loved setting about a new routine with a daily morning stroll with Merle to take in the scenery and their new neighborhood.

He kept busy, enjoying his new garden, and Merle had created a *honey-do list* that would keep him occupied for quite some time.

He quickly fell into a simple lifestyle: after their morning walks, he'd work in the garden, watch the incredible bird life, and enjoy dinner with his wife before watching their favourite television programs in the evenings.

Afterward, Merle would retire to bed, and he would wander off to his study, sit at his desk and go through old files. He kept in touch with Hughes and some other men he had worked with and would get nostalgic, remembering the good and bad cases. He'd look around at his certificates and commendations from his long service in the police force, which now hung here on the wall in their new house. Merle called it his wall of distinction.

There was one case that still haunted him, still unresolved. Each night alone with his thoughts, he would open the top drawer of his desk and remove a small kangaroo leather pouch. Without fail, he would open the drawstring of the pouch and remove the ring. It was like his secret treasure trove, and he would pour himself a scotch and stare at it wistfully, hoping for an answer.

No missing baby had ever been mentioned in the press or on television. There was never any word from any of the local police stations. Incredible, he thought.

PART TWO

PART TWO

Chapter Ten

C hester Jones had received another large inquiry order for mining equipment from a huge Australian consortium. The email was from someone he once met at the exclusive Albert Park Golf Course, who was interested in a bucket-wheel excavator, two new hydraulic shovels, a massive dozer, a borer, and several dump trucks.

Chester's eyes widened in ecstatic disbelief. If Chester's optician had to check his eyes, he would have seen dollar signs instead of pupils. If this deal went through, it would make him richer than some countries in the world.

Chester's job took him all over the world. He regularly travelled for periods of several weeks or more to the huge mining shows in the USA and Germany. There he would meet and visit international trade stands and connect with his main suppliers from China, Canada, and Japan. Recent rumors suggested that an Israeli company was supplying the most advanced software, which would reduce the technology clutter in the mining sector.

There was some serious work and travel ahead; it would be arduous at times.

Meanwhile, little Fern was growing up fast, and amazingly, it wasn't long before Fern was eleven years old, her tragic beginning not even a memory.

She excelled at school, and on the recommendation of the principal, she enrolled in middle school a year early. She was also an excellent athlete, finishing in the top three in the swimming events, and her leadership skills were beginning to emerge as she captained the hockey team to the school championships.

It was tough keeping up with their young daughter's exuberance, so Megan installed a full-sized trampoline in their garden alongside their pool. Meanwhile, Chester arranged to have her IQ tested and her score of 140 confirmed she was highly intelligent.

Fern's natural energy made it easy to make friends and she wasn't afraid to stand up for herself when she was teased about her different colored eyes. She was quick to put them in their place by replying that they should check the back of their head to see the different colored patches of hair growing. It never failed. They would hastily run to the mirror or ask a friend to check to see if it was true. Most of the kids, though, found her different colored eyes fascinating.

"Have you seen her eyes lately?" Chester asked his wife one day.

"Well, we know they are not the same color," Megan replied.

"My dear, I am talking about the way she looks at things inquisitively. For example, when she has friends around, her eyes dart from person to person, to the windows to the door. However, when you say something, she looks at you steadily, but then if there are others in the room, she will lock eyes onto the one expected to reply. She has an uncanny knack of always being spot on."

"Are you saying she is psychic in some way?" Megan asked with raised eyebrows.

"Not at all dear, I am just pointing out how sharp and quick she is. She is highly alert and perceptive, don't you think?"

Unbeknownst to Chester, Fern was taking a keen interest in his company and was observing closely how he conducted his business.

Every few days, when she was not tackling extra homework or bouncing on the trampoline, she would eavesdrop on Chester's calls. When he was not at home, she would often wander into his study and go through his papers, and calendar and take notes.

One afternoon, Megan dropped Fern off at home after school and went into town for a hair appointment.

"Will you be alright?" she asked. "Dad is coming home early. He should be here in about 20-minutes. I can change my appointment if you like, or you can come with me?"

"I'm not a little girl anymore, Mom. I'll be okay," she replied quickly, pleased at the thought of having some alone time at home.

"We know that honey; it's just that we care so much."

Megan dropped Fern off at the front door and headed to her appointment.

Bonzo greeted Fern wagging his tail. He was starting to slow down at 11 years but was still following Fern around and went with her to the bedroom.

She put her school bag down on her bed and wandered into Chester's study.

She loved being in her father's study and amongst his things. She took in the smell and the power of his success. She sat in his chair and admired the clinical neatness, the wooden walls, the wide olive desk, and the bronze statue of a horse, all emanating prosperity.

She looked around, taking in the opulence, and then she opened one of the drawers. A private old telephone book caught her inquisitive eye.

Her eyes darted over the names and numbers, and a few stood out from the rest.

On one line under *D* was the name Danny and in parenthesis *papers*. She wondered what papers they were. Then under *P*, there was just the word *Pilot*. Fern then flicked back slowly, and under *M* saw the word *Muscle*.

She suddenly heard a noise while she was quietly snooping and quickly and softly closed the drawer. She immediately sat back in his chair, rubbing the chair arms as if she was pretending to be the boss.

"And who have we got here in Daddy's office? Ah, I see it's my new secretary," Chester smiled, surprised.

"Bonzo, Bonzo, where are you, boy?" Fern hastily called, looking under the desk and averting an inquisition.

"Hi, Dad, I was just looking for Bonzo. I needed some company, you know, and I thought he had wandered in here."

Luckily for Fern, Bonzo had heard his name called and, at that moment, came trotting into the study.

Chester walked up to his daughter and kissed her on the forehead affectionately.

"How was school? Come and have tea with me, Fern, and tell me." He put his hand on her shoulder and guided her out of his office.

"Rain check, Dad; I need to finish my homework."

"So be it, see you later. Go study. There's an engineer or scientist or actuary in you yet," he said proudly.

Fern smiled as she blew her dad a kiss and went back to her room.

After finishing her homework, she went out to the trampoline to blow off steam. She had become quite efficient; her fearlessness regularly gave her mother a heart attack watching her. She bounced and flipped and sailed through the air as if she was flying, twisting and somersaulting for nearly an hour. She felt like a graceful ballet dancer and a strong gymnast. Her imagination ran wild, and she fantasized about jumping as high as a young kangaroo joey, or as fast as an African cheetah, or soaring in the wind like a regal eagle in the sky. This was Fern's sacred time, where she could get lost in her own world.

Exhausted, she lay on the trampoline on her back, gazing up at the sky and thinking about how lucky she was to lack for nothing. She thought about her parents and wondered why she looked so different from them. She was blonde, and they were both dark-haired. Earlier, a boy at school, who had not met her parents, had asked her if her family was from Scandinavia.

During dinner that night in the kitchen, Chester's favorite piano music was softly emanating from the stereo in the lounge.

"Dad, Mom, there's something I've been meaning to ask you both," Fern casually asked...

"Yes, my dear?" Chester responded, enjoying the rockling fish that Megan had fried.

"Sure, what is it, honey?" Megan encouraged.

"It's just that I've been thinking, I'm a pure blonde. Mom, your hair is naturally black, and dad's hair is pure grey, but in all the photos that I've seen, like the ones in your study, Dad, your hair was pitch black when you were young."

A second or two of silence followed.

Chester and Megan had thought that this day might come. When Fern was a baby, they said they would tell her she was adopted but as time had passed it had seemed easier to let things lie. They were both worried if they told her she was adopted it would lead to other questions.

Chester looked at Fern sharply and immediately replied, "It is not very unusual, Fern. A human being carries thousands and thousands of genes, up to one-hundred thousand in fact. There are two-types of genes: dominant and recessive. The recessive genes often skip a generation or two before their true impact is really known." Chester took another bite to give Fern time to take in his answer.

"So, it is possible for parents with black hair to have a redhead or blonde even though it is more normal for the child to have the same color hair as their parents. You know, my late father was born blond, and eventually when he grew up, he was as ginger as a tom cat."

"Yuck! Does that mean I will turn into a redhead?"

"No, I don't see that happening. My late father was born blond and had turned completely ginger by the age of four."

"There, glad that's settled then," Megan responded with a relieved smile, although she reckoned it wouldn't be long before they wouldn't be able to fob her off that easily.

"I was not concerned, just inquisitive," Fern replied.

"Well, now that's settled. My gorgeous girls, I have news," Chester said, happy to change the subject, "The day after tomorrow I'm flying abroad and will be away for a few weeks on business. I have some intense business dealings to take care of. You'll need to look after each other, the house, and Bonzo, of course."

"Oh, Daddy, can I come?" Fern asked jokingly as she jumped up.

"Chester, this is sudden! Normally you give me more notice," Megan said with a slight edge of annoyance to her voice.

"You knew I'm attending the mining expos in two weeks. Well, something else has cropped up, and I need to secure some additional heavy equipment before the show. My Asian contact has come through with a good deal I can't pass up."

"Where are you going exactly, Daddy?" Fern asked.

"To Asia, America, and Europe. In Europe, I will be visiting Germany and the UK at this stage. There is also a possibility I might tag on Canada as well."

Later that evening, Chester's loyal pilot, Oliver, came by, as arranged, to finalize Chester's trip. Oliver had been Chester's private pilot for the past seven years, and the two men had formed a strong bond and healthy respect for one another. Oliver was in his early twenties, full of confidence and the swagger to go with a successful, globally savvy pilot. The two men sat in the study with the door shut. When his office door was closed, Chester's family knew that he was not to be disturbed under any circumstances. It was important for them to focus on the flight plan and all the relevant permits and costs involved.

At 24, Oliver was a much sought-after freelance pilot who flew the best planes, jets, and choppers for top executives — the ones who could afford his fee. Born in the USA, his father had taught him to fly when he was just a teenager and he now could afford to maintain two homes, in Sydney and Melbourne, and a lavish playboy lifestyle.

Good-looking and carefree, he was not overly ambitious: just give him a plane to fly and a beautiful woman to charm, and he was happy.

Chester liked him because he was good at his job, reliable, and above all, discreet. Megan didn't care for her husband's choice in the pilot. She thought him cocky and too arrogant for his own good.

"Oliver, how's your father?" Chester asked as he sat down to settle in for the long meeting.

"Never better, thanks. How's your little girl?" Oliver opened his briefcase to spread out the map of the flight plan. "Last time I saw her, she was just a tot. She's gonna be a stunner. You're going to have to keep an eye on her!" he grinned mischievously. "I bet a lot of boys are already suffering from stiff necks."

Chester chuckled good-naturedly, although he made a mental note to keep Fern away from Oliver. "Don't worry, kid, it's all taken care of. Can I pour you a scotch? I'm having one."

"Won't say no, thank you."

Chester opened the liquor cabinet and produced a Johnnie Walker Blue Label.

"My, my, are we celebrating?" Oliver commented.

"I think this is cause for celebration, to toast a successful trip with a twenty-five-year-old, exquisite label. Cheers!"

They clinked glasses, and each took a gulp. After savoring the signature taste of the malt, Oliver got down to business.

"Chester, I've gone ahead and arranged our flight details with all the airports. It's going to be a beautiful flight. I've secured a Gulfstream G200. It's the latest luxury jet that came on the market last year. I've piloted this particular plane many times. I think you'll love riding in her. She does require two pilots, and I'll arrange for a couple of attendants as part of this package deal."

"The other pilot has to be trustworthy, Oliver," Chester stated looking squarely at him.

"Oh, of course! He's good and reliable. I've flown with him many times. Obviously, I haven't told him about our cargo, and he will never know. As Captain, I'm first on and last off, like all good aviators, so there are no worries there. Talking about cargo, can I see?"

Chester took another sip of his platinum label, put the glass down on a leather coaster, and removed the so-called cargo from his inner jacket pocket. It was a small cardboard box, the size of a cigarette case, and inside Chester removed a tiny velvet pouch and opened it up on his desk, revealing seven clean-cut sparkling diamonds.

Oliver nodded, showing no surprise. He had collaborated on trips like this many times for Chester.

"Here are the magnificent seven, my pilot. Look after them. This one here is the smallest—a three-carat white, the others range from three to six carats, and the queen here is a pink five and a half carat." Chester picked it up, almost drooling with admiration of the radiant gem. "The colors range from D to E in quality—the very best! They are flawless in the 4C's—Clarity, Color, Cut, and Carat Weight. This makes them the fucking cream of the crop!"

"Which one is my cut, Chester?" Oliver joked.

Chester looked at him with a raised eyebrow. "They're all spoken for kid. Don't worry, I've factored in a more than generous bonus, above and beyond your fees and the cost to hire the jet. How does $150K sound?"

"Jesus, Chester!" was all Oliver could say. He then drained the rest of his whisky in one gulp without pulling a face.

"And" Chester added. "I foresee more trips in the future, if all goes well."

Megan soaked in the tub to calm her rattled nerves. It wasn't like Chester to spring a last-minute trip on her. He was up to something.

Fern took Bonzo into the courtyard out back and gave him a large knucklebone to chew and occupy him while she quietly tip-toed to her father's study to listen outside. She knew she was taking a risk, but at least Bonzo wouldn't give her away by whimpering or clawing the screen. She put her ear to the study door.

"Oliver, I know last time you unscrewed the padding of the Lear jet door and put them in there. Where are you going to hide them in the Gulf?"

"I've already checked it out. There are many safe places. No need to worry, Chester. In London, for example, the co-pilot will disembark first, and we will make sure we are a few minutes behind him so we are the last to leave. I've arranged for us to land when *our* custom official, the one we look after, is on duty. We will then take a cab to the Ritz and check in."

"Let's hope the Mossad hasn't bugged our rooms," he smirked.

Chester was stony-faced.

"Only joking, Mr. Jones," he tried to make light of it because they were indeed taking a huge risk with enormous consequences. "I heard that they've bugged rooms at the Ritz before. Someone even said that the Mossad supplied MI5 with recordings about someone famous before they were killed."

Fern was shocked and decided it was best not to eavesdrop after all. She tiptoed away as silently as she could and then ran as quickly as possible to the safety of her bedroom.

"It's getting late, Oliver." Chester was finishing his second glass. "I assume we have covered all the necessary papers for tonight?"

"You bet, boss, all the required stamps and dates for the certificates and all the necessary signatures for my privileges, validations, and instrument ratings.

"We will fly direct to Cairns, refuel, then off to Hong Kong. After that, Mumbai, and then onto London. And then, when you are ready, we will head to Washington DC and the rest we will schedule from there."

"Great, sounds like everything is in order." Chester smiled, relaxing a little. "Here's the box, Oliver. Don't fucking lose it! Remember, your bonus will be waiting for you when we get back if all goes well." But just to make sure his pilot had a better incentive, he added, "Seriously, if any of the magnificent seven get lost or don't make their destination, I have a very loyal associate who will happily cut your tool off and stick it behind your ear." He chortled sinisterly, "At least when you scratch your ear, you can have an orgasm!"

Oliver smiled. He knew his boss was half-joking, but the message was received loud and clear. He played along, "Might be worth losing a couple then."

He changed the subject to ease the tension in the room and started to put away his papers. "One last thing, the jet seats up to ten comfortably. There is room for six beds. Plenty for us and the crew."

"Aren't you concerned this would arouse suspicion from custom officials?" Chester queried.

"Not necessarily," Oliver assured him. "I mean corrupt leaders in Africa sometimes fly a fricking Boeing just for their family to go shopping in Hong Kong—they do it all the time, while their people starve to death. I wouldn't worry. I can always get a bevy of beauties over to fill the seats if you want?" Oliver joked.

Chester smiled without comment, "OK, good, let me walk you out." He put his hand on Oliver's shoulder to give fatherly advice, "Until then, get some rest and no screwing around. We need all your energy to concentrate on flying."

Bonzo was crying and scratching the kitchen screen door to be let in when Chester went to the fridge looking for a late-night snack. Bonzo came bounding in as if he had just spent a week in the kennels. Chester snuck the pooch a piece of cold ham, puzzled why he had been locked outside in the courtyard.

Fern lay on her bed, struggling to sleep. The words she had heard ran through her head. None of it made sense—money, diamonds, bugging hotel rooms, looking after a custom's official, and even death. She was scared, hearing her dad talk of things like this. She remembered seeing the letter *P* in her Dad's address book and now knew this was for *pilot*. Oliver was obviously *P*, her father's private pilot.

She tossed and turned, her mind racing; what did her dad really do, until she eventually fell asleep.

Chester was as good as his word and gave Oliver his bonus as soon as they arrived back in Melbourne six weeks later.

Megan was delighted with her brilliant diamond and sapphire platinum ring, a three-carat diamond of exceptional quality with two matching sapphires on either side. Fern also loved and treasured her stunning heart-shaped diamond pendant in yellow gold. His extended trip and the nature of his business were immediately forgotten as their happiness in life went back to normal.

Chapter Eleven

Over the next few years, Fern continued to sneak into Chester's study without anyone noticing whenever he was abroad. She wanted to figure this mystery out. She soon discovered her father had a secret safe hidden in the wall behind files and books. It was the size of perhaps two shoeboxes and housed a manual key mechanism as well as a combination lock with dozens of numbers. Fern reckoned her father kept more diamonds there. Well, maybe it wasn't that surprising; he did indeed work in the mining business.

One morning, while Nash was sitting quietly on the patio enjoying his morning coffee, mesmerized by the vibrant colors, Merle shouted from the driveway that she was off to run errands.

"Bruce, is there anything you need at the stores?"

"Just check up on the fruit, dear," he responded.

"Do you still have enough seed for your birds?"

"I believe, but perhaps you can get another multi-grain loaf of bread for them?"

"Will do, Bruce. Shan't be long." And with that, Nash heard the car pull out of the driveway.

Bruce realized how much he loved her; she was a true friend. He was lucky to have such a devoted partner in life. They made a good team.

At midday, the phone rang, but he didn't hear it as he was scrubbing down the birdbath and hosing off the soap. As usual, he'd totally lost track of time, and when he finally looked at his watch, it was two o'clock.

Strange, Merle was still not back. He went inside to get a cool drink and noticed he had missed several calls from the same number. He called Merle on her cell. There was no answer. He then called the number of the missed calls.

"Hello, MacAlpine here," a stranger's voice answered.

"Hello, this is Nash here, Bruce Nash. I seem to have had some missed calls from this number. Can I help you?"

"Mr. Nash, I am a surgeon at the local hospital here. I'm afraid your wife has had a bad accident. Can you get to the Dandenong hospital as soon as possible?"

"What!" Nash froze. "How bad? Oh my God!"

"I'll explain everything when you get here, Mr. Nash; please drive safely."

Nash hung up and rushed to grab his keys and wallet. "Merle! No, no, please God, let her be all right," he muttered under his breath, and he drove carefully but fast to the hospital.

The receptionist paged Dr. MacAlpine over the intercom. He arrived a few minutes later and introduced himself.

"Mr. Nash, please come with me. Let's sit here for a moment." Nash did not like this at all. He had been around a number of family notifications during his service on the force. A cold chill ran through his body.

"I'm afraid your wife had an accident; a serious one, and we are doing everything we can for her." Nash felt his heart stop.

"She has a punctured lung, both legs are crushed, numerous lacerations. She has a bad concussion and is in a coma. I'm terribly sorry." Dr. MacAlpine reached out his hand in support.

Nash felt he was going to faint, and Dr. MacAlpine snapped a command at a nurse nearby. He was immediately placed in a wheelchair, and she gave him a cup of cold water. They helped him onto a gurney and raised his feet. Within a few minutes, the room stopped spinning and he felt a little better. They escorted him to his wife's room.

Merle was unrecognizable. She lay there in a spaghetti of pipes and tubes, and needles and drips with an oxygen mask, surrounded by monitors and machines that were blinking and bleeping. She was covered in bandages, pins, and pulleys. Her face was ashen almost grey.

Nash stood frozen. His tears quietly trickled down his cheeks like an old tap needing a new washer. He didn't know what to say or do.

"When did you last eat, Mr. Nash?" the doctor asked concerned.

"Early this morning," he said absently.

"Nurse, please organize a sandwich and a hot drink for Mr. Nash," Dr. MacAlpine kindly asked.

The nurse quickly disappeared into the corridor to carry out the doctor's order.

"W-w-will she make it, doc?" Nash stuttered.

"There is a chance, a good one, but she will never walk again. She is in an induced coma right now. We must wait for the swelling to come down before we will know more. Be prepared, there is a small chance she will lose her ability to talk." He put a comforting hand on Nash's shoulder, but it had little effect.

Nash was shattered.

He later learnt from the Police Officer assigned to the case that the accident had occurred on the Burwood Highway just outside Ferntree Gully. Another car, apparently traveling at speed, had experienced a blowout, and flipped right into Merle's car. They rolled for some distance before coming to a halt upside down on the road. The other driver had been killed instantly. There was nobody else involved.

The policeman drove Nash home. There was nothing he could do. The doctor had advised him to rest and freshen up. It would be a long recovery and he would need his strength. Nash could take a taxi to the hospital in the morning and pick his car up.

"Will you be alright, inspector?" the officer asked as he pulled up outside his home.

"I will have to be," Nash replied climbing out of the police car.

Over the next few months, Nash hardly left his beloved wife's bedside. He practically lived there, and the nursing staff became like family.

When he did spend time alone at home, his mood was sombre. He thought he had been delivered one of the worst hands, to lose a life partner, who was barely still alive, paralyzed and could not talk. She needed help with everything from bathing to wearing a catheter that constantly needed changing. It was worse, he thought than being widowed because he had lost his wife, and yet she still lived.

He lost weight and aged; the garden was neglected, and so was the house. He became forgetful. One evening, sitting feeling sorry for himself alone on the patio, he looked in the direction of the birdbath and watched a beautiful galah in its tri-colored feathered suit of pink, grey and white teaching its young one to fly. It was comical and clumsy. He shouted out, "Merle, come look!" and then wept at the emptiness.

Chapter Twelve

Fern graduated high school with the highest honors and as class valedictorian in the summer of 2005. She had been accepted into Melbourne University, one of the top schools in the country to study architecture. She decided to take a gap year like most of her other classmates before she immersed herself in the seven-year course.

She turned down numerous invitations from friends to visit Thailand and Bali and even declined an extended trip through Europe. She had never taken to experimenting with drugs or alcohol and actually disliked the taste of wine and any liquor. In fact, she avoided crowds and congested city social gatherings altogether.

As a single child, she enjoyed her own company and loved exploring the city sights and admiring the various different building designs in her own time. She excelled in art and history, and she was very interested in environmental concerns, as well as in the design of buildings.

Chester loved this about his daughter. Even though he knew she was not going to be an engineer, scientist, or actuary, he could see she was a lateral thinker and a problem solver. With these qualities, Fern entered university to earn her MBA in architecture.

Fern was popular and easily settled into university life. She was admired by her lecturers and peers, and she did turn heads with the boys, just as Oliver had predicted. Her long wavy blonde hair and unique colored eyes with a genuine smile melted many admirers and attracted many approving looks.

She was disciplined and fearless. She was quick to deflect any inappropriate behavior or pass toward her and was happy to stand up for a colleague or friend against bullies or unwanted admirers.

For the first year, she shared a ride with a friend to the University campus or borrowed Megan's car when she had late classes.

She was excelling so well that Chester and Megan decided to buy her a small zippy Audi sports car for her eighteenth birthday.

She had also recently passed her driver's license exam, and this would be a wonderful way to celebrate her new independence.

Chester wanted it to be a huge surprise, so he talked to the dealership to arrange for the car to be delivered gift-wrapped in specially made blue and white paper with thin gold stripes. They also agreed to make sure that an enormous red ribbon bow would be perched on top of the roof.

In the meantime, Chester arranged with the dealership to visit their used car lot on a Sunday when they were closed, where he could show his daughter some older models to choose from.

That Friday night over dinner, while they sat at the kitchen table sharing the weekly events, Chester broached the subject.

"Fern, do you have any plans for the weekend? I want to show you something. It is your birthday on Monday, and I have an idea what you might like."

"Like what, Dad? Where do you want to go?"

"It's a surprise, honey." Megan chimed in.

"Tell you what, Sunday after breakfast we'll go for a ride."

"But Dad! What is it?"

"Patience is a virtue," Chester teased while winking at Megan.

"Oh, Daddy, I can't believe it! Wow... wow!" Fern exclaimed as they pulled up to the Used Car Dealership.

"I looked at that Holden the other day," Chester said. "It's been well looked after with just one previous owner. It is only six years old with under fifty-thousand kilometres on the clock. What do you think?"

They started to walk over to the blue car, Fern happy with excitement. As they got closer, her mood deflated.

"Ah no, Daddy, there is a sold sticker on it."

Chester took Fern's hand and smile, "Of course! I bought it for you! The sold sticker is for you!" Fern couldn't believe it.

"When you come home tomorrow night, it will be waiting for you," he grinned.

Fern let out a whoop of joy and hugged Chester. She was genuinely overjoyed.

On Monday morning, Fern couldn't wait to tell her friends about her new car and to give them a ride.

While she was in class, Chester arranged for the new Audi to be delivered to the house. The flatbed tow truck parked it outside the double garage, gift wrapped as arranged with a huge red bow fluttering in the breeze.

Megan and Chester were just as excited to present their special gift and couldn't wait to see Fern's face when she returned at the end of the day.

She came home running down the long driveway, all smiles and laughing with excitement to try out her first car. She stopped when she saw it was all wrapped up. She hadn't expected this, but her mom and dad were full of surprises.

"Surprise," they both beamed.

Fern laughed, enjoying the moment.

"Go on, open it, Fern," Megan encouraged, just as excited as her daughter.

"It is a little bit too heavy for me to pick up and hand you," Chester joked, grinning.

Ecstatic, Fern started to tear the paper off, ripping off the roof first.

"Dad, it's not blue. I thought the Holden was blue. I don't understand?" she stopped for a second, looking at him.

"Patience—remember?" Chester gently insisted.

Fern then noticed the brand-new shiny red paintwork and looked enquiringly at her dad. He just shrugged his shoulders, so she pulled off more wrapping paper to reveal another logo. It took a while to register before she recognized the iconic Audi symbol of the four overlapping circles.

"Oh my God! Oh my God!" Fern started jumping up and down. "Thank you, thank you, Daddy." She ran up to him and hugged him. Then she turned around to her mother.

"Thank you, thank you, Mommy" and she squeezed her tightly.

"I don't believe it! An Audi, yahoo!" she screamed.

Bonzo barked hysterically in all the excitement and furor.

Chester removed something from his pocket; it was the car keys, which he dangled in front of Fern, "Happy Birthday, my darling daughter! Ready for a test drive?"

Megan smiled and kissed Fern. "Congratulations, darling. I am making something special for dinner tonight for your eighteenth. Go and have fun!

Fern hugged her and grabbed the keys from Chester and climbed into the driver's seat.

"Don't forget to check the glove box," he smirked mischievously.

Fern shrugged inquisitively. "Just smell this leather; I love it,' she smiled.

"Fern, the glove box."

Fern opened it and removed a sealed envelope with her name on it.

She tore the envelope open; inside there was a beautiful birthday card and inside a deposit slip. She read the loving words. She was so lucky to have such doting parents. She knew she was a daddy's girl and looked up at her adoring father. Chester indicated to take a closer look. Her eyes widened. She put her hand over her mouth and was finally speechless.

Chester smiled and cleared his throat. He was serious.

"That is a deposit slip for two million dollars, Fern. It has to last you for seven years while you are studying at university. This allowance will only let you draw up to a maximum of a hundred thousand per annum. It should be plenty to provide you with whatever you need."

Fern didn't know what to say.

"All I ask is for you not to change and to continue to be the most loving, caring, and compassionate daughter—to always know who you are. I loved the fact that you were so excited and appreciative about the prospect of getting the old Holden. I hope you will never stop appreciating things and never expect things." As he spoke these words, tears welled up in Fern's eyes.

"No more surprises, I promise," he put his hands up in defeat. "Let's go for a spin before dinner and see what this little tyke can do, eh?"

Chapter Thirteen

It was about two years later when Megan walked into the bathroom after Chester had stepped out of the shower and was busy shaving.

"I don't know if I'm imagining it, darling, but it seems like you have lost a bit of weight," she said curiously.

"Hmm, I thought so too," he said, patting his stomach. "I've had to fasten my belt a couple of notches tighter in the last couple of weeks. Must be the stress of the job. There have been a few deals that have been pretty intense to close." He didn't add that he had also been a bit lethargic so as not to worry his wife. He was concerned though as he was also experiencing some odd sharp pains in his stomach.

"Maybe I should set up a doctor's appointment for you just so we know nothing is wrong. Have you weighed yourself lately?"

"No, and maybe I'll give Lance a call instead. I don't have time right now to make an appointment. We have a big deadline we are trying to meet at the moment."

"Oh, okay. You know best," Megan said and leaned forward and kissed him on the cheek, and left.

Chester looked in the mirror and studied his body. He turned sideways. He was in pretty good shape for his age. He leaned closer to the mirror and noticed a nasty dark bruise on the side of his shoulder. He became a bit more concerned and decided that he would speak to his brother.

When he arrived at Collins Street, he immediately jumped on the phone to put out the little fires that were burning. He spent an hour or two catching up on emails. He noticed how tired he was again. He started to worry and question himself. Where did the bruise come from? He couldn't recall bumping into anything and certainly hadn't knocked that area. He would have remembered such an impact to cause a bruise like that.

He fumbled for his mobile and immediately called Lance.

He picked up on the second ring. "Chester! How are you? Is everything okay? You don't normally call at this time of day?"

"I've not been feeling well, and I'm starting to get worried."

It was very unusual for his brother to complain about his health. Alarm bells went off in Lance's head. "Can you come by today? I'll make sure I fit you in."

"Perhaps on my way home around 5 pm. Does that suit you?"

"Perfect. You'll be my last patient, and we will have more time. See you then."

The bruise did not look too serious to Lance, but Chester's weight loss was a concern. He normally weighed about 175lbs, and today the scales read 165lbs.

"Did you know you've lost ten pounds? Hop up on the bed."

"Ouch!" Chester winced as Lance probed and pressed.

"Sorry, brother, but I think we are going to have to do some blood tests to give us more information. Get dressed, and let's chat."

"What is it?" Chester asked in a worried voice.

"Not sure, but go get these tests done tomorrow at one of the path labs. I should have the results in a couple of days. Your blood pressure is good, by the way, so that's a good sign."

"Jesus Lance! I hope it's nothing serious?"

"Perhaps you should take a few days off. Are you under a lot of stress?"

"No more than usual."

"Well, it might be good to take it easy for a while. Don't worry too much, we'll find some answers and figure it out. Give the girls a kiss for me."

Chester left Lance's office and headed home.

Chester brought Megan up to speed when he got home. They were in the kitchen chatting over coffee when Fern arrived. She came in full of energy, and her usual radiant smile lighting up the room.

"Hi, Mom. Hi, Dad," she said, going straight to the fridge to see if there was anything to snack on. "Crazy day, I'm starving. What's for dinner, Mom?"

"Fern, darling. Your dad isn't feeling too well. He went to see Uncle Lance today."

"Dad, are you all right? What's wrong?" Fern asked apprehensively.

"I'm okay. I've just lost a bit of weight," he told her.

"You don't look so good. You look tired," she observed.

"Oh, huh—when Lance checked me out, he touched a spot on my stomach. I nearly hit the roof."

"Chester, you never told me that part," Megan looked at him with alarm.

He stood up and put his hands on his wife's shoulder. "Let's wait for the results to come through. We will then have more information for Lance to prescribe the right meds. In the meantime, best to carry on as normal."

They ate dinner in a somber mood, the unspoken uneasiness dampening the atmosphere.

A few days later, Lance phoned Chester and said he needed to see him.

"Is it that bad, Lance? Tell me over the phone, we are family, you know."

"Chester, it is not great news, but let's chat in person," Lance stated firmly.

A cold chill ran through Chester's body. "I'm on my way," he responded.

The tone in his brother's voice was unnerving. He immediately thought the worst. *Not great news* could mean cancer. How many years had he left? he wondered.

Lance ushered Chester into his consulting room. The look on his face was serious.

"Please sit, brother," Lance said as he shook his brother's hand and indicated the chair.

"Sock it to me, doc." Chester tried to lighten the mood and put on a brave face.

"There is good and bad news. Your liver and spleen are swollen, which we can fix with the right medications." Chester nodded, knowing Lance hadn't finished with his diagnosis.

"The acute pain you experienced when I touched you is caused by your appendix. It is very swollen and needs to be removed as soon as possible before it becomes dangerous. I've already arranged for you to see the surgeon today."

Chester looked stunned. "Today?" he questioned.

"If it doesn't get treated straight away, it could burst. But that isn't all. Your blood work also indicates you have some form of leukemia. We need to do more tests which will involve doing a bone marrow biopsy. Come, I'm taking you."

Suddenly Chester found his world turned upside down. In the days that followed, the tests were conclusive. He had advanced leukemia, and it had spread.

Lance had the worst news he had ever had to deliver in his career — a death sentence to his own brother.

The drive over to his home was torturous. He dreaded delivering this kind of news to his patients but to a family member, it was unbearable. Chester was resting when he arrived. Megan told him Fern was at the gym and wouldn't be home for another hour.

Megan walked with Lance to the lounge, where Chester was quietly napping in his favorite recliner.

"My darling family, it is not good news. The tests came back and show that you have cancer, and it has been going on for a long time undetected. It has spread considerably and gone into your liver and bones." Chester paused to let the news sink in.

Chester was quiet and reached out his hand to Megan, who began to cry.

"We need to admit you immediately for intensive chemotherapy treatment amongst other things."

"Be honest Lance. What are my chances and how much longer do I have?" He was trying to be stoic for Megan's sake.

"One can never be definitive with these things …"

"How long have I got, Lance?" Chester repeated firmly.

Lance took a breath to compose himself. "With treatment, a few months. Without treatment, a couple of weeks, if we're lucky."

Megan gasped, panicked. She broke down sobbing, her wet face buried in her hands.

"I am not dying in hospital," Chester said vehemently, swallowing any kind of emotion that was welling up inside. "I will stay home, maintain my grace and say my goodbyes here."

"I know you are a proud man, Chester, but please, let me admit you. You will have twenty-four-hour care and attention, only the best, please, I beg of you."

"Lance, that's like being on the Titanic. You know you are sinking, and it is just a matter of time before you die from drowning or hypothermia. I'd rather go quickly rather than suffer. You can't avoid the inevitable."

Megan was starting to compose herself. She blew her nose and wiped her eyes, and suddenly chimed. "Let him decide, Lance. Please." Megan, with swollen red eyes, looked up at her brother-in-law.

"So be it," Lance said disappointedly. He knew it was no use arguing with them. "Have it your own way. I will visit you daily and prescribe strong painkillers to help you with the pain. I will need to give you injections around the clock, and we will make you as comfortable as possible." He had seen this too many times in his long career and knew most patients had no idea what they would be facing on a day-to-day basis. "We will have to set up hospice care further down the road as well. This won't be easy for you either, Megan."

Fern was pulling into the driveway as Lance was leaving. As she was about to get out of her car, Uncle Lance snapped at her.

"I need to leave. Please move your car now, I have patients to visit in the hospital."

"Sure, okay," Fern responded, wondering what brought on the cold and unfriendly manner, which was so unlike her Uncle.

Fern reversed and as soon as there was room, Lance sped off. He never even waved goodbye.

Fern parked and went inside. She followed the voices emanating from the lounge. Her mother sat opposite her father, holding his hands.

"What's the matter with Uncle Lance? He was so unfriendly." Then she noticed something was very wrong.

"Mom, you're crying?"

"Come here, darling, come sit by me." She reached out her hand to her daughter. "Uncle Lance has just delivered the worst news in the world."

Fern stared at her parents, her mind racing. She was about to go to her mother when Chester said, "No, please come sit with me."

She stepped towards him when Chester, very wobbly, stood up and gave Fern a huge hug. She could feel his strength and his great love for her. He hugged her tightly for a few seconds before letting go.

"Sit in my chair," he offered.

"Daddy, what is it? You're scaring me."

"It's your chair now."

Fern sat down as she was told. "What do you mean it's my chair? Please tell me what's wrong, please."

"My darling daughter, Fern. I have stage four cancer. Uncle Lance thinks I have a few months at best. I am riddled with it. It is all over my body." Fern couldn't believe her ears and started to sob.

Chester leaned heavily on the back of the chair for support and took charge as he always did when taking care of his girls. This was not going to be an exception.

"I have decided I will not die in a hospital even if it means I have less time here on this planet. I want to be at home with my girls and enjoy what little time I have left. Being at home with you is all the comfort I need and cherish. It is important that life carries on as normal." Chester was beginning to tire. "There is not much time to organize everything and put my affairs in order, so it is imperative we discuss everything tonight. It is also important to me that you both continue on with your lives and steer the Jones legacy into the future and do good in the world."

"Why don't I go and make some tea before you continue?" Megan suggested as she saw her husband's energy drop and helped him sit down on the couch. She also realized she needed a break too. "Fern, why don't you grab a notepad as well while I make tea."

A few minutes later, they reconvened, and Chester continued with his thoughts and wishes:

"In my safe is my last will and testament. Basically, my money is divided equally between both of you, to the tune of some two hundred million each. The properties that are in my name are worth another fifty million or so. It will be your choice to keep or sell, but all proceeds are to be divided equally. Megan, you must arrange this with our lawyer, Stanley Isaacs from Hoffman & Isaacs. I have already spoken to him. He is expecting a call from you. Our home here I leave to you, Megan, so you can stay in Toorak; and my business I leave to you, Fern. It is worth a fortune. Also, in the safe is a small fortune in diamonds, which I have acquired over the years for a rainy day. That rainy day has arrived. It is a long story, but basically, I sold some equipment on consignment, and the client gave me the diamonds as collateral. In the end, I kept the diamonds as the client never paid. These magnificent gemstones I leave to you, my darling wife," he smiled at Megan, "and it is up to you if you want to give one or two to Fern." Megan was still speechless, reeling from the news and now this. It was impossible to take all this in.

"I will also arrange with my friend Oliver, the pilot, to sell them and transfer the proceeds to you. I will give him a ten percent commission fee for taking care of this for me. There should be another good few million there. Now I really am tired. Fern, would you be a dear and pour me a double scotch, and then I'll turn in for the night. What time is your first class tomorrow?"

Fern was also in shock like her mother. She was emotionally spent from the sudden news. She got up and went to the liquor cabinet.

"Do you really think school is important, especially now, Daddy?"

"Of course it is! Your whole future depends on it."

"I'm actually off tomorrow."

"Good, that settles it because you and I are going for a short drive tomorrow."

"Where?" Megan asked, surprised. She was used to him making unilateral decisions without consulting her. She mostly let it slide because he always had her best interest at heart. But, this time, she felt betrayed. Things were moving too quickly without any discussions. They were running out of time for any more hidden secrets.

"Yes, where Daddy?"

"You will see tomorrow."

Megan had a bad feeling about this proposed trip, but she didn't say anything; she was too exhausted to object. It was getting late.

None of them slept well that night; Megan lay for a while in Chester's arms until he pushed her away. She reached out for him. "You'll have to get used to being alone sooner or later, darling."

"Not yet," she said, putting her arm around him again.

Chapter Fourteen

Physically, Chester didn't feel as badly as he thought he would. He was up early and ready for the short journey.

They left a little while later, leaving Megan gazing at them from the upstairs window, her expression troubled.

"Where are you taking me, Dad?" Fern asked curiously.

"We are going for coffee."

"Just coffee?"

"And a chat, my gorgeous daughter."

They drove past the police station that Chester had avoided nearly twenty years ago and a couple of blocks later pulled into a small strip mall.

"This place makes good coffee," Chester said, pointing to a picturesque café.

The manager greeted them with a faint smile as they entered.

They sat down at a table furthest from the entrance and away from other patrons. Chester threw his car keys onto the table and ordered coffee for both of them.

Fern was puzzled. Her eyes darted around as she wondered why they could not talk at home. What was all the secrecy, and why away from her mother too?

Chester waited for their coffees to arrive before talking. "There is something I need to tell you. It is very important. It's been bottled up inside me for a very long time."

Chester hesitated; he had not forgotten the promise he had made to his brother all those years ago, but Fern was now a young woman, not a child. . Soon, he would not be around, and she deserved the truth.

"Honey," he said, leaning in to hold her hands. "Just over twenty years ago, you came into our lives and changed our lives forever," he started and then paused again. Taking a deep breath, he continued, "Do you remember challenging us over dinner once? You wanted to know why you were blonde, and we weren't."

"I'm not thick, Dad. I figured it out ages ago that you and Mom had adopted me. If that's what you are trying to tell me, I'm okay about it. It doesn't bother me that I'm adopted. You're my parents and the best parents anyone could have. That's all that matters to me."

Chester's phone rang. It was Megan. He chose to let it go to voicemail.

"Oh, we are so blessed to have you in more ways than one. Thank you, my darling girl. Your Mom and I could not have children, and then I found you."

Fern noticed her Dad said *I* and not *we* and chose not to question.

The manager walked over, and Chester raised his hand, stopping the approach. The manager backed away. He understood that something serious was taking place.

"Go on, Dad," Fern said, keen to hear more.

"It was a cold, bitter winter evening. It was early but already dark. I had just bought my first new Audi to celebrate the first massive deal I had clinched that day. I was on cloud nine and took the car for a spin. I felt like a teenager. I had the music on full volume, put my foot on the accelerator, and hit the road. I was enjoying the freedom of driving an open road and was cruising along the main Tourist Road in the Dandenong, not far from where we are now. Something caught my eye in the headlights, and I turned around."

Chester sipped his coffee. Fern was engrossed.

"I pulled up to the side of the road amongst the gum trees, the moss, and ferns. I left the car lights on when I saw what I thought was a small dirty basket. But then, I couldn't believe my ears when I heard crying. As I got closer, I realized it was a small bassinet with a tiny baby inside and a fluffy koala for company. There was no one around. I was shocked and devastated that this infant had been left to die in the cold. The baby was wet and hungry and close to death. I brought her home, and your Uncle Lance worked his magic and saved you."

Chester paused again, letting Fern digest what he had just told her. He waited for a reaction. None came. There was a heavy silence between them, and he could feel the tension in Fern's body.

He went to speak again, but she startled him by suddenly snatching his car keys off the table and running outside, knocking a chair over in haste. She opened the car door and sobbed hysterically in the driver's seat. Chester quickly dropped some cash on the table and raced after her. As he approached the car, she locked all the doors.

He banged on the car window. A sharp pain tore through his body; his abdomen was burning like there were a thousand fires inside. He was puffing, trying to catch his breath. His shoulders were heaving up and down like a pump.

"Fern, Fern, please, please, please forgive me, and open the door, my darling. Let me finish. Let me explain more."

" I just want to be alone!" Fern shouted while pounding the steering wheel.

Chester sat down on the pavement a few feet away from the Audi. A few people stopped to stare.

Chester's phone rang again. Megan. He put the phone on silent.

Fern looked at the small crowd gathering. She wished the ground would swallow her up. She just wanted to disappear, to vanish for good. The butcher came out to see what was happening; an elderly lady stood leaning on her walking frame and gazed wide-eyed while a young couple with three kids looked on curiously. Fern wanted to yell at all of them — leave us alone, you fucking vultures, you magpies, scavengers, go to fucking hell! She didn't know what to do with the rage burning inside her. She was stunned and frozen from the betrayal and the lie she had lived all these years.

All of a sudden, she released the central locking system.

Chester heard this and jumped up. "Move over, Fern, let me take us home." He was wheezing now, finding it difficult to breathe.

"No, Chester, no! You hop in!" Fern snapped.

For the first time in her life, she addressed him as Chester, not Daddy or Dad. He sat down heavily in the front passenger seat.

"Fern, please let me drive," he whimpered.

"No, Chester, no! No!" Fern replied, taking charge.

Fern turned the ignition on, reversed out of the parking lot, and turned right.

"What are you doing, Fern? You should have turned left."

"We are going to the Tourist Road in Dandenong. I want you to show me exactly where you found me, do you hear?" she barked.

"Oh Fern, please don't put me through this. Please I am begging you."

Fern drove fast. It was unnerving. She kept cold eyes on the road and looked nowhere else.

Chester held on tight. In a short while, they came to the turn-off up ahead.

"Where now, Chester?" she snapped again.

He inwardly winced again at being addressed by his first name. "Left at the yield sign, that's the Tourist Road. Left here," he said, holding onto the grip bar to steady himself.

Fern tapped the brakes and slowed down a bit. She was still driving too fast to make the turn ahead. She tapped the brakes again and the Audi stuck like glue to the road as she took the corner and managed to make the turn safely. She slowed down a bit when she realized the risk ,she had taken, going so fast.

"Where?" she shouted, hurt creeping into her voice. "Show me, Chester. Where's the spot? Tell me, show me, show me now."

"Just slow down. I don't mind dying since death is days away for me anyway, but I do not want you to die from driving recklessly. You have your whole life ahead of you."

The Audi climbed the hill. She stayed silent and then...

"Chester, where to now?" She was getting hysterical.

"Watch it; there's a sharp bend up ahead," he mumbled.

Fern had to slow down; there was a truck in front of them, but only for a moment. She pulled out of the bend and hit the accelerator, overtaking the truck.

"How much further, Chester?" she screamed.

"Any second after that next bend, up on the left."

Fern finally slowed down, the car now crawling, and the truck was now right behind them.

"Pull up there," Chester indicated. "There, there by that clump of trees," he pointed.

Fern swerved off the road; the truck driver waved his arm and flipped them the bird as he passed by, shouting obscenities.

Fern switched off the ignition and jumped out of the car. Chester followed.

"Show me exactly where, Chester," she said in a slightly calmer voice.

With great effort, Chester walked up the road for about thirty feet, then turned. He went downhill for about a couple of dozen paces, and suddenly he saw the roots of the tree and, further off the road, the dense bush and ferns.

Fern came running up.

Chester fell onto his knees and sobbed. "Just here, Fern, that's the exact spot."

Fern stood silent, rigid, her bottom lip trembling, then she bit it hard in anguish.

She sat down next to Chester

and started to moan. A deep torment rising out of the depth of her soul, the grief overwhelming, she mumbled, slurring her words.

"Mamma, where are you? Why? Why here? Why so cruel? You left me to die, this horrible death. You treated me like garbage chucked out onto the road like junk. I was crap, and you treated me just like a fuckin' piece of fucking trash!" She screamed, and Chester sat there letting her vent, but he could not console her. It was painful for him to witness.

It seemed like an eternity, but eventually Fern was spent. Her eyes were red and swollen, she took a breath. Chester stood up, and Fern copied him.

They hugged each other tight and hard, not wanting to let go. Chester felt excruciating stabs running up and down his spine, but he would not let on. While Chester stood, Fern slipped to her knees, holding on to his legs, clutching them tight for dear life as if she had received the death penalty. Chester put his hand on her head for comfort, and then she stood up and stepped away. She placed both trembling hands across her chest and looked up into the sky to the heavens, standing dead still and alone. Chester thought that if Michelangelo had been present, he would have sculptured a statue of her in that desperate position.

"Thank you, Daddy. I'm okay. Let's go home to Mom. I will drive."

They climbed back into the car. The silence was deafening. Each in their own thoughts.

Twenty years ago, Chester had made an inexplicable, impromptu stop that had produced a miracle. Today the same spur-of-the-moment stop by the side of the road had turned into doom and gloom, he thought. He had shattered Fern's world, and he was nearly dead.

Chester phoned Megan; the call was short, just to say they were on their way home.

"Why did you decide to tell me, Daddy?" Fern asked.

"Difficult to die with such a secret. I wanted to get it off my chest. I wanted to show you how much we love you, and how much you have meant to us. But I realize it was inconsiderate and selfish of me. It was cruel and unkind to expect you to take it in. It must be a great shock."

"That's for sure!" Fern said sarcastically.

"Fern, I've made a grave mistake. I, we, should have told you sooner. Gently broken the news to you. It is the greatest mistake I have made in my life, and I will forever feel guilty for hurting you like this." He looked out the window at the passing scenery.

"Forgive me, Fern, please forgive your dying father. Now, I know what it is like to be an innocent man being sent to the gallows for a murder that he did not commit." He turned and looked at her, deeply remorseful.

Fern remained silent and did not look back at him.

They arrived home an hour later. Megan knew something was wrong and was waiting for them in the driveway.

Megan went to kiss Fern, but she turned her head. "No, don't. My lip is bleeding."

"Good heavens! What happened, darling?"

"Everything!" Fern said and excused herself before she broke down in sobs again. She ran inside, grabbed a glass of juice from the fridge, and went out into the backyard. She removed her shoes and climbed onto the trampoline; her morale rock bottom.

Megan shouted out something about lunch, but it fell on deaf ears.

Fern jumped and jumped and jumped. She somersaulted forwards and backward. She cut through the air like a whip.

Chester went straight to the liquor cabinet and poured himself a double scotch. He swallowed half in one gulp.

When Chester told Megan what had happened, she was furious. She had never felt so angry towards him. It was rare.

"Why, Chester, why?"

"I felt she had a right to know. She's a woman now. And, I didn't want to go to my maker with this burden on my conscience about what I did back then."

"So, you were thinking only of yourself, eh? I've always known you were a self-centered, self-important man, Chester, and I've loved you anyway. But this, this is too much."

Chester was shocked at Megan's tone. She had never spoken to him like this before. His face crumpled, and Megan felt a stab of pity.

In a quieter tone, she asked, "Could you not at least have told me what you were going to do? If you had to tell her, don't you think it would have been better to tell her together and at home?"

Chester's response was typical, "I thought you would try to stop me," he said simply and shrugged.

Megan sighed. She wanted to storm out of the house to teach him a lesson, but what was the point? Chester had always been a law unto himself, and now he was on his last legs. It was too late for lessons, too late to try to change him.

Fern jumped higher and higher still.

Chester poured another double, and Megan busied herself in the kitchen.

Fern jumped, landing on her stomach and bouncing back onto her feet.

Chester snuck in another drink, this time a single. He tried to stand, but his head was spinning, and he sat down again.

Fern did another somersault, landed sharply on her feet, and bounced on her back this time.

Megan looked out the lounge window; Fern was going full steam, her blonde hair flying up and down, sparkling in the sun as if she had tinsel in it. She began to worry and went to talk to Chester.

"I'm concerned. She's been jumping for two hours."

"Huh, uh," was all he could say. The booze was winning.

Megan took his shoes off and moved his legs onto the couch, and then she went outside.

"Fern, honey, you'll get sick. Your face is red! Come off the trampoline now, for God's sake. You've been jumping for two hours."

"Later, later," was the response.

Megan phoned Lance. She needed support. He said he would be there soon.

Fern continued on the trampoline, half twists and full twists, landing on her feet and on her knees; there were tuck jumps just as she had done as a child.

Her head was spinning, but she continued to bounce more, on her feet, higher and higher, and then she went into a tucked back somersault. She landed askew, falling heavily.

She lay where she fell, uninjured but exhausted finally.

When Lance arrived an hour later, Fern was still lying motionless on her back on the trampoline. Megan briefed him, and he went outside.

"Fern, Fern, it's me. Uncle Lance. Please come off now. You must be thirsty."

Surprisingly, Fern obeyed and climbed down, standing unsteadily next to her uncle, the doctor.

"Were you in on this too? Did you know that I was thrown out like garbage?"

"My darling niece, I wasn't in on what happened today. I am so sorry I wouldn't have agreed to it." He put his arm around her shoulders. "Let me have a look. Your lip looks like it needs attention. Let's go sit down on that garden bench for a few minutes."

They walked together with Lance's hand on her shoulder, his other hand carrying his doctor's bag.

They sat down in the shade, "Let's see that lip first."

"It doesn't hurt."

"You don't need any stitches, but I need to clean it," he said soothingly.

"Sure," she reluctantly agreed.

Lance produced an alcohol wipe from his bag.

"This will sting a bit." He wiped her lip gently clean, "Your dad should never have put you through what he did today. I'm not siding with him, but remember, if he lives another two weeks, he'll be lucky. You're in a tough situation: between a rock and a hard place. It's not fair, but we have to be aware of this."

"Don't you think I am not aware?" she retorted.

"I know you are, but strange things can happen when you have just days left to live. It is amazing how your priorities shift for you and your loved ones. It gives life a different perspective."

"Thanks. I am all right now."

"You do not look it. Let's go inside and get some liquids inside you. You must be dehydrated. Your face is burnt from the sun, and I want you to drink more and rest. You've had an emotional shock."

Inside the house, Fern swilled down three glasses of water while Megan made tea.

"Where's Chester?" Lance asked.

"He is sleeping it off too much to drink," Megan replied.

Lance checked Fern again. Physically she seemed fine, but he gave her a couple of sedatives to take to calm her down; it had been a long and harsh day.

Fern excused herself and went to her room. She lay on her bed in deep thought.

After a while, she got up and went to her dresser. She took the little koala sitting on top and climbed back on her bed. She felt the poignancy exuding from the well-worn toy. It had been with her all her life. Tears streamed down her cheeks. She knew now it had been a gift from her birth mother.

Downstairs, Lance went to check on his brother, who was still dozing on the couch. He stood there for a few seconds watching him, knowing he would lose him soon. Chester stirred and opened his eyes, and yawned. He lifted his head.

"Lance, I've given it some thought. There isn't much point in having my appendix removed if I am already staring death in the face. Having it out will not delay my journey to the cemetery."

"Perhaps, but if it bursts, it will be a very painful death."

"That is a chance I am willing to take." Chester rolled his eyes. He yawned once more and was almost instantly asleep.

Lance vacated the room and said goodbye to Megan in the kitchen. As he walked up to his car, he had another shock. He stopped suddenly in his tracks. He couldn't believe it. Bonzo was lying motionlessly on the ground. Poor Bonzo, he had finally succumbed to old age.

This was more than enough in one day. Lance just stood there aghast. He started to tremble, and his shoulders shook. The weight of the world came tumbling down as he stood there all alone. After a while, he gathered himself and grabbed a blanket from his car. He covered Bonzo, gently picked him up, and put him into the back of his car without anyone noticing. He would arrange for the vet to come to his home and collect him from sparing Megan and his niece any more heartache.

Megan knocked on Fern's door, then entered.

Fern jumped up, leaving the toy on the bed.

"Are you all right, darling?" Megan asked kindly while studying Fern.

"Feeling better, thank you," she lied.

Megan hesitated and then added gently, "Darling, I know this has come as an enormous shock to you, and I don't agree with Dad telling you like he did. But please, you must understand that if your dad hadn't found you when he did … in a way, it was your Dad who gave you your life."

"I know, Mom," Fern interrupted. She understood, but somehow it didn't make the pain disappear. She would never understand why she had been thrown out like garbage, probably by her own mother. The horror would remain with her for the rest of her life.

"I suggest you have a good shower and then come downstairs for dinner. I've made you something special—it's a surprise."

"I will," Fern said as she looked furtively at her running shoes on the floor near her cupboard.

Megan left and went downstairs. Fern picked up her running shoes; she looked at them and then put them back next to her bed.

She then went downstairs to eat.

"There, you look much better, and I'm sure you'll feel better," Megan greeted her.

"Thanks, I do."

"That's my girl," Chester exclaimed. He looked like death warmed over; he was slower and had lost his color.

After dinner and while Megan had gone upstairs to shower, Chester asked Fern to come into his study for a minute.

Fern complied but felt a stab of worry that he might be about to divulge more things she would rather not know.

"Fern, please forgive me for my shocking behavior today. You will one day be one of Australia's most successful architects and businesswomen. You are rich, talented, and gorgeous. Sadly, it is my biggest regret. I will not see that day. Nor will I see you marry or my grandchildren playing on the slide or jumping on the trampoline. Fern, you are powerful, I know it, you are shrewd, you are taller than the trees, taller than the mountains, taller than my office block, and no one can ever take that away from you."

"Thank you, Dad; I will cherish those words." And she meant it.

Chester wrote something down on a piece of paper.

"This is the safe combination. When I check out, give it to your mother." He sat down in his chair, exhausted. "Now I need to sleep." He kissed her on the forehead. "Good night, sleep well."

In her room, Fern knew her father was half gone. Even his once fine writing was all over the place. She looked at the numbers on the paper; they were 2229632.

Chapter Fifteen

Lance had already telephoned Megan to break the sad news about Bonzo. Megan was terribly upset; the timing could not have been worse. Lance said that delivery of the new Bonzo was in motion, and Megan appreciated it.

Fern had left early and driven to the Toorak Railway Station in Armadale.

In the car, she swallowed the two tablets Lance had given her.

She parked her car and went straight to platform 4, where she knew the express train to Cranbourne was due in a few minutes.

The station was busy with people going to work. She noticed a young man looking at her and moved away.

He had noticed she had not scanned her Metro card to travel on Melbourne's public transport. He thought she was obviously chancing it and trying to ride for free.

Fern walked to the end of the platform, where it was less crowded. The curious young man followed her at a discreet distance.

Every now and then, Fern glanced in the direction from where the train would approach. She had tied the laces of her running shoes very tight; she could not afford to slip or for a shoe to come off.

She wriggled her toes and took in a deep breath, exhaling slowly. To avoid suspicion, she stayed well behind the yellow line on the platform.

She heard the deafening, high-pitched horn of the express train appearing. It was some two hundred feet down the track. Fern breathed in again deeply and wriggled her toes for the last time. She placed her left foot forward with her tense arms hanging, just like an athlete ready for the starter's pistol.

She looked up. The train was fifty feet away; any second now, she was ready. It was traveling at speed and had no intention of slowing down.

The metal train was massive, over ten carriages long, carrying about five hundred people on board. It was traveling at approximately one hundred and four kilometres per hour.

Fern placed all her weight on her right foot, her heart exploding with thunderous beats. She was about to spring forward when a voice spoke from behind her.

"Are you all right there?" It was the young man.

Instinctively Fern turned towards the voice just as the express train sounded the horn again, accelerating.

She was out of breath but nodded her head up and down. The train whooshed past. The stranger waved and turned away.

She left the train station and walked to her car. She sat inside for some time, crying. Her mind was racing faster than the express train. And then she had a thought. She had a plan. This would be the way to make sense of her fate. She could do it.

She hit the ignition and drove home.

When she pulled up in the driveway, new Bonzo came out to greet and investigate her. Fern stooped down and hugged the dog. Where was old Bonzo, and who was this puppy. . The dog followed her inside with his tail wagging like a farmer's scythe cutting the long grass.

"Fern, darling, where have you been?" her mother called out.

"Just went to see a friend to help her with her studies." She wandered into the kitchen and picked up the puppy, "Mom, what's with this little guy? Where's Bonzo?"

"Fern, please be brave but old Bonzo has passed from old age, and Uncle Lance brought us a new puppy."

"What? Oh no! This is too much."

"We have to be strong for your father's sake. Our love for each other is even more important than ever. We must appreciate and be thankful for every day we have together."

Fern was distraught. Megan reached out and hugged her, and she hugged her mother even tighter and held on to her for a little longer than usual. Megan looked at her closely. Fern hadn't hugged her like that since she was a little girl.

"Where's Dad?" Fern asked.

"He's in bed resting. He's having a tough day, my sweet thing," Megan turned away so her daughter wouldn't see her own tears. She busied herself at the sink. "It's really hard to see him waste away like this...."

Fern didn't know what to say. She made herself a long black coffee and toast and went to check in on him. He was on his back, snoring loudly. She went downstairs; her mother was still busy concocting something for dinner, which smelled divine.

She went quickly to Chester's study and looked around. She took his telephone book, his notebook and his diary that was on top of his desk. He wouldn't miss them.

She decided she would come back when her mother went out and checked the safe just out of curiosity. There was something else she would take, but that was still next to Chester's bed. She could wait.

The epiphany she had at the train station was percolating in her soul, and her energy invigorated, she jumped on her bed and opened up her laptop.

The Google search results were mind-boggling and depressing. She read that 50 million births go unregistered every year worldwide; over half a million children live on the streets; there were 135,000 abortions carried out daily; 250 million children were engaged in child labor; 10 million children were enslaved in prostitution with about one million entering the sex trade every year; and there were hundreds of millions of undocumented orphans, with Africa and Asia leading the epidemic.

The search also revealed horror stories about dumped babies found dead and alive in public toilets, abandoned in the bush, or in city dumpsters, or left next to the roadside in either cities or parks and other bizarre and sad places. If they were lucky, some were dropped off anonymously in hospital parking lots. There was even a gruesome article about starving dogs eating babies left in garbage dumps in third-world countries.

Reading this, Fern realized how incredibly lucky she was. It was certainly a miracle she had been found by such a loving couple. She knew exactly what she had to do to show her appreciation and pay it forward. Her epiphany was her mission.

Chapter Sixteen

"Chester?" Megan rolled over in bed and gently touched his shoulder to wake her husband.

"Chester, wake up!" Megan shook him a little harder but still no movement. She was wide awake now.

"Fern, Fern come quick!" she screamed.

Fern was quietly dozing in her bed. She jumped out of bed and quickly ran to her parents' room.

"Oh my God!" Fern cried.

They tried to wake him, calling his name in the hopes he would open his eyes.

Megan grabbed the phone and called 911 while Fern tried to find a pulse. There was none.

Someone on the end of the phone asked, "What is your emergency?"

"My husband is dead," Megan sobbed into the phone.

"Ma'am, what's your name?"

"I… I am Megan Jones, his wife."

"Does anyone know how to do CPR?"

"For God's sake, he's cold; there's no pulse," Megan howled with despair.

She could no longer talk, so Fern took the phone, "My father is definitely dead," she said emphatically. "He had cancer and died overnight. Please send an ambulance immediately."

"Your name, please."

"Fern, Fern Jones. I am his daughter." Then she gave the Call Center woman their address in Toorak.

"I'm sorry for your loss," she said. "An ambulance has been dispatched and will be with you shortly."

"Mom," Fern interrupted her mother's crying. "I think it's best if you phone Uncle Lance now before the paramedics get here."

Megan called her brother-in-law. While she was distracted talking to Lance, Fern quietly took Chester's phone from his bedside table. She felt bad, but she would need all his personal belongings to take care of all the immediate needs and necessary arrangements in the next forty-eight hours. She already had her father's vital contact information, his notebook, and his diary from his study, as well as the safe combination. She gave her mother privacy and went downstairs to make some tea.

Lance arrived a short while later, a few minutes before the ambulance pulled into the driveway.

The EMTs went with Lance to Chester's bedside while Megan and Fern hung out in the kitchen. It was obvious nothing could be done. He was long gone.

Soon the ambulance crew left, and Lance joined them in the kitchen. Fern made her Uncle tea and a second cup for her mom and herself. They sat around talking about the last few difficult days and the huge gap Chester left in their lives.

They started to talk about the necessary funeral arrangements until it became too much for Megan. She excused herself to get dressed as they were still in their night clothes.

Lance stayed on a bit longer to finish his tea and to check in with his niece. He was concerned about how she was coping with everything in general, and after he was reassured that she was okay, he departed.

They had drawn up a list of things for Megan to do. Keeping busy was good for her. It kept her mind from dwelling on her loss. She had to phone their church and liaise with the priest, the funeral home, and the cemetery. She also needed to talk to their lawyer Stanley Hoffman in due course and action Chester's will and last testament. It reminded Megan that she should also think about drawing up a will.

She was doing well, considering the shock she had been through waking up next to her dead husband. It was impossible to digest that the man she loved, with whom she had spent the most part of her life, was gone. The ache inside was unbearable, and she wondered if she would be able to endure it. She took comfort in the wonderful life he had provided for her and Fern. She would cherish those memories forever.

Later that day, there was a never-ending stream of friends of the couple who popped in to pay their respects. It was touching to know he was loved and respected by so many, but it was also exhausting.

When finally, the last person had left, and the house was all quiet, Megan was able to go upstairs and rest; the emotional strain had taken its toll. She put her phone on silent and took another Valium that Lance had given her.

Fern went to Chester's study.

She immediately opened the safe. There were two boxes, one small and another about the size of a cigarette box, an older cell phone, and a copy of Chester's will, which was rolled up and fastened with an elastic band. Fern removed the items from the safe and placed them on his desk.

She opened the tiny jewel box first. Before her was a set of gold cufflinks. Each one housed a flat, black stone with the initials RDJ. She closed the tiny box, and then she opened the small velvet-lined, navy blue box.

Fern whispered a soft *wow*. Inside there were nine diamond stones, and they all sparkled.

There was also a typed list.

8 CT, IF-D. Value $190,000
7 CT, VV S1-E value $140,000
5 CT Pink-flawless $11,000000.
11 CT, IF $2,000,000,
3 CT, VS 1D $61,000,
2x2 CT, VV S1, both F both $54,000 each
I CT IF-D $27,000
1.5 CT blue & flawless—Oliver getting back to me with price
(roughly $600,000)
Grand total value $14,000,000

Fern was hypnotized for a while—she hadn't expected this. She was looking at over fourteen million dollars in diamonds.

This was a vast sum of money and didn't even include the other assets; the multi-million-dollar business, the commercial properties, the house, as well as other portfolio investments and cash in the bank.

Fern photographed Chester's will and the diamond list with her cell phone.

She couldn't help herself and picked up the pink one that was worth eleven million to admire and feel what it was like to hold such a valuable gem. She then put it back with all the other stones and put everything in the safe the way she had found it. As she was doing this, she felt the base of the safe was a bit loose. Curious, she carefully pressed and pulled until, eventually, the floor moved, and she saw a secret cavity underneath. She was stunned. Inside was a massive black opal, the likes of which she had never seen before. It was interlaced with flaming colors of red, green, and blue. She picked it up, and she held it to the light and saw what appeared to be a double-curved vein with thin slopes that looked like the iconic Sydney Harbour Bridge.

It must be worth a fortune, she thought. Then she noticed something else, a small black plastic container. Her father was full of surprises and secrets, but this time Fern was flabbergasted when she saw the contents. It was a full set of false teeth sitting in a black denture box.

Completely thrown by the last discovery, Fern returned to her room.

The service was small at Chester's request. In attendance at the crematorium were Megan, Fern, Lance, a few close friends, and the priest. Chester did not want a fuss or hundreds of people milling about. He wanted it to be private and intimate for his family and not turned into a corporate networking event.

"God is our refuge and our strength," intoned the priest, surveying the congregation over his tiny reading glasses, "a help when in trouble and worry. Peace, he gives to you, Chester Jones, and to loved ones left behind. Eternal God is your dwelling place. Blessed are those that mourn, and God will comfort them."

Then the coffin was removed to the crematorium. Lance handed Megan a handkerchief so she could dab her eyes.

They had fulfilled Chester's final wishes, and he was cremated.

A few more consoling words were spoken by the priest, and soon it was all over.

They all moved out into the grey weather outside.

Fern drove, and Megan was silent, except for asking that Fern switch off the music.

When they arrived home, Megan went to rest, and Fern spent a few hours on her laptop.

After a light meal, they sat in the kitchen alone.

"It feels so strange and sad that it is only us now," Megan commented.

"I know, Mom. Even our new Bonzo is bereft; he keeps going to the front door expecting Dad to come home. But we all have to learn to deal with it. And, Mom, there's something else."

"What is it, dear?"

"Mom, I'm going to take a break from university. I don't know for how long at this stage."

"Why, Fern? As you said, we have to be strong and move on."

"We promised Dad we would build his legacy and not let his name fade away. I intend to honor this promise. It's going to be hard to attend school and take care of his business. I cannot let it stagnate. . I've decided to take time to learn more and meet with his accountant and find out about the feasibility of selling it and using the assets for other ventures. I have some ideas I have been mulling over. I will use Dad's study but take care of any serious work at his office in Collins Street."

Fern knew her mother would never stand in her way and, besides, her father had left the business to her without any conditions.

"Fern, you must do what is best for you. I trust you. You are your father's daughter. He always had my best interest in mind, and I know you'll do the same."

"Dad gave me the combination code to his safe to give to you, Mom. Why don't we go there now and check it out?"

"Oh, honey, I'm exhausted. It's way too soon. I'm emotionally drained — tomorrow, perhaps? We'll see."

Fern was disappointed. She was itching to get going with her plans, although she understood. Out of consideration for her mother's feelings, she sat with her for a while longer, but after half an hour, she excused herself.

Chapter Seventeen

Over the last few months, Bruce Nash had carved out a daily early morning routine to walk around the neighborhood that got him out of the house for an hour or so while Merle slept. His keen police sense had made mental notes of the homes' security systems and which homes had friendly dogs and which ones were best to avoid. He also enjoyed admiring the various cars in the driveways and instinctively tried to profile the characteristics of the owners and their careers.

Nash was naturally reserved, and his chosen professional had made him come across as somewhat aloof, but after Merle's accident, he changed. As the months went by, he became increasingly lonely and craved human companionship. So, when the opportunity presented itself, he became positively garrulous in the company of others. With so much time on his hands, he welcomed any chance to stop and talk with anyone he ran into.

He would hang out and shoot the breeze in the nearby stores to catch up on local gossip as if he was gathering information for a case, and, on occasion, he would join a fellow walker for the latest news. The folks in the area got to know about his former career and his wife's tragic accident. They were kind and compassionate towards him, knowing he was adjusting to a life of solitude.

This morning, he closed the gate behind him, removed the mail and newspaper from his letterbox, and went inside. The odor greeted him. It was the worst part of being a caretaker. He knew Merle needed attention.

"Hello, dear. How are we today?"

Merle looked at him with a crooked smile and nodded her head.

"Come, come dear, we have to get you changed."

He removed the soiled diaper and cleaned her with great care, all the time breathing through his mouth to lessen the stench. Afterward, he washed up and came back to her.

"Are you hungry, dear?"

She shook her head.

"Perhaps I can get you a nice cup of tea then?"

"Mmm," she tried to mumble in an attempt to speak.

"Good, then I'll go and make it. Back in a minute."

They had slowly developed a new way of communicating. Nash had learned to keep asking questions until Merle nodded, indicating her agreement.

Nash came back five minutes later with two mugs of tea for him and his wife.

"Merle, dear, I do need to talk to you about some changes. Are you up for talking now?"

She nodded.

"You know, I love you with all my heart, but I realize I can't do this on my own anymore. I need help looking after you," he looked at his wife and saw she was listening and understanding.

"We do get some government assistance, and we can afford to employ a full-time assistant. I think it would be best if this person could help with cleaning around the house and help take care of you. What do you think, my dear?"

Merle nodded.

What he also wanted to tell her was that he needed to move into the guest room, so he could sleep more easily without the smell permeating their bedroom. But he could not bring himself to do that just yet.

"Come, Mom, come see my new office," Fern urged tugging Megan's hand. Fern had been rearranging her father's study in preparation for her new vision.

"I know it is still early days, but Dad..."

"I understand. He wouldn't want you wasting your days and would be happy you were busy occupying yourself with the business."

They entered Chester's study. Fern was keen to show her mother the contents of the safe and see her surprise.

Fern had put her laptop on the desk next to Chester's computer. She had hung a new photo of Megan, Chester, and Fern on the wall facing the door. A few items on the desk had been cleared away too.

"Mom, I think it's time to open the safe too and see what is in there for you." Fern didn't wait for a response and entered the combination. The door popped open. First, Fern removed the box with the gold cufflinks and handed it to Megan.

"My, my, so Chester kept these through all the years," Megan marveled, with a lump in her throat. "These were his dad's cufflinks; RDJ stands for Roland Daniel Jones. The initials are in gold, and the black stones are opals. Dad always spoke of how good and generous his father was."

Megan looked up at Fern. "You don't know too much about his family. His dad originally came from Britain and arrived here with little money. He worked hard in a little convenience store and later bought it. He opened a few more branches that were very profitable. He saved hard and bought a small commercial property. He continued to work just as hard in spite of his success and bought more real estate. Melbourne was starting to boom at that time, and he was in on the ground. He eventually sold all his real estate and commercial properties when he retired. He and his wife, Ilana, had a good life and never suffered, thank Heavens. They both died of old age."

"Umm, wow, that's fascinating," Fern didn't want to go down memory lane. "I see now how Dad had so much capital to start his business—interesting," she commented. She wanted to keep her Mom focused on the task at hand.

"Here's another box." Fern took out the box with the leather pouch and placed it on the desk with its list of diamond contents.

"Oh my God, diamonds! How exquisite! How beautiful. Wow, some are really huge. Look at this pink one." Megan picked it up and handed it to Fern.

"Mom, did you see the list? They are worth fourteen million dollars, fourteen million!!"

Megan sat down bewildered. "It's too much for me. Too much for me to take in. Your dad never ever mentioned this to me." She started to tear up. "Why? Why?"

"Dad was known to be secretive at times, but Mom, they usually were pleasant surprises. Here, look. There's an old cell phone and a rolled-up piece of paper."

Megan picked up the paper. "It's his will." Megan's heart sank. The extent of the situation was beginning to sink in, and the enormous task ahead of adjusting to a whole new life.

"I have a copy and will be meeting with Stanley Hoffman soon. What shall we do about these diamonds? I think we should sell them all, but I don't know who to talk to."

She looked directly at her daughter.

"Fern, I want you to have one. I know Dad didn't mean to upset you by taking you up into the Dandenong just before he died. I know he caused you a lot of pain, and I am so sorry. I want you to choose anyone you like."

"Mom, not now, but leave it to me. I will get them valued at the current rate and sell them. It is kind of you to offer me first choice, but there is no hurry. The first thing to do is to set up an appointment with the accountant and attorney as soon as possible, so we know where we stand. I do not want us to procrastinate. Dad would not have wanted it."

"Ah, you are right, dear. You are so like your father and even your grandfather. You won't let any grass grow under your feet. Here, let's put everything back for now."

Fern put the stones, the list, and the cufflinks back in the safe. The two cell phones that belonged to Chester she placed in the desk drawer. She would need them and planned to check them out in the next day or two. She did not mention the black opal to her mother, the one hidden under the floor of the safe, nor did she mention the false teeth. She decided to keep both in reserve, just as Chester had done.

Bruce Nash eventually hired a pleasant Philippine lady. Her name was Kate; she was quiet and sweet, efficient, and worked hard. Both Bruce and Merle were appreciative and liked her.

Nash paid her weekly, and every month or so, he threw in a few extra dollars to spend on her children.

With Kate around, he was able to spend more time in his study. The old case of the prostitute's missing baby still haunted him. He removed the ring from the desk drawer. He felt frustrated that the police never solved it. The case had been closed a long time ago.

Aggravated, he walked into Merle's old sewing room. It had been abandoned for a while now. She would never sew again. He looked around and then went to check on his wife.

Kate was feeding Merle her lunch. It was a sad and pitiful sight to watch her being hand fed. Life was so unfair. It didn't feel right to tell Merle he wanted to move into her sewing room and set up a bedroom for himself. He thought he would spare her the misery and decided to tell her instead the police department had asked him to work on some old unsolved *cold* cases. This way, he could work from home and not have to leave her alone. He would also tell her, that it would entail him working late into the night, so he would purchase a bed to put in the sewing room so as not to disturb her. He planned to tell her his little white lie idea after Kate had left for the day.

She understood, of course. It hurt her, he could tell nevertheless, as he looked into her sad, empty eyes lying there on the bed. But he did not hesitate. He moved into the sewing room that same day. He put the old, faithful sewing machine in its case and into the spare closet forever.

He actually preferred this room. It had a beautiful clear view of the garden and above all it smelt better.

Megan Jones received the brass and ceramic urn containing Chester's ashes. The priest was kind enough to deliver them. The urn fit perfectly on her dressing table behind an enlarged old photograph of their wedding day.

Fern spent some time at Chester's office on Collins Street. She carefully studied her father's notes and created a detailed spreadsheet with all his contacts from both his cell phones.

She had separated out the important names and numbers and placed them at the top of the excel document. Of course, she knew her uncle, Lance Jones, and Oliver, the pilot. The other key names were Danny, who was categorized in the book as the professional forger, and Mike Barzel, who was listed as security. Another seventy-five names followed that were an assortment of associates and colleagues.

Fern googled private investigators. One who caught her eye was George Spiros. He was licensed and bonded and had twenty-five years of experience. She called his number.

A smooth voice answered, "Spiros here."

"Mr. Spiros, hello, my name is Fern Jones. I have some business I would like to discuss with you today."

"I'm afraid I have a full calendar and don't have an opening until sometime next week."

"It is important, Mr. Spiros. If you do a quick search for Chester Jones or IME, you will see who we are, and it will be worth your while. I only need five minutes of your time, and your office is around the corner from mine."

Spiros was indeed already doing a quick search and agreed. "I can do 6 pm on my way to my next appointment."

"That's fine. I'll be waiting, Mr. Spiros. I will send you my address. Look forward to meeting you later. Goodbye." She hung up without waiting for his response. She had learned that from Chester.

George Spiros did conduct a more detailed search on Fern Jones and soon saw she was the daughter of one of Melbourne's richest people. The family-owned Infinite Mining Equipment, properties, and other investments, and the founder had recently passed away. His heir Fern Jones was very young — not yet twenty-one.

Fern smiled to herself as she walked around the office, examining and taking in the empire that had been built and commanded from this very desk. She went through the contents of the desk drawers, and the fridge bar and admired the pictures on the wall of her Dad with various colleagues at award presentations. There was a custom-built wooden unit that ran along the length of one wall. On the shelf was a CD player with several CDs.

She hit the play button, and soon the ambient electronic music of Vangelis was vibrating through the office.

She lowered the volume and phoned her accountant to tell her she wanted to sell IME.

She made an appointment to see her the next day.

She searched for Oliver's number and then decided against calling him until she had met with the PI and got his feedback.

A couple of minutes before 6 pm, Fern opened the office door and waited for the private investigator. He appeared on the dot of six.

"Come in, Mr. Spiros. Do sit," Fern said with a smile.

"Good evening, Ms. Jones. Nice to meet you, George Spiros, at your service." He gave Fern his business card.

"I do not as yet have a card of my own to give you, but I will give you one of my late father's," Fern said, very business-like. She wrote her name on one of Chester's business cards and handed it to the private eye.

"Thank you. What …" The investigator was about to say something, but Fern was quicker.

"Mr. Spiros, here is a short list. On the list, there are three first names. I don't have last names, but I do have cell phone numbers. The job is simple, Mr. Spiros. All I need is some information on each one—their full names, addresses, and some background details.

He took the list from Fern and gazed down at it for a second or two.

"All I have here is Oliver, perhaps a pilot with a number, Danny with a mobile number, and Mike Barzel followed by the word *muscleman* and also with a mobile number.

"I believe you'll be able to do a reverse search using their numbers. I'm not asking for their autobiographies and who they sleep with, or the aftershave they use. I just want a few important facts about what they do and who they are. That's all."

"I will see what I can do," he said pleasantly.

"Can do, Mr. Spiros, or will do?" Fern looked at him directly. She knew it was important to let him know who was boss.

"I will see what I can do, Ms. Jones," he repeated, realizing he was not dealing with a normal twenty-year-old.

"When will I have your results? How soon?" Fern emphasized the urgency.

"It could take a few weeks, I guess," he said, looking at Fern.

"Mr. Spiros, I am a busy person, and I take it you are as well. You have one week—that is all I am prepared to wait."

Spiros cleared his throat, "I take a fifty percent deposit up front for all jobs. A credit card will suffice, and the balance is payable on delivery of the information."

Fern had learned a number of negotiating tips through listening in on Chester's meetings and knew offering bonuses and promising big paychecks kept the power and control in his hands.

"Mr. Spiros, I will pay cash on completion of your investigation, no credit cards and know I will pay generously. Who knows, I may need your services again soon." Her father played hardball, and it always worked. She smiled and waited for his response.

Spiros thought for a few seconds. He knew what she was worth.

"OK, Fern. You have a deal, I accept."

"Good, and please call me Ms. Jones."

Spiros stood up and extended his right hand, "Goodbye, Ms. Jones, thank you. I'll be back in touch in a week."

"A pleasure, Mr. Spiros. One week, not a day late."

"Jesus!" he muttered to himself. "What a hard bitch," he thought as he made his way down to the foyer of the building. What in life had made her so cold?

Fern locked up her new office and went down to the garage below, to her car.

On the way home, she stopped at the local grocery store and purchased a small bag of cat litter.

She felt like a new person; the paradigm had shifted. Pumped up and motivated, she was determined she would now call all the shots and that no one, no one would cross her path ever again. The plan would soon come together, no matter what. Perhaps she was her father's daughter, after all.

Chapter Eighteen

The morning sun was streaming through Fern's window when she rolled over and checked her phone.

Meeting today 2 pm my office with accountant.

It was still early. She quickly dressed in shorts, a t-shirt, and running shoes.

Megan was coming downstairs. "You are up early, honey."

"Yes, Mom, going for a run, then meetings later on."

"Okay, you'll be pleased to hear I've taken your advice, and I am going to join a friend who hosts a book club every week. It is at ten this morning, and then a few of us are going to have lunch at a new restaurant in Toorak. I'll be back later this afternoon."

"Oh, I'm glad. Have fun, Mom. I'll be back soon, so I'll see you before you go."

It was lovely and fresh outside. She paced herself for the first fifteen minutes and then slowed down as she headed home.

After she had eaten breakfast, she put Bonzo outside in the yard and went upstairs to her mother's room. She went straight to the urn on her dresser with Chester's ashes. She went outside and emptied the contents into a large zip lock bag. She then poured most of the cat litter into the urn, making sure it was similar weight.

She dusted it off, closed the lid tightly, and returned it to the exact same spot in her mother's room.

She looked at her watch. She still had time.

She grabbed her keys, the zip lock with Chester's ashes, and the remaining cat litter to dispose of elsewhere so there was no chance Megan would see it in the trash.

She drove out of the gates, and as soon as she saw a public dumpster by the local stores, she parked and discarded the litter and packaging before accelerating away.

The traffic was against her, and an hour and a bit later, she arrived in Dandenong. She drove straight to the spot where Chester had taken her a few weeks back, which was embedded in her memory for the rest of her life. Pulling off the road carefully, she turned the engine off. Clutching the bag containing his ashes, she waited for the few cars to pass by and disappear around the bend. Her hands were shaking a bit, but with a deep breath, she scattered Chester's cremated remains over the ferns, weeds, stones, and bushes. She said aloud, "There, Chester, buried at last."

Without any more ceremony, she hopped back into her car, turned around, and made her way back to the city, arriving before lunch.

She prepared the coffee machine and settled down to wait for her father's accountant.

Fern had met her very briefly in the past when she had come to meet Chester at home.

Fern heard a soft knock on the door to announce her arrival and was glad she was punctual.

"Come in, Anne, come and make yourself comfortable," she said warmly.

The attractive Asian lady smiled and offered Fern her hand. "I am very sorry to hear about your loss, Fern; my condolences." She sat down.

"Thank you, Anne. Nice to see you again. Can I get you a coffee? I'm having one."

"Thank you, Fern. A cappuccino would be great. I think the last time I saw you were a few years ago. Your father was very proud of you, and you've certainly grown up to be a fine young lady."

"'Thank you." Fern acknowledged the compliment as she passed her a cappuccino.

"You wanted to discuss your father's business, IME, I understand."

"Yes. My father bequeathed me the business, but he also made me a silent partner some years ago. I understand this avoids a long drawn out probate and that I can take charge as sole owner and take action to sell it immediately," Fern stated, getting straight to the point. "What is it worth?"

"I cannot give you an exact estimate off the top of my head, but I could get that to you within the next day or two."

"I appreciate that, but just give me a ballpark figure."

"Well, there is no stock nor business equipment, but the long-term contracts are worth a vast amount. The goodwill, coupled with the fact that it has been operating for nearly thirty years, would make it worth between thirty and thirty-five million dollars, I would say as a very rough estimate."

"Good, my lawyer will be in touch with you once you email me a breakdown with all the figures. Is there anything else I need to know?"

"No, Fern, I will email you within a day or two, and please don't hesitate to contact me if you have any questions."

"Thank you, Anne, thank you," Fern smiled and walked her to the door, pleased with achieving another step in her plan.

Fern spent the rest of the day googling some real estate offices and making numerous calls. She explained she was looking for a vacant piece of land, a couple of acres, and if there was nothing suitable, she would buy a few adjacent properties by offering them inflated prices.

The agent explained there was beautiful land available between Sassafras and Olinda, just over two acres off the Mount Dandenong

Tourist Road. The asking price was two million, eight hundred thousand dollars.

Fern arranged to meet her the next day in Sassafras.

That night Fern and Megan discussed Chester's finances, and they were both very up front with each other about their intentions.

It came as a shock to Megan when Fern told her she planned to move out within a few months and find her own place. She saw how disappointed and hurt this news was to her mother and quickly suggested she might like to move with her. A change would do them good, she told her firmly, although she didn't let on about her search for vacant land or her inquiries with the real estate agent.

Megan had noticed Fern had become very single-minded since the day she found out the truth about how she was adopted. Her anger seemed misguided to Megan, but there was nothing Megan could do at this time but go along and be supportive.

It seemed, Megan thought, that Fern was turning into Chester.

Later that week, Fern headed out to Sassafras to meet the property agent. It was a beautiful day, and Fern drove with a purpose of freedom. As she got close, goose bumps erupted all over her upper arms.

She met the agent at her office, and they drove out to the property in the agent's car.

Fern was immediately taken and charmed at how the land nestled among the tall trees; everything was green, and the sunlight was penetrating the canopy in a way that was breath-taking. She was careful, though, not to show too much excitement in front of the agent.

The agent was attentive and pointed out the boundary lines and the many benefits of living in the area.

Fern took the honest and direct approach and told the agent she would be interested in purchasing the property for a cash price of two-and-a-half million only, and that would be her final offer.

The agent called the owners while Fern took more time walking about the property.

After a short time, she approached Fern with an outstretched hand and a big smile. "Fern, you've got a deal. Let me draw up the paperwork, and you will be the new owner."

Fern shook her hand, "Good, thank you," she said in a business-like tone without displaying any emotion.

The agent drove them back and dropped Fern off at her car.

"I will send over the documents to you next week to sign. Congratulations again, Fern!"

Fern gave a brief smile.

When the agent drove off, Fern sat in her car until she was out of sight. Only then did she let out a huge sigh and grinned from ear to ear. It was the first time she had felt joy in a long time.

A week to the day, private investigator Spiros sat in Fern's office on Collins Street.

"Ms. Jones, here are my results. You will be happy, perhaps interested is a better word, with the facts, I am sure." He handed Fern a large, slim envelope.

"Thank you, Mr. Spiros." She took the envelope and opened it.

Inside there were just three A4 pages, which consisted of notes on each character together with the cash invoice for seven thousand dollars.

Fern glanced at the pages for a minute, scanning the notes to be sure what he had brought her was useful. Then, without saying anything, she unlocked and pulled out her desk drawer to count out the money in one-hundred-dollar notes from the ten thousand she had put aside for the job.

She put the cash in the envelope and handed it back to Spiros.

"Thank you, Mr. Spiros, for your time and hard work."

Fern stood up and shook his hand.

As soon as he was gone, she started to closely read the facts and examine the background checks he had uncovered.

> ***Danny Smyth***—*Known as Danny, married twice and divorced twice. Aged 45. Born in Melbourne, Australia, to parents originally from Ireland. The average student in high school excelled in art, particularly in detailed sketching. After school, he assisted with chores in various jobs ranging from department stores to Foreign Affairs, where an aunt worked. Advanced computer skills. Traveled extensively for several years and eventually ended up in the Philippines, where he lived for fifteen years. No one knows what he did there or how he earned a living. He spent most of his time in Manila. My contact informed me that he frequented The Quiapo District, known as the hub of major counterfeit syndicates and individuals. My contact reliably tells me for a high price you can secure any passport, Ivy league University diplomas from even Oxford or Harvard, or order a professional license for a gynecologist, engineer degree, or Nuclear scientist certificate. Subject is well off. No criminal record. No exposure on any of the social media platforms.*

Fern read a few more details and then turned her attention to her late father's pilot.

> ***Oliver Hall***—*qualified charter pilot. Very experienced and licensed to fly any plane, jet, or helicopter. Travels extensively, flying business executives all over the country and the world. Many clients include the mining industry personnel. Wealthy and holds a black American Express card. Thirty-two years of age. Marital status single. He is known for his playboy lifestyle*

and has been seen with many top models, including Camilla, one of America's highest-paid fashion models. Lives in Brighton, just outside Melbourne. I did a drive-by, and he owns several sports cars and a six-car garage. High-sophisticated security system and cameras monitor every inch of his property. Well-known in the diamond world. No criminal record. No other information is available. No profiles were uploaded on LinkedIn or Facebook.

Fern turned to the third sheet of paper:

Mike Barzel—Muscleman, also known as 'M' and 'the Mike'. Aged 35. Gained a lot of respect in his early career as a bodyguard. Extremely well connected worldwide. Has worked with many local Canberra embassy executives and as well as Consulates in other major Australian cities. No info on where he was born. Single. Son of a Jewish Israeli and a Lebanese Christian mother. Father's whereabout unknown. Mother lives in Italy, somewhere north of Milan. Speaks several languages. He is tough, fearless, and smart. Ironically, his last name Barzel means 'iron' in Hebrew. Address unknown. No social media presence. Started out by selling genuine generic drugs to compete with major brand-name narcotics at very competitive prices. Imported the most popular generic drugs for Viagra, antibiotics, and AIDS and carved out a very successful market for his company. He has no history of drug abuse. He recruited an assortment of distributors in the more rural areas until his network spread across the continent of Australia, New Zealand, the Cook Islands, Papua New Guinea, and Indonesia. The product was originated and manufactured by a major Indian pharmaceutical company. No criminal record. I am told he currently frequents the Trombetta coffee bar near Flinders Lane.

She was somewhat surprised by the brief information provided and had expected more but she didn't have anything to compare the job with. However, this valuable background nonetheless was valuable to know.

Fern's cell phone rang. She looked at the caller id. It was Anne, the accountant.

"You will receive my email in the next few minutes," she said, "but I thought that I'd let you know over the phone before you receive it the value of the business."

"OK, I am listening."

"When we met, I gave you a ballpark figure that it would be somewhere between thirty to thirty-five million. After going over the numbers, it looks more like twenty-five in today's market."

Fern took a deep breath. "Twenty-five, only twenty-five? And what do you mean by today's value?" her voice rising in surprise.

"Well, there are two mining companies that still owe a substantial amount of money. One is in good standing, and they are a solid client. They pay two hundred-thousand dollars a month on their account against a balance owed of just over two million." Anne took a slight pause to let the good news in.

"But here is the small glitch; the other company owes five million, and, after doing a little bit of digging, things are not looking good for them."

"What can we do?"

"Well, in the event of liquidation, they still have some serious assets invested in machinery and equipment. And this is the collateral your father supplied, and the transfer of ownership remains with IME until the balance is completely paid off. Your lawyer and I had a chat, and it won't be too difficult to resell the machinery to recoup the outstanding amount."

"Okay, Anne, thanks. I will wait for your email, but please keep me updated."

"Will do, Fern. Have a good day."

Fern returned to her laptop and googled architecture companies. She also put a call to the real estate agent regarding the property in Dandenong.

The agent arrived later that day with the documents for Fern to sign. The land was now officially Fern's.

After she left, Fern made an appointment for next Tuesday with the top architect firm she had selected from her research.

She sat down in the big leather chair behind the mahogany desk that used to belong to her father..

Fern smiled to herself as she picked up the phone. It was now time to let everyone know.

Chapter Nineteen

The first call Fern made was to her Uncle Lance. It was late Friday afternoon, and she explained to him she had to see him.

Lance had a busy weekend planned, but he had appointments scheduled in the city on Monday. Fern explained she wanted to meet privately, so he agreed to come by her office at 8 am before the work day began on his way to his consulting rooms on the French side of Collins.

The second call was to Oliver Hall. She used her father's cell phone so when he answered, she heard a very hesitant, "Hello, who's this?"

When Fern told him who it was, Oliver was even more surprised.

He told her he was busy on Monday, but Fern used her beguiling female charm after reading the PI background notes and soon, he was making arrangements to see her on Monday at 10 am.

The third call was to Danny Smyth. Again. she used Chester's phone.

Danny was startled and very reserved at first when Fern introduced herself.

Despite his reluctance, Fern managed to cajole him with the promise of a lucrative and worthwhile proposition that would challenge his talents. She knew he couldn't refuse. She set the meeting after Oliver at 11 am on Monday.

The fourth and last call was to Mike Barzel.

Mike had just returned from overseas after a long trip and didn't know that Chester had passed away. He was sad to hear the news, he said, although he didn't know Chester very well, although he had done two *deeds* for him many years back. He would come by the office at noon on Monday.

Fern smiled satisfactorily, happy with the way the phone calls had gone. Monday would certainly be an interesting day and the beginning of something special.

She walked to the window, gazing thoughtfully out onto the street below.

There was a quiet knock at the door and in the doorway, clutching a bucket stood the cleaner.

"Can I help you?" Fern asked.

"Good day, Miss. I'm Maggie. I clean Mr. Jones's office and many other offices here."

"Nice to meet you, Maggie. I am Fern Jones, his daughter. Can you come back in ten minutes? Do you have a key?"

"Key? No, I don't, Miss," Maggie said, shaking her head.

"That's okay. Next time then. The office is clean anyway. It can wait until another time. Thank you, Maggie."

"Alright, Miss. Where is Mr. Jones?"

"He's resting, Maggie. He's at peace. He passed away recently."

She visibly gasped. "I'm so sorry to hear that," she replied, shocked. "He was a nice man, a real gentleman," she added.

"Thank you, Maggie. We all miss him."

The cleaner departed.

Fern thought about Monday and the four separate meetings. If she was successful and everything went to plan, it would culminate into one major speech with all four characters present.

Fern drove home. She did not see the dark blacked-out BMW parked on the other side of the road about 100 feet from her gate. Megan was cooking roast chicken in the kitchen.

"Hello, sweetheart. How is my girl today?"

"All good, Mom. Wow, that smells delicious! Is that your recipe or Gordon Ramsay's?"

Megan laughed, "A combination of both."

"Mom, I'm off to shower. Do I have time?"

Megan smiled and nodded. She wondered why Fern was in such a good mood.

After clearing away the dishes, Megan was tired and excused herself early for the evening. Fern was anxious and excited about Monday, so she grabbed herself a coffee and some Swiss chocolate to nibble on and went to the study to work on her laptop to keep herself busy. She researched a number of commercial and residential architectural styles and landscape designers. Fern started sketching and drafting ideas for her new venture.

Fern spent the entire weekend holed up in the study, researching, drawing, cross-referencing information from the Internet, and visualizing her dream. She even wrote out the bullet points for Monday's meetings in front of her bedroom mirror.

Chapter Twenty

The next morning, Fern put on navy slacks and an elegant floral top and wore the pendant her father had bought all those years ago. She slipped on comfortable heels and admired her presentation in the mirror.

The sun had been up for nearly an hour as Fern drove into the city. The homeless were stirring, waking up on their cement mattresses. The trains and trams were starting to fill up, and the first of the tourists were lining up for the horse carriage rides and the Yarra River cruises. The seagulls and pigeons were mingling about in search of scraps in Federation Square, which was in full swing with early bird officer workers walking briskly, well caffeinated, dodging and overtaking one another to get to their destiny on time, while other small groups stood around smoking their first cigarettes of the day staring at their cell phones engrossed.

Fern parked her vehicle in the underground parking structure and, a few minutes later, was in her office making coffee. She looked at her watch. It was nearly 8 am.

Spiro's report lay in front of her.

Lance entered the office punctually. They hugged for a second or two, Fern pulling away first.

"Thanks for coming, Uncle Lance."

"My, my, look at you, what a beautiful, professional lady you have grown up to be. You look right at home!"

"Thank you, Uncle Lance. . Can I pour you a coffee? I've also got cold orange juice in the fridge."

"No, thank you, I just had breakfast. So what's this all about."

"I don't want to mince words. You know me too well, and besides, I can't fool you."

"I'm glad to hear it."

"I've decided to launch an adoption center. I've purchased a piece of land in the Dandenong and propose to build a brand-new complex and have it ready within the next few months." Her uncle looked taken aback.

"I plan to live there as well. It will be my new home and a home for orphaned babies. I figure we will need a very experienced doctor. This is highly, highly confidential. I hope you understand this is not to be discussed with anyone?"

"Fern, I couldn't be more happy for you, but why so secretive? This is something to be proud of; it is such an innovative idea that will do so much good, we should celebrate."

"Do you agree to keep this confidential and not leave this room?"

"Of course."

"My plan is to bring babies from all over the world to give them a better life. I will employ a personal pilot to fly to various poverty-stricken areas from all corners of the globe. I have determined this would require a full-time medical doctor to be on staff to travel with my pilot and oversee the care of the babies at the center. Some of these babies will need to be checked for serious illnesses, such as AIDS or neonatal abstinence syndrome. We will not bring any infant into Australia with highly infectious diseases that cannot be cured beforehand."

"Fern, this is extremely risky. You won't be able to check for every disease under these conditions, especially not AIDS. What happens if a serious disease is discovered later when the child is already in Australia? And, if it's discovered before you bring them into the country, have you thought what will happen to them in their own city?"

"If anything is discovered on the onset, I will arrange with my contacts to deliver them anonymously to local clinics or hospitals. We will do everything we can to bring back healthy babies. As for diseases that might appear later, that will be the responsibility of the adoptive parents. We will make that risk clear to them, and it will be part of the contract they sign. This is the other part of the equation. My goal is to only sign up affluent couples who can comfortably afford to deal with anything that arises, like medical issues. The doctor's role will be to ensure our babies are healthy. If any babies are sick, then it will be the doctor's duty to ascertain the seriousness of the illness and the recovery prospects. They will be the ones to determine whether to find medical care in the child's country or prescribe the right plan and medications to bring them back to full health to be available for adoption."

"Fern, this is very admirable, but you are living in a fantasy world. Why babies from overseas at all? There are many Australian babies that need adopting, and it would be a lot easier. We would be able to check their history, less likely to have any disease and, not to mention, logistically simpler."

"I've thought about that, but it is too dangerous. This is a private enterprise. The red tape would be tougher to bypass, and I would risk everything. If anything went wrong, I would be looking at jail time, and I am not willing to do that."

"But how on earth do you intend to start all this? How will you obtain the babies? How will you get them into Australia? What about birth certificates? Who will be the adoptive parents? You will need licenses and permits, not to mention government permission. You are legally required to register a business. The bureaucratic tape and documentation alone will take you a lot longer than a mere three or four months. The big issue is, if money changes hands and it is not done legally, it will amount to trafficking, and you will be facing a serious prison sentence."

Fern stood up and started to pace the room. She let him sit there while she pretended to compose her next thought.

"Lance, I did some research, and I am guessing you earn about a hundred and twenty to a hundred and forty thousand dollars a year as a GP. Is that right?"

"Wait, just wait a minute! Do you think that I would embark on this type of business, or whatever you call it, for money? Do you think you can buy me?" he said indignantly.

"Uncle Lance, I need you on board. You saved my life once, you remember? You were the one who cared for me, and saved me from certain death. You were the one who knew what to do in such an extreme emergency. You became my Uncle the moment you said yes to helping my mom and dad. If you come to work for me, I will not only double your salary, I will pay you a five-hundred thousand dollar bonus per annum with every perk imaginable. It is time I take care of you." She looked at him resolutely. She had no intention of letting him refuse her offer nor her dream.

"I will conduct a thorough background check on all prospective parents, which will include detailed financial reports. I will also make sure they don't have any criminal records or drug or alcohol history. We will check every skeleton in the closet to ensure there are no sex offenders or pedophiles with them or other family members. We will be targeting couples who genuinely yearn for a child, and they are all out of other options."

"This is still absurd, Fern! I will not entertain this idea. It is ludicrous and dangerous." Lance looked at his watch; he felt trapped and very uncomfortable by his niece's ambush.

"These loving parents will pay top price for a baby, and I will set up the business as a 401K so that a certain percentage will go to various worthwhile charities and support humane societies. In other words, I will donate to the needy and the desperately underprivileged in this world. This will include orphanages, abused women and children centers that have a great need for financial assistance, as well as many more. You will play an important and crucial part in this. This is how we will honor your brother and my father's wishes and create a legacy that will do good in the world. You are the perfect person and the only medical doctor I want on my team. The work will be the reward. Can you imagine the joy we will bring to childless couples like my parents and the brand-new life we will give to a new baby? I get chills just thinking about the joy we can create together! You don't have any major commitments, no wife, no children. Mom and I are your only family. Can't you see, this is an amazing opportunity to give back and be part of something special." She turned and looked at her Uncle, daring him to defy her dream.

Lance squinted and rubbed his face in disbelief, "I can't see myself agreeing. This goes against all my medical vows. How dare you put me in this predicament. I must go now, Fern." He stood up and turned. "And I caution you to be very careful."

Fern ignored him, not giving up so easily. "Forty-eight hours, uncle. Please, at least think about it for 48 hours. I am meeting my team on Wednesday evening at 6 pm. It will be the first time everyone will be together to introduce one another. I will go over the plans in more detail then." As Lance headed for the door, Fern went over to hug him and made one final bid. "If you come on board, you know you will be part of a huge domino effect that will ripple out into the world and make it a better place."

Lance left the meeting with his brows knit. He wondered about the lasting damage his brother's final confession had had on his daughter after all.

Fern looked at her watch. It was just past nine and Oliver was due at ten. She made herself a fresh coffee and went to the bathroom to freshen up. She stared into the mirror for a few seconds. Am I crazy? she wondered.

While she waited for her meeting with Oliver, she browsed the internet, looking for new office furniture.

She ordered a solid walnut mini boardroom table and six comfortable chairs in black leather. Stock was available, and delivery was scheduled for the next day.

She was busy on her laptop when Oliver Hall arrived on time. He entered the office tall, dark, handsome, and wearing a winning smile.

"Good morning, Fern," he greeted her, "To what do I owe this pleasure?"

"Hi Oliver, you will hear in a minute. Coffee?"

"Any coffee will go down well, thank you."

As Fern stood up and walked over to the machine, Oliver's eyes followed and admired her tall, elegant body. When she leaned over to put his coffee cup on the desk in front of him, Oliver took a sly look at her breasts. He reddened slightly as Fern sat back down behind her desk. He quickly reached for his coffee, hoping she didn't notice.

"Thank you," he said as he smelt the coffee, trying to cover up his discomfort, which was unusual for him.

"Oliver," Fern said, taking control. "I need a pilot."

"No problem, you're talking to the right person. Just say when and where to, and I'll take care of the rest."

"What I mean is, I need a permanent pilot, one who will fly exclusively for me. It will be extensive travel that will require knowledge of all the major international airports and custom protocols."

"Wow," he didn't expect this. He took another sip. "That's some request. Doing what?"

"In three months, I will have my own luxurious, state-of-the-art baby adoption center in the Dandenong," Fern responded confidently. "I will also be living on site. I need a permanent pilot who can fly to any country at short notice. It will require staying in top hotels around the world and flying back here with babies to Australia. In between gigs will be your free time, but you must be constantly on standby at a moment's notice to fuel up and fly."

Oliver smiled slightly, "That's some tall order, young lady." He rubbed his hand through his thick dark hair. "It begs a lot of questions: Whose plane do we use, or what type of plane? Who will deliver the babies to me? And, who will look after the babies once aboard the aircraft? These are only a few of the immediate questions that come to mind."

"You choose the aircraft. Maybe similar to the ones that you flew for my late father. I will buy the jet once you find the right one. It should be luxurious and only seat a few people. We will modify the interior slightly to accommodate our special cargo." Fern looked across at Oliver to assess his reaction. He was giving nothing away. She ignored the butterflies in her stomach and the effect his uncanny good looks were having on her.

"I am at the moment in the midst of securing couriers or international contacts that will facilitate locating and finding abandoned babies. I intend to employ local people through the couriers so they will be delivered to you at the airport where you will be waiting. On board with you will be a full-time doctor and/or a nurse, and perhaps the occasional extra staff member when necessary."

"Uh huh," Oliver nodded, taking in this incredible vision. "How do you intend to get the babies on the plane? This is not a parent fetching his or her kid from daycare, you know — there is such a thing as customs and passport control. There is a lot of paperwork involved and documentation that needs an official stamp, and don't forget a valid passport."

"I will take care of all of that. There will be an in-depth briefing in two days if you agree to come on board, and all these questions will be addressed."

"Seems like an audacious operation. What kind of package do you have in mind for me?"

Fern smiled, a clear indication he was interested. "30K per month, all expenses paid, including accommodation, meals, and per diems included. There will also be a massive bonus for successful delivery to be determined later on."

"Ah, sorry, Fern, I can make more than that if I stayed non-exclusive. Plus, this is not a legal operation, and risks cost money, especially great risk." He looked at her directly, oozing confidence. He was a man's man, she observed.

"What's more?" Fern fired back.

"At least fifty," he said without batting an eyelid.

"Okay, you have a deal. That's six-hundred thousand a year excluding perks," Fern quickly calculated.

"When do you need to know by?"

"Now," she said firmly. She knew she was taking a chance, but she was her father's daughter.

"Hell! You really mean it, don't you?"

"Damn right, I do." She glared at him, challenging him. "And, Oliver, the bonus will be substantial."

Oliver stared back at her with no expression. She held her breath, and silence hung in the air. He stood up and smiled. "You've got a deal, young lady," and he put his hand out to shake.

Fern smiled but more to herself. "Oliver, the world needs people like you, and so do I. We'll meet here at 6 pm on Wednesday. Congratulations and welcome aboard." She couldn't help but notice the shiver that went down her spine when they shook hands to seal the deal.

As Oliver got into the elevator to take him down to the garage, he wondered just what she meant when she said that the world needed people like him.

Fern was happy with the way things were going, two down with two to go. Oliver was in the bag, and she was still hopeful that Uncle Lance would come through. It had been easier with Oliver — with guys like him, money talked. But with Uncle Lance, it was more complicated. It was going to have to be something other than money.

Fern looked at the clock. Danny Smyth was late. He hadn't phoned. She hoped he was still going to show up. Fern called him and as it rang, he appeared in the doorway.

"Mr. Smyth, please come in."

There was no apology for his lateness which Fern did not like. He was the complete opposite of Oliver. He wore black-framed glasses and had a couple of days of stubble and unkempt light brown hair. She could see that he was somewhat reserved, almost hesitant.

"Good day, Ms. Jones," he said, shaking her hand. His grip was limp.

"Please call me Fern. Have a seat."

Danny pushed his glasses back higher on his nose with his index finger and sat down. Fern continued, "Look, Danny, I know you are perhaps a bit shocked. I am like my father, a straight shooter, so I will be candid with you. I've put two and two together, and I know it was you who forged my birth certificate."

Danny visibly jolted and stood up. He felt awkward and wanted to leave. He was embarrassed and didn't know whether, to be honest, or sidestep the question.

"Ms. Jones, I am not sure what you want, but perhaps it is better that I leave."

"Danny," Fern said more gently. She saw she had spooked him. "Please sit. I have a vast amount of work for you. I owe you big time. Sorry, I shouldn't have ambushed you like that. Let's start again."

He sat back down. Fern opened the top drawer of her desk and produced a tube holder. He watched her as she unscrewed the lid. Then, while smiling, she removed her birth certificate.

At long last, he spoke. "That must be nearly twenty years old, Ms. Jones," he said, shaking his head. "I am terribly sorry to hear about your father, Chester. I hope he didn't suffer," he said kindly.

"Thank you. Unfortunately, he did suffer but luckily it was only for a short while. He went quickly. Can I offer you something to drink—tea, coffee or tea? What do you prefer?"

"Do you have anything cold, perhaps?"

"Sure! I have water or a soda?"

"Thanks, I'll settle for a soda."

As Fern handed him his drink, she confirmed with him, "What I am about to tell you is confidential. Within three months, I will need many more birth certificates, and this will be ongoing work." She paused.

"Carry on." He took a sip straight from the bottle.

"I will be bringing babies into the country for adoption to be placed in kind, loving forever homes. They will only go to the best and most affluent couples. I will be vetting the cream of the crop families. I am looking for someone with your expertise to help expedite the necessary paperwork. Someone who can create birth certificates exactly like the originals. I may need other types of sensitive documents but know this is ongoing work. Do you understand what I am saying?"

"Of course, Ms. Jones."

"I insist that you call me Fern. I do not know how long it takes to produce such a certificate, but we will need to place many orders on a regular basis. In the beginning, we will start out with a handful of missions per month, but my vision is to grow from there. At this time, I don't know if this is a part-time or a full-time job, but I am willing to explore and be open to your advice. I am sure my late father paid you handsomely for my certificate, and so will I, but you need to take the volume into consideration. Are we on the same page, Danny?"

"Hundred percent. It makes perfect sense, Fern. Anything for Chester's daughter."

"Excellent. In two days, I am holding a meeting with all the key players involved for a briefing and to answer any questions. There's no need to be concerned as I have hand-picked and only selected the best and most discrete associates from my father's confidential contacts for this sensitive operation. I trust you will be able to attend?"

Danny thought for a second or two. "Is that such a good idea? One of the reasons why I am the best and most sought-after artist in the world is because I am faceless and work behind the scenes. I work from home, and the fewer people that see me, the better." Danny eyed her warily. "It's safer that way."

"I understand, but at some stage, the other team members will have to coordinate with you regarding documents that they may need. It is imperative that we all meet at the beginning just once, and then the rest can be handled by communication. They are all highly regarded professionals in their own fields of expertise and are all taking a risk too. I am loyal and affluent. I will make you richer and expect the same loyalty in return."

For a moment, she was unsure what his reaction would be. His index finger covered his mouth as he sat in deep thought, and then his finger scratched his cheek, and his head started to nod up and down slightly.

"Okay, I'm in. I will see you Wednesday at 6pm."

Fern smiled. She stood up and shook his hand, and with the other hand, she touched his elbow for a mere second. She needed him in the business.

"Welcome aboard, Danny, welcome. Now, if you need to reach me, you have my number — just be careful what you say over the phone. Thank you for coming over. I really appreciate you making the time to see me today." She walked him to the door.

Fern was thrilled it had gone so well, especially as she could see he was a cautious person and rightly so given his services.

Mike Barzel liked to know everything about anyone he was meeting. He checked LinkedIn, Facebook, and any article that was written on his subject. He also checked various internet sites to see if his subject was insolvent or operating under the government's radar. He did whatever it took to know all about Fern Jones. He also researched whatever he could on Chester Jones and confirmed he had recently died.

Armed with Fern's address, he watched her drive home one day in her Audi. He noted she was blonde and beautiful. He checked the registration, and over the weekend, he passed her house a few times in his BMW. Her car was always there. He observed her through his binoculars in her home as she walked past windows. She never went out, so he knew she was busy with something. He knew all about Chester's mining business and that it was worth a fortune. She would have inherited and was now very rich. He took photographs. Mike Barzel had one philosophy in life. He was faithful to the people he worked with but double cross him, and he was ruthless. He had no intention of harming her. He was just doing his due diligence and carrying out a thorough background check, so he knew everything there was to know about people who wanted to meet him.

Everyone knew almost everyone in the underworld, and one of his sources had advised him that the mining girl was asking questions.

Mike entered the building and walked straight past the concierge, his eyes taking in everything.

In the elevator, while several people stared at the floor awkwardly, Mike stared at each person intently, and the ones who noticed almost melted in embarrassment.

When he got off at his floor, he turned left and walked for a couple of feet before stopping. After the elevator door closed, he looked around and continued down the passage.

Standing outside IME offices, he briefly studied his subject before he knocked. He greeted her at the same time as he knocked.

Fern looked up, "Hello, Mr. Barzel, please come in."

"Hello, Fern, nice to meet you," he said as he approached.

Fern stood up and moved forward to shake his hand. It was firm, not limp like Danny's, but not so tight as to crush her hand. She was impressed. She liked what she saw: very athletic and striking, he obviously worked out, and his steady, intelligent gaze exuded a powerful presence that pleased her while at the same time slightly unnerving her.

"Can I get you a coffee or soda?" she asked, adopting a brisk, business-like tone that belied her nerves.

"I would love a coffee, thanks, black," he said, smiling into her eyes. Fern felt her knees go a little wobbly.

She stepped towards the coffee machine. His eyes did not follow her, nor did he peer furtively at her assets, as Oliver had done. By ordering a coffee, he had bought at least a minute to study her desk.

He saw a couple of stapled A4 sheets turned upside down and quickly turned them over and put them back in the exact same spot. He also checked to see if her cell phone was on the desk. Instinctively, he wanted to check if she was recording this conversation.

There was no phone. His eyes flickered around the room. There were no alarm sensors or CCTV. He didn't know whether to be disturbed or relieved.

Fern returned with his coffee and a glass of water for herself.

"Sorry to hear about your father, my condolences for your family's loss."

"Thank you, that is kind of you," Fern said and meant it.

"May I call you Mike?" she asked.

"Of course, that's my name," he answered with another quick smile that made Fern glad she was sitting down.

"Mike, it is not my style to beat about the bush. I want you to work for me."

"A job offer without explanation! That's different. What is the job description?"

"I am starting an adoption center for the elite. The babies will be brought into Australia from all over the world. I plan to do this on a large scale. I have already made arrangements to purchase a jet for the center, and I am in the process of recruiting the crème de la crème in the industry to assist in the operation."

"What would my position be?"

"Mike, I would be looking to you to head up worldwide operations."

"Bringing little ones in from overseas would be political suicide to the government. Ah, I get it! You're talking about smuggling babies. Who are these babies for? Everyone has principles, and I, for one, will not be part of any baby trafficking or prostitution. I am serious. Do you understand me?"

"Mike, listen, this is certainly not the case at all. You will see at the meeting on Wednesday.'

"What meeting? Isn't this the meeting?"

"Mike, please just bear with me, and hear me out."

Mike paused for a moment and then asked. "If I were to accept, which I am not agreeing to, when would I start?"

"Yesterday?" Fern said in earnest.

"Give me a rough idea of the package and I'll get back to you," Mike replied and took a sip of his coffee.

Fern wanted him on board more than anything. He had muscle, brains, and connections worldwide, along with years of experience. She knew she would not be able to run an operation like this without someone like Mike at her side.

"One hundred thousand dollars."

"Are you playing with me? You're wasting my time." Mike's facial expression was cold, like a crypt.

"This is my offer, Mike. It is extremely generous, and non-negotiable. Just as I said, one hundred thousand dollars — *per month*."

Mike smiled, "Now we are talking… now we are talking."

Those few seconds of silence in Fern's office felt like a year or a decade, she thought.

"If I am to drop my other commitments and turn this business into a viable and successful one, I will need more information."

"What do you have in mind, Mike?"

"A one-on-one with you after the Wednesday meeting."

"No problem. By the way, the package includes all travel and accommodation, meals, and entertainment. There will also be a significant budget for various incentives to open the necessary doors or information needed and, of course, an annual bonus yet to be agreed upon."

"Thank you, Fern, for your generous offer. I will let you know tomorrow morning. Do I reach you on the same number?"

"I need an answer now. If it's no, you can leave and pretend this meeting never happened. If it is, yes, we will reconvene on Wednesday this week at 6pm, and you can meet the rest of the team. I will brief everyone then and all at the same time."

"Well, I guess I'll see you on Wednesday, Fern," he responded, smiling. "As long as you shred that report on your desk about me and get another cell phone number," he continued smiling. "Also, I want the names of the other team members before we meet. Text me their names and numbers from your current cell. Where is your phone, by the way?"

"In my desk drawer."

"Can I see it?" Mike said as he stood up. He watched closely as she leaned over the desk and removed it from the drawer. It was not recording.

"Welcome on board, Mike! I look forward to a long-term relationship," she said, hoping her voice did not betray her nervousness. In Mike, she knew she had met someone she could not manipulate.

"So do I," he acknowledged. For a few seconds, they observed each other in silence.

Mike offered his hand and disappeared. Fern was relieved. She had just hired a very dynamic man with intellect and a commanding presence whose connection spread across the globe. She realized that no one could pull the wool over his eyes. He had even known his profile was on her desk, despite it being face down. He was being paid an enormous amount, but he was worth every cent.

Chapter Twenty-One

Megan, nibbling on a piece of raisin toast, was watching the morning news. "My, my, you look like you are seeing someone important today, honey."

"Yep, you're right, Mom. I'm running late so I only have time to gulp down a quick coffee and hit the road."

"Do you fancy anything special for dinner tonight?" Megan had already lost her husband, and now she was watching her daughter disappear into her work.

"Surprise me, Mom," she said as she headed out the door.

Megan's shoulders slumped. "I'll try, dear."

Fern climbed into her Audi and was soon gone.

She was on the way to Richmond to see the architect.

While driving, she called her Uncle.

"I was going to call you in the next hour," he said as he answered his phone. "I guess, mental telepathy." He didn't wait for Fern to respond.

"Look, Fern, there is absolutely no way that I can be part of your new venture. I know this will upset you, but I have my practice, my patients, and my reputation to consider."

Fern didn't say anything and kept her eyes on the road.

"And, Fern, I think you should seriously rethink this for your own sake. What you're proposing is well-meaning, but it's way more complicated than you imagine. It is highly risky, and it could be very dangerous for you. You'll have the law and the authorities to contend with on one side and some pretty unsavory characters on the other. This is a very sensitive raw topic, and it can bring out some very passionate dogmatic people, where young children are involved. I would hate your good intentions to backfire on you."

Fern sighed. "I'm really sorry to hear that, Uncle Lance, but I respect your decision. I can hear you have certainly given it much thought."

She terminated the call without saying goodbye and hit the accelerator.

Fern parked the car in a guest parking space and slammed the door. She was annoyed. Uncle Lance had never turned her down before. Her heels clicked on the cement ground as she walked briskly to the stairs.

She took the few steps to the entrance way and noted the sign on the building: *Jaffe and Murphy—The Architects.* It was etched in gold on the large automatic glass door. Fern admired the emphasis on the word *the.*

Inside, she looked around, and goose bumps erupted again on her arms. The reception area was warm and modern. The skylight was shaped like a cloud. She knew that these partners were chic.

The receptionist was friendly and offered Fern a seat. Soon a good-looking young man approached and extended his hand, "Good morning, Ms. Jones. I'm David Jaffe. Come meet my partner, Blythe Murphy. Please follow me."

They entered a boardroom, and Jaffe's partner approached and introduced himself in the same easy manner. Blythe was also striking and well-groomed. He wore his hair long, and Fern thought that the bright rainbow bowtie complemented his looks and suited his occupation.

"I insist you have coffee with us, Fern," he said. "What will it be?"

"A strong cappuccino, thank you."

David picked up the phone and ordered the coffees and a plate of croissants.

"What can we do for you today, Fern?" Blythe asked.

"To begin with, I would like your assurance that what I'm about to discuss with you will remain confidential between us, regardless of whether we move forward together."

They both assured her that they always respected client confidentiality, including prospective clients; their business would not survive long without it. "In fact, the company has a standard NDA that we would be happy to sign," David said. "I can ask our assistant to bring one in now."

Satisfied, Fern removed some rough pencil sketches and typed notes she had prepared over the weekend. She handed each of the men a copy.

They both looked at their copies, and Fern waited for a response.

"Is it my understanding you intend to build a sophisticated state-of-the-art baby center?" Blythe enquired inquisitively.

"Yes, that's right. It will be a modern adoption center for orphan babies."

"I see," David responded cautiously. "Can you elaborate a bit more?"

Just as Fern was to launch into her pitch, there was a knock at the door. The assistant arrived with the coffees and croissants and a couple of copies of the Non-Disclosure Agreement documents to be signed.

"Sure, gentlemen, but my biggest question is that I am on a very tight deadline, and I need to know if your company would be able to meet it and deliver on time. As you can see, I have come up with a design to accommodate up to twenty-four cots and beds. There is a main room, a clinic, and sick room, a couple of playrooms, and a luxury visitor's lounge to interact with the babies. There is a special hygiene room for the babies alongside the adult restrooms. A large kitchen to be able to prepare all the necessary meals. I have included a couple of on-sight bedrooms with en-suite bathrooms and a suite of offices with a manager's private quarters to interview prospective clients."

Fern glanced over at the men. They were astounded.

"And, here," she pointed to one of her sketches. "there will be two luxury two-bedroom units for the nurses. Each will have a large bedroom, small but fully equipped kitchen, bathroom, and a separate living room."

"What is this area at the back? All I see is a large empty circle," Blythe asked while sipping his coffee.

"That's for you to design and build. That will be my private residence. I want it to have a three-hundred-and-sixty-degree view of the whole property with one-way glass windows and doors all around. It will be a two-and-a-half thousand-foot home with three bedrooms and en-suite marble bathrooms, and a separate guest bathroom on the ground floor. I want a chef's kitchen, a large reception, and a separate dining room as well as a spacious office with a walk-in safe attached to a boardroom. Outside I want a secluded courtyard with a jacuzzi and pool and a manicured landscape garden."

"This is a sensational project," David commented, getting caught up in Fern's vision. "I can see a lot of thought has gone into this. Is there anything else that we need to know?"

"Yes, it is imperative the latest security systems are installed, and I will need to be able to monitor activity on the property in a separate room. I will be looking to your company to design and furnish the entire complex. Of course, there will need to be a commercial central air system that can be controlled in the individual rooms, and all rooms will have to be soundproof. Finally, I want a small two-bedroom guest cottage designed and built separately that will also have the ability to monitor the front-gate camera and the babies' area.

There was silence in the room, which lasted for several awkward seconds. Fern helped herself to a glass of water.

David's eyes darted to his partner, then back to Fern.

"You said earlier on *if we can deliver*," Blythe commented.

"Yes, I want it built and up and running in three months, no longer," she said emphatically.

"That's not only absurd, ,but it's also impossible," David answered, shaking his head.

"What will something like this cost?" Fern asked. "A rough estimate figure?"

"We will have to crunch some numbers, but you will be looking at probably around twenty million, and it will take a good year to build," Blythe replied while looking again at David, perhaps for some support.

"Then I will have to go elsewhere," Fern said and stood up.

"Sit, sit please, Fern," David hastily encouraged.

"You have caught us by surprise. Please allow my partner and me time to discuss this more fully. Another coffee?"

"No, thanks," Fern declined the coffee. "But let me say that I might be prepared to wait up to six months, provided my home is ready for me to move-in in three."

The two architects froze in their tracks.

Fern continued, "Here are my terms: I am prepared to pay you a fifty percent deposit by the end of the day. You agree contractually to have the complex up and ready in six months tops, and for every week that it is built and ready, beforehand, I will throw in an extra fifty thousand dollars per week. However, my home must be ready in three months while the rest of the complex is being built, or there will be no bonus," Fern stated with conviction.

"Just give us a minute, please," David answered.

The two left the boardroom, shutting the door behind them.

About ten minutes later, they came back and sat down.

David cleared his throat, "Most clients want three things when they come to see us: a good price, high quality, and a tight deadline. We have to explain that it's only humanly possible to have at most two of these things, and they usually choose quality and a good price, so they are flexible on the deadline. In your case, you have chosen quality and a tight deadline, and the price is flexible. Yes? If so, it's doable. We can agree to your terms," David said, smiling while Blythe offered his hand.

Fern shook hands with both men.

"We will outline a schedule and an itemized budget for you to review," David confirmed.

"I will arrange for my lawyer to be in touch so you can draw up the terms of the contract stipulating the conditions that we have agreed upon with them," Fern responded. "Oh, and, gentlemen, one last thing, for every week that the building is late, Jaffe and Murphy partners will deduct fifty thousand dollars per week," Fern said, shaking David's hands, effectively locking him into her final request.

Blythe quickly stepped up to open the boardroom door in haste to end the meeting before they unwillingly agreed to any other outlandish terms.

"Jesus Christ," David grimaced to his partner. "That's one hot, tough mamma, full of chutzpah," David grimaced to his partner.

"Shit! Tough isn't a strong enough fuckin' word. Do you know who she is? She's the only child of the late Chester Jones. He was a mining magnate supplier and the owner of Infinity Mining Equipment. She's not only full of chutzpah, ,but she's also full of money. She's worth at least a billion dollars."

Chapter Twenty-Two

On Wednesday, Fern sat down at her desk, confident everything was in order. She opened up her laptop and searched for *The Art of War* the popular book by Sun-Tzu, the ancient Chinese military strategist .

She took notes and made bullet points to reference, and also wrote down a famous quote from Sun-Tzu that she planned to use later as part of her pitch to the team.

It was already late afternoon when she finally finished with her preparations.

She walked to the window, gazing out for a short while, just like her father used to do when he was deep in thought, looking out over the city to calm or inspire himself.

It was 5:25pm. She couldn't eat, even if she was hungry, her nerves were restless so she made herself some coffee. Her mind wandered as she sipped the hot liquid. *What if no one is interested in adopting the babies?* She got up and paced to wipe any negative thoughts out of her mind, as *The Art of War* had taught.

She busied herself quickly, setting the stage, laying out the snacks, glasses, and napkins, and opening the liquor cabinet to show off its contents.

At 6 pm, Fern opened her office door, but it would not stay open. She remembered seeing a few golf tees in the desk drawer. Using a golf tee, she pushed it under the door to jar it open. While she was bending down, Oliver Hall appeared in the carpeted passage. Being focused on the tee, Fern did not hear or see him.

Oliver, once again, admired her figure.

"Here, let me help you, Fern," he offered softly.

Fern jumped a little and stood up, blushing slightly. "Hi, Oliver, I think I've got it, thanks. I just wanted to keep the door ajar until everyone arrived. How are you?"

"Very well, thanks," he said with a teasing smile.

Ignoring his flirting, she said, "Come, let's go inside. The others should arrive any second."

As they sat down at the boardroom table, Danny knocked and paused in the doorway. "Hello, hello," he called.

"Hi, Danny, please come inside and have a seat. Let me introduce you to Oliver Hall," Fern offered as she shook Danny's hand.

"Good to meet you, Danny," Oliver said.

"Gents, please make yourself at home and help yourself to a drink," Fern encouraged while glancing at her watch.

"Who else are we expecting?" Oliver enquired.

"Just waiting for one more, Mike Barzel."

"Mike!" Oliver commented with a smirk on his face.

"You know him?" Fern asked with a raised eyebrow.

"Did a bit of business with him some time ago."

His timing was appropriate as the last figure appeared at the door.

"I heard my name, and I heard Oliver's voice. Hello everyone," Mike said as he entered the room. Oliver got up and looked Mike straight in the eye. They not only shook hands but they hugged briefly, clobbering each other hard on the back with flat hands. Fern wondered how Oliver and Mike had met and what they had done together in the past to forge such a strong bond.

"I guess you two do not need an introduction, but Mike, please meet Danny Smythe," Fern said. "Mike, please help yourself to a drink.

I'm going to have a small glass of red wine. This one is the best from the Hunter Valley. Can I pour for anyone?"

After they all had their drinks, they sat around the large boardroom table. Fern went to take the golf tee out from under the door to close it when there was a timid knock. All heads turned in the direction of the doorway, and Fern looked up. It was the pleasant cleaning lady. "Sorry to disturb you, Miss Fern, but I was just checking if you needed any more help?"

"We are in a meeting now, Maggie. Thank you for your kind gesture, but if you don't mind, pop back in the morning to clean up if you can?"

"Certainly, Miss Fern. Have a good evening."

Fern shut the door and rejoined the group. She took her seat at the top of the table. She took a sip of her drink and cleared her throat. The men turned to look at her. She smiled, hiding her nervousness, and raised her glass. "This is a special evening for me, and I am very excited you were all able to attend. In a couple of minutes, I will explain what this is all about and go into more detail, but first, a warm welcome and here's to a successful and productive meeting. Cheers!"

"Cheers," Oliver said, followed by echoes from the others.

Fern looked around the table, "I have had one-on-one meetings with each of you, so you all got the gist of this new venture I am launching, which is very personal to me, so I am very grateful that each one of you shares my passion. So, let me outline and explain this operation in more detail."

Fern paused for effect as she had practiced but didn't expect the profound silence her opening remarks would have until another soft knock at the door amplified the room.

"Didn't the cleaner get the message?" Danny commented, looking at Fern, annoyed at the interruption. But Fern was smiling from ear to ear.

"Gentlemen," she announced. "We are complete. Our fourth and final team member. May I have the privilege of introducing you to Dr. Lance Jones, my uncle? Come in, please, Doctor Jones."

"Good evening all," Lance said in his professional manner without any expression.

"Please help yourself to a drink and snacks," as she pulled out a chair next to her.

While Lance poured a stiff whiskey, Fern introduced the others to him and continued.

"Okay, let's resume. I was about to share with you a true story." She leaned on the back of her chair towards the group to emphasize the secrecy of what she was about to share.

"One cold, freezing night in August twenty years ago, a baby was discarded on the roadside, amongst the long grass and fern bushes in the Dandenong. She would have died there had not a kind and loving man come along in his car at that time and found her. It so happened that this man was rich. He and his wife had everything they could ever want, except a child. At that moment, the man decided not to take her to the authorities and put her into the foster care system but to take the baby home to his wife and raise her as their own. It was touch and go for a while, but luckily his brother was a doctor, and he was able to provide the right medical care at home without admitting her to the hospital."

There was utter silence in the room. Fern felt a lump in her throat, which she didn't expect. This was the very first time she had told her own story. She looked at her Uncle, who smiled. Her eyes teared up a little.

"Yes, the wealthy kind couple was Chester and Megan Jones, and his brother Dr. Lance Jones saved the baby, and the baby was named Fern. I was nursed back to life by my new parents and my uncle to whom I owe my life."

Everyone turned to look at the person Fern addressed and then turned back to Fern, just like the turning heads of spectators at Wimbledon.

"So," Fern continued, "this team, which I have personally hand selected from my father's trusted contacts, sits around this table and will be given the ongoing task to rescue not dozens but perhaps hundreds of other babies worldwide. Oliver is a well-qualified pilot and the best of the best. He flies choppers and jets and will run transportation and get clearance for all necessary customs and permits. Mike has the intel; he is fearless and well-connected. He will head operations and recruit field agents to gather information abroad. Danny is an expert forger and was responsible for creating my birth certificate. He will be in charge of all the paperwork needed for transportation, including the birth certificates for the babies.Our babies. If you are not aware, Danny is the Picasso of forgery, and his work is impossible to tell the difference between the originals. Thank you, Danny. We are very privileged you're joining us."

"Last but not least is Lance, my uncle. Dr. Jones will ensure and oversee the health of the babies and carry out thorough examinations when Oliver brings them into Australia.

"As we speak, plans are being drawn up to establish our headquarters in the Dandenong. There will be a comprehensive on-site medical clinic with two full-time nurses. Dr. Jones will hire the nurses and regularly check in on our babies. The goal is to open in three months."

Fern looked at her team; they were hanging on every word. No one balked at the tight deadline.

"Once the babies are settled and have a clean bill of health with all the necessary documentation and vaccinations, I will place them with new loving parents who will adopt them and give them a forever home.

"The adoptive parents will be screened with a full background check, including financial stability, and character references from employers, employees, friends, and neighbors. They will have no criminal records, no history of abuse or pedophilia in any way. Only then, after a strict vetting process, will I part with our babies. The couples will be charged a significant fee to clearly demonstrate their serious commitment to these little souls. Of course, the cost of this operation will be substantial, but I will arrange for a large proportion of the monies to be distributed to select charities around the world to support the welfare of children. The rest will be retained to cover the overhead of the operation.

"We know there are abandoned and ill-treated children in Australia, but it would be too dangerous to rescue babies from our own backyard. All babies will come from overseas and will be taken to the Dandenong center, where the adoption will formally take place. They will never know their birth parents. The couples who will be adopting will be Australian citizens and listed as the official biological parents on their birth certificates. They will be extremely wealthy and influential, not because they are more deserving than others, but they will be able to afford our fee and will have much to lose if they are exposed."

Fern paused to look around at each face, assessing their reaction.

"Don't misunderstand me — this is dangerous work we are embarking upon. There are serious risks involved, which you have all agreed to undertake, but the rewards will be great. I'm not talking about money but the indescribable gift of giving a new life a real home.

"Any questions?"

Suddenly all of them spoke at once, each with a plethora of different questions.

"One at a time, please, gentlemen. Oliver?"

"There will no doubt be a huge amount of travel abroad, is that so?" Oliver asked.

"Yes, Oliver, but spread out," she replied, and then she pointed to Mike, who was keen to speak.

"I think it will be me traveling the most. What countries or continents are we targeting?"

"On initial research, I found the Americas, USA, Canada, Mexico, South America, Europe, and Asia show considerable numbers of at-risk children. We may include Africa, which has an appalling record of children in the millions living in the streets and gutters. Do you know, fifty million births go unregistered every year worldwide?" Fern stopped for a moment to let in these shocking statistics.

Then she piled on the most unconscionable facts. "Do you know, I discovered babies are dumped in public toilets, and some are found dead, and some lucky few are found barely alive. The same goes for places like the bush, in hospital parking lots, in garbage dumps, by the roadside, in park cities and streets and other bizarre and sad places. There was even a horrific article of starving dogs eating babies in garbage wastelands in third-world countries. And the rich are not all innocent either. Some have aborted their babies because they did not want a girl or vice versa. Gentlemen, this is my vocation, and I am going to make this my mission to help as many babies as possible have a better life no matter what happened before or what cruel parent abandoned them."

The room was silent, and Fern felt she had hit her target—their hearts.

"How many do you envisage bringing into the country?" Danny asked.

"Difficult to give an exact number, Danny, but I'd like to think along the lines of roughly 100 a year." Danny nodded his head in acknowledgment, deep in thought. "Okay, I get the picture, thanks," he replied sombrely.

Lance was the only one who had not spoken, but Fern knew privately he would have plenty of suggestions and questions.

"Gents, I will be available to meet with each of you as and when necessary and when questions arise as we move forward. Before we close, I would like to share these inspirational words..." She looked at the piece of paper in her hand, which shook a bit not from nerves but from excitement. "Sun-Tsu, the great military strategist, once said,

Victory belongs to the man who can master the stratagem of the crooked and the straight. You must weigh the situation carefully before you make a move to extend your territory. Again, she paused while looking at each of them.

"And, in my father's own words, you will need marrow in your bones and a bit of steel in your spine. Please remember that what has been discussed is totally confidential. Mike will see to this as well. I need your commitment and your unwavering dedication because once *we cross the Rubicon,* there is no turning back."

Oliver was in awe and raised his glass, 'To the Stork Center!"

"Hmm, I love that, yes, to our Stork Center," Fern said smiling.

Lance remained behind, and Fern poured him another drink. She thanked him again for coming.

"What made you change your mind?" she asked.

He sighed. "Well, Fern, I haven't changed my mind. Not about the inadvisability of this entire enterprise. But I realize you're my niece, and you are still very young. You have no father now, and I know he would want me to watch over you. Your heart is in the right place. I'm not interested in the money, only in what happens to you. So, if there's anything I can do to make this idea of yours work, I'll do it."

Fern stood up and silently put her arms around her uncle. There were no words that expressed her gratitude at that moment.

Fern knew Maggie would be cleaning the office in the morning. She crumpled up a fifty-dollar note and threw it on top of the trash can where it would most likely be found. She locked the office and, with Amy Winehouse's music blaring in her car, she hit the road for home. She had not felt this happy since before she'd learned about being dumped and abandoned in the Dandenong.

Chapter Twenty-Three

A few weeks later, very early in the morning, Fern took a drive out to the Dandenong site. The sun was just getting up when she left the house in Toorak. It was an invigorating ride speeding along the road before any commuter traffic was about. She arrived a little after 7 am and parked off the side of the road, next to the entrance of the property. Only heavy-duty vehicles and four-wheel drives could manage the current terrain of the land. Some workmen were already onsite and acknowledged her as she walked towards the activity with a nod or a wave. The foreman came over and greeted her in a sonorous voice, "Good morning, Ms. Jones. Let me show you around so you can get an idea where we are at." It was early days, and the workforce was in the midst of clearing the area and prepping the site. He left Fern shortly after the brief tour so she could wander around on her own and take in the lay-of-the-land and the new foundation being laid, as well as enjoy the moment for herself.

After about fifteen minutes of surveying the work, she walked towards her car. She turned and waved to the foreman and crew, acknowledging their work.

Bruce Nash was out on his daily morning exercise and approaching the construction site just as Fern walked out of the entrance to her Audi. He saw her as she turned back to admire her hew property.

Fern did not see him until he was within touching distance.

"Good morning!" Nash said in a bright, friendly voice.

Fern was a bit startled. She turned to him, "Good morning," she responded quickly. He seemed to have come out of nowhere.

"May I ask if this is the construction project that you are visiting?"

Fern smiled briefly, "No, no, it is my new home they are building. Why do you ask?"

"Oh, it's just that I've never seen a construction crew work so quickly. I'm impressed!"

Fern looked at him through her dark sunglasses. He seemed like a pleasant old man.

"Do you live in the area?"

"Yes, I do, just a few blocks, in fact. It is beautiful up here; been here for many years now," he nodded.

Fern could tell he wanted to talk more and probably had a lot of time on his hands as well, but she didn't want to get cornered with questions. "I'm rushing to my office. I'm going to be late if I don't get going. I'm Fern, by the way, Fern Jones."

"Pleased to meet you," Nash offered his hand. "I'm Bruce Nash, and welcome to the Dandenong."

Fern smiled as she opened her car door and put her hand up in acknowledgment before climbing into the front seat.

Nash carried on his walk as he thought how pleasant she seemed. He also took in her expensive Audi and her couture designer outfit. She was obviously very wealthy for someone so young and exuded success—her good looks didn't go unnoticed either.

Fern was already refocused on her day. She looked over her shoulder and in her side mirrors before doing a U-turn and heading back to her office in the city.

Nash also turned around and stood for a few moments more at the construction site. He couldn't believe how fast the luxury home was springing up. He was used to houses taking a year at least to build and, in most cases, closer to two years, but this building site was a different kettle of fish. The activity was full on. An extra-large number of crew were on site six days a week, and construction vehicles and cement trucks were constantly in and out with deliveries. Ms. Jones was certainly in a hurry to move in.

. Nash continued his walk, his mind rambling over Merle. She had begun to lose weight, ate little, and was soiling her bed more frequently. As much as the house was cleaned and Kate scrubbed, sprayed, wiped, and disinfected, the stench lingered, and there was no getting away from it.

He wasn't sure what to do.

On the way to the city Fern thought about how her mother had seemed to age overnight. She must try to spend more time with her.

She made some calls and checked in with the architects while on the road back. She instructed them to make sure they saved the tall Gum and Algerian oak trees on the property. She wanted to also be put in direct touch with landscapers to discuss the color design and the various plants and shrubs to be used for the garden.

When Fern reached her office, she found that Maggie had already been by to clean that day. Everything as usual, was immaculate. She also found the fifty-dollar note on her desk with a handwritten note stating Maggie had found the money amongst discarded rubbish and questioning whether someone had lost it. Interesting, Fern thought.

Chester's mining equipment business IME was sold for twenty-eight million dollars. Fern's attorney and accountant also made separate arrangements for the one account receivable to continue the payment schedule owed directly to Fern within 180 days. The other delinquent client filed for bankruptcy with the agreement Fern could sell off the equipment held as collateral to pay off their debt.

She also sold a few commercial properties that were left to her by Chester's estate. All in all, Fern's bank account stood at well over hundred-million-dollars.

Fern still retained some properties left in her name, which would provide a healthy rental income for the years to come. One sought-after real estate asset was a block from Collins street near the French quarter, and there were some smaller properties in Richmond and a double empty stand in Toorak that overlooked the Yarra River.

Fern was sitting at her desk, going over the paperwork from the real estate transactions, when there was a soft knock on the door, and Maggie entered.

"Hello, Maggie. I was keeping an eye out for you. Come in, please." Fern said kindly.

"Thank you, ma'am. How are you? I forgot to ask if you found the money I left on your desk after your big meeting the other week?"

"Yes, Maggie, thank you for your honesty, but that's not why I wanted to see you. Please sit down. Have you a little time?"

Maggie sat down slowly, a little concerned. "Yes, I have a few minutes, ma'am," she said after glancing at her watch.

"Would you like a soda, Maggie?"

"No, thank you, ma'am." Maggie would have loved a soda but was too shy.

"My name is Fern. Please call me Fern. You are working full time. Am I right in saying this?'

"Yes, I am, Fern," she said timidly, unsure of the direction the conversation was going in.

"May I be inquisitive and ask what you get paid?"

"Yes, I earn $38,000 a year. Why, ma'am — sorry, I mean Fern?"

"Maggie, you do a great job, and I can see how meticulous you are, and I appreciate it. You are also very honest, which is not easy to find.

I am going to be direct with you and not beat around the bush. I am hiring and want to know if you would be interested in working just for me?"

Maggie's mind was racing. She felt a bit confused but, at the same time excited.

"Doing what? Cleaning? This isn't a very big office Ms. Jones. I mean Fern."

"Oh no, Maggie, I am setting up a new business and will need a competent housekeeper for the business as well as my new home, which will be on the same property. I want this person to do cleaning, of course, but more than that. I would like them to also take an interest in the overall running of the domestic side of things — you know, making sure the supplies are well stocked, and we have everything we need to operate efficiently. Would this interest you at all?"

Maggie's eyes widened at the prospect of a more interesting job. "Yes, ma'am," she said quickly.

"Where do you live, Maggie?"

"In Belgrave South."

"Excellent, that will be another bonus as the complex will be even closer. It is in the Dandenong, near the Sassafras area. I plan to have it up and running in a few months. Are you interested?"

"Yes, yes, for sure!" Maggie couldn't believe her luck. She got a little choked up. The thought of less of a commute and the opportunity to save money on public transport was just what she needed.

"That's really great news, Maggie. Because I know what a great worker you are, and I trust you. I will pay you fifty-eight-thousand a year, plus three weeks of paid leave, and a Christmas bonus. Also, if we find you need extra help, come speak to me, and then we can hire assistants for you. Would this be acceptable?"

Maggie blushed and teared up. She was lost for words. "Thank you, thank you!" she finally said.

"Your job title will be *Head Housekeeper*. Before you go, write down your details, and I will draw up an employment contract. In the meantime, carry on working your current job until I'm ready. It will not be long."

Maggie was a bit speechless. "Thank you—"

"Thank you, Maggie. I am looking forward to welcoming you. I will be in touch. Have a lovely day."

As Maggie left, Fern picked up her phone, smiling to herself. Having money might not buy happiness, she thought, but giving it out to deserving people was certainly a lot of fun.

She remembered the promise she made to herself and called her mother to offer to bring home dinner or to take her out so she wouldn't have to prepare anything.

Before she called it a day, she rang Mike Barzel to schedule a one-to-one meeting to go over details in depth. She also set up another meeting with Danny, but there was no answer from Oliver, so she left a message.

While she waited for him to call her back, she googled the name Bruce Nash, the stranger she had met at her construction site earlier that morning.

Detective Inspector Nash was a retired policeman.

The internet is a wonderful source of information, she thought and made a note to mention Nash to Mike when they met.

She wasn't unduly worried but retired police officers, like Nash, probably had too much time on their hands, and she couldn't afford to have him nosing around.

The sound of her mobile broke into her thoughts; it was Oliver.

"Hi, this is Fern," she answered, making sure she remained professional with him.

"I know. You called me, Fern," he jokingly replied. "I was under a friend's plane doing a safety check."

"I was calling to schedule our one-on-one follow-up meeting I mentioned at the meeting. Can you do tomorrow?"

"Sure. Where do you want to meet?"

"My office, say 9 am? I'll order breakfast to be delivered."

"Nine is good. How long do you reckon we'll need?"

"I'm anticipating a couple of hours or so."

"Fern, I tell you what, I've got a proposition for you. You've been working really hard these last few weeks, and you need a break. Why don't you let me fly you to Noosa so you can experience my work first-hand? Noosa is a lovely part of the world. I would really like to show you. It would be a good opportunity to get to know each other. I did want to invite you face to face, but there's been no chance."

There was a pause at the other end of the line. "We are, after all, going to be collaborating in a clandestine operation, so we need to know who we are jumping in the fire with, don't you think?"

Fern was silent for a moment. "What do you envisage?"

"I'll book the best accommodation. We'll go to the beach, feel the soft sand cracking beneath our feet, relax while gazing at the blue ocean, and…"

Fern cut him off, "And what?"

"And eat. I know the best restaurant there. We'll drink another toast to the Stork Center. Let's just get out of Melbourne. No rules, no strings attached. Let's go and enjoy the weather on the Sunshine Coast. It beats damn Melbourne's four seasons in a day."

"I'm tempted, Oliver. Give me another good reason."

Oliver wanted to say because he wanted to make love to her all night long but didn't.

"We will hire a couple of bikes and ride between Coolum and Noosa Heads. In my backpack, I'll have a blanket, the best bottle of wine, a couple of ciabatta rolls with salami, and, wait for it, served by the best waiter in the world."

"What's his name?"

"His name, I only know his first name, it's Oliver. I think his last name is Good-looking, no wait, I'm getting forgetful. It's actually Big-boy."

"I guess you had better book two tickets, Mr. Vain Big-boy," Fern said with a smile of mischief.

"With me you never have to book. I'm the pilot."

Chapter Twenty-Four

Fern took her mother out for dinner and told her that she was going away for the weekend. She did not say with whom, letting her mother assume it was a girlfriend.

Megan had met Oliver numerous times when Chester was alive and would be well aware of his reputation. Fern wasn't sure she approved herself; it was risky business having a fling with an employee.

She also told Megan that it was only a matter of weeks before they would be moving into their new home and promised she would drive her there soon.

Megan had faith in her daughter, and so driving back home after dinner, the silence in the car was comfortable.

Fern's first call when she entered the house was to Lance. A date was set to meet a few days after she came back from her weekend trip.

Fern slept fitfully that night. She lay awake thinking how stupid she was to get involved with Oliver, especially as she was not remotely interested in him. He was fun to be around, but she could see through his charm and what he was after. However, she was young, rich, and no different from any other girl of her age, therefore not totally immune to flattery. She had to be honest with herself. She did enjoy the flirting and the excitement it brought.

She was just about to doze off. Bonzo II scrambled out of his dog door, barking like mad at a couple of opossums that dared to venture into his garden. The commotion eventually stopped, and she soon fell asleep.

In the morning, she packed an overnight bag and breakfasted with her mom before heading out. She walked to the main gate of their home and waited by the roadside so her mom wouldn't see Oliver's car.

A few minutes later, a flashy yellow Lamborghini sports car pulled up, and Oliver jumped out to open the door for Fern. He put her overnight bag in the front trunk and slammed it shut.

"Good morning, Fern, good to see," he smiled charmingly.

"Morning, Oliver. Nice car. I'm a bit tired as I didn't sleep well last night. I guess I really need this break."

"How's your mom doing?" he enquired, changing the subject.

"She's fine," Fern responded feeling a little self-conscious. "Look, Oliver, I know you probably think it's a bit weird that I came out to meet you on the road. I didn't exactly tell my mom I was going away with you this weekend. I know, I am an adult, but she wouldn't approve."

"No worries," he grinned beguilingly. "By the way, rhetorical question, you did pack your two-piece, I assume?"

"Yes, captain," she saluted, starting to relax. "And, can I ask, have you packed your waiter's uniform for when you serve dinner later?"

"Of course," and Oliver floored the accelerator. The drive to Essendon Airport was relatively quick and pleasant. Fern felt more at ease. At the airport, Oliver parked his car and escorted her through a different door and onto the tarmac near a couple of new hangars. He greeted another pilot amid the airport activity. They watched an old non-flyable small plane being towed out of a hangar. Oliver knew it was destined to be an exhibit for the Moorabbin airport museum not far away.

"Here, Fern. Here's our plane. Come, let's get aboard," he joked with a straight face.

"You're kidding. You mean we are flying to Noosa in that rusty heap?" she said, alarmed.

"Why not? The old bird has still got life in her."

Fern raised an eyebrow and smiled, "Come on, you are having me on. I can see by your body language that you are bullshitting me. You can't fib a fibber, captain."

Oliver chuckled and then moved his head to the side and gestured for Fern to look to her right.

She followed his eyes and looked. A sleek small jet was being towed towards them, but it was much larger when she came up close to it.

"Is that our bird, captain?" she asked somewhat in awe.

"Sure is. She's a Learjet. She is the largest, fastest long-range plane in the family. She's ultra-comfortable. Perhaps not top of the range but I tell you what, at 869 kilometres per an hour, we will land at the Sunshine Coast Airport before you can say *Black Caviar*."

Fern smiled, "Why do you guys refer to a jet or a cool car as *she*?"

"Why not? *She* depicts beauty. Look at you," he admired.

Fern smiled, and she covered her eyes from the sun.

With the stairs down, Oliver and Fern entered the Learjet.

Fern was a little taken back to see another pilot in the cockpit.

"Meet Morris, aka Morrie, my co-pilot," Oliver happily introduced Fern. "He's the best in the west. If we hit a flock of birds or a hail storm, Morrie is *The Man*. He is one of the few who will still get you out of any mess anywhere, anytime."

"Don't exaggerate, dude. Welcome aboard, Ms. Jones," Morrie said, extending his hand.

"Hi," was all Fern could say at that moment. She had assumed Oliver would be discreet and keep their little getaway secret. She chided herself for not clarifying this beforehand.

Oliver showed Fern her seat.

"Why another pilot?" she asked under her breath.

"Aviation laws require two pilots for a jet this powerful. It's based on the number of controls, speed, and other avionics," he explained.

"What if I want to come and talk with you during the flight? You can't sit with me in the cockpit. Anyway, don't worry, sit back and relax. Morrie is the soul of discretion." He bent down and kissed her on her forehead. "Belt-up now. We leave very soon."

She heard the engines roar into life and the jet started to move. Fern could somewhat overhear muffled aviator jargon; "ADT 2 pm. Essendon Tower Learjet, Tango 40 ready for take-off." Then she heard another voice, which Fern assumed was the tower; "runway three-niner Tango 40, winds two nine zero at fourteen, cleared for take-off."

Oliver's smooth voice came through the sound system, "Fern, we have been cleared for take-off. Sit back and enjoy the flight. We will be in Noosa in just over a couple of hours."

She smiled and relaxed into the comfortable leather seat.

In seconds the jet was in the air. Unlike the big Boeing commercial passenger planes, the noise was not so intrusive, a more comfortable hum with a pleasant smooth whistle.

During the flight, Oliver did come back into the cabin a couple of times to visit and make sure Fern was happy. He also spoke to her over the PA system, pointing out points of interest and major landmarks.

Touchdown was as smooth as velvet. After Oliver completed the necessary pilot landing checks and handed the reigns to Morrie, he took Fern's hand, and they stepped down onto the tarmac and went to collect the Land Cruiser from the Toyota rental desk.

The drive to Noosa was stunning. They were immediately engulfed in a beautiful clean sandy beach, green bush, and palm trees. There was a special feel to the place. The air was warm and fresh, the sea was blue and clear, and seagulls patrolled over the beaches, eyes as sharp as eagles looking out for an occasional tidbit from the sunbathers and surfers.

They checked into their five-star chalet, a few hundred metres from the beach.

Oliver dropped their bags on the couch and looked around, making sure the kitchen was well stocked with all the food and beverages he had ordered. There were many little touches the staff had undertaken on their own, including a welcome gift basket with a bottle of wine with cheeses and fruit and local gooseberry jam and premium honeys from Queensland.

Fern stood on the patio, her back to Oliver, facing the sea.

"It's gorgeous here, Oliver." She was genuinely mesmerized.

Oliver eyed Fern's body against the backdrop of the sea. The brilliant sun giving a seductive silhouette look. "Glad you like it. I always like a room with a view."

After they unpacked their few belongings and changed, they took a stroll to the beach. They started to talk about the Stork Center, but after the flight and the lack of sleep the night before, Fern was desperate for a nap.

When they arrived back at their chalet, they found the hotel staff had brought over two mountain bikes and put them on the patio.

"Wow, everything meticulously arranged," Fern marveled, but her eyes were already closing, so she excused herself and went to lie down.

Oliver relaxed in the living room and checked on her every so often. He looked at her, lying fast asleep on the queen-sized bed. He had always admired beauty. It was late afternoon, and he sat on the patio, sipping a beer and staring at the infinite horizon and the sparkling sea. When he finished his beer, he woke her. She had been sleeping for nearly four hours.

"Wakey-wakey, my blue-eyed, brown-eyed princess." He kissed her naked shoulder.

"Mmm," Fern mumbled.

"What can I make you to drink? There are all sorts of teas here, and there's juices, sodas, coffee, or wines, or a cold beer perhaps?"

"Is there mango juice?"

"Yep, there is mango, orange, and also lychee."

"Mango, please, waiter—with ice."

"Yes, ma'am, coming up in five."

Oliver put a white napkin over his left forearm and served her mango juice on a tray with a small bowl of cashew nuts.

Fern smiled at Oliver, "Does a cook come with the chalet by any chance?" she teased.

"Yes, ma'am, chef Oliver is on duty tonight, and he has arranged fresh delivery of the best Gulf White shrimp in the southern hemisphere. Hope that meets with your approval, madam?"

"Can't wait, captain."

Fern excused herself and went to shower and change. Oliver found the CD player and put an old one by Dusty Springfield, *The Look of Love*. The gentle yet powerful tune filtered through the chalet as Fern stepped out of the shower and began to dry herself.

She smiled at Oliver as she came into the living room, her hair still wet. "Wow, thanks for letting me sleep. I really needed it. Your turn. There's still plenty of hot water."

He smiled back and disappeared.

Fern took out a YSL perfume bottle and sprayed a little around her neck, the top of her ears, a tiny amount on her belly button, and a little behind her knees.

Oliver came out of the shower in a fresh, white cotton robe.

He walked towards her, teasing her with his eyes. They stood facing each other. He put his hands on Fern's shoulders and eased her bathrobe over them, dropping it to the floor. She stood there naked, her nipples erect in anticipation. He kissed her long and hard. Their tongues finding each other. He gently picked her up in his strong arms and carried her to the bedroom.

"Wait, be gentle. I am new at this," she looked up at him with Bambi eyes. Oliver paused, taking this in. He didn't expect this.

"Okay, hold on while I choose another song." He left the room and found Katy Perry's *I Kissed a Girl*. He then went into the open-plan kitchen and opened a cupboard and removed one of the bottles of honey, and returned to the bedroom. Fern had one bedside lamp on dim, and the curtains closed; she didn't see what he had. Oliver put the bottle down next to her side of the bed, and they kissed passionately.

Almost immediately, he took hold of her hand and guided her to gently take hold of his cock, massaging it up and down and encouraging her to insert it into her mouth. She didn't want to disappoint him, so she sucked hard whilst he moaned gently in delight. In a flash, he plucked the honey from the table and squeezed the honey all over his penis.

It felt warm and sticky and gave a pleasant sensation. She looked up and smiled and continued to lick and suck, then she came up and kissed him on the mouth.

"You taste sweet," he moaned with ecstasy.

"Mmm," she whispered back.

"Aww, I'm ready. Now Oliver, get inside me."

He mounted her gently, rhythmically moving up and down, up and down, down and up. At one stage, he was on top of her, and while her legs rested on his shoulder, he enjoyed the aromatic perfume behind her knees.

She climaxed, and a few seconds later, he did as well.

Then something happened that he'd never experienced. She took his rod again in her mouth and sucked it clean.

In the late evening, he barbequed the large shrimp that had been marinating in melted butter, lemon juice, and garlic. He cooked the baked potatoes wrapped in aluminum foil and served them with butter, a dash of salt, and dried parsley while Fern made a salad. They sipped a perfectly chilled bottle of Sancerre and ate outside against a gentle moonlit ocean.

Fern looked at him, "Oliver, I'd like to present you with the distinguished medals for being the best pilot, driver, lover, waiter, and executive chef in the world." They chinked glasses.

"Thanks, Fern, I'm honored, but where are the medals?" he winked.

"We only have one more night here; I guess I'll have to present them in kind," her eyes twinkled back. She was having the time of her life away from family and all the responsibilities she had inherited and taken on.

After the delicious meal, they made love again and fell asleep to the sound of the waves washing the white sands while the moon waned in Noosa.

In the morning, Oliver prepared a mushroom and cheese omelet with toast and fresh juice, and coffee so Fern could enjoy breakfast in bed. Afterward, they took the Land Cruiser and the two mountain bikes off into Noosa National Park, where they rode for a couple of hours. After an invigorating ride through the gorgeous landscape vistas, they stopped for a break, and Oliver laid out a picnic made up of exquisite cheeses and fruit. In the afternoon, they swam in the sea near their chalet and later lay in the sun to dry below the few fluffy clouds discussing plans for the massive operation of saving babies from around the world.

In the evening, they dined in the local restaurant that Oliver recommended, and true to his word, the food was incredible. They washed it down with Penfold Grange worth ten times more than the meal itself.

They drove back to their beach chalet, chatting and laughing, both so happy and enthusiastically looking forward to their future endeavor.

Fern turned to look at Oliver as he was driving, and he glanced back at her.

"Oliver, I keep meaning to ask you, where do you know Mike Barzel from?"

"We've known each other for many years when I flew him around. Mike is loyal and a tough guy. You are lucky to have him on board."

"What about my dad? You flew for him many times, too, didn't you?"

"Sure did, many business trips for his mining business."

Fern knew that there was more to his answer but left it at that. She didn't want to spoil the weekend. It could wait.

Back at the chalet, when he opened the door for her, she kissed him, and he pulled her closer, their arms wrapping around each other. He kissed her neck, then her lips as they made their way to the bedroom.

"Wait for a second. I need to use the little girl's room," she gasped with pleasure.

He released her and let her go while he undressed and climbed in under the covers naked. He switched off the main light and turned on his bedside lamp. He looked up and saw Fern had returned and was smiling with a clenched fist.

"What have you got, Fern?" he asked, pretending to be scared.

"Your medals that I promised you," she giggled.

He looked puzzled, then she opened her fist, and it was empty. They laughed, and she jumped on top of him.

"I'm paying you in kind, remember." There was more laughter and even more laughter when the bed started to squeak.

In the morning, they left for the airport, returned the Land Cruiser, and were soon climbing aboard the Learjet. Morrie, the co-pilot, was waiting.

Once the jet was in the air, Oliver's voice came through on the audio system, "Fern, it's the last time for a while that we will see that exquisite sea in this part of the world. Look out your window now as we bank to the right and the sea disappears."

She gazed out the window and smiled at all that perfection..

Back in Melbourne, while Oliver was driving Fern home, she called Lance, Danny, and Mike to let them know that she was looking forward to their next individual meetings. As he pulled up to her gate, she used her remote, and Oliver drove into the driveway and up to the front door.

Fern was pleased to see her mother was out.

Oliver climbed out and opened Fern's door. He took her bag out from the trunk, and suddenly Fern became all formal, "Oliver, thank you so much for the lovely weekend. I'll see you soon."

"It was my pleasure, Fern," taking her cue. "I look forward to working with you."

As he turned to get back into his car, she said casually, "By the way, I forgot to mention, there's one more important thing to discuss. We will need our own jet."

Oliver looked blankly at her.

"Seriously, I mean it. Arrange it. We will need to purchase a new Learjet, like the one we just flew in. A few seats will have to be removed and replaced with carrycots so they will be safe for young babies. I want two or three car seats that can be detachable but clamped to the floor for safety reasons. Can you take care of this?"

Oliver smiled, "Sure. I'll look into it today and call you back with choices and costs. The jet we just used may be available, and it has low mileage on the clock. You would save a few bucks as well. Let me check this out and get back to you later."

"Sounds good," Fern kissed him goodbye, and Oliver took off.

Chapter Twenty-Five

"Good afternoon," David welcomed her with a smile as she climbed out of the car for a site visit.

Fern nodded. "Good afternoon to you too."

"You look well. Excited, I bet," Blythe said and led the way.

Fern looked around as they chatted, taking in progress. The framework of the building and roof had been completed, and there were huge neat piles of bricks, molds of sand and cement, and stacks of wood under enormous tarp coverings. They walked towards the temporary construction site office.

"This main driveway must be able to take you to the front door and around to the double garage; it also has to fork off to the building by the kitchen back door and to the baby center building as well," she instructed.

"We can do that. Luckily the area is flat, and there are no trees in the way," Blythe assured her.

David smiled, "Ms. Jones, I am pleased to tell you that my partner and I are ahead of schedule. We've put immense pressure on the builder, and we will be presenting you with your keys to your new home in two to three weeks."

Just then, in the distance, about a hundred feet away, Fern saw someone walking past the front of her property. The man stopped for a second and waved. It was Bruce Nash, and before Fern could react, Nash was on his way again.

"Thank you, Gentlemen. The faster, the better, thank you."

Fern drove home to Toorak. She decided not to go back to the office but to work at home and go over her notes and crucial points in preparation for her meetings with her crew.

She also took some time to research property values in Toorak and checked out the homes for sale. She was curious to estimate what their home was worth if her mom ever agreed to sell. Toorak was a much sought-after area, and the high-end houses were fetching between three to three-and-a-half million.

She also continued her google search for more information on adoption and was amazed to see some couples actually advertised that they were looking for babies.

Lying in bed that night going over everything in her mind, Fern thought everything was really being well attended to. She had even thought to instruct the architects to make sure the driveway would go all the way to the back of the building. This tiny detail would allow them to unload the babies out of sight of passers-by. No one would have any idea of the activity going on.

Fern expected to see Maggie as it was her day to clean, but she wasn't there. She left word on her voicemail to give her a better idea of her start date.

There was a soft knock on the door. That must be Mike. They had a meeting scheduled.

"Come in," Fern said as she glanced at her watch, pleased with his punctuality.

"Hi, Fern. Nice to see you again. Did you enjoy your weekend in Noosa?"

"Yes, it was okay, thanks." Fern was taken by surprise at Oliver's lack of discretion. It was unnerving.

"Come sit," she invited, quickly recovering.

"I hear you test drove the jet," Mike commented as he pulled up a chair and sat down.

"So, where's the best place to begin?" she enquired, ignoring his comment.

Mike was impressed by her confidence as she looked directly at his right eye showing a sign of trust. From his years of experience, only trusted ones or family members are able to look at your right eye when talking.

"First priority is the security," he said. "Have you had this discussion with the architects? It would be best if you put me in touch with them so I can oversee the design and CCTV surveillance cameras equipment?"

"I had a brief conversation with them about security, and I will get them to call you to discuss, no problem."

"Great. I will also need to start planning a field trip to start scouting cities and identifying places where we are most likely to locate abandoned and neglected babies. To begin with, I must reconnect with my connections and informants to get the ball rolling."

Fern nodded and smiled; it was so good to have someone with whom she could share this..

"Now, I've given this some thought. I believe the best way to gain access to these slums will be with press credentials. We can ask Danny to create a press ID card for us. That way, there will be less suspicion. My angle is that when I meet with people, I will tell them that I am gathering information for a news article about street kids and the people living in extreme poverty. I will explain that I am visiting a number of countries and comparing how the different governments deal with their forgotten society. I will have my digital camera to take pictures for the fictitious article and let them know I will be sending a follow-up television crew to film in the future."

"Great idea." She was glad she'd been smart enough to hire him.

"Of course, the press card is just a ruse so we can move about freely and avoid questions and minimize trouble. The Press is known to be a nuisance and ask awkward questions, but once I locate prospective informants, they will be our intel gatherers. We will have to reward them generously for their information and their silence. They'll soon realize I am not press, and the money will ensure their loyalty and secure delivery. I need time to befriend them to gain their trust."

Mike looked at some notes he had brought with him and paused.

"I've also been thinking that every major city in the world has slums, so I would hit up the Americas first. The Favella district in Brazil will be a good starting point. The shantytowns around São Paulo and Rio have got to be rife with unwanted discarded infants."

Fern was thinking. Mike waited.

"It sounds like you need to leave soon. Our center will be ready in a few weeks. I've also been thinking that maybe it would look less dubious if you fly outbound on a commercial airline and then, when you are ready to return, Oliver can fly out to meet you wherever you are in our Learjet and bring you home."

"Our Learjet? Did you purchase one?"

"Yes, Oliver is taking care of it."

Mike was secretly amazed. Fern's maturity and professionalism were impressive for her young age. "One other thing. Best to use the word *parcel*—it will be safer and more secure if we attract attention."

Fern smiled. "Cute."

"Also," Mike interrupted her thoughts. "I will, from time to time, have to use a burner phone."

"What do you mean?"

"An untraceable phone. Once this operation gets up and running, we don't know what kind of attention we will attract. The less, the better, and, of course, phones are the easiest way to connect the dots. I plan to only use a phone once or twice before I ditch it so it can never be traced. It will be safer for all."

"Sounds like these expenses will add up. Open a new account, and I will transfer a hundred thousand in cash, as soon as you send me the details. You let me know if this is enough, but it should get you going and covered for your maiden voyage."

Mike nodded.

"Are you hungry? I'm starved. I have an hour or so before Danny will be here. You got time to grab something downstairs?"

"Sounds good," Mike stood up and waited for Fern to join him.

Fern locked her office and the two of them, a lot more relaxed now, sauntered over to the diner a block away. Fern noticed how Mike's eyes constantly kept vigilance of his surroundings.

Mike opened the restaurant door for Fern, "Grab a booth. This is on me. There's an open booth just behind you towards the window," he pointed.

As Mike waited in line to order, he noticed a man talking to Fern. She did not look too pleased. He ordered quickly and went over to their table.

"I was just telling this person that we are together," Fern looked to Mike for reassurance.

"Can I help you?" Mike asked imposingly. "Do you know this lady?" he said in a soft, deep voice.

"No, man, just passed her a compliment; thought she was alone," he said, backing off.

Mike's eyes widened. He took a step closer to the stranger. "She's with me. I'm not your fucking man, and my partner is not on the menu, so take a walk before someone has to call an ambulance for you," he growled quietly.

He didn't need to be asked twice.

"Jeez, what a frigging freak. I mean, I only just sat down, and he came out of nowhere. Who the hell does he think he is? Thanks, Mike," Fern said, relieved.

They ate and talked a bit more. It was good to know that her operations manager meant business. He seemed fearless.

They finished eating and left. Again, Mike took in his surroundings, scanning for the creep or anything else lurking nearby.

"Thanks, Mike. I will talk to you soon. Don't forget to send me your bank details."

"Wait, wait—I'll walk you back to your office." The incident had made him realize he was with a vulnerable young heiress, who was extremely wealthy and naïve to potential danger.

"Don't worry, Mike, he's gone. I think you put the fear of God into him."

"Not negotiable," he said firmly. He couldn't let anything happen to Chester Jones' daughter on his watch.

Mike escorted Fern up to her office and departed.

Fern sat down at her desk to revisit her notes. The phone rang. It was Oliver.

"Hi!" he said softly. "How are you doing?"

"All good," she said in a bright professional manner. "Danny will be here any moment."

"Oh, okay. Good news. I got a better deal on the jet for you."

"Great job. When will it be officially ours?"

"I'll send over the payment details. The paperwork will take a few days at most before we can register the change of ownership. Then I'll need a day or two to remove seats and set it up for our specifications."

"Of course, for *the parcels*."

There was a knock on the door. Danny poked his head around. Fern motioned for him to come in.

She put her hand over the phone, "I won't be long. Help yourself." Danny smiled and turned to grab a water.

"Fern, I will email you the transfer details and figures. We can chat later," Oliver said.

"Ok, good. See you later." She hung up.

"Hope you did not hurry on my account," Danny said.

"No, not at all. How are you, Danny? I just met with Mike, and we decided we need press credentials for him. It will make it easier for him to move around and ask questions. Suggest we have an extra set just in case. Choose any name for the second one.

"No problem. I will need to take a passport photo of him, so I have the original to manipulate."

"What will the card look like?" Fern asked curiously.

"I'll make sure it looks a bit old and worn, and the photo somewhat faded, so it gives the impression he has been on the road for a long time. I'll create an employee number and call it something like a diplomatic journalist."

"Cool, I like that. Now, here's the big thing, I need a website up and running. Call it *The Stork Center*. It needs to be stylish and chic, oozing elite and exclusivity. Less is more, so simple and elegant with only a few images from stock photos or something. We need to create an inviting ambiance, perhaps with an evocative entrance way and the user rings the doorbell to reveal a cute smiling baby face. The contact info should only be my cell phone number. No address, no email, just my number."

"Of course."

" It also needs a heavy-duty firewall so that we can control who gets access."

"How soon do you need this up?"

"The sooner, the better. I will compose some wording for the description. I am thinking something along the lines of: *everyone needs a home, and every home deserves a family.*"

Danny was quiet. "I like it."

"I will get onto it immediately."

"Good. I just need your bank details."

Danny smiled as he removed a pen from his pocket. Fern automatically handed him a piece of paper. After taking the details, Fern stood up and shook Danny's hand.

"Thank you, Fern."

"The pleasure is mine, and in a couple of weeks, we will all be able to meet at our brand-new headquarters, in our very own Stork Center, to celebrate the opening."

"Looking forward to it, Fern."

"Wow, I nearly forgot the most important thing. We must create a business license and any permits or paperwork necessary to operate a legal adoption center in Australia. Also, we will need the mandatory State license certificates for everyone to work with children. I will give you the names later. There will be me, there will be a nurse or two, and a helper as well."

"No worries. I've already started work on the company license. That's part of my job, remember? You've hired me, so you don't have to think of every little detail."

"Awesome, thank you! And yes, my uncle Lance Jones will also require a new ID with a different doctor's license number, so it is not associated with his current GP credentials. Something to the effect of Dr. Lance Jones, Head Physician of International Doctors Beyond Boundaries."

"Sounds good—will do!" And with that, Danny took off.

Fern looked at her watch. It was 6.10 pm, and no Lance.

She phoned him, and there was no answer.

At 6.20 pm, Lance walked into her office. "Sorry, my dear, my apologies, I had a small emergency. I was just about to leave when someone in my building needed a few stitches."

"Of course. Are they alright? Would you like tea or a real drink?"

"They are going to be fine. Tea would be good, thanks. So, where are we at? How is the building going?"

"Everything is on track. I move in about two weeks."

Fern poured the tea.

"You're doing great. I've also got good news for you. I have recruited a full-time nurse for you. She's worked for me before. She happened to phone me last week to see if I had a job for her or if I knew of anything."

"That's great. How do I contact her?"

"Here's her number. Her name is Alice Wilson, and she is expecting a call from you. That's not all, a friend of mine is a highly respected gynecologist and only yesterday said to me that he knows a couple who will do anything to adopt a baby. The couple has had every test under the sun with fertility specialists, and she's had more in vitro fertilization than anyone I know. They got the official word this week that, sadly, they cannot have kids. Just like your poor Mom and Dad when they were young."

"Are they wealthy?"

"Yes," he nodded, happyto be sharing this news with his niece.

"Wow, Uncle Lance! This is really happening," Fern looked at him excitedly. Her eyes glistened.

"Fern, I tell you what, leave it with me. I will phone my friend. In fact, we are playing golf together on Sunday, and I will mention something to him."

"That's fantastic. Thank you so much, Uncle Lance."

"I don't have a lot of time. I need to leave in a half hour or so."

"That's okay. We will be finished by then. I also need to get home to Mom as well."

Lance sat back in his chair.

"I see your job as mainly to inspect every baby as soon as the jet lands with the babies. We will have to have a full medical check-up, blood work, and all the tests and analyses you recommend. We will also need any diagnostics and treatment analysis and any observation reports if any. Occasionally, you or Alice Wilson will need to accompany Oliver on the flights. Not often, perhaps, but it is a possibility. Your doctor's card is being addressed as we speak."

Lance listened carefully.

"Alright," he said," all sounds good. But I must add that certain countries carry different diseases and my advice is to concentrate on countries with fewer health issues. Africa is prevalent with AIDS and malaria, as well as the upper parts of South America, the far east, and other areas. Diseases to be aware of are yellow fever and other related mosquito bites as dengue fever, which is in Africa, Asia, and South America. There have been cases even here, up in the Northern Territory, Queensland, and northern Western Australia."

"What do you suggest?"

"Concentrate on Europe and the USA. Believe it or not, there are also slums there, homelessness, and street kids. Yes, everyone thinks Europe is free of slums. Forget it. Slums are all over, in France, in Spain. In Rome, there are a good few thousand children living with rats in shocking conditions, also Turkey, Romania, Slovakia and on, and on."

Fern loved her uncle, but sometimes he could be a tad infuriating with his gloominess.

"Uncle Lance, come on, I'm aware that even in the richest countries, babies are discarded—"

"But they don't carry malaria and other frightening illnesses, Fern."

Chapter Twenty-Six

"Mom, I'd like to take you for a drive." It was 8 am, and Fern was standing at the kitchen door in her bathrobe.

"Oh?" Megan was caught off-guard. Fern was always so busy. "Where to?"

"It's a surprise." Fern winked playfully.

"You're like your father," Megan laughed.

As they pulled up to the entrance of the Dandenong property and drove through the gates, Fern looked over at her mom. Her eyes were wide, and her jaw dropped. She looked at Fern, wondering what was going on.

There had been much improvement since Fern last visited. There was a flurry of the crew putting together last-minute touches and a number of gardeners planting shrubs and flowers while another group cleaned and swept and generally tidied up outside. It was a hive of activity.

"What is all this, Fern? Is this what you have been up to these past few months?"

"Yes, let me show you around." Fern was so excited and happy. "This is my new home!"

"What? It is so big. Won't you get lonely? You'll rattle around here all by yourself." Megan knew Fern had been working on some big secret project but had no idea to what extent.

"Come on—you'll love it!" she urged, ignoring her mother's comments. "I plan to move in a few weeks. I was thinking a change will do us both some good, and I want you to move with me!"

"Look, I am also building an adoption center," she said with sweeping arms to express the enormity of the project. "I want you to be part of this. I am going to find forever homes for abandoned babies like me and match them with wonderful parents, like you and dad. What do you think?"

Megan was floored, deeply touched. . Her daughter had found both her vocation and was honoring her father, her husband. Her eyes filled with tears. "Oh, honey. I am so proud of you. Your dad would have been so proud of you. I honestly don't know what to say," she stepped towards her and hugged her tight. She looked around and saw the beautiful landscape, the vista of trees, and mother nature holding the space for something special to be birthed.

Fern interrupted her thoughts, "I want you to sell the house in Toorak and move in here. I want you to be involved. You are the one with first-hand experience of how to handle a newborn, lost and separated from its mother. You know how to comfort and help them feel loved and nurtured. You can assist and oversee the running of the place, you know, make sure it's clean and supervise the housekeeper's responsibilities."

"Ah, Fern, dear, I'm a bit old for house chores."

"No, no, no, mom, what I meant is just to keep an eye on things as an interest; I have already employed a full-time housekeeper/cleaner. There will be a full-time nurse to start and as we expand, I expect to hire another one. I am arranging all new furniture for the center and would love your help decorating the nursery and the nurse quarters. It would be great to discuss and plan together what is needed, and then you can oversee everything just as you did when I first arrived home."

"Darling, I love my home. It was where I made my first home with your father. I have so many memories of Toorak. Happy memories…" she said.

"But if I am not there, I think you will be lonely," Fern said, trying to prompt her mom into her way of thinking.

"I'll have to think about it. You are all I have left. Let me sleep on it."

"Thanks, mom. That's all I ask," Fern smiled and hugged her mom, knowing she would come around. "Let's go for ice cream and check out the baby stores."

When they arrived home, Fern arranged to meet Alice, the nurse, the next day.

Over dinner, she and Megan talked more about furnishing the center. She told her Mom to go ahead and start ordering the cots and whatever else she felt was needed. "I want the bedding and drapes to be colorful and bright. We will obviously need diapers, baby wipes, creams, and bins for the soiled diapers. I leave it all up to you and the nurse."

"When do you want them delivered?"

"I'll know more in a few days. I'll arrange for a company credit card so you can charge everything to The Stork Center."

Megan smiled and looked energized. It was good to see her mother get some spark back into her eyes."

Fern then phoned the architects and was put through to Blythe.

"Blythe, it's Fern. I've just been to my home. I'm impressed. Can I move in tomorrow?" Fern was being facetious but maintained a formal tone. There was silence for a second or two, then she heard Blythe say to someone in the background, "She wants to move in tomorrow!"

Fern assumed he was talking to David.

Blythe cleared his throat, "Actually, we just need a few more days. You can move in on Thursday this week. The arborist will still be planting all the trees, and the horticulturist will be taking care of the shrubs and flowers and laying the lawn."

"Tell you what, I will move in on Friday, which gives me the weekend to work. Liaise with the greenery people and tell them I want it all completed by Friday. The little things like the ground cover, small plants, and flowers can be finished during next week."

"Okay, that will work."

"I've been speaking with my mother, and she is going to take over all the baby equipment and stuff needed. You can call her directly and coordinate everything with her. What about the wallpaper for the babies' area that I chose?"

"Being put up straight after the cleaning, don't worry."

"Fine, Blythe, just keep me posted daily now, even if you have to phone me several times a day. Another thing just entered my mind — how is the sound system going for the nursery? I want them to hear soft, light, instrumental scores that will be soothing and good for the babies and nurse."

"Okay, we will take care of it."

"Mom, mom!" she shouted as she hung up and went in search of Megan.

"What, darling, what's up?"

"We move on Friday."

Fern called Mike Barzel and instructed him to push the architects and to check out the CCTV, perimeter beams, access control, and the electronics of the place.

Fern phoned the architects again and got the contact information for the building contractor, the landscaper, and the interior designer. She called each of them to let them know there would be a bonus if they completed the job by Friday. The bonus would include flight and five-star accommodation for a weekend away for two anywhere in Australia of their choice. Fern would also cover all expenses for a staff company BBQ and a $250 gift voucher for each member.

Meanwhile, Oliver was busy at the airport. He'd just taken delivery of the Learjet and installed the carrycots, making sure they were safely secured and anchored in the cabin.

Oliver also had done a thorough safety check of the jet before taking delivery and was now inspecting it for his own personal pleasure, savoring the moment and thrilled to have his own plane to look after, albeit his boss's. He sat in the cockpit and examined the instrument panel, and then he ran his hands over the interior leather seats in the cabin, admiring the elegance of the sleek design. Outside he caressed the fuselage, whispering to her and getting to know her as if he was soothing and complimenting a full-blooded racehorse.

He called Fern before he hopped onto his Harley Davidson to ride back to Melbourne.

"Great news, the stork has landed!" he laughed down the phone.

"Wow! You mean, we've got our jet!"

"You bet. When do I report for duty?"

"Aha, very soon. Next week we will have our first meeting at our new headquarters.."

"The generals will all meet," Oliver said.

"Aye, aye, captain, we sure will."

"You bet, honey. Keep in touch soon,' he said with a saucy voice. He ended the call with a smile, and so did Fern.

Jaffe & Murphy decided to organize a small celebration to mark the opening of The Stork Center for Fern. They hired a catering company to serve appetizers and offer glasses of chilled Moet and Chandon to guests. They also put in a special order with their favorite bakery to design a cake with one round section in blue icing with the words *It's a boy!* and the other round section in pink icing, saying *It's a girl!* The company also designed a large beautiful gold ribbon to put around the front door of Fern's new home.

The opening day was set for Tuesday the following week.

Chapter Twenty-Seven

Nurse Alice Wilson stepped out of the elevator and paused, looking left, then right, down the hallway. She followed the correct number sequence to Fern's office and poked her head inside.

Fern was on her phone and waved her in.

Fern finished her call.

"Alice, thank you for coming into the city to meet with me. My uncle, Dr. Jones, has given you a glowing reference. What part of the world are you from, Alice?"

"I live in Ringwood with my husband."

"Do you have children?"

"Yep, but they are grown up now. My daughter's at college, and my son just graduated high school last year and is working in England. He intends to see Europe before he comes back and decides his future."

"I believe you have worked as a nurse for some time now?"

"Yes, seventeen years, to be exact."

"What type of nursing?"

"I spent several years in the neonatal unit as a senior nurse looking after newborns. I looked after premature babies and neonates and a number of poor infants born with very distressing illnesses."

Fern started to think about her entry into the world and how she was found. She was quiet for a moment.

"Did you enjoy the work?"

Alice nodded, "It was extremely challenging but very rewarding."

"Any setbacks?"

"Yes, unfortunately. It is hard when a baby doesn't make it and very tough on the parents. I've also spent time nursing older kids, from toddlers to kindergarten. I love children and caring for them. It's in my blood, Fern."

Alice handed Fern an A4-size envelope.

"This is my résumé, with references and contact information."

Fern opened it and glanced quickly over the document. She was excellent.

"What are you looking to earn, Alice?"

"With my qualifications and experience, I can earn anywhere between $80 and $90K per annum, but I do not mind earning a bit less if there is stability and long-term prospects."

Fern listened, then perused her résumé again. She was perfect for the position, and she knew her Uncle wouldn't recommend her unless he trusted Alice professionally and personally.

"Why don't we start you on $120K and, after three months, if you fit in and prove yourself, I'll make it $130K. I can assure you that if you stay on board long term, you will see that I treasure my staff and reward loyalty."

Alice's eyes widened at the unexpected offer. Smiling from ear to ear, she jumped up, "Thank you. Thank you. You will not regret this, Fern," she said, shaking hands.

"I will expect total confidentiality, and you will need to sign an NDA."

"Of course, not a problem," Alice agreed.

"Great, I will be in touch to finalize the paperwork and get you on the payroll. Can you start Monday?"

"Definitely, yes. Just tell me the exact address. Do you have your own car?"

"I do," Alice couldn't stop grinning.

Fern stood up, also smiling. "Then welcome aboard. You will meet the rest of the team in the next few days.

Chapter Twenty-Eight

As they all prepared for moving in and the opening, Mike was there checking the layout and security, barking orders to the technicians as they finished installing the array of security cameras and perimeter sensors. The electronic front gate had been completed earlier that morning.

Mike was the first to jerk his head up at the familiar sound.

Fern walked over to him to see what he was looking at.

Mike glanced at Fern but kept his focus on the spot in the sky.

"What is it, Mike?"

"Wait," was all he said as the noise became louder, and closer. The rotary blades of a helicopter cut the air until the chopper came into sight and circled above them.

"It's Oliver," Mike smiled.

Everyone by now was looking up.

Oliver lowered the chopper, and the noise was deafening. He made sure he didn't get too close and create a major dust storm, spoiling all the cleaning and hard work to have the place spotless for the opening.

He hovered above for a few seconds while watching the wind speed and direction.

He dipped a bit lower, and tilted the chopper while sticking his hand out with a thumbs up. And as fast as he arrived, he turned sharply, banking at an incredible angle, and sped off until he was a mere speck in the distance with the thunderous, ricocheting noise fading across the sky.

"I knew it was him," Mike said, smiling.

"His way of saying hello, I guess," she replied.

"Yes, but he just broke an aviation rule. He's not meant to fly lower than one-thousand feet over built-up areas, but that's Oliver. Always pushing the boundaries, but he's a good pilot. I've flown with him many times and in choppers as well. Best pilot to be found."

"Going where?"

"Oh, business here and there."

"That secretive, ay?"

"No, not at all, just don't want to bore you with business," he said and grinned.

"Okay, Mike, have it your own way. I'm going to check on the team. I will see you at the grand opening."

"You bet, but I'm going to stick around a while. Shout if you need any help."

Fern trotted off, and Mike gazed at her retreating figure.

Slowly but surely, things were starting to take shape, and the number of frantic workers decreased. Fern ordered a delivery lunch for everybody, which was much appreciated.

The furniture removal guys worked tirelessly, unpacked, and placed the furniture as directed. Soon they were removing all the packaging and gathering up empty boxes to take away with them.

Mike left an hour later. He told Fern he was going to check out the local area and head into Sassafras and Olinda to get to know the lay of the land of the quaint places. As he pulled out of the entrance and turned left, he noticed an older guy walking down the hill with a bunch of flowers in his hand.

He had better walk more quickly, Mike thought, as the afternoon sky had clouded over and thunder clouds were rumbling over the Dandenong forest and hills.

Bruce Nash had picked a nice selection of flowers from his garden and thought it would be an appropriate gesture to drop by and welcome his new neighbor.

From a distance, he had seen the furniture removal truck leaving for the day.

The sky darkened some more, and the security installer called out to Fern. He needed to show her something at the gate.

Fern called her mother.

"Mom, it's getting pitch black. We are in for a massive storm. I'm just going to the gate to check something; then I am going to put my car away in the garage. I'm worried about possible hail."

"Sure, dear," Megan responded while surveying the gun-metal-colored dark clouds.

Fern approached the gate, feeling a couple of drops of rain on her face.

Bruce Nash quickened his pace; he wanted to avoid the downpour too.

The installer showed Fern a small switch in the motor housing that controlled the electronic gate. "Ms. Jones, your business partner Mike insisted I show this to you. He instructed me to install it."

Fern bent down to look and didn't see Nash approaching as her back was facing him.

"What does this little switch do?" she asked the installer.

"That's what I want to show you. It is an ingenious device that must always be in the up position. In simple terms, you can see that the tiny switch is difficult to see and forms part of the housing. In the event that someone wants to jump over the gate and illegally gain access, they would normally put the motor into manual override and merely slide the gate open. With this gadget, that will not work unless you see and flick the tiny switch over, and, trust me, it is so tiny and hidden no one will find it."

"Okay, is that it?" Fern said without much interest.

"Yes. And, if there is a power failure, there is a backup battery, so you will never have access problems."

"Thank you."

The installer walked back to his vehicle. Fern stood up, and as she turned, Nash was right next to her.

"Oops, you gave me a fright. You're Mr. Nash, aren't you? I'm sorry, I've forgotten your first name."

Nash immediately noticed Fern's one brown eye and one blue eye and was jolted back many years to that day on the beach near Lorne when that pretty woman was found half-eaten by a shark. He physically took a step back.

"Are you all right, Mr. Nash? You don't look well."

Nash gathered himself quickly. "Yes, I'm fine, just been walking a bit too long today. Bruce is my name. I live up the road, remember? I thought I'd pop over when I saw the removal truck and give you these to welcome you to the neighborhood. I picked them myself from my garden."

"Why, thank you, Bruce. They're lovely. I have the perfect place to put them. I'm afraid I still have lots to do today and must run. Maybe we can catch up another time. What is your address by the way?"

"51 Upper Hill Road."

"Great. Thank you again for the flowers. They are gorgeous," Fern smiled, nodded her head once, turned, and walked back to the house to move her car into the garage. Fern was generally a friendly person, but she was somewhat perturbed by the way Nash had snuck up on her. It wasn't the first time he had done it. She did not mind seeing him from time to time, but she had not forgotten that he used to be a detective.

Still, she felt she should be polite. Maybe have one of the workmen drive him home. But this guy might pepper him with questions. Better not. "See you, Mr Nash, and thanks again," Bruce heard from her retreating back. He watched her until she was near the house. He pulled his hat down further over his head and zipped his jacket as the rain began to come down in earnest.

On his way home, he could not erase that scene from his head when he saw the shark mangled body of Sophia Semenov more than twenty years ago now. He recalled vividly the young lady with one blue eye and one brown eye lying on the beach with the crab scurrying for safety, fat from feeding on human flesh and tissue. He almost wrenched again as he remembered the mass of flies, the seagulls squawking up above, and Max Blumenthal from forensics confirmed that she had recently given birth.

It was raining hard now, but Nash didn't notice. All he was thinking about was how Max told him then, that people with different colored eyes were rare, and the gene had to be passed down the lineage. Nash still had the gold ring found in the shark's belly inscribed with *Sophia*. He had not looked at the ring in ages. And now, a beautiful, stunning young woman of the right age, with blonde hair, one brown eye and one blue eye, and looking like a dead ringer of the dead prostitute. "Jesus, holy Christ," Nash muttered aloud as he neared his home.

When he entered his house, he passed his wife's room. She was sleeping, thankfully and so he didn't have to look at her open, suffering face. It was too painful to watch her disintegrate before his eyes. For a second, he imagined it was the shark-eaten cadaver in her bed and rushed to his study to shake off the illusion. On the way, he saw Kate, the carer, and asked her to clean and change his wife and spray her room.

Nash sat at his desk and opened one of the drawers. He rummaged around for a while and finally found the small packet containing the ring that belonged to Sophia Semenov, the beautiful hooker. Impulsively, he slipped the ring on his smallest finger, looking at it as he swiveled it on his finger, wishing it could speak to him. Then he took it off and placed it back in his drawer.

"Hmm, he pondered, and then he poured himself a beer.

A short while later, Kate knocked on Nash's door.

"I don't mean to worry you, sir, but I need to take some time off later this month. I have family visiting from abroad, and I was just wondering ...."

"How long do you need?"

"A week would be good, sir."

"I see. As long as I have enough time to find a temporary replacement, it shouldn't be a problem. My wife needs 24/7 care, as you know. What are your exact dates?"

"In about ten days time, sir, which will be from the 15th of this month."

"Okay, Kate. Give me some time to secure a replacement. I am sure we can make this work."

"Thank you, sir," she said appreciatively and turned back to her work.

Chapter Twenty-Nine

Today was the Opening. Fern was up and dressed in her jeans and a casual top and went downstairs to get the day going. There was a lot to do.

The entire team would be here, along with the architects.

Fern looked over the guest list. David Jaffe and Blythe Murphy, the architects; her mother, Megan Jones; her uncle, Dr. Lance Jones; Mike Barzel, Head of Operations; Danny Smyth, Head of Business Affairs and IT; Oliver Hall, Head of Transportation; Alice Wilson, the newly appointed Head Nurse; and Maggie Watson, Head Housekeeper.

It was only a handful of people but this suited Fern. It was important to keep it a close-knit group of loyal and trusted associates. The Stork Center would only thrive under a cloak of secrecy.

Fern had arranged for the first formal meeting after the opening celebrations.

Maggie was the first to arrive at 6.30 am as arranged, and Mike showed up half an hour later. He made it clear that he was available to help with anything needed. He had a spare remote control for the front entrance and drove in and parked at the back of the building, out of sight from the road.

The weather was perfect — there was a light breeze, smattering of white fluffy clouds, and the sky was tinged with a lovely blue and fading pink hue. There was no rain in the forecast.

A white catering vehicle pulled up to the gate, and the driver pressed the buzzer. Mike answered the intercom while looking at the monitor.

"This is Garden of Eating caterers, here to set up for the event," the driver announced.

"Who booked you?" Mike questioned.

"Jaffe & Murphy, the architects," came the answer.

"One second," Mike said and turned to Fern.

"It's okay, Mike. It has all been arranged. I know about it. Let them in."

Mike hit the button, and while they drove up, he turned to Fern.

"Fern, as head of security, I need to know and be advised of any visitors in advance. I don't want to sound brazen but never ever do this again, please. Never. Your safety and this whole operation depend on me and my ability to keep this secret. This has to be a very tight top-secret confidential compound that will only function as long as it remains private and classified. I must be briefed on every event and on every visitor. I have to know who is at the gate before they arrive."

"My apologies, Mike. I understand and will implement new procedures for everyone to follow. It will not happen again."

"No worries this time, but you must be aware of the potential dangers, so we are on the same page. It is imperative to our success. Let's make sure we bring this point up at the meeting later."

Fern went to meet the caterers who unloaded the trestle tables and unpacked the appetizers and drinks. She then led them to the front of the house and showed them where to set up. A few minutes later, David and Blythe arrived in a silver blue BMW.

They exchanged greetings, and Fern introduced them around.

"Just before we start, I will put up the beautiful ribbon across the front door, and when it is time, Fern, you will cut it and announce The Stork Center officially open," David said enthusiastically.

"Why not, sure, why not?" Fern smiled.

Lance arrived and was greeted and embraced by Megan and Fern. Soon afterward Oliver arrived on his Harley Davidson motorbike. Fern made a point to stand next to Mike as Oliver approached.

"Good to see you, Oliver. From jets to helicopters, to cars and Harley Davidsons, I guess if there were water here you would have arrived in a speedboat," she joked playfully.

"Talking about boats, a great friend of mine has a super luxury yacht, which is crewed and a fifty-foot motor cruiser. He has offered either for my use while he is abroad."

"Maybe but the, launch of our operation is a priority at the moment," Fern tactfully side-stepped the invitation while looking around.

Mike and Oliver chatted warmly, and Fern went to speak to her mother.

Megan asked Fern if she had invited anyone else and wondered if their accountant and attorney would be part of the celebrations.

Fern told her she wanted to keep it small and that it was only for members of her new team. Of course, with their connections, they could have turned the day into a major media event with the mayor, other local dignitaries, and influential elected officials in attendance. Megan would have liked to see Chester's former business associates and executive giants from the mining industry, but discretion was primary before anything.

Everyone started to gather. The enormous gold ribbon took center stage in front of the entrance. The tables were beautifully decorated in blue and gold tablecloths, especially ordered by Jaffe & Murphy, complemented by gorgeous yellow desert flame and blood red waratah flower centerpieces.

A waiter passed around a tray of appetizers and a barman poured chilled bottles of Moet & Chandon into long stem champagne glasses. Exquisite fresh mango juice and Cape gooseberry juice from South Africa accompanied the small setting.

Danny proudly handed Fern a large envelope. "You are official. Here is the company's registration certificate and signed license papers to operate as of today," he smiled.

"Theatrical timing, "Fern joked. "Thank you."

While they all chatted, Megan ushered everybody to the front area of the house. Only Fern, David, and Blythe remained on the top of the steps.

Megan was the first to request silence.

Fern looked at everyone with a gleam in her eyes as she felt the incipient pride building up.

"Welcome, welcome. Ladies and gentlemen, it gives me great pleasure to welcome you all today. First, I want to thank Jaffe & Blythe, the architects, for making this all possible in record time. And, as you can see, they did this with no compromise in style, design or quality." Fern turned and smiled at both men. She put her hands together, and everyone joined in the clapping.

"To my indelible team, a very special thank you for coming on board at this moment in time when millions of babies out there are crying in pain, crying to be fed and to be loved. We cannot save them all, but the ones that we do will enrich the lives of many loving couples. To my amazing mom, Megan, if I had to thank you for everything you have done for me, I would still be standing here a year later. Thank you, Mom. I love you and know that my late father, Chester Jones, is looking down on us, so let's make him proud." There was more applause.

"To my very dear Uncle Lance, thank you for everything, thank you. I am so immensely happy you are part of this worthwhile endeavor.

"Our adoption business has been officially registered today, and tomorrow I am already meeting our first potential couple who want to adopt." There were more smiles and clapping with this latest news.

"Last but not least, I want to welcome on board our newest staff members, Nurse Alice Wilson, who will be in charge of the nursery, and

Maggie Watson, our housekeeper. Before I take you on a tour of the center, and we raise our glasses...." Fern turned towards the architects.

Blythe and David approached, and Blythe opened a beautiful wooden box made from Tasmanian oak. The box was lined with velvet, and inside was a pair of scissors. He offered the open box to Fern ,and she removed the scissors.

She held the scissors up in the air with one hand and immediately lowered them to cut the ribbon.

"I now declare the Stork Center open!" Fern said jubilantly.

There was more cheering and congratulations, and the waiters poured the champagne and brought out the blue and pink cake to cut and serve.

Everyone mingled, enjoying the moment and excited at the prospect of doing good in the world.

Fern quietly slipped an envelope with the final payment to David and thanked him and Blythe privately for their professionalism and excellent work.

Soon the small party was over; the caterers packed up and left. Fern told Alice there was no need for her to stay and would phone her when the first baby or babies arrived, which she expected to be in the next couple of weeks. Before David & Blythe left, they presented Fern with a small sentimental gift: the Tasmanian oak box and scissors.

Maggie cleaned up, and Megan retired to the kitchen for a well-earned cup of tea.

After a tour of the entire place, the team entered the boardroom that had a stunning wooden oval table with ten emu-leather chairs. On the far side of the wall was a large television screen hooked up to a computer, and the other wall was full of security monitors with real-time coverage from all the security cameras around the property. There was a bar with a small fridge and a coffee machine on a wood-paneled counter and liquor cabinet. The floor was huge, with non-slip terracotta quarry tiles with a luxurious rug. Behind Fern's chair was a large framed aerial shot of the entire complex.

There were no windows in the boardroom, but the room was brightly lit by several skylights.

"Help yourself to coffee. I expect the meeting will go on for a few hours, and if it goes into the night, don't despair. There is a fully equipped guest cottage at the back which sleeps four."

"I've got time but not the entire day," Lance said. "I have patients to see later."

"No problem. In fact, I think if you can manage a couple of hours at most, that will be good.

"I want everyone to have a chance to ask as many questions as you wish as well as chime in on your recommendations about your departments and the operation. We need as many different opinions, and perspectives as possible as we are dealing with different countries and cultures, and any concerns or ideas will be welcomed."

"Danny here will talk about all the documents that we will need. Oliver will discuss the different airports, the various idiosyncrasies and scenarios he knows from his connections, and where there maybemay be gaps in crucial information. And, of course, Mike will have a lot to present. Some of it will not concern all of you; therefore, it is probably Mike who will need to stay longer. Danny, you will most likely be able to leave early too.

"Anyway, gentlemen, before we begin, I would like to welcome everyone on board again. Before I hand it over to Lance for his presentation, please be aware that Alice believes this is a legit organization and adoption center, and that is the way it will stay. She will be the head nurse and in charge of the nursery. Likewise, Maggie knows no more. I have not told my mother, but she is no fool and will come to her own conclusions in time. She will not be officially involved as she is retired but will be the ultimate mother figure to see to it that all the staff are happy. And anything else that needs mothering.

"There is one other important thing to mention; I have been running into an elderly gentleman who seems to be very interested in what is happening here. His name is Bruce Nash, and is a retired detective. He is very pleasant but a bit too nosy for my liking. Yesterday he gave me a small bunch of flowers to welcome me to the neighborhood. I have his address. Mike, if you can review the CCTV footage and burn an image of Mr. Nash's face and circulate it so everyone knows who he is; and can keep an eye out? Also, this goes for any other suspicious activity. It must be reported at once and brought to mine or Mike's attention."

"Fern, I have a suggestion," Mike commented.

"Go ahead," Fern said.

"It was a good move on your part to get his address. That's vital. He is obviously neighborly since he gave you flowers, so here is your opportunity to reciprocate. When are you meeting with the couple, your first clients looking for a bambino?"

"Tomorrow," she said.

"I suggest you take this Nash guy a cake or a couple of sweet treats so you can learn more about him. I'll grab the address from you just so I can see where he lives and do some digging on my end. Is he slim, like a lot of older men, average height, and loves to wear khaki, neutral-colored clothes?"

"How the hell do you know that? Don't tell me you met him as well," Fern asked, surprised.

"When I left your place yesterday to check out Sassafras and Olinda, I saw him walking with flowers about a few hundred feet towards your gate."

"That's it! That's when I nearly jumped out of my skin. I was checking the gate and turned around, and there he was right behind me with the flowers!"

Mike looked like he was thinking. "Well, don't worry about it. Let's go on."

Chapter Thirty

L ance was up first, focusing on the health benefits of seeking out abandoned babies in Europe. He also stressed it was important for Oliver to make sure he achieved as smooth take-offs and landings as possible because their eardrums were still tender and very sensitive to noise. Likewise, it would help keep their stomachs settled so Alice could make sure they kept their milk down during the long flight.

Danny was next. He passed around the bogus press card for a local journalist for Mike and two foreign correspondent cards for Mike and Oliver. As promised, he had even doctored their headshots to look like they were taken years ago. They were also given diplomatic cards, flight permits, various border control and customs documents, and two perfectly forged American passports.

He then opened his laptop and connected it to the large screen on the wall to show them the new website. It was tasteful and elegant, and Fern loved it. It was a huge risk uploading the website live, but now that the paperwork was in order, Fern felt better.

Fern handed Danny the list of the fifty names of the boys and girls for him to start making the first batch of birth certificates.

Danny asked that once Mike and Oliver had determined which cities they would target, he would create the City Mayor's official formal letters acknowledging full cooperation for their work and research.

Oliver's presentation was also short and to the point. He was the pilot and confirmed his navigator was on standby 24/7. He was absolutely trustworthy, and could vouch for him. Oliver would handle everything regarding flights, intel for the local airports and customs, and mapping out the flight plan to get them to point A and back in the quickest manner possible. He announced that he would assist Mike wherever Mike needed him. He was available as a driver as well as security if necessary.

At 2 pm, they broke for a late lunch. Mike went to the security surveillance room to check on the digital video recorder to view the CCTV footage of Bruce Nash the day he presented the flowers to Fern. It didn't take long as all he had to do was punch in the date and approximate time, and there was Bruce Nash standing over Fern at the gate with flowers in his hand. Mike was pleased, the footage was crystal clear, and he could make a clean ID of Nash's face, body siz,e and type, and khaki clothing down to the smallest detail and zoom in on a pen in his pocket.

When the others returned to the boardroom, Mike was sitting down in front of a clear pause,d picture of Bruce Nash on the big screen.

"Ahh, folks, I have some important news update to share. I googled Bruce Nash, our retired detective from Melbourne. You won't believe what I've discovered. A newspaper article in 2006 ran a profile piece on Inspector Bruce Nash, which states he was responsible for arresting and capturing some of Australia's most wanted criminals. It appears he retired soon after that article and was named as one of Australia's top police officers." Mike looked at his team, his head slightly tilted.

Fern was stunned and cleared her throat, "What does that mean for us?"

"You must not get too friendly with him. The less said, the better but be relaxed when you bump into him. We have nothing to be afraid of and tomorrow, take that cake to him."

Fern felt a chill go down her spine. "Guys, at this point, I do not think it necessary for all of you to remain. Mike and I need to spend some time going over more in-depth details. Uncle Lance, you do not need to stay. Same for you, Danny. You can head off too."

She turned to Oliver, "It would be good if you could stick around for a bit longer and be part of some of the discussion I have with Mike."

Fern stood up, "I am just going to see Lance and Danny out, be back in a few."

Mike went to the counter and made some fresh coffee. Oliver went outside for some air. When he saw Fern returning, he approached her.

"Fern, I wasn't kidding when I said a good friend left me a crewed yacht and a luxury cruiser at my disposal. If there's no time now or in the near future to visit Tassie, then maybe we could just go for a weekend and sail around Lorne, the Twelve Apostles, by Apollo Bay and the Cape Otway coast. You'll love it."

"Oliver," Fern said firmly. "My main focus now is The Stork Center.. For heaven's sake, I'm meeting our first couple tomorr,ow and there's a lot of work and preparation to be done."

Oliver wasn't going to give up that easily. "You know how the saying goes; work hard and play hard. Besides, we had such a good time in Noosa," he said with his winning smile.

"I'm serious,s Oliver. I appreciate the offer, but no hard feelings. The answer is no thanks. Come, Mike is waiting," she said in a business tone and entered the boardroom.

Mike was silhouetted against a world map displayed on the huge High Definition TV screen.

"If I had to point to any part of the map, any country, you can bet your bottom dollar that there are kids, babies of all ages that need a loving home. Africa has millions; India, Brazil, and Indonesia have shocking numbers. Pakistan is one of the worst. It is a very sad picture in the Philippines and Romania, and Russia is just shocking. I've also taken a closer look at Europe, given Lance's input earlier, and it too has its share in vast numbers. And, believe it or not, the US is heading towards the two million mark, which is very alarming, yes?"

Mike pursed his lips into a bulldog shape, disgusted. "The most shocking is there are more homeless Caucasian children and females on the streets than males in America, and they are most vulnerable to the worldwide exploitation of human trafficking and the sex tourism business. Yes, it's appalling—it is part of the tourist trade."

The room was silent. "Let me say this. After seeing these figures, we need to spread our tentacles like an octopus. We cannot focus on one country. We would risk putting ourselves on the radar screen and in too much danger from the authorities. I tend to agree with Lance; better to spread our goal across Europe, America, and maybe in parts of Brazil and pursue other countries further down the road. We are roughly thirteen-thousand kilometres from the USA, sixteen-thousand from Europe, and eight-thousand from Bulgaria."

Mike pointed to the map and tapped the location of Sofia.

"Sofia has plenty of homeless kids sleeping in and around the railway stations. According to my research, it is horrific that as young as three are living rough. I believe it will be easier to bring back young children under five than an infant at this point. I intend to get in and out quickly."

Mike looked at Oliver. "Keep those fuel tanks full, as I will be calling youatt a moment's notice. I will leave in a few days to suss out the area, set up a cont,act and gather intel on the security cameras around the stations. We need to be a ghost."

Fern nodded her head.

"Is that a green light from you, Fern?"

"Yes, it is."

Oliver turned to Mike. "Are you intending to just steal them off the streets? Surely, they will need to be persuaded or how will they agree to go with you? The last thing we need is howling kids on a twenty-hour flight, screaming to go home?"

"Join me on the collection and you can see first-hand, Oliver." Mike retorted firmly.

Mike then turned quickly to Fern. "I know some time back you had me checked out and found out, I am fluent in several languages. I speak Italian, French, Spanish, and a bit of German. I also know Hebrew and Arabic. But I confess I am most fluent in Bulgarian thanks to a gorgeous lady I once had the pleasure of living with for years."

"Flight path to Sofia, Mike?" Oliver interjected, spoiling the reverie.

"That's your domain. In the past, I have flown from Melbourne to Darwin, Bangkok, Oman, and then Sofia. I leave it to your expertise to finesse the route."

"If this is the case, I must get Mom to order a couple of children's beds; a little child cannot sleep in a cot," Fern added.

"Yes, but first things first. Meet with the new prospective parents and see if they are open to adopting a toddler. Tell them once their references and background checks have been completed and they have been given a clean bill of health, they could have the patter of tiny feet sooner rather than later."

Mike looked at his watch, "Time to hit the road folks. Let's focus on our priorities: Oliver, you've got your work cut out for you. Fern, I will talk to Danny regarding all the paperwork for the Sofia trip; and the website."

He pushed his chair back and stood up. "Fern, I discovered a neat little bakery in Sassafras. I suggest you go there tomorrow and take something tasty to Mr. Bruce Nash." He gave a half-hearted salute and said "Night all," and strode out of the boardroom.

Fern felt a stab of jealousy about the gorgeous lady in Bulgaria. No one likes a man extolling the beauty of another woman, especially when she wants him to notice her.

Chapter Thirty-One

Fern looked at the house in Caulfield hard and long. She sat in her car, which was parked in the shade across the street. She was about to meet Mr. and Mrs. Jack Harris, Uncle Lance's contact.

Fern intended to verify they had a stable marriage and did indeed live at this address.

The first thing she did was check the mailbox, an old simple trick that Mike had taught her. He told her it was the best way to quickly establish you are at the correct place and validate the names addressed on the mail.

There were a couple of letters and both were addressed to the Harrises.

Fern left the letters in the box and walked down the garden path and pushed the front doorbell. She noticed the outside of the house was clean, and the garden well maintained.

Fern heard footsteps and the door was opened by a smiling brunette lady who appeared to be in her mid to late thirties, well dressed and attractive.

"Hi there, you must be Wendy Harris."

"Indeed, I am and you must be Fern Jones. Do come in," she gestured with her outstretched arm.

"Let's go into the lounge just here on the left," Wendy invited.

They sat down. Fern removed her small laptop.

"May I call you Wendy?"

"Of course, you can."

"Thank you. Wendy. Please tell me a bit about yourself and is your husband going to be able to join us?"

"He will be here any minute. He's upstairs washing — he's just varnished the patio deck outside."

Just then Jack appeared. He was tanned, clean cut, and dressed smart-casual.

Fern stood up.

"Sit please, I'm Jack, thank you for driving over to see us. Much appreciated."

"My pleasure," Fern smiled.

"Fern, what can I get you to drink—tea, coffee?"

"Something cold, water is fine, thank you, Wendy."

"Jack, dear, anything for you?"

"Water is perfect. Melbourne water is one of the best you know? It's the best in all of Australia, you know," he said nervously, trying to fill the awkwardness of the moment.

Fern smiled and Wendy disappeared. She was back within a minute.

"Folks," Fern began. "This is the first interview of many. This is a *get-to-know-you* meeting so I can have a better understanding of your background and lifestyle. I need to know your likes and dislikes, how often you traveand l, where you vacation. This will ve me insight into your personalities and characters. I will also do an extended background check into knowing about your parents and siblings and other family members. You will also have to agree to a credit and financial audit to demoncan ability to raise a child."

"Yes, sure," they both acknowledged.

"The uniqueness about the Stork Center is that it is not a long drawn out process but the background checks are more aggressive and thorough. We will need to spend more time getting to know you and garner more information. Does this make sense?"

They both nodded. "Of course," Jack said.

"Have you tried to adopt before?"

"No, never. Simply because we have been focusing on all the treatments for Wendy and sad to say none of them worked."

Wendy turned to Fern, "That is correct. All the IFVs were unsuccessful. You see, under thirty-five years o,f age there's a thirtypercentr cent chance of having a baby. Over forty it drops percent ten per cent and I am pushing forty. We have tried everything," her eyes watered. "Do you think you can help us? she implored

"That's why I am here," Fern smiled encouragingly. "We have a solution, but there is a difference. Our screening process is very strict as I mentioned, but we move fast. We have a tight-knit infrastructure and can cut through a string of red tape a mile long to ensure you get to hold a healthy baby in your arms. You must understand the major difference is that we exchange money for our services. We incur huge operating costs so we can remain discreet and I personally hand pick only the cream of the crop clients. We also ensure the babies are healthy and have gone through a complete health check before placing them in loving homes. We donate half of the proceeds to worthwhile children's charities around the world. The Stork Center only donates to charities such as education centers struggling financially as well as centers for abused women and orphanages."

Fern looked directly at Jack, "Your support goes a lot further than you think and so many will benefit."

"What kind of money are we talking about?" he asked.

"Our minimum fee is two-hundred thousand, but it all depends on what's involved and each case is different. We do offer twenty-four-hour support and we invite new parents to visit and interact regularly with their children before delivery takes place to train and familiarize what is involved in handling an infant. We provide hands-on instructions for everything; from feeding to changing, but also the little things; like how to hold them properly, lay them down to sleep to coping with any allergies and so much more."

Wendy looked at Fern, she couldn't believe what she was hearing. She glanced back atat her husband.

"We're in, Fern. Let's proceed," Jack said taking control.

Fern kept a poker face. "Congratulations and thank you. You are about to make a big difference in a little boy or little girl's life, I will email you a lengthy questionnaire and a list of requirements. As soon as you complete it, we will begin the process. I can say I trust the person who referred you, so don't anticipate any problems. We will be in touch to invite you both to our center and introduce you to our qualified neonatal nurse who will teach you everything you need to know for your first year. It will be a series of two-hour lessons and include some medical training for basic children's health issues.

Fern crossed her legs and smiled. She pulled out a couple of sheets of paper. "I will need you to sign this form with all your details and contact information and acknowledge this is a private and confidential agreement. And, here is the form for you to complete regarding payment. We require 50% up front and the balance will be due when we have located your nbeforeand prior to taking him or her home."

"Thanks," Jack said taking the paperwork. "That seems fine."

"How old will the baby be?" Wendy asked. "Can we choose between a girl and a boy?"

"They are normally anything from a few months up to a year old. In extreme cases, we have older ones around four or five years old. Sometimes we find homes for siblings as it would be cruel to separate them."

Wendy turned to her husband, "Jack, how do you feel about a baby, or a toddler, or a small child?"

"Sweetheart, I will be happy with either. And you?"

"I'd prefer a baby or toddler if there is a choice. I've always wanted to hold my baby in my arms."

Fern smiled again, "As you can imagine, we cannot guarantee the gender. It is more important that we find the right match and you will only know once you meet them."

The Harrises nodded in unison, beaming with joy and anticipation.

"Thank you, Jack, thank you, Wendy." Fern stood up and gathered her things.

They walked Fern to the gate. "Oh, I nearly forgot, here's my card," Fern said, pulling one out from her pocket to hand it to them.

"Do you have one, Jack?"

He removed a card from his wallet and gave it to Fern.

Fern got into her car and waved. In the car, she looked at his card, "Hmm," she murmured to herself.

Jack Harris MD. He was the MD of one of the largest IT companies in Australia and the southern hemisphere.

She would speak to Mike to make sure he took extra precautions to safeguard thecenter from potentially prying eyes. Theyneed to check up on . Mr. Harris' company to corroborate he didn't use his connections to snoop. It would be important to step up security before delivery took place as well as periodically afterward, just in case.

As Fern drove off, Jack showed Fern's card to his wife. It said Fern Jones, Managing Director of the Stork Center.

She arrived home in time for lunch. Megan was happy to see her but Bonzo was beside himself with excitement, as though she'd been away forever. His tail banged the table legs, the door, the kitchen cupboard, and the bin with different drumming sounds. Fern laughed, "He's like a one-dog drumming band!"

She put her bag down on the counter, "Mom, I want to drop off a cake as a gift for someone tomorrow. Where's the best home-style bakery around here?"

"If you'd have told me earlier, I would have been happy to bake something. I don't think I have all the ingredients now. I suggest the bakery next to the gift shop, in Sassafras, run by that Frenchman. The cakes are double-story high and are absolutely delicious. They melt in your mouth."

"Okay, thanks. By the way, can you order a couple of good quality children's beds? Wait, I've just realized we can use the ones in the guest cottage if necessary. I take it back, ignore me."

"What do you want single beds for?" Megan asked with an inquisitive look.

"Ah, there may be some cases where we get a toddler or are a few years older. Don't worry now."

They finished lunch and Fern phoned all the members of the team, letting them know of the latest developments with Mr. and Mrs. Harris. She spoke to Mike the longest. She emailed the Harrises to follow up on their meeting and to send them more forms and questionnaires. Then she phoned Alice to discuss with her all the essentials they would need for the new arrival and to plan for any age up to five years. Fern would let her know soon when she would be required to report for duty.

The next day, chocolate cake in hand, Fern headed over to Nash's house at 51 Upper Hill Road.

She parked the car outside and looked at the property. It had a low wall but there were plenty of trees, shrubs, and tall Yucca plants to protect inquisitive eyes.

There was no sign of a car and Fern presumed he was either out or the car was in the garage. There was also no gate so Fern walked up the driveway to the front door.

She pushed the doorbell attached to the old screen door. The bell was dirty white and was loose when she pushed it. She didn't hear any chime or ringing. Perhaps the battery needed replacing. She wasn't sure what to do so she left the cake box by the front door under the porch and decided to take a peek through the front windows.

She looked around to make sure no one was watching and stepped into the flower beds to get a closer look. Putting her face up to the window, with both her hands blocking her reflection, she peered in. The drapes were partially drawn. All she saw was a room that looked like a study but it was vacant. She then pushed aside some more shrubbery and looked in the next window. The drapes were also closed, saved for a small gap. She squinted almost touching the glass. There was one fan light on, and she saw what appeared to be Nash walking down a very small visible section of the passage. Without wasting time, she walked quickly to the front door and pushed the bell again. There was still no reply. She tried the screen door but it was locked.

Fern attempted to knock on the screen door but it wasn't possible to make contact with the front door, even with her car keys.

She decided to call it a day and come back the next day. For some reason, as she approached her car, she hesitated and looked back.

"Dammit," she mumbled. There was a third window.

She turned around and approached the last window. It was a similar scenario. The drapes were closed but there was a small gap of about half an inch.

The room was dimly lit and the tall rose bush in front prevented her from getting too close. There was no sign of Nash, but she made out there was part of an armrest and a wheel; it looked like a wheelchair.

Then she caught a flicker of a movement to the right. Cupping her hands on the side of her face to minimize the sun's reflection, she saw Nash bending down over what appeared to be a person lying in bed but Fern could not see a face.

She gasped slightly. She saw Nash sit down on the bed and start pushing something down. It was weird and, with sinister curiosity, she fought the roses and pushed her face up against the window pane. What the hell was happening? Then Nash stood up and did it again. He bent over and pushed his arms down while still standing up.

He moved slightly and Fern's mouth opened. Her jaw dropped as if it was suddenly broken. Her eyes widened. She realized he was pushing a pillow down over the person's head. Fern was shattered, she nearly pummelled the window with her fist but instantly stopped. There was no way, she wanted to be caught up in a police matter. What if she was implicated? Without wasting any time, she whipped out her phone from her purse and began to film.

Her hands were shaking and it was difficult to hold the cell phone still. Nash suddenly stood straight up. Fern ducked to the side catching her cheekbone on a thorn. She did not feel it, she was in total shock from what she was observing. She carried on filming. Nash was still standing, breathing hard, and released the pillow. He stood for a while longer, then he dropped the pillow on the floor.

As he walked away, Fern saw a limp body lying very still as if fast asleep.

Jesus Christ, Fern thought, she had to get out of there. She quickly turned away from the window and then she remembered the cake. She scurried to the front door and snatched the cake and high-tailed it to her car running on the front lawn to avoid any noise on the driveway. She hit the ignition and jerked the gear into drive and skidded off.

Bruce Nash walked to the dining room and opened the liquor cabinet. He clutched the bottle of whisky and poured himself a double shot. He took a small sip, then he downed the rest in a second, in one big gulp. Some saliva mixed with alcohol ran down his chin.

He made one call, to the Homecare agency, "Good morning, this is Relief Care Workers, how can I help?" a voice asked brightly.

"Yes, good day, this is Mr. Nash here, Bruce Nash. I arranged for a replacement care worker to start here today from lunchtime. Can you please cancel this request? My permanent care assistant has canceled her holiday and won't be taking time off after all."

"Can you please repeat Mr. Nash, we have static on the line?"

"I said to cancel tbackup-up temporary carer who is supposed to be arriving this afternoon."

"What is your address, Mr. Nash?"

"Oh, for God's sake! It's 51 Upper Hill Road, Sassafras and the zip is 3787."

"Thank you, Mr. Nash. We can take care of that for you but you are aware that there is a late notice cancellation fee?"

"No, yes, whatever, just do it. Just make sure you contact the person on their cell phone so they do not show up here."

"Will do, Mr. Nash. Have a good day."

Bruce felt like he needed another shot of booze but decided against it.

He walked to the kitchen table and picked up his phone. He only dialed three digits.

"911—what is the emergency?"

Fern arrived home and before she left her car, she made a call.

"Mike get here now, something has happened!"

"What's up? You sound stressed."

"Just come now please, I'm home."

"Okay, I'm on my way."

Mike was getting to know Fern during these past months. She was strong but obviously, something had shaken her badly. He wondered if Bruce Nash was playing *I spy* again. Then he remembered, she was going to take him a cake that day.

Fern dashed out to meet him as soon as he arrived.

Mike saw a long thin dried trickle of blood coming from Fern's cheekbone.

"What the fuck happened to you? Did Nash do this to you?"

"Oh, it's nothing. Just a thorn from a rose bush," she said feeling the cut with her finger. "Mike, I just witnessed a murder! Well, I think I did."

"Murder?" he snapped.

"Come inside. Don't say anything to Mom. Let's go straight to the boardroom."

Mike followed Fern who was walking quickly.

They entered the boardroom and Mike shut the door.

"Murder?" he looked at her incredulously.

"Here! Take a look at this—I recorded it."

Mike was calm. He watched the video carefully.

"Shit a brick, you've got him killing someone on camera. Did he see you at all?"

"No, I don't think so. Should we call the cops?"

"Uh-huh. We've got Nash just where we need him," Mike smiled sardonically. His street-smart mind was doing overtime. "We have to act now, this minute."

Fern looked deeply surprised. "Do what?"

"Go wash your face, and freshen up quickly. Put something on that is warm and friendly. Grab the cake or whatever you bought. Where is it?"

"In the kitchen. Why?"

"Because you and I need to establish right now for sure if Inspector Bruce Nash saw you. I will go say hi to your mom and get the cake. We are going to have tea with Nash."

"Jesus, Mike, you mean it, really?"

"Absolutely. We've got to take full advantage of this and spin it in our direction," he grinned.

Fern left the boardroom and Mike went to the kitchen to retrieve the cake. There he found a perplexed-looking Megan.

"How are you today, Mrs. Jones?"

"I am well, thank you. Is everything okay, Mike? I didn't think Fern was expecting you?"

"Sure, why should it not be?" he answered nonchalantly.

"Fern said she was taking a cake to someone but she is already back and I see the cake is here on the table. And, there are some spots that look like blood?"

"Let me see." Mike walked to the cake. He saw fresh spots of blood on the top of the closed box.

Mike laughed lightly. "We met earlier in the village and I couldn't resist a hotdog, damn ketchup."

He stretched out his index finger and scooped up a drop of blood, bringing the finger to his mouth. He quickly switched to his middle finger, tucking his index under his thumb. "Mmm, ketchup," he smirked as he pretended to suck his finger clean. "I wonder what brand it is?"

Megan smiled and rolled her eyes.

"By the way, have you any Glad Wrap?" he asked.

"Sure, over there next to the microwave."

"Thank you, Mrs. Jones." Mike tore off a piece. "Do you have scissors, Mrs. J?"

Megan fetched a pair of scissors and Mike cut the cardboard lid off. He then crumpled the lid up and threw it in the trash. Then he covered the box with the glad wrap.

Fern appeared in the doorway, "Let's go, Mike. See you soon, Mom!"

"Excuse us, Mrs. J, we have a few errands to do," Mike smiled and scooped up the cake.

Megan smiled and indulged in the image of the departing couple. She liked Mike. People said he was a *muscleman* but to her, he was always a gentleman. She preferred him to Olive, and wished Fern did too.

Mike told Fern about the blood spots and the bullshit story he had spun. When they arrived at Nash's residence, they saw an ambulance with flashing lights outside. "Mike, is this a good idea, now?"

"Even better. Come, you bring the cake," he said confidently.

They walked up to the front door. It was ajar.

Mike knocked hard. "Hello, there, hello," he called out.

Bruce Nash approached looking shockingly pale and very disturbed. Mike noticed his trembling hands.

"Yes? Oh," Nash looked a bit startled. "It's you, the lady from up the road. I'm terribly sorry but you have come at a bad time. I'm afraid my wife has just passed away. The paramedics are with her now."

"Mr. Nash, I am so sorry to hear," Fern replied, with the appropriate amount of sadness in her voice. "Please forgive us for just showing up, but I wanted to bring you a cake in exchange for the flowers. I couldn't quite remember your address. I was not sure if you said 51 or 61."

"Thank you, my dear, you didn't have to do that. I hope you will excuse me. I must go and talk to the paramedics."

"Sure, of course! I am so sorry," Fern said and retreated.

Nash took the cake and disappeared back inside.

Mike took Fern's arm and they walked back to his car.

"Well done, Fern. You make an excellent actress! It's clear he has no idea that you were here earlier. Did you smell his breath, by the way? He's been drinking alcohol. Come, let's go home. I think you have earned a tea or coffee. Pity there's no cake."

PART THREE

PART THREE

Chapter Thirty-Two

Alone star, divorced from its companions, flickered in the distance and the Learjet taxied to runway A14 ready for take-off.

Behind the controls, Oliver sat with his co-pilot Morrie. Mike settled himself in the front passenger seat of the cabin. He noted the carry-cots, housed on raised carpeting and bolted down, had replaced a few of the passenger seats around him.

Mike was happy. Everything had gone well so far. They'd arrived at the airport on time and gone through the usual checks flawlessly.

He called out to Oliver in the cockpit while the jet was in line for take-off. "Final flight path, Skipper?"

"Darwin, Bangkok, Qatar, and then onto our destination: Sofia."

"Oh, so we are not landing in Oman after all?" Mike queried.

"It is much of a muchness, buddy," Oliver replied.

Mike grabbed a bottle of water from his backpack in the overhead compartment and

curiously opened another overhead compartment. There he saw plenty of diapers, bottled water, baby bottles, and various formulas. There were also several other baby items such as pacifiers, blankets, and even a couple of cute stuffed animals.

Oliver joked into his microphone that they would soon be landing on the moon and Mike laughed, "Well, we have all the equipment to keep us going there—we certainly have enough panties for all of us!" Oliver and Morrie laughed. "And pablum to eat. We've got plenty."

The tower came through on the radio. Clearance for take-off.

Mike looked out his window as the jet commenced to gain speed; the airport terminal disappeared fast and so did all the other buildings and soon they were a graceful speck in the sky as the metal bird roared smoothly towards the heavens.

When they had reached their cruising altitude, Oliver shortly pointed out Lake Eyre and later the Simpson Desert as they flew over. A little while later, they saw the MacDonnell Ranges, and then the Tanami Desert with Darwin not far off. They were eating up the kilometres at an incredible rate, Mike thought.

In Darwin, while Oliver and Morrie refuelled, Mike sipped a cold drink in the terminal building and thought about what lay ahead. The others joined him for a bacon and egg breakfast to fortify them before they continued on their way. Next stop Bangkok.

Bruce Nash was slightly more relaxed sitting on his patio overlooking his bird garden. His care worker Kate was due back in a few days and Nash decided to give her the option to stay on and look after him. It would be nice to have a housekeeper and, besides, it would be good company.

He felt remorse about what he had done but relief at the same time. He had done it more out of compassion for Merle than himself. She had suffered enough and he knew she would have hated becoming more disabled and dependent. He knew what he did was wrong but he also knew it wasn't fair to either of them. Both were suffering with the inevitable outcome lingering.

To distract himself from his painful thoughts, he started again to ponder the enigma of Ms. Fern Jones. Her likeness to the shark attack victim was eerie. None of this would add up if the age difference didn't match right — but it did. Two and two does equal four. Sophie's baby, if it had survived, would be the same age as Fern.

He wondered who lived with her and what she did for a living. It was clear she had landed on her feet and money was no object. Had she followed her mother's footsteps but had high-class clients? Her luxury mansion had been built so quickly. They must be very powerful influential and prominent clients with so much security around the place.

Fern sat at her laptop thinking about Mike and what he'd said. If Nash did dig deeper and became a nuisance or, heaven forbid, found out about the center, they had the videotape as collateral. There would be no way he would want to jeopardize his decorated police career.

Fern was leaning more and more on Mike for his reliance. At first, her feeling was simply one of satisfaction in her own perceptiveness in hiring someone so capable. Of course, his good looks didn't hurt either. Now she wondered if her feelings were changing. She liked how protective he was, but she felt it was more than that. She wondered what he thought of her. Did he just see her as his boss? She felt he admired her. But how far did that admiration go?

She shook her head and told herself to stop behaving like a schoolgirl. There was too much hard work and uncertainty ahead to be speculating about romantic feelings.

Resolutely, she put such thoughts out of her mind. Fern phoned Lance to focus her attention elsewhere. She wanted reassurance that everything was going well from his point of view. He told her, he was happy with Alice and her level of knowledge and competence. He'd discussed medications, vaccinat,ions and appropriate nutrition. Fern was in good hands.

With the help of her mother and Alice, Fern completed all the final purchases for the Stork Center. They were ready for the first arrivals. Now, the long wait began.

At the other end of the globe, the jet had landed in Bangkok, refueled, and taken off again. It was now well on the way to the penultimate stop: Qatar.

In Qatar, Mike stayed with Oliver and Morrie during the pitstop to fill up. Before long Qatar, too, had disappeared and it was all systems go for Sofia, Bulgaria.

They slept and ate but as the long-haul flights took their toll and time passed, the conversations became more relaxed. Smal talk disappeared and benign topics had been abandoned in Qatar. Mike and Oliver now spoke freely in front of Morrie on the last leg to Sophia. Amazingly, Morrie didn't twig that he was unwittingly involved in an illegal operation and that most of their flight documentation was false. He never questioned the speed and efficierefueling refuelling landings and take-offs.

The touchdown at Sofia was smooth. With most passengers and crew entering terminals one and two, the three boys entered the VIP arrival section, just west of terminal one. Here, VIPs had their own entrance and clearance protocols.

Oliver whispered to Mike, "We could have used the government terminal, the one for heads of state, but Morrie does not have a diplomatic passport. Maybe we should talk to Danny about that for next time?" he suggested.

"Would you like to be a president or a king, Morrie?" Oliver joked.

"I'll settle for either one,'" Morrie chuckled, convinced Oliver was not being serious.

Then Mike spoke rapidly in Bulgarian to the customs officer and soon they were on the other side.

"Shit a brick, the customs guy stamped my passport like he was swatting a frigging cockroach. The frigging stamp nearly went through the whole passport," Morrie complained.

"Let's go and get our rental car, guys," Mike suggested, changing the subject.

It was a silver BMW 335 and they were on the highway within half an hour with Oliver behind the wheel.

Mike looked at Oliver and grinned at Morrie, "Give Oliver a motorbike, a chopper, a jet, or a speedboat and he's happy as a clam."

"You're right," Oliver responded, "I love machines and speed. If you guys weren't such a bunch of ladies, I'd take you into space. Problem is there's no fucking atmosphere there." The boys laughed again.

"Jesus, that sign says Brussels Boulevard. Thank God the other sign says Sofia Ring Road, otherwise, I wouldn't know if we were in the right country. For all we know we could be on the Melbourne Ring Road going to Sunshine West. Jesus, why can't they just have a frigging sign that says *City*? Oh shit! Hold on we are in the wrong lane, hang on, guys."

Oliver's reflexes were fast. His eyeballs darting to the blind-spot sensor on his mirror, he floored the accelerator and crossed two lanes, following the sign to the city center.

"Look at those statues — frigging lions—four of them!" Oliver said aloud.

Mike saw them. "Yep, we are going over the famous Lions' Bridge, buddy. Welcome to the center of Sofia. Go past the lions and then take the third right. There's a hotel, not bad. Looks a bit like Fawlty Towers, but ifive-starstar and it is good. Suggest we check in and you boys et some rest, and grab a shower. I'll hook up with you later and we can meet for dinner."

"What about you?"

"I've got work to do. I need to do a full reconnaissance of the train and bus stations. Ask around and chat to the street people, and the kids. We are not here on vacation. We need to strategize and be heading home as soon as possible."

"Okay, buddy, I guess we are in your hands," Oliver said.

They pulled into the hotel and were greeted by the doorman.

"We don't need help, thanks! We only have hand luggage," Mike told the porter in Bulgarian. "But you can park our car or is there a valet?"

The skinny doorman acknowledged he could attend to the car and took the keys from Oliver.

They checked in at reception. They were each assigned a room on the third floor. They rode up in the elevator in silence. Mike dropped his backpack off in his room and then knocked on Oliver's door.

"I will see you later, around 9 pm. It's nearly 5 pm now local time — doesn't leave me much time."

"Stay in touch," Oliver said as Mike disappeared.

On the ground floor, Mike smiled at the attractive blonde receptionist. She smiled back and the doorman stood to attention and opened the door for Mike.

He stepped out onto the street, and soon he was lost amongst the pedestrians on the sidewalk, watching, listening, and looking about heading towards the station.

Chapter Thirty-Three

Mike walked down the boulevard that led to the train station nearly a mile away. As he neared the central bus station, which was on the way, he made a quick sweep of the area and went inside.

It hadn't changed much since he was last there — uncomfortable back-to-back seats, and the famous Marlboro cigarettes poster ad still on the back wall. The shops were the same but now there was a sign advertising free Wi-Fi above the arrival and departure gates.

As he left the bus station, a beggar approached him. Mike surmised he was no more than twelve or thirteen years old.

He spoke to him in his native language. He asked the kid if he was hungry and the sad and dirty kid nodded yes. Mike took out some loose change from his pocket. He asked the kid where all the homeless kids hung out, and the youngster gestured by pointing and muttered a few words.

Mike thanked him and told him the money was for him and to not give it to anyone else.

Mike made a mental note of the kid's directions and carried on towards the railway station.

It took him about twelve minutes to walk and when he arrived, he saw the throngs of people coming and going and milling about on the concourse. He also observed the increased numbers of beggars hanging about hoping to receive charity from the travellers. The majority of them were older in their teens or mature adults. Mike looked around and saw the many security cameras, so he left and headed towards the park that the kid had mentioned.

Now and then a stray dog went by. He sat down on a street bench and reminisced about the last time he was in the city.

He decided it would be better to target the small streets and alleyways without the intrusion of surveillance cameras.

He took off in another direction and soon he was engulfed in the foot traffic passing small kiosks, and a handful of beggars with nothing to do but loiter. It reminded him of Flinders Street Station, back home. There was a junkie or two stoned having difficulty focusing; a hooker smoking, waiting for business, and another hungry stray dog looking for its next meal. Like any major city in the world, Sofia had its fair share of pigeons, dozens of them, pecking for scraps, their heads bobbing up and down leaving their unhygienic trademarks.

Mike recalled seeing a lot more beggars and street children when he was here some years back. He saw a small grassy area with a few trees and walked towards it. It was getting dark. He glanced at his watch; the night scene was emerging. A few kids were kicking an empty can around the trees. A homeless man was preparing his bed for the night; a flattened cardboard box and a dirty blanket.

There were a couple of swings and the children were taking turns pushing each other. They were dirty and grimy and hadn't seen a bathtub in months.

"Bingo!' Mike mumbled to himself under his breath.

One young girl, who couldn't have been older than ten or eleven years old, wore a tattered but clean, blue sweat top and an odd pair of sweat black pants laced up at the waist. In one hand she clutched a dirty doll. She did not notice Mike watching them. He saw a bench nearby that faced the swings and sat down.

The girl with the doll shouted to one of the kids not to push the swing so hard. Mike admired that.

After a while, he got up and approached the girl he had been observing.

"Don't be afraid," he said gently, putting his hand out indicating he was friendly. "I'm doing charity work in the area. Shouldn't you kids be in a shelter of some kind?" he asked concerned to show her he meant no harm.

She looked at Mike while clutching the doll tighter to her body.

"It's getting dark. Shouldn't you be off the street and out of the park, no?" he added.

She did not answer but walked back about ten feet giving herself some space. Mike stayed where he was. "Listen, all I want to do is help. Tomorrow morning, I will be here at 9 am. I want to help homeless children like you, particularly babies. If you know of any baby that needs help, milk, food, and a safe home. Meet me in the morning. Let me meet any babies that want a home. I will make it worth your while." Mike smiled showing her some coins.

The girl shouted to the others. "Let's go. It's time to go." She accidentally tripped in her hurry to leave this weird stranger.

Mike stepped forward and caught her. His strong arms easily prevented her from falling hard. She looked up into his eyes that were surprisingly warm and caring.

"I've got you. Are you okay?"

She indignantly stood up on her own and brushed herself off, shouting at the others to come.

"Don't forget, I will have money and chocolate. What's your name, by the way?"

The children gathered together sensing something was up and followed the girl down the street with her doll.

As they walked away, the girl glanced over her shoulder at him. "Anna, my name is Anna."

Mike smiled and waved, "Be safe, little one, be safe."

Just then he felt his phone vibrate. "Everything okay, Oliver? I'll be at the hotel in less than an hour."

"Christ, we're starved, man!"

"Less than an hour, I'll meet you in the bar."

Mike looked around. The children were gone.

When he arrived back, he saw Oliver and Morris sitting on the bar stools.

"Hi, what are you boys drinking?"

They both turned to face Mike.

"I'm having a beer, and as you can see, good old Morrie here is eating a pound of peanuts and enjoying a scotch. Anything we need to know?"

"Is the jet ready and fuelled?"

"Yes, why?" Oliver replied, sipping the end of his beer.

"I've possibly made good contact. She's a young kid, but we will see. I'm meeting her hopefully at 9 am tomorrow. There's a chance we will get lucky in a day or so. The point is, if we do, we need to be ready to leave at a moment's notice."

"Well, let's take it a step at a time. You know the city. What's good here?" Oliver asked, letting his stomach do the talking.

"How about a traditional Bulgarian meal? I know this great place. Up for walking?"

Mike took them a few blocks to a charming rustic restaurant that was busy with locals enjoying dinner on the covered patio out front. Delicious aromas met them when they stepped inside, and Mike arranged a table for them with the hostess.

They ordered soup to start, and the waitress brought them hunks of bread and olive oil.

"One thing that I overlooked," Mike said, dipping his bread in the oil. "We should have brought Alice on this trip with us. We could potentially be returning with a young baby, and it slipped my attention. Someone has to look after the baby not only during the flights but also during the overlays to refuel. Hell, it means bottled milk and...."

"… and changing diapers. Many, many, dirty diapers," Oliver finished and chuckled.

"Fucking hell!"

Morrie, who was slurping away, wasn't paying any notice. He wiped his mouth and commented, "Nice soup. It's got a pleasant spicy taste."

"Yep, that's chubritsa. It's like oregano. It is very common here. They mainly use it in soups and stews, amongst other things," Mike responded, ilmomentarily distracted, before returning to problem at hand. "Fucking hell, I've got to change endless diapers and feed a little one for twenty-odd hours!"

Morrie smiled, and Oliver laughed again.

Mike chuckled too, but underneath he was touched by the plight of these homeless kids. It also hit him forcibly that here they were eating like kings and staying in a five-star hotel while a short distance away, there were kids sleeping in the streets, on park benches, in shelters, and going to bed without a proper meal and without love and care. He knew this was not a problem just in Bulgaria; the whole damn world had this problem.

He was quiet for the rest of the meal and pensive. Oliver and Morrie continued shooting the breeze like they were on vacation. Mike started to find it slightly irritating, although he knew they would be acting differently if they had seen what he had today.

Finally, Oliver noticed. 'You look serious, man. What's up?"

"Oh, just running things around in my mind, that's all. I do need to call Fern soon." Mike looked at his watch, "Melbourne is nine hours behind."

They walked back to the hotel for a well-earned night's rest and a proper bed. Mike reminded them he would be up at dawn and heading into the city early. Oliver and Morrie could take their time and enjoy breakfast but afterward to make sure they were ready for any eventuality. Just in case, he texted Oliver with the cross streets near the place where he was meeting little Anna at 9 am.

After he showered, Mike called Fern, who was by then anxiously pacing up and down, waiting to hear from him.

She answered it, the split second her phone rang, "Yes?"

"You're quick on the draw. How're you doing?"

"Mike, I was concerned. No word from you."

"All good, but there is a small issue. Tomorrow I'm meeting someone who may have a parcel or two. The parcels may be a bit heavy for me on my own. I think you should send someone here to help. I mean, with four stopovers or more, it's going to be difficult and a tough ride."

"That also entered my mind. What do you suggest?"

Mike remembered the public phone on the corner.

"I tell you what, I'll call you in an hour."

He dressed quickly and called her from the public phone.

"Okay, I'm here now in a public booth. We can talk freely. Jesus, Fern, I don't mind changing an odd diaper, but hell, we've got four stopovers. It means changing, feeding, and God knows what else. I tell you what, get Alice here now. When she arrives, I'll brief her. We'll all head back to Australia together. I need to be more on my toes, strategizing and recruiting, instead, I'll be treating diaper rash. In fact, second thoughts, I should stay here and spend more time gathering intel. I can get a commercial flight home. Remember, I am your stork," he grinned down the receiver.

Fern listened carefully and then responded, "I agree we need Alice to be involved on all the trips, and we should have had her involved on this one, but it is too late now. You are going to have to be mom and dad for this one. We need to talk about how we are going to present this to Alice, and we need to do this together. But I promise I will recruit a second nurse immediately, so when Alice is flying, we will have a trained nurse back here."

"Shit, you're right. Tomorrow I am meeting a young girl at 9 am and just in case something comes out of it, have Lance on standby with guidance and instructions."

"Okay, keep me in the loop, please."

"Sure will. See you later."

At one in the morning, Mike climbed into bed and was asleep in seconds.

A few hours later, he was up, showered, and dressed. He grabbed a few bites from his room service breakfast tray and headed back into the city in a cab. His mood was fatalistic. If Anna didn't show, he would recruit someone else.

By 8.30 am, he had checked the area out and settled down to wait from across the road in case Anna showed up early.

At fifteen minutes past nine, he saw someone who looked like Anna approaching. She was holding something small in the crook of one arm, and her other hand was clasping the hand of a little kid.

Mike looked around and, with the coast clear, he hot trotted across the road to meet her.

"Anna, so nice to see you again. I see you have a baby," he said in Bulgarian.

She nodded, "This little boy is four years old, and this is his baby sister."

"Where did you get them, Anna? It's very important you tell me the truth."

"From a run-down derelict housing estate. Their mommy leaves them alone a lot, sometimes for a day or even two. They don't know their daddy."

Mike looked at the little boy. He noticed a couple of bruises on his arm. Then he looked back at Anna and at the baby she was holding. The baby cried briefly, and Anna rocked her gently.

"He will not leave his sister," Anna said.

"What's your name, little man?" Mike hunched over and asked.

"Ivan."

Anna chipped in, "His English is not bad. He watches American cartoons all day when he is alone."

Mike tested him and spoke to Ivan in English and Bulgarian.

"Ivan, would you like to come with me and your little sister in an airplane?"

"No." He blushed.

"Why not?"

"I don't know you. Why do you want to take me, take us?"

"Because no one is looking after you, and you deserve a loving, nice home, with new clothes and food, and you will never get bruises, do you hear?"

The little boy was quiet. Mike almost thought he had him.

"Do you like soccer, Ivan?"

"Yes," he nodded.

"What if I buy you a pair of new soccer boots and a proper ball?"

Little Ivan's eyes lit up.

"Do you like puppies? I can get you a little dog."

Ivan was smiling, "Yes, please, sir."

Mike, who was as hard as nails, had a lump in his throat. He crouched down to Ivan's eye level.

"Now listen very carefully. We can fly this morning, but it will take a whole day and even a night because we'll have to stop to put fuel in our airplane. If you promise to be a good boy, we will make you very happy. Do you understand?"

"Yes, sir."

Mike looked at Anna, "Where do you live, Anna?"

"In a one-room flat with my mother."

"Is your mom good to you, Anna?"

"Yes, she is. She is in a lot of pain, though."

"What kind of pain?"

"Her tooth is rotten."

"Anna, I have something for you. I promise I will come back in a few weeks. I must leave, but I want to help you and your mother."

"Yes, Uncle Mike."

Mike was touched at her calling him uncle. "Good girl," he said, putting his hand on her shoulder.

He took out his wallet. "Here is some money to buy food for a week, and here is extra for your mom so she can take care of her tooth."

"Uh-huh," she replied with a smile taking the money, not quite believing what was happening. Then she was serious again as Mike reached out for the baby.

"Okay, good. Give me the baby, and I'll take the blanket too." He offered his hand to Ivan, "Come, you're not so little, are you?"

"No, sir," he answered solemnly.

"What is your baby sister's name?"

Ivan shrugged his shoulders.

"She is so cute. She must have a name. What is it, Ivan?"

He shrugged again, lifting his shoulders high, and pulling in his upper lip. Then it dawned on Mike. The baby didn't have a name.

"Nikol. Who do you think? Shall we call her Nikol?"

Ivan gave a shy little nod.

Mike looked around, pleased that everything was going so smoothly.

"Okay, Anna. We must go. Where can I find you again?"

"We always play by the swings, Uncle Mike."

"Okay, good. When I come back, I will meet you here. Before I go, this is for you," Mike took out a chocolate bar and gave it to her.

"Now, go straight home and give your mamma the money."

Anna gave him a big heartfelt smile. Then she turned and ran.

Mike stood under the tree with a little baby in his arms and a child holding his hand. He thought he might cry. They were so vulnerable. He swallowed, took a deep breath, and phoned Oliver.

"Are you in position? I've got parcels."

"Affirmative. Did you say parcel or parcels?"

Mike ignored the question. "Great. See you shortly."

Mike held the baby and little Ivan's hand and walked quickly to the rendezvous point he had given Oliver the night before.

Thankfully they were waiting. They hopped into the back of the BMW and were on the way to the airport. While Oliver returned the rental, Morrie babysat Nikol. He was a natural, his children had grown, and he was used to caring for his grandchildren. Mike took Ivan to the men's room to clean him up a bit. Then he took him to the airport clothing store and bought him clean clothes and a pair of small Nike shoes. Poor kid nearly tripped several times as he had hardly worn shoes in his life before, let alone a pair of Nikes. He kept looking down proudly at his new shoes more than once and nearly walked into someone.

Then the men struck a problem. They would have to leave via the diplomatic side of the airport because it was the only way to exit their jet.

Mike and the crew already had their forged diplomatic papers but the baby and little Ivan did not.

Mike called Danny. It was 4 am in Melbourne.

Luckily, Danny answered straightaway. "No problem. I can email you a signed letter from the Bulgarian Foreign Affairs Minister confirming you have permission to escort the two little ones to a hospital in Melbourne for a rare bone marrow transplant. Give me an hour or so."

"Oh, thank God—great idea," Mike sighed with relief.

"I'll also attach a letter from the Chief Administrator of the hospital to say that they had just acquired a suitable stem cell donor for the transplant. That ought to do it," Danny said confidently down the phone.

"You're the best," Mike said in genuine awe. "Truly, the best. Do you think you can also write a letter from the orphanage releasing these two youngsters into my custody? I'll come back to you with some Bulgarian last names. Ivan is a 4-year-old little boy and his sister Nikol is probably about one month."

They were still taking a chance, but it was the quickest solution.

The baby started crying. Mike left Ivan with Morrie and went to buy immediate supplies for the baby at the pharmacy before taking her to the family room to change her.

He washed his hands and whipped up a bottle to feed the starving infant. She sucked the bottle dry in no time. He burped her, and she brought up some formula.

"Ah shit," Mike mumbled under his breath as he tried to clean himself off.

True to his word, in less than two hours, Danny's forged letters arrived via email. Mike headed over to the business class lounge and used his Frequent Flyer gold status card and powers of persuasion to enter and use the facilities to print them.

With the proper papers in order, they went through the diplomatic security area. Mike played the role perfectly, abrupt and jingoistic, just the way many politicians behaved. He sounded just like them.

There were several questions at the desk, but little Nikol was crying so hard that the official gave the letters a cursory glance and waved them on. In a few minutes, they were on the tarmac, walking toward their jet.

While waiting for clearance for take-off, Oliver showed little Ivan the cockpit, and Mike changed another diaper.

Mike swore it would be the last time he would fly without Alice, and then he turned to Ivan.

"Ivan, I am sure you have never been in a jet before."

"No, I haven't, Uncle Mike. It was also my first time riding in a car."

Mike patted the kid's head, smiled, and then called Fern.

"The Stork has good news, my lady."

"You do?" she said eagerly.

"I have two parcels. One is light, and the other one weighs four pounds. We are shortly leaving on our first leg. Will be in touch soon."

Fern was excited and a bit shocked. She understood Mike's coded message. He also had a four-year-old. What were they? A boy or a girl or both? It had happened so quickly, but she knew Mike had to keep all calls brief and encrypted for the sake of safety.

She longed to phone the Harrises with the good news but decided it would be premature. She ran to find Megan and Alice.

"Guess what? Good news! In a day or so, we are taking delivery of our first two children. All I know is that one is a baby, and the other is four years old," she said, grinning with delight.

"Lovely dear, lovely, I can't wait," Megan said, hugging her.

"Are they boys or girls or one of each?" Alice asked.

Fern looked at Alice. "No idea, but I can tell you one thing — we need another Alice, someone just like you. Celebrations aside, Alice, we must find another nurse. We need two of you. I mean, we will be busy, and what happens when you are off duty?"

"I've been thinking that too. I will get someone."

"They have to be very experienced and discreet and be able to start asap. It looks like you will soon be flying around the world."

Fern excused herself and went to her office. She phoned Danny.

The phone rang for nearly half a minute. Danny answered very sleepily.

"Hello, Fern," he yawned.

"Gee, you sound half asleep. What's up?"

"Got to bed late. Mike woke me around 4 am—didn't you hear?"

"No! What the hell for?"

"He needed some more urgent papers for the two kids."

"Oh, so you know everything?" she was a little perturbed.

"Not a lot to know. I organized some papers for Nikol, a baby girl, and her four-year-old brother, Ivan."

"Wow!" There were a few seconds of silence.

"I see. I was calling you to rework the heading on our website. I was thinking something like *Ever thought of adoption? Let us help change your life so you can change another!*" Danny was yawning again.

"All right, Danny, don't worry. I'll email you. Get some sleep. Thanks!"

"Cheers, Fern."

Fern rushed back to Megan and Alice with the latest news.

Several hours later, Mike phoned again.

"Fern, hi, it's me again. We land tomorrow morning in Melbourne in the early hours."

She put down the phone, and she couldn't help thinking, This is a man who always comes through.

Chapter Thirty-Four

They landed just before sunrise, and less than an hour later, Morrie headed home. He would be on standby for the next trip. Mike also confirmed with him the Stork Center was now his top priority, and he would be generously compensated. Oliver would be his line of communication.

Oliver and Mike had left their cars at the airport. But, since they now had the little ones, Oliver drove Mike and the kids to the center.

Baby Nikol was asleep in Mike's arms in the back after feeding her before disembarking. Ivan was able to ride up front like a little prince and loved every minute of it. He was excited when Mike welcomed him to Australia as they landed and was looking about him eagerly, wondering what *Australia* was.

It was about one hundred and five kilometres from Avalon Airport to Fern's home, and it took them well over an hour even though the traffic was not heavy.

Mike opened the main gate with his remote and drove around to the drop-off zone at the back, where the three ladies were there to welcome them with open arms.

Fern felt a tear trickle down her cheek, a tear of joy. Alice immediately took Nikol and disappeared into the building. Megan took little Ivan's hand happily.

Fern hugged Mike first, then Oliver.

"You boys must be tired and hungry. Come inside. You can shower and freshen up in the guest cottage if you want. Ivan, I am sure you are hungry. There is a big breakfast waiting for you. And then Alice will show you where your room is. She will help you get cleaned up as well."

They went to the kitchen, where Megan had prepared a full-on English breakfast. They all quickly devoured bacon, eggs and toast washed down with copious amounts of coffee and fresh orange juice. Ivan happily munched away.

Megan smiled at Ivan enjoying his breakfast. "What would you normally eat back in Bulgaria?"

'Two-minute noodles," he said between mouthfuls. "Every day and sometimes we had to share half a portion as there was not enough to go around," he said.

Everyone went quiet for a moment.

"I must say," Megan said, "Ivan, your English is wonderful."

"Cartoons," he smiled.

"Maybe we should use them for adults," Mike said, "but you know kids pick up languages like nothing."

Mike ruffled Ivan's hair.

Fern suggested Megan take Ivan shopping when he woke up from a nap later that day for clothes and toys.

"Ivan, how would you like to go with my mom and buy a soccer ball and some books? You can pick out some lovely picture books, and maybe Alice or my mom can read to you when you get back?"

Ivan nodded enthusiastically, but his eyes were beginning to droop. Young Bonzo put his head in Ivan's lap and looked up at him with sorrowful eyes. Ivan squealed with delight and patted him. "Is this my puppy, Uncle Mike promised me?"

At that point, Alice walked back into the kitchen to fetch him and take him for a bath.

"Come, Ivan, let's get you cleaned up. I am Alice, and I am a nurse. I take good care of everyone, and I am going to check you out to make sure you are as fit as a king!" She grabbed his hand and smiled. He smiled faintly back. He felt safe even though he was in a strange place.

In the boardroom, Mike sat opposite Oliver with Fern at the head. "Great job, and thank you again. Congratulations on our first collection, both of you. I know you boys are exhausted, so let's keep the debrief quick. Mike, fire away..."

"First of all, since we need a nurse on board for obvious reasons, Alice needs to be informed and sworn to secrecy. She's smart and has been around the block. She'll put two and two together any way that the babies are not coming through the proper channels but straight from the field." Mike paused. He wanted his words to land.

Fern looked at him, "What do you propose?"

"Morrie also needs to be included in this conversation. I suggest we hold off until we have successfully completed two or three collections and not before. If Alice is told now, she could pull out. It will be easier to convince her after she witnesses successful placements and see how the little ones transform. Once they get to her heart, it won't be so hard to talk her around. As for the additional nurse, the same; if we lay our cards on the table before she commences work, we could jeopardize the whole operation. It is important we get them emotionally attached through being involved." Mike took a large breath. The toll of the trip was kicking in. He was also emotionally drained.

"Two last points. If Alice had been with us on this last trip, I could have stayed behind in Sofia and worked on developing a relationship with my contact there. It might have been possible to obtain more kids in a few days. My last point is that Oliver's co-pilot, Morrie proved himself to be a valuable team player, and I recommend he be employed full-time by us. And that's it from me for now." He yawned and tried to hide it behind his hand.

"Thanks," Fern acknowledged, looking at Mike with a serious expression. Then she quickly turned to Oliver. "You obviously agree with Mike regarding your co-pilot?"

"Certainly. I also looked at the numbers, and it's terribly costly to fly to one country with several stop-overs just for one, even two kids. Mike needs to go ahead of us and prepare several pick-ups, and we need to be ready for his call. That is pretty much all I have to say for now, other than I need a good long sleep."

Fern nodded, "Okay, guys, Oliver, employ your co-pilot, find out what he earns monthly and add on twenty-five percent and let me know."

"For the record, I've had many inquiries on our website, and I have two more appointments lined up this week with prospective parents. Mike, if you have made agood contact in Sofia, go back. I suggest you fly out after a couple of days of rest. Book a ticket with a major airline. I agree with you. When you are ready, notify us, and then Oliver can fly out with Morrie to join you. That's it for now, guys. Get some well-deserved rest."

"No argument here," Oliver said, pushing back his chair.

"Likewise, come, Oliver, let's hit the road. I need a ride, remember," Mike said.

They walked out together, Oliver turning at the door to give Fern a wink.

She smiled briefly.

"Cheers, guys. I'm off to check up on little Ivan and baby Nikol."

"I have good news," Alice whispered happily as Fern entered the nursery. "Both babies Nikol and Ivan appear to be healthy. I feel confident when Dr. Lance comes to examine them, he will be of the same opinion."

Fern smiled, "Excellent, Alice," and tiptoed over to the cot to peek in on a sleeping Nikol. Ivan was cleaned up and fast asleep on his back in the new bed that Megan had organized at the last minute.

"The sooner you get on the phone and find another nurse, the better, don't you think?" Fern said in a hushed tone.

"Certainly, I intend to do that today," Alice said while thinking about the overseas travel and why they were bringing in babies from so far away.

Megan was all smiles, and a little teary-eyed as she helped put away clothes and tidy up. "I'll take Ivan out for ice cream when he wakes up. It will be fun going to a center to buy clothing and toys for a little boy."

"Good, I have to work now. Alice, I am available today to interview any nurses if that's possible to arrange?"

"I'll see if I can do that."

"Mom, can I have a quick word?"

Ushering her mother out of earshot, Fern was keen to know how Ivan had been behaving and if he had been fretting at all.

"Has he been asking for anyone? His mother?"

"No, dear. He hasn't asked for anyone except he wants to make sure his little sister is alright. Why?"

"I was worried he might be fretting for his parents — they were recently killed in a car accident, you know," Fern calmly lied to her mother without batting an eye.

"No, dear, nothing like that. He seems a happy little boy, provided his sister is nearby."

Relieved, Fern left for her office. Her first call was to give some good news to Jack and Wendy Harris.

Later, Megan drove little Ivan to the Westfield Knox shopping center. Like a fond grandmother, she treated him galore to clothes and shoes as well as books, video games, toys, and the all-important soccer ball. Ivan couldn't stop grinning, even all the way back home. As Megan looked in her mirror at an ecstatic Ivan, she realized in a few short hours, this little boy had become like a grandson to her. She knew he would soon be with his new adopted family, and she warned herself not to become too attached.

Oliver dropped Mike at home and then called Morrie and made him an offer his co-pilot couldn't refuse.

As he dropped his bags in the hallway, Oliver wondered about Fern and her less than enthusiastic response to his wink. It was time to get her in the sack again, he thought.

Chapter Thirty-Five

Bruce Nash began to settle down after ending his wife's misery. He thought about it every minute of the day and had to keep reminding himself she was no longer suffering and free of pain and shame.

Almost as much as he thought about his late wife, he thought about Fern. The same question kept circling in his head: could she be the missing baby, the daughter of the Russian prostitute?

Nash was unsure how to proceed without access to the resources he once had as a police officer. One option was to confront Fern but would she even know? Maybe he could track down her parents, but how? He couldn't exactly loiter around the gate every day with flowers in the hope her parents showed up. And, still, there was no guarantee they would know anything. Adoption papers remain sealed without a court order.

There was always Google, of course. Jones was a common name, but *Fern Jones* was not so common. Impulsively, he entered her name into the google search bar and was surprised by the results. It did not take him long to come across an obituary for one of Australia's wealthiest men, Chester Jones, 75, deceased, survived by a wife and a daughter Fern Jones, heiress to his multi-million-dollar company IME. She was definitely the right age. This, at least, explained her massive fortune. Nash also noted the large age gap between father and daughter. Surely his widow Megan would be a lot younger with a 20-year- old daughter.

The other option was to simply keep snooping around, as he had been doing, building a rapport with Fern to see if he could find out any more information that way.

After giving it some serious thought, Nash decided to resort to good old fashion police work. She had brought him a cake as a neighborly gesture. It was now his turn to return the favor. He showered and shaved and headed into the village to buy a reciprocal gift.

He ended up in the popular French cake patisserie and chose a beautiful box of exquisite chocolates. He placed it carefully on the floor of the passenger seat, out of the sun..

When he arrived at Fern's house, he parked outside in the tree-lined street. As he climbed out of his car, he heard the cackling laughter of a territorial kookaburra in the tree above.

Nash glanced up at the bird as he pressed the intercom bell at the gate.

Megan heard the buzzer and walked to the intercom, wondering who it could be, and looked at the camera.

"Hello, can I help you?"

"It's Bruce Nash. I live around the corner and have met Fern a few times. She was kind to me recently when my wife died. I'd like to drop off a gift in appreciation," he spoke into the box.

"Ah yes, Mr. Nash, I remember something like that vaguely. I believe we may have met for a second or two a few weeks ago. I'm Fern's mother. Please come in," Megan invited. She pushed the button, and the gate opened.

Nash walked up the driveway, and Megan was at the front door, ready to receive him. He was immediately struck by how unlike Fern she was in appearance. And, by the fact she could easily have been Fern's grandmother and immediately noticed her kind brown eyes.

Megan smiled at the sight of the box of chocolates, "Why that is very considerate of you. Please come in."

"Thank you, I do not want to keep you from your schedule. I am sure you are busy."

"Not at all, please. I have just boiled the kettle. Follow me." She liked the thought of a chat with someone closer to her own age. She was on her own a lot, and sometimes she got lonely. Fern was like Chester, very secretive with her work and always busy.

Megan led him to the kitchen. "Do sit, Mr. Nash."

Nash chose a chair that faced the kitchen door. "Thank you, much appreciated, Mrs. Jones. It is Mrs. Jones?" he pressed.

"Please call me Megan."

"Okay, in that case, please call me Bruce."

They both laughed awkwardly.

"Will it be tea or coffee, Bruce?"

"Tea please, Megan, with milk." Nash looked around, "You have a lovely place. I watched it being built as I went by on my daily walks. It must have been built in record time."

"Yes, thank you, it is very comfortable," Megan replied, ignoring his comment about the construction schedule.

Fern had heard the gate buzzer and followed the voices to the kitchen.

When she entered the kitchen, she could feel her face burn red with surprise.

"Why, look who is here, darling? I believe you have met Bruce before?"

Fern was fighting her flushed cheeks but without much success.

"Hello, Bruce. How are you? How have you been coping?" she asked, quickly recovering her thoughts."

"Bruce has kindly brought these delicious chocolates to share. Join us, dear."

"Yes, please do. I brought it over for you to thank you for the other day," Nash added.

"I am terribly busy at the moment, but certainly, I'll sit for a few minutes," she said politely, trying to control her nerves running through her body.

"Can I pour you something to drink, darling?" Megan asked, oblivious of her daughter's uneasy manner.

"No thanks, mom. I have a meeting soon and need to prepare. Later perhaps, thanks."

"What do you do, may I ask?" Nash asked casually, looking at Fern and then her mother.

Fern responded quickly before her mother could say anything. "I manage a guest house, an exclusive guest house for people wanting privacy." This was the party-line Mike had advised during one of their many meetings if there were any questions about the activities going on at the property.

"Is it nearby?" he probed as nonchalantly as possible.

"You are sitting in it, Bruce, well alongside it, I must say."

She did not like the way the conversation was going. She stood up.

Megan was surprised by her daughter's seemingly evasive behavior. Why is Fern making up stories? she wondered.

"Well, Bruce," Fern said, looking at the clock on the wall. "Nice to see you again. Excuse me, but I see I need to run. Mom, I will talk to you later."

"Sure, dear."

Nash stood up. "Good to see you again, Fern."

Fern walked slowly to the door, then, once out the door, she ran to her office and grabbed her phone. She called her mother, hoping against hope that Megan would have the gumption not to greet her by name.

Megan's phone rang, and she excused herself and walked towards the table with the large bowl of fruit where she had left her phone. She looked at the caller ID and saw it was Fern. She instantly realized something was not right. She had more common sense than her daughter gave her credit for.

"Hello," she answered in her normal greeting and for the sake of her guest.

"Mom, don't indicate you are talking to me. Listen, the man you are talking to is not to be trusted. I do not want him in my house. Please finish your tea quickly and excuse yourself. Do you understand?"

"Why yes, of course. Thanks for calling, goodbye."

Megan looked at Nash. "That was my hairdresser," she informed him, looking at her watch. "She's asked me to come in a little earlier for my appointment today."

"No problem. Thank you for the tea, Megan." She walked him to the door. At the door, Nash turned and said, "Congratulations again on your new home. Your daughter is lovely, by the way. She must take after her father as she doesn't resemble her beautiful mother."

Hearing a reference to Chester by a stranger made Megan drop her guard. "Yes. in business anyway. Fern is adopted. My husband passed away last year."

"Oh, I see. Sorry to hear. I recently lost my wife. It's not easy, is it?" Nash prodded, hoping to prolong the conversation and connect.

"Yes. I am sorry, I really must go," Megan did want the company, but something in Fern's voice warned her.

Nash left and walked briskly back to the front gate.

Under his breath, he mumbled to himself, "*Adopted* — now I know Fern is almost certainly the missing baby."

Fern rushed back to the kitchen.

"Mom, that man is known to be a swindler and a crook! Everyone in Sassafras and Olinda knows it. He is dangerous and not safe to be around. Don't ever let him in again!"

Fern purposely embellished the accusations. She did not want to tell her mother the truth about what she had witnessed, and she certainly did not want her silence to result in her own mother getting involved with a wife killer.

Megan was startled by her daughter's vehement tone. "He seemed pleasant enough, darling. I hope you don't mind but…"

Fern cut her off, "But what, Mom?"

"I accidentally told him that you were adopted."

"Why on earth would you do that, Mom? It's none of his damn business!"

"He was nice. It was nice to be with someone of my own age, and I felt comfortable with him," she sighed, crestfallen. "He also said that you must have looked like your father, and that's when I told him you were adopted. I'm sorry, I didn't know."

"Jeez, Mom, don't you know con artists are famous for making people feel comfortable? But what's done is done. Just don't see that man again, here or anywhere. I am warning you."

"Yes, dear." Megan was genuinely disappointed, but, as with her husband, it was no use arguing.

Fern walked out of the kitchen, shaking her head. She went to check up on the two little ones. They were settling in well, and Ivan was playing quietly in the nursery with Alice supervising.

She then phoned Mike and explained to him what had happened. He told her that perhaps a day would arrive when he would have to confront Nash with the video. He also confirmed he was flying out soon; procrastination was the thief of time, and there were many parcels to collect.

Even though she never wanted Nash in her home, Fern was pleased she got the opportunity to tell Nash she operated a guest house. Now, when exercising his old bones in the neighborhood, he would not find the different cars going in and out of the complex suspicious.

She walked into the garden and called Jack Harris.

He answered promptly, and straightaway asked if she had good news.

"I sure do, Jack. I have the pleasure of inviting you and Wendy to visit the center for a personal tour and to meet a beautiful baby girl who needs a special home!" she said gleefully.

"Wow, that is so exciting. When can we meet? I know Wendy will be so happy."

"Does tomorrow work? Anytime from 11 am onwards."

"It sure does, and if my stubborn dairy disagrees, we will make the time."

"Jack, just so you know, the procedure will be to visit for around an hour. We will introduce you to the baby, and if this seems a fit, we will sit down and work out an agenda to complete the necessary process to finalize everything. We will also require both of you to have up-to-date vaccinations, including one for whooping cough. We will also need to do a home inspection to make sure you have everything set up to welcome a newborn into your home. Once you can provide these necessary documents, the final payment will be due." Fern stopped to pause to let all this information sink in.

"How old is she? Does she have a name?" was all Jack asked.

"She is one month old and her name is Nikol. As soon as we receive full payment, you will officially be the proud parents of little Nikol Harris. You do still have the opportunity to change her name if you wish, and we can take care of that and apply to the Victoria registrar department for a new birth certificate and name change.

"By the way, Nikol has a little brother looking for a home too. His name is Ivan, and he is four years old. Both parents were killed in a car crash, and there was no family member who could afford to take the kids. Sadly, there are no other relatives either."

"Gosh, I do not know what to say. Let me talk to Wendy. Maybe we can meet them first and then decide?"

"Of course! It's tough to separate siblings, as I mentioned before, but you do not have to take Ivan as well," Fern said, gambling on the fact that they would not be able to resist Ivan once they saw him.

"Splendid. See you tomorrow."

"Thanks, Jack!"

"Cheers."

This was all going so well. She grinned to herself that she was able to come up with such a convincing story about the parents being killed in an accident. She would have to come up with other similar tales for future placements as well, she realized. But, now, she would invent something for Ivan's bruises while living temporarily in Bulgaria to explain his accent.

Fern returned to her office and checked her emails. Her eyes widened. She had a couple of inquiries, and one looked serious. It was from a Mr. and Mrs. Mwangi expressing an interest in an African baby. They explained in the email they were both Australian citizens and had immigrated here several years ago from Kenya. They very much wanted to adopt a child from their native country. The message was signed Bayana and Dinka Mwangi.

Fern googled their names and found there was only one Dinka Mwangi on Facebook residing in Sydney and she was married to Bayana Mwangi. His LinkedIn profile stated he was a very wealthy investment banker. This couple was seriously rich.

In the middle of the night, Fern was awoken by the buzzer. Someone was at the front gate. She rolled over in bed and looked at the monitor from the high-resolution security camera, and screamed. She started to shake uncontrollably, and she began breathing heavily. She gasped for air like a mountaineer would near the summit. She was shocked to see Chester Jones and Bruce Nash looking up at the camera, asking to be let in. Fern screamed. She felt faint and tiny spots of perspiration broke out on her forehead.

Then her mother came rushing into her bedroom.

"Fern, are you alright? You've had a bad dream," she said soothingly, sitting on the bed, stroking her forehead.

Fern opened her eyes and sat up in bed. The bedside clock read 3 am.

"Mom, I had a terrible nightmare. I dreamt that Dad was pushing the bell at the gate, and he was with that monster, Bruce Nash. My God, it was so real!" She couldn't stop shaking.

"Hush, my darling, go back to sleep. I'll stay with you for a while. We have a very important day ahead of us tomorrow. Do you want a glass of water?"

"No thanks, Mom. I'll be just fine. God, what a nightmare," she said, shaking her head.

"Alright, darling, I'm going back to bed. Sleep well, just relax," Megan gently dabbed Fern's forehead with a tissue.

Megan left her room, and Fern eventually settled down and went back to sleep without any more bad dreams that night.

Chapter Thirty-Six

Fern and Megan were up early at 6 am and sat at the kitchen counter, mulling over their morning coffee, each preoccupied with their own thoughts.

Fern was still fighting off the horrible nightmare and trying to focus on the day ahead. She had instructed Maggie to show up an hour earlier. Alice slept on site and was on call throughout the night for both babies, Nikol and Ivan. She hoped she had had a better night.

Megan looked at Fern, "Are you alright? Did you get enough sleep? That was a terrible dream you had only a few hours ago."

"I'm fine, Mom. Let's move on and forget it."

"No worries, dear. So, what's on the agenda today?"

"Well, first and foremost, the Harrises are coming here at 11 am to see baby Nikol. I would love for you to look after little Ivan today. Alice will be with the baby. Alice has also arranged for a second nurse to pop in for an interview after the Harrises leave."

"I'd love to!" Megan beamed. "Look at them now, little sleeping beauties," she said, looking at the screen monitor in the top corner of the kitchen.

"Ah, yes. Great. Thanks for the coffee. I'm going to check on the tiny tots now and speak with Alice, then I am going to get dressed."

Ivan was sound asleep, curled up like a cat, clutching his new stuffed kangaroo toy Megan had given him. Fern peeked into the crib to watch Nikol breathing peacefully. Alice appeared and tip-toed in, fully dressed and ready for the day.

They stepped outside the door to talk.

"Good morning Alice! Did you have a good night?" she nodded yes.

"I did indeed. It was very comfortable, thank you."

"Everything is going well, and I will be meeting the new nurse today. But I was thinking, as we grow, it will be inevitable that we will need further backup support. You know, if you are overseas and your assistant gets sick or is on leave, we will be stuck. Perhaps Maggie can spend a couple of hours every day with you, watching and learning, so she can jump in if we get short-staffed? She has grown kids of her own, so she'll know the basic stuff, but if you could teach her some routine medical procedures, that'll be great?"

"Sure, of course, Fern. Will you tell her?"

"Yes, I'll talk to her when she arrives and send her to you before the Harrises get here. Two on duty will look more professional."

"Okay, good." Alice turned to go back into the nursery as she could hear baby Nikol stirring.

"And another thing. I have asked Mom to fetch Ivan when he wakes and look after him for the morning while the Harrises visit, so you can just be with the baby. Oh, and, one more thing, I would like you to sit in with me for a short while when your colleague comes at noon for her interview."

"Absolutely, she's a lovely lady. Her name is Sheelah. She was born here, and her husband is charming; his name is Ugo. He immigrated here from Italy many years ago."

"What's their last name?"

"Carrera, Sheelah Carrera, and her name is spelt differently to the normal S.h.e.i.l.a. It is S.h.e.e.l.a.h."

"Good, now please excuse me. I will send Maggie here shortly."

Fern left and went to shower and spent some time on her appearance. She selected an elegant charcoal pantsuit for the upcoming meetings.

Fern went downstairs to the kitchen and found a happy Megan proudly watching over little Ivan, who was dressed and eating cereal at the kitchen table.

Fern sat at the kitchen counter and could not take her eyes off the front gate. A few minutes to 11 am, a Mercedes pulled up outside, and the buzzer went.

She checked the monitor and gave Jack and Wendy Harris directions to the back of the house, and opened the gate for them.

The Mercedes drove slowly and carefully to the back.

"Welcome to the Stork Center," Fern said with a smile. "Come this way, folks. I'll introduce you shortly to baby Nikol, but first, let's sit down and catch up."

The couple followed, looking around curiously as they walked behind Fern.

Fern led them to the boardroom and closed the door.

"How are you both feeling? Do you have the latest paperwork filled out?"

They both smiled and nodded, anxious to meet Nikol. Jack gave Fern an envelope, "All here. And the certificates confirming our whooping cough shots."

"Marvellous," Fern said, her heart beating fast with excitement. She knew it was a done deal.

"Good. The normal routine is that I take you to the nursery. We will introduce you to the baby. You are welcome to hold her and ask any questions. Alice, the nurse, will be there. Take your time. I'll leave you and give you time on your own. I'll come and collect you a little later. We can then come back here and talk more and decide what needs to be done next."

"Great. Shall we?" Jack responded, and his wife nodded approval.

Fern could see that Wendy looked flushed and nervous but hopeful, oh so hopeful.

"Excellent," Fern smiled warmly.

Again, they followed Fern to the heart of the building.

"Just over there is baby Nikol. Come…" Fern indicated.

They all walked over to the cot. Fern was watching their faces carefully.

"Allow me," Alice said after being introduced. "Nikol is a lovely little healthy girl. She is very placid. She has a good appetite, sleeps well, and loves her baths," Alice said while picking up the baby.

The faces of the couple erupted into huge smiles of joy.

"May I?" Wendy said, putting her arms out to take the baby.

"Of course," Alice replied while passing baby Nikol over.

Wendy took the baby in her arms, and Alice showed her how to support her tiny head.

A tear ran down Wendy's cheek. "Forgive me, but I've prayed so long for this day to happen."

"Feel free to cry, Wendy. You deserve this moment. Nothing whatsoever to be embarrassed by," Fern encouraged gently, pushing back her own tears.

Jack put his arm around his wife and patted her upper back a few times. Fern could tell he was just as touched and moved as his wife. Baby Nikol didn't stir. She lay there very content in Wendy's arms.

"What is the next step, Fern?" Jack asked.

"Well, let's go and have tea, and I will explain everything."

"What is happening with the little boy?"

"It is just a matter of time before I will find a suitable home for her brother."

"Can we see him?" asked Jack, thinking about the notion of having a son too.

"Sure, just for a minute or two."

Fern excused herself and went to see Megan.

She was sitting with Ivan on her lap and was reading him a story in the living room.

"Mom, would you bring Ivan," she smiled happily. "The Harrises want to meet him!"

Megan followed Fern back to the nursery, holding Ivan's hand. She was a little bit depressed as she knew that one day the little guy would be gone.

Fern smiled at Ivan, who was still clutching his book with his other hand to his chest. "Ivan, this is Jack and Wendy Harris. I told them what a big boy you are."

Jack proffered his hand, "Pleased to meet you, Ivan."

Ivan ignored his hand and held Megan's hand tighter. Jack then said, "Give me a five, big guy!"

Thankfully, Ivan handed his book to Megan and pushed his hand slowly forward until it collided with Jack's.

"There you go! High five!" Jack said encouragingly.

"This is my mother, Megan Jones," Fern said, acknowledging her mother. "Okay, Mom, you can take him back and carry on reading him his book. Thank you, Alice. I will see you later when Sheelah arrives."

As Megan was leading Ivan back to the house, he turned and ran back to his baby sister and kissed her on her cheek. Everyone's hearts just melted.

"Shall we go back and talk over tea?" Fern turned to Wendy and Jack. They followed Fern out the door, and Jack winked at Ivan.

Fern made tea for both of them and coffee for herself.

"Well, how do you both feel?"

"Couldn't be more delighted and thrilled," Wendy said.

"And you, Jack?" Fern asked.

"Same goes for me. I'm just a bit hesitant, that's all."

Before Fern could ask why, Wendy looked surprised and said, "What is it, Jack? We are saying yes to baby Nikol, aren't we?"

"Of course we are!"

Wendy exhaled deeply with relief.

"It's just that we will be separating a sister from her brother, that's all." Jack paused to explain. "Little Nikol is costing us two hundred thousand but paying four hundred thousand is a lot of money."

"What are you saying, Jack?" Wendy asked.

"I think it's unfair to separate them, that's all."

"Jack, I tell you what," Fern interjected, having been affected too. "Why don't you think about taking Ivan too, and we can lower our fee? I would be happy to, if it helps, say one-fifty. Don't feel obligated, but I know these siblings are close, and if this is all that is preventing from keeping them together, I can work with you on this."

Everyone sat in silence.

"You don't have to decide now. It is a lot to think about waking up to a ready-made family of four." Fern peeked at Wendy to see how she was reacting.

"Jack? What do you think?" his wife urged.

He looked at his wife and smiled. "Why not? We have wanted a family for years. And now we have this opportunity…"

"Aww, Jack, I'm so happy. Are you sure?" Wendy asked.

"Yes, darling, absolutely, I am sure!"

Fern's heart glowed. She saw first-hand what her own parents had experienced when she arrived into their lives. She realized what a sacred moment this was and why she was truly driven to undertake such a risk. It was nothing short of momentous.

"Congratulations!" she beamed, her hands clasped in excitement.

"Well, okay, I will send you the paperwork to confirm if you can arrange the payment."

"We will schedule for Alice to visit and help you organize all the necessary things like a crib for Nikol, a child's bed for Ivan and the right car seat for Nikol, and all the other necessary basics. She will also help you baby-proof your home. We will get going on this end to finalize all the official documents and make sure their birth certificates will have Harris as their last name. This will take about a week."

"For the next couple of weeks, we will schedule regular visits so you can get to know them. It will give Ivan a chance to become more comfortable and a chance to bond with you more before you take him. Alice will be available for lessons so you both can be familiar with changing and feeding a newborn and more confident bathing, which can be a little daunting for new parents. Alice is excellent. She covers everything and more."

Fern took a breath, "My heartiest congratulations, I am so happy for you both, and I know Ivan and Nikol will love their new home."

"Fern, you don't know how great you have been. I will take care of the payment as soon as I return to my office today."

"Wonderful! Wendy, tell me when it would be convenient to come back and spend some quality time with your new son and daughter?"

Wendy smiled girlishly at the words of son and daughter, "Tomorrow, is tomorrow good? The earlier, the better?"

"How about 9am? I'll let Alice know to expect you," Fern smiled.

Fern called Megan on the internal phone extension to bring Ivan to the boardroom to meet his new parents.

Jack immediately couched down and patted Ivan gently on the shoulder.

"Ivan, I know you have had a rough start, and life hasn't been too good, but don't worry, things are going to get better. You have a new mom and dad now, and we are going to take care of you. You're safe, and we are going to have a lot of fun!"

Ivan looked up, concerned, "But, but will you keep me tomorrow? Will you keep my sister and me tomorrow and the day after that?"

Wendy bent down and looked at Ivan face to face. "Forever, my son, forever," she whispered into his ear, fighting the lump in her throat.

Fern wiped a tear from the corner of her eye with her little finger. This was beyond her wildest imagination and took her by surprise at how deeply touched she felt.

A few minutes later, Fern waved goodbye to the Harrises as they drove out of the driveway. At the same time, Mike Barzel was coming down the street in his car to visit. He saw someone standing at the gate, and he decelerated and edged forward slowly, not wishing to scare the pedestrian.

Then Mike saw the gate to the center open, and a Mercedes drove out, and the pedestrian moved on and walked in Mike's direction.

Mike pulled up next to the man and opened his passenger window.

"Hello, Mr. Nash. I see you are out exercising again. Good for you! Walking is healthy and good for the soul."

"Do I know you?" Nash replied, surprised.

"Mr. Nash, I am Fern's right-hand man. We brought you a cake the day your wife died, and the paramedics were there."

"'Of course, of course, how is the lady, er Miss, er, it's on the tip of my tongue." Nash had started to notice he couldn't always remember words. He was getting forgetful.

"That depends on who you are referring to. It could be Ms. Jones or Mrs. Jones. Which one is it, Bruce?" Mike said with a little bit of a caustic tone.

Nash was mad with himself and frustrated in front of this healthy and fit younger man.

"Both of them. I met both of them. How are they, how are they both?" he recovered.

"Both well, Bruce, thank you. By the way, I need to chat with you in confidence and soon. When and where would suit you?"

"About what?" his sixth sense kicked in again.

"I believe you are a retired cop, one of distinction, is that correct?"

"Yes, uh huh. How do you know?"

"Google is a great resource, and I have some information I know you will love to hear."

Nash relaxed a bit. His mind raced ahead. He had a feeling it was about Ms. Jones, who was adopted. Perhaps this man knew more about her history and her real parents.

"We can do it now if you want. I'm keen to hear what you have to say."

"Good, hop in," Mike said with a grin.

"We can go to my house. It's not far."

"I know. It's fifty-one Upper Hill Road," Mike nodded.

Mike walked with Nash, passed all the foliage blocking the street view to the house, and strolled next to him up the wide slated, paved garden path. About ten feet from the front door, Mike stopped and looked at Nash.

"My Bruce, what a lovely garden," Mike took a few steps toward the roses growing up against the infamous window.

"Here," he said, "these are gorgeous. Come here and tell me what these are called," he asked, gesturing to Nash to join him.

"Certainly." Nash came over next to Mike.

Mike put his face up against the glass and peered into the window in the gap between the drapes.

"What on earth are you doing? What the hell are you looking at?"

Mike turned to Nash and made the instant decision not to implicate Fern. He looked at Nash with those penetrating eyes of his.

"I happened to pop by some time ago, and being a lover of gardens, I parked my car outside and walked up to this exact spot to admire these roses. This was only after I'd tried to ring the front door bell, but it wasn't working. Then while examining the flora, I saw through this exact window..." he paused a moment for full effect. "Mr. Nash, I saw you suffocate your wife. Can you imagine my surprise?"

Nash visibly gasped and went pale. He started to breathe loudly and deeply. The shock was enormous.

"What hogwash are you talking about?"

Mike removed his cell phone from his pocket and immediately went to the gallery and recorded videos on his phone. "A video paints a thousand words, as you know, Bruce, from your police days. In this case, a video paints a million pictures." Mike hit the play button, maximizing his screen. "Come, let's watch together, or perhaps we should go inside so we can see better."

Nash was ashen. The part where he placed a pillow over Merle's head while she slept and pushed down hard was displayed on Mike's screen.

Nash knew the chips were down. He had been checked-mate, his face now the color of putty.

"Please, yes, let's go inside."

Mike followed him, noting that Nash's pace was a tad wobbly.

Inside, Nash went straight to the cabinet in his dining room and removed a bottle of scotch. It was the first time that he'd indulged in alcohol before lunch since his wife's death. He poured a double with shaking hands and knocked at least half back in one gulp. Then he pulled up a chair and sat.

"Spell it out. What do you want? How much? I don't even know your name."

"Pleased to meet you officially, Bruce. I am Mike. Some call me mad Mike. What I want isn't money. I have plenty of that. What I want is that you never, never ever walk past the Jones' house ever again. Never! That if by any chance you bump into one of the Jones women anywhere, whether it be in the local village, the city, or Timbuktu, you walk past, you do not stop, you do not say hello. Because, Bruce, if you ever do one of these things again, the video of you murdering your helpless wife will be sent to the police and to the media. And, with my connections, we can upload it to YouTube and let it become viral. I don't think you would like that. Your life would be so miserable you'd wish someone would put a pillow over your head. Do you understand me loud and clear?"

Nash had dealt with lots of low-lifes during his days on the force. He had faced countless petty criminals and some of Melbourne's notorious felons, including rapists, murderers, and drug smugglersHe had never feared for his life. There was something sinister about this man that made him know he would follow through on his threat. This man was deadly.

"You have m-m-my, word, Mike," he stammered in fear. "What, w-w-what the hell are they hiding that you do not w-want me near the property?" chills ran through his body.

"They are hiding nothing. Who would feel safe with a killer lurking about? Would you invite a murderer over for tea?" Mike laughed and walked towards the front door but stopped and faced Nash again in the hallway.

"Oh, one last thing. I have duplicate backup copies of this brutal killing not only on my mobile but also on my laptop, on a disk, and a couple of memory sticks, so we are fully covered."

Mike then walked out the door and slammed it shut.

Nash was shocked, lost for words. He sat with his head in his hands for a few minutes, gathering his thoughts. He then went to his study and removed the ring from the drawer. He twirled it around. Poor, poor Sophia Semenov. Forgotten and abandoned. Even Fern, her own daughter, who shared her body, doesn't know of her existence. Lost and drowned under the influence of drugs, the young Russian shared her body with everyone, including a shark.

Chapter Thirty-Seven

The Stork Center's back door was open, but Mike knocked loudly before entering.

Fern met him in the doorway.

"Hey,, how're you doing?" she said, glad to see him, in spite of wanting to seem distant.

"When you are happy, I am happy. I heard it went well with the Harrises."

"You know? Is there anything you don't know?" she laughed. "How do you know, by the way?"

"By your eyes and your smile. I also saw them leaving. They looked pretty ecstatic too! Come, let's go to the boardroom. We need to talk."

"Sure, what's up?"

Mike ignored Fern's question. "Where's your mom?" he asked.

"She took Ivan for ice cream and shopping. It will probably be the last time she gets to spend any time with him. She's grown fond of him."

"Ah, the Harrises are taking the little boy as well? Now, *that's* something I didn't know. Well done! I'm glad to hear it. It would have been sad to separate them."

"Yep, done deal," Fern said elatedly.

"Money in your account?"

"Will be by tonight."

"Fern, when the money's in, *then* it is a done deal," Mike corrected.

Fern sat at the head of the boardroom table and Mike took a seat to her right. She looked at him quizzically.

"Nash is no longer a problem," he said matter-of-factly.

"Why, what's happened?" Nothing rash, she hoped.

"When the Harrises were leaving, I was coming up the road. I saw Nash gazing at your property outside the gate and we had a little discussion. And, then we went to the movies together," he said, shrugging his shoulders and smirking.

Fern knew instantly what he meant.

"Jeez, Mike — you showed him the video?"

"Yep, the one you directed. What was it called? Something like *The Cop Who Kills*. But don't worry, I let him think I filmed it."

"How the hell did *you* get it? It's on my phone."

"The other day I sent it from your cell to mine."

"When did you do that?"

"Not important."

Fern was silent, annoyed, but, a few seconds later, she burst out laughing.

"Wow, you really are something, aren't you? I should be mad with you for going behind my back," she said, her grin belying her words.

Mike started to laugh too, and she felt something stir within her. It was such a warm feeling knowing that someone had her back.

Then her smile slipped.

"And now you look worried again. Spit it out, Fern. What's troubling you?"

"Last night, I had a nightmare that Dad was not dead. He was pushing the buzzer at the front gate, and guess what? He was with Nash."

"You serious? This guy really has gotten under your skin."

"Mom heard me shout out, but she managed to calm me down."

"Your mom is a special lady. But you don't have to worry anymore. Believe me, Nash is no longer a threat to you or to any of us. You have my word."

Their eyes locked for a moment. Then Mike suddenly became businesslike.

"You told Nash you're running a guest house here. Now it's official, I'll get on to Danny about doing the necessary permits and licenses so we can deflect any suspicion. How about calling it *Rainbow Creek Guest House*? We'll make some elegant gold plaques to put on the front doors of the cottages. This will serve to discriminate between your home and the guests' quarters. You can order them online. Don't put any guest-house signage on the front gate, however. If anyone questions you about that, just say we are respecting our high-profile guests' privacy. It is not our policy to advertise. Discretion is our priority. Otherwise, signage like that might put off prospective parents."

"I agree." It made her happy they were so in sync.

"By the way. I fly out tomorrow on Qantas Airlines back to Bulgaria. I'm going to connect with the young girl again — the one I told you about, Anna. Also, did you contact Danny? He needs to do the birth certificates for Ivan and Nikol Harris?"

"It's being taken care of."

"Good. Anything else I need to know?"

"Yes, I received an email from an African couple wanting an African baby. They live in Sydney. You might have to fly to Africa. At least you can go on safari, you lucky bugger."

"I don't have to go to Africa to go on safari, Fern. I can go right here in Australia. Africa has the *Big Five*, but we've got the KKK."

Fern lifted her eyebrows, "KKK, what do you mean? Not Ku Klux Klan I hope."

Mike chuckled, "KKK stands for kangaroos, kookaburras, and koalas, dear girl."

Fern laughed, and so did Mike.

"Mike, you are something."

"I know. You said that already," he retorted somewhat sheepishly.

"On a serious note, here's where I am at. I fly out tomorrow. I will spend a week or two locating babies who need homes. In the meantime, you do research on the slums of Africa; they are not short of them. I think Kenya has the largest poverty level and sprawling kilometres of shantytowns in Africa and possibly in the world."

Fern nodded.

"Also, you need to prep Alice. She will need to be ready to fly out with Oliver as soon as I have confirmed the new arrivals to come and pick them up—thank God, my diaper duty and feeding days are over!"

"Methinks the gentleman doth protest too much," Fern teased. "Come on, Mike, fess up. You loved playing daddy to baby Nikol?"

Mike rolled his eyes. Fern chuckled and then assumed a businesslike manner.

"So, do you think you will be flying back with Alice and the parcels?"

"Time will tell, maybe. But, depending on the information you find out, I may head over to Africa. Anyway, we will stay in close contact and will make that decision when we have more intel."

Just then, Alice walked into the boardroom to announce Sheelah's arrival.

"Sheelah?" Mike raised his eyebrows.

"Hopefully, our new nurse," Fern explained. "Alice recommended her. Sheelah also specializes in newborns."

"Good, I'm glad that's in hand. I will walk with you."

They arrived at the Center's reception area, and Alice performed the introductions.

Fern looked at Maggie, who was busy with baby Nikol. "Maggie, can you hold the fort for a short while? I want Alice to spend some time with us in our meeting."

"Sure, Ma'am," Maggie replied.

"Mike, you are welcome to join us," Fern added.

"I'll sit in for a short while, then I have errands to run."

They left Maggie with the baby, and the four of them walked to the boardroom.

Fern asked Alice to explain how she and Sheelah knew each other and then asked Sheelah to explain why she wanted the position. Afterward, Fern excused Alice and Mike took the opportunity to leave at the same time.

As Fern walked him to the boardroom door, he said to her in a low voice, "First impression, I like her. She seems ideal."

"Thanks, Mike. Safe flight, keep in touch."

"A hug? You deserve one."

They hugged briefly. It was the first time she had hugged him properly, and it felt good. Mike was family.

Mike departed, and Fern carried on the interview with Sheelah Carrera.

It turned out Sheelah was very much like Alice, a solid person, dedicated to her profession and thorough.

Fern stood up. "Thank you, Sheelah, for your time."

Sheelah stood and shook hands. "When do you think you'll be making a decision, Ms. Jones?'

"I'm not."

"Gosh, I don't understand," Sheelah said in a confused voice. She thought the interview had gone well.

Fern smiled, "No need to get back to you, Sheelah. I like what I see, and I am offering you the job today."

Sheelah's smile lit up her face.

They walked back together, and Fern immediately approached Alice.

"Alice, you can welcome Sheelah to the Stork Center. She is our newest staff member!"

"Why, that's marvelous!" Alice said, smiling too.

"Good, and how has Maggie been doing?" Fern asked.

"'Very well. We have a really good team now."

"We need one as we will soon be taking delivery of a few new babies. I don't think I mentioned to you, baby Nikol and baby Ivan have been officially adopted by the Harrises."

"Oh, I am so glad. They seemed a nice couple," Alice commented.

Fern turned to Sheelah, "I nearly forgot. Sheelah, when can you start?"

"In two weeks, if I give notice tomorrow."

"Give your notice in tomorrow, and I will arrange a doctor's certificate to say you are sick with something like bronchitis. I need you here this week."

"Ms. Jones, I have never done anything like that in my life. It's just not me," Sheelah protested.

Fern never took her eyes off Sheelah. "Sheelah, that's good to know. But I simply need you to start by the weekend. Why don't you tell your boss this new job will only be on the table if you can start in a week, and I'm sure it will be okay," Fern encouraged confidently. "They won't want to stand in your way. The ball's in your court."

Sheelah thought seriously for a moment. She wanted the job.

"Okay, I'll do it. Yes, I'll do it!"

"Alice will give me your details, and I will email you our contract and offer by tomorrow."

"Thank you, Fern. I will see you soon then." Sheelah was grinning.

Fern left Alice and Sheelah to check to see if the funds had arrived in her account from the Harrises, although it was probably still a bit too soon. She also needed to chase up with Danny about the progress of the birth certificates.

The money had not arrived yet. Danny confirmed he was working on the birth certificates for Ivan and Nikol and would have them within a couple of days.

Nash sat on his veranda, Mike's words still reverberating in his head. He was ashamed and devastated that he had been seen carrying out the mercy killing of his wife. But he was equally troubled by the fact Mike said he would not report it but use it against him. Why not report it? His detective mind was doing overtime again. What was the hidden agenda? What was behind the gates to the phony guest house? Was it even a guest house? Something fishy was going on, but Nash knew he had been cornered. He had to keep away.

Now that Merle was gone, Nash spent more time with his retired colleagues. He also changed his route and walked in the opposite direction of the Jones place. His mind was constantly churning, and he talked more often to himself, especially on his daily walk. As much as he still kept fit, he did not like what he saw in the mirror. He noticed his face was more wrinkled, and puffy bags had started to develop under his eyes. He was also becoming more forgetful.

That night Fern ate dinner with Megan and Ivan, then she excused herself and went to work on her laptop. The money was still not in, but there were a few email queries about potential new adoptions.

The first one she read was from a Kenyan couple who lived in Sydney. Mr. Bayana Mwangi wrote he was due to visit Melbourne on business and wished to meet her during the week. Fern replied she would be in touch to set up an appointment soon.

Then there was an email from a gentleman from St Kilda in Melbourne who expressed interest in adopting a baby boy. Fern let him know there was a procedure, and first, they would have to meet.

Fern researched the slums of Kenya and established that Kibera, just outside the capital of Nairobi, was the largest shantytown in all of Africa. It was listed as among the top ten poorest areas in the world. She sent a one-word text message to Mike: *Kibera*.

She checked her account one last time before turning in for the night. Fern smiled devilishly. The three-hundred and fifty-thousand dollars had been deposited.

The following day Jack and Wendy Harris came and collected baby Nikol and little Ivan. It was a happy day for the Harrises. Ivan was smiling, too, though he didn't understand why Megan wasn't there to wave him off or why she had cried when she made him breakfast this morning. But he liked the way his new father kept his hand on his shoulder as everyone said goodbye. Ivan could tell it was going to a good home.

Chapter Thirty-Eight

M r. Bayana Mwangi's flight from Sydney landed in Melbourne as the sun was waking up, and he went straight to the rental car office to pick up his car for the trip. He drove directly from the airport to his business meeting in the city and afterward drove out to the Dandenong.

He was happy to experience the change of scenery and was amazed to witness the contrast. He noticed a forest of trees and interesting places to walk and explore.

He arrived at the front gate, and he stretched his arm out the car window and pushed the buzzer. Fern answered and instructed him to drive around to the back and park.

The grounds were beautifully landscaped and well kept. Bayana was immediately hit by the peaceful ambiance and the sounds of birds in the trees.

Fern stood smiling as he exited his car.

"Welcome to Melbourne, Mr. Mwangi, and welcome to the Stork Center."

"Hello, Fern. You have a delightful place here."

"Thank you. Come, let us first go to my office. I'm sure you would love a coffee?"

"Most considerate, and thank you."

Fern opened her office door, and Bayana Mwangi indicated to Fern to enter first. She liked that.

"Please sit, Mr. Mwangi, and make yourself comfortable."

"Thank you, Fern. I insist you call me Bayana."

"Will do. How do you like your coffee Bayana?"

"As it comes, do you have a machine?"

"Sure do. There's one in our kitchen."

"In that case, a cappuccino will be lovely."

Fern phoned her mother and asked her to arrange it.

Bayana asked to use the bathroom and excused himself. Fern guessed what he really wanted to do was have a quick look around on his own. She liked that too — it showed he wanted to be sure they were a well-run operation.

When he returned, he was greeted by Maggie, who placed the coffee tray on the table.

"Thank you," he said.

"Bayana, let's chat, and then I will show you my center. We just had two adoptions a couple of days ago, and so the center is empty at the moment. We are expecting new arrivals in the next week or so."

Bayana swallowed another mouthful of coffee.

"Fern, I will get to the point. My wife, Dinka, and I have been happily married for a decade now, but six years ago, we suffered a major tragedy. In two weeks time, it will be exactly six years that we lost our only hope," he looked down, avoiding eye contact. "You see, Dinka was five months' pregnant when her appendix burst. Thankfully Dinka survived but not our unborn child. There were complications, and, sad to say, she cannot carry a child ever again." Bayana paused for a moment and looked away off to his right as if gazing back into the past. Then he gave his head a brief shake and looked directly at Fern.

"So," he said, clearing his throat. "What can you do for us, Fern? My wife has never really recovered emotionally, and the anniversary is around the corner. It is always particularly hard for her. I am convinced my *old* Dinka would return if a child were to be placed in her arms. I would like this to happen as soon as possible, and I do not care about the cost. What I care about is that the child is African, for obvious reasons. Is there any chance you can do whatever it takes to give us a son or daughter for the anniversary of our lost baby?"

Fern thought deeply for a few seconds. "I am sorry for your loss, Bayana. That must have been a devastating time for you and your wife," she gently smiled.

"All our babies are Australian. However, we are well connected, and I think it might be possible to arrange for an African baby. However, this would entail a massive amount of logistics and all kinds of red tape and planning. I believe it is achievable, but it would be costly. We also ensure that all our babies are healthy and documented."

"What do you mean by logistics?"

"We would have to fly a plane to Africa once we have located a healthy baby that is up for adoption; the costs involved in doing that are enormous. Also, it could take up to a year or more to apply for an adoption visa."

"Heavens, I never thought about this kind of detail," a concerned Bayana said.

"And, of course, finding a healthy baby in Africa is tantamount and takes time given the prolific diseases to run health checks and make sure any medical concerns are completed."

"Oh, of course!"

"Bayana, what if I could wave a magic wand for you?"

"Then I would pay all costs, and I would throw in a million-dollar bonus on top of that."

"I see. You know, with an adoption visa, your baby would enter Australia as a permanent resident, and he or she would be eligible immediately for healthcare and citizenship after a while," Fern said.

Bayana thought for a second or two. He could put two and two together and could see what Fern was proposing might not be above board. But he decided he didn't care. He hated watching his wife disappear and suffer in agony over their loss. "You make it happen, and so will I," he said, looking her in the eye acknowledging the deal and game plan.

"Okay, great! To get the ball rolling, you need to scan every page of your passport, including the front and back covers, and email me. You must include your wife's passport details as well. I will also need scanned color copies of your citizenship certificates, a letter of employment, and a full police criminal background check from both of you as well as bank statements and financials from your accountant. If you can get this to me asap, I will do my best to make this happen in six weeks. Also, here are our own forms for you to fill out. When this is all done, I will need the full amount up front. I will email you the exact figure and bank details for the wire before the day is over."

"Excellent," Bayana nodded in agreement. "I look forward to that," Bayana said.

"In my email, I will confirm everything and the documents required. Now let me take you on tour."

Meanwhile, Mike had landed in Sofia and had booked into a different hotel. It had been a long flight. He napped for an hour and then showered as he knew he had to be fresh and alert later.

He took a cab a few long blocks down to the park where he'd met Anna by the swing. Again, he sat on a bench, watching and waiting to no avail. A few kids played, but there was no Anna. He was hungry, but he could go without food. He waited, and still no Anna.

He saw a small group of kids and approached them. He asked if they knew who Anna was and described her to them in their language. He explained that he had arranged to meet her and her mother, who was his cousin.

They all shook their heads. No one knew Anna or of her. Mike left and returned to his hotel.

This was not good. He needed a contact here, and he was also concerned for her safety and welfare.

He ordered room service and opened up his laptop.

He knew there was a large ghetto area where the poverty was extreme and hundreds lived on the streets just outside the city. He checked with the concierge and found out Plovdiv was about ninety minutes or not much more by car.

He weighed up his options and decided to go there first thing in the morning.

Bayana was impressed with his short tour of the Stork Center. Fern walked him to his car. Bayana opened his car door and sat inside a moment with the door open, lost in thought. He slipped his key into the ignition, and Fern swung the door shut. Bayana rolled down his window.

"Fern, give me an idea of what I am in for, more or less?"

"A lifetime of happiness! If I can locate a healthy baby from Kenya and cut through all the red tape in record time, you will be looking at about a million bucks. And, then, there is your bonus…"

"Do it! I'll send you a million by the end of the day, and if you deliver within two weeks, I will transfer another million. I guess the ball, madam, is in your court. Thank you, Fern. I am impressed."

"Be well, Bayana. By the way, you didn't say whether you have a preference—a boy or girl?"

"Healthy is all we ask! In my heart, I would like a boy; my wife would say a girl. So, it makes no difference."

As he drove out, he thought that Fern must have connections in the highest places — or the lowest. He also knew it was a crazy amount of money, but he had more, and his wife was the love of his life.

Fern phoned Mike and told him to finish up in Sofia and be in Kenya within a couple of days.

Mike responded by telling her to prepare Alice, Sheelah, and even Maggie for an overseas flight. He also told her to phone Danny and let him know she would be emailing all the documentation from Bayana to him so he could get cracking on the necessary documents, including an adoption visa for Australia.

Fern slept well that night.

The morning crept in. The sun was all but hidden behind a veil of pollution that engulfed the city of Sofia.

Mike realized he was fighting time. He left early by bus for Plovdiv, which was the second largest city in Bulgaria. The trip took a good two hours. As he got off the bus, he saw a rough-looking person talking on his cell phone. Mike approached him, and he hung up.

"Hey, mister, I see you have a cell phone."

The heavily tattooed man looked at Mike. "So? Everyone has one."

"Do you know where I can get one? I could do with one, you know, one that someone has lost?" he asked cautiously, showing the man some bills.

The man was no stranger to the streets and knew Mike was looking for a *burner*. This man didn't want his calls traced and would ditch it within a few days. He looked at Mike, taking in his appearance and sizing up his wallet. He figured he would pay good money to assure the safety of his calls.

"Loud and clear, mister. I can get you one in an hour, but it will cost you a thousand leva."

"My budget is four hundred," Mike snapped back. "No more." This was not his first rodeo.

"No way, mister."

"Can you get me one sooner?"

"Ten minutes."

"If you're back in ten minutes, I will give you eight hundred. One minute over ten, the price drops to four. I'll be gone in twenty minutes. Deal?"

"Deal, mister, where will I find you?"

"Right here."

He disappeared, and Mike crossed the street. He walked about a hundred feet and took up surveillance of the area.

Fifteen minutes later, Mike saw the man return. He was looking everywhere for Mike, anxiety written all over his face. Mike crossed the street and approached the man from behind.

"Hey! Buddy, where's the phone?"

"Right here." He extracted the cell phone from his inner pocket.

"You're late, never made it in ten. Four hundred is the deal unless you give me your SIM card."

"Why not? Makes no difference to me!" he shrugged, doubling his money for a stolen SIM card. He happily removed the SIM cards from both phones and swapped them.

Mike gave him the cash and left.

Mike walked a few blocks and saw a group of men lounging on the sidewalk smoking. He approached them, asking for a smoke. They eyed him up and down. One guy who looked like he was in his fifties with grey hair and a goatee offered him a cigarette from his packet. Mike helped himself, "I'm looking for a ride to Stolipinovo?" He lit it and, without inhaling blew the smoke out slowly. "Do you own a car? There is three hundred in it for you if you're interested?"

The man nodded and pulled out his car keys. He indicated for Mike to follow him around the corner. He walked up to an old brown Skoda and got in the driver's seat.

They drove to the fringe of the gypsy slum district, and the smell told Mike they had arrived. The driver turned to Mike and asked him where he wanted to go. Mike told him to drive in deeper.

He drove slowly, and in minutes hundreds and hundreds of shacks and shanties with warped walls surrounded them on the filthy potholed road littered with trash. Mike saw kids playing in the muck and filth; one group was feeding a fire with broken pieces of wood from a dumped and broken baby crib. Some of the kids stared at the car, and two even grinned at them. There was a dirty kid with bare feet, who couldn't have been older than ten, dragging on a cigarette and staring as the car went by. The stench, Mike saw, came from the open sewerage lines overflowing and trickling across the road. There were broken bottles, discarded soda cans, plastic bags, papers flying around, and large pieces of rusted, broken fencing by the side of the road. Children sat on rocks passing the time of day as weeds invaded the area.

The stench in the air forced Mike to breathe through his mouth.

He then saw a few men and women milling around.

"Stop, stop here!" Mike ordered the driver.

He looked at Mike, "You know, mister, there are more murders here and robberies than in the entire country. What you doing here?"

"I'm looking for an old friend. Tell me, driver, what is your name?"

"Peter. Why do you ask?"

"Peter, I am going to need a ride out of here today and a driver for the next couple of days."

"What are you proposing?"

"How much do you make in a day? I bet no more than fifty leva? Sixty, seventy — you tell me, Peter."

"Mister, some days I can make one hundred and fifty in a day and into the night. I also do odd jobs for all kinds of people."

"Okay, Peter. Here's the deal: you work for me now and every day and sometimes at night too for a short while. I'll pay you five hundred leva a day in cash and even a little extra for gas. If you do a good job, and keep your mouth shut, there will be a bonus. Understand? That is over two hundred and fifty US dollars per day, Peter."

Peter smiled. "Yes, boss, sure boss, you got a deal."

"Okay, now you follow me in your car while I get out and walk. If I disappear, you wait where you last saw me. Now, give me your phone number."

Mike punched it in and hit the call button. Peter's phone rang, and Mike immediately terminated the call and added Peter's name next to it.

"You now have my number." Mike climbed out of the car and headed toward the small group of women. As he got closer, a rat scurried for safety from a pile of garbage.

The group of women spotted Mike coming toward them and started to split up and walk in different directions. He chose the best-dressed one and caught up to her.

"Ma'am, no reason to be afraid, I am not a policeman nor a pimp, and I do not want sex, please. Just give me a minute of your time. I am looking for someone. I am an Australian."

The lady stopped and looked at Mike.

"So, what do you want?"

"My name is Mike. What's yours?"

"Stella."

"Stella, is there somewhere we can talk? Too many prying eyes here. Is there a place close?"

"Why? I do not know you. What are you after? Leave—go away!"

"Stella, I am just looking for some information. You help me, I help you. For a few minutes of your time, a few questions and I will pay you one hundred leva. If you can help, there will be more, much more money. Now take me to a place where we can get a coffee and talk."

"Come," was all she said while pointing up ahead to the right that led to a dilapidated path.

Mike followed and glanced over his shoulder and saw with relief Peter edging behind them in his car.

"So, what is it you want to know?" Stella asked while they walked.

"I represent an international humanitarian group that finds loving homes for abandoned babies. We also offer money to parents who cannot afford their babies and want to find homes for them. Our clients are couples who cannot have children of their own and want to adopt."

"Carry on," she said with curiosity.

"We locate healthy babies for good, wealthy people who want children to raise as their own. They have been to the best doctors for help but without success. They have given up hope. We check out these people thoroughly. We go out of our way to make sure these couples have no criminal record and are not associated with any human or sex trafficking organizations in any way."

Stella took this all in without comment. She then glanced at Mike a couple of times.

"Up here, we go up here," she said, pointing to a staircase.

Mike was forced to walk behind her as the rickety stairway was so narrow.

He saw they were going into someone's home.

Stella removed a tiny drawstring pouch bag from her bra and pulled out a key, and unlocked the door. Inside they were greeted by an old woman who eyed Mike very suspiciously.

"This is my grandmother. She rules this area and is known as *the iron lady*. Take no notice of her age. She knows everything that goes on around here."

"'Pleased to meet you," Mike offered his hand, giving his most friendly face.

"Ah, even though you have a foreign accent, you speak our language," the old lady commented, warming to Mike's charm.

"I do."

Stella held her hand up in the direction of her grandmother. Then she turned to Mike.

"Tell her what you do and why you are here, Mr. Mike."

Mike explained again what he was doing in the area. He showed her his ID. Director of *United Children of the World Relief and Safety Fund*. Danny had carefully given the laminated card a worn look, with a slightly younger headshot of Mike, giving it great authenticity.

The old lady smiled and said it would take time.

Mike said he was looking for three babies now and more in the days ahead.

He offered her a thousand dollars for each baby. The old woman's eyes lit up, and soon Mike was making arrangements to return in two days. He gave them his new phone number. Stella's grandmother was suddenly very happy and hospitable. She insisted Mike stay and enjoy a coffee. She even produced some cake which went down very well. He didn't realize how hungry he was.

Grandmother obviously took note as, when he got up to leave, she stuffed a ripe banana in his hand for the road trip back.

"Thank you again for your kind hospitality," Mike smiled. "I will see you in two days to pick up any packages you have."

Stella walked Mike down the stairs. He was behind her again and now that he was more relaxed, he was able to eye her figure. She was slender and attractive. She also had a pretty face with dark eyes and high cheekbones. He thought all she needed was a good makeover, and she would be very desirable. But Mike reminded himself that she was going to be his contact in the field, and he needed to be professional, not proposition her. He also felt instinctively it would not be a good idea to get on the wrong side of Stella's grandmother.

At the bottom of the stairs, Mike bid her farewell and made his way across the large, sandy, littered patch of ground in the direction where Peter had dropped him off.

He instantly saw three people up ahead on his right, and they were walking directly toward him. He smelt trouble but continued until he could see their faces clearly.

314 STEVEN IRWIN FINE

There were two adults and a youngster. Mike recognized the youngster as the one he had seen smoking when he arrived. He quickly sized up the two adults; one was solid and tough looking in his dirty black string tank top, but Mike was more concerned about the skinny guy with the grey and maroon windbreaker. He knew this could mean a concealed weapon.

As their paths crossed, the solid guy gripped Mike by the arm and pulled him close. Mike had no space to throw a punch. In a split second, he pulled his own head back as far as he could and, with all his might, head-butted the guy square on the nose. He stumbled awkwardly. The skinny guy went for something under his windbreaker. Mike immediately hooked him with a hard punch to the side of his head, and he went down. Mike then turned and swung a right hook at the big guy, who was swearing and clutching a badly broken split nose, the blood splattering down like twin waterfalls from his nose. Mike then kneed him hard in the balls and punched his eye as he went down.

The kid ran away, and Mike swore. This may have complicated the operation.

Peter, who had witnessed Mike's confrontation, drove up as quickly as he could tooting his horn for Mike to get in.

Mike didn't need a second invitation. "Let's get the hell out of here," and leaped into the car.

"You bet, boss, you bet. Where to?"

"Sofia, back to the city."

"Gee, boss, you sure know how to take care of yourself."

Mike ignored the comment. He was in deep thought and relieved to be leaving the slums.

Peter dropped Mike off a block away from his hotel. Mike wanted it that way. He told Peter to be on standby, as tomorrow or the next day, he would need to return to Plovdiv and Stolipinovo.

Chapter Thirty-Nine

Fern smiled to herself as she sat in front of her laptop, looking at her growing bank balance. Bayana was a man of his word. After so many expenses, it was good to see funds coming in.

Without wasting time, Fern picked up the intercom, "Alice, would you and Sheelah come through to the boardroom, please? I need a word."

Alice wondered what was up — maybe they were being sent home. Things were really quiet.

The two did not know what to expect as they sat down.

Fern smiled quickly to put them at their ease and was then immediately serious.

"Do you two have valid passports?"

"Why, Fern?" Alice asked, taken aback.

"We need you to go overseas just for a couple of days."

"What for? I mean, yes, I was abroad recently. My passport is valid," Alice confirmed.

"And you, Sheelah?" Fern asked.

"Oh, I got a new passport when I went to Italy last year."

"Great!" Fern folded her arms and sat back in her chair. "As you already know, we rescue babies abandoned by their mothers. What you don't know is that we rescue them from all over the globe. Mike, our operations manager, visits the shelters in various countries to find suitable matches for our parents. He now needs your help."

"The long Easter weekend is coming up next month, Fern. Would we be going before or after Easter?" Alice enquired.

"I am waiting for a call today or tomorrow from Mike. If, as I expect, you'll fly out within a day or two."

"Wow, so soon, Fern!" Sheelah exclaimed.

"Short notice, and how long will we be gone, Fern?" Alice asked.

"As I mentioned before, ladies, traveling on short notice is part of our work."

Alice looked at Sheelah as if waiting for another comment, then back to Fern.

"Where are we going?"

"Bulgaria. There will be a couple of stop-overs but just for refueling and time to stretch your legs and freshen up."

The nurses didn't look so keen.

"Look, I know it is short notice, but as we grow, I will employ more people, which should take the pressure off."

"I guess we need to go home and pack. Which airline?" Alice asked.

"My airline. I forgot to mention, we have our own Learjet and full-time pilots, who are excellent. It is very comfortable, and you'll be in great hands." Fern smiled, knowing this would soften the deal.

"Wow!" Alice and Sheelah looked at each other, and their eyes sparkled with excitement. "Where exactly in Bulgaria?" Alice asked.

"Sofia, the capital."

"And then back home?" Sheelah asked.

"More than likely."

"Fern, please, I'm lost. What do you exactly mean by *more than likely*?" Alice was leery.

"Okay, you'll hook up with Mike in Sofia for a short while, and then you'll bring the babies back home. I'm just guessing until I know more, but I believe there will be two or three traveling with you."

Fern looked at Sheelah, "You'll stay here and look after the new babies," and then she turned to Alice, "You'll probably only be home for a night, and then the pilots will fly you to Kenya. Mike will take a commercial flight there and be at the airport to meet you. He will arrange hotel accommodation so you can stay a night, or two, maybe three at most, before heading home. You see, Mr. Bayana Mwangi, who came to visit, he and his wife are adopting a baby from Kenya."

"Fern, if there are three from Bulgaria, surely we will need an extra pair of hands?" Alice suggested. "Maybe Maggie can help out?"

"Good thinking. I had thought of that and am looking into it. Leave it with me. Suggest you go home early and leave now. Get some rest. You will need it. Stay home until I call you both."

It was an hour away without heavy traffic, but Fern liked to leave early for appointments to give herself plenty of time to find parking, a premium in many parts of Melbourne.

On the way to the coffee shop to meet Bill Pinkston in St Kilda, he called her and said he was standing outside and would wait for her. Fern was just a block away, and a few minutes later, she saw him. He was dressed in a dark suit and was bald with a mustache. He looked like he was in his sixties. A bit old to be an adopted parent, she thought.

He saw her at the same time.

"Ah, Fern Jones?"

"That's me, Mr. ..."

He put his hand out, and she noticed he had a limp handshake.

"Pinkie, please, everyone calls me that. Shall we? Let's go have a coffee. Are you hungry?"

"Not really. I had a bite earlier."

A waiter greeted them and ushered them to a table.

They sat, and he flung his car keys on the table. They ordered coffee and exchanged business cards.

"I'll get to the point, Ms. Jones. I want to adopt a little boy."

"Sure, Pinkie. You say *I*. Are you married?"

"No, but soon will be."

"Pinkie, we provide babies to couples who are in stable relationships and who, for whatever reason, can't have children of their own. Does that make sense to you?"

"No, it does not."

"Why not?"

"Look, let's just leave it then."

"Why? Firstly, adoption is about finding a suitable home for a baby. It's about me knowing everything about you and your partner. We do thorough background checks; on your history, where you live, character references, your financial ability to raise a child, and many other aspects. Our process is strict and takes time, so my company's reputation is built on a match par excellence. A match where I know the baby will be happy, and grows up in a healthy family environment and is well educated."

Fern paused before delivering the bottom line, "Forgive me, but you seem to be a bit old to adopt, you are not married, and you haven't offered any information about your fiancée and whether she is also interested in adopting. It is mandatory for me to meet both sets of parents to ascertain that it is a joint decision and a harmonious one."

"And what if I have no family?"

"Well, it is not our practice to cater to single parents. Of course, we have nothing against a single person. Many single parents do an excellent job. But nonetheless, research shows children are generally more confident and adjusted to life better in a two-parent home. When a child grows up without a strong family structure, it has an impact. I am not saying my answer is a definitive *no,* but I can promise you, I will discuss this with my team and get back to you." He looked at her, rather annoyed. "So," she said, "I need to look into it before we meet again."

Fern stood up, leaving her coffee on the table.

"Thank you for your time, Pinkie. I'll be in touch."

Before she could take a step to leave, he stood up abruptly, knocking over his chair and snatching his bunch of keys from the table. He brushed past Fern, furious. One of his metal keys caught her tan-colored Fendi purse near the bottom buckle. It locked for a second or two on the prong of the buckle, and with infuriating force, he yanked his keys loose and stormed off, cursing under his breath.

"Waste of my bloody time," he said.

Fern stood flabbergasted, embarrassed, and mad as hell. There was a momentary silence in the coffee shop as the other customers stared at her. They soon resumed their chatter, and Fern went to the cash register to pay for their coffees.

When she opened her bag to take out her wallet, she noticed a deep scratch, an inch-long cut gouged in the leather of her expensive purse. She pulled the purse closer to look and saw a small chip where a tiny piece of leather had been ripped off.

"Bastard!'" she vehemently mumbled under her breath and then realized the café manager was waiting to take her money.

"I apologize. Did you see what happened?"

"Afraid so," the manager said.

She was annoyed walking back to her car. There was something about that man that made her shudder, something creepy. She thought about the warning Uncle Lance had given her at the start about unsavory characters emerging whenever young children were involved.

Back in his hotel room, Mike showered, grateful to wash the Stolipinovo dirt and grime off his body. His fist still throbbed from the scuffle, and he had a headache from the head butt, but he didn't let any of this bother him.

He went straight back out again to the park with the hope of seeing Anna. At least, he didn't need to rely on her exclusively as he was confident Stella and her grandmother would deliver. He just wanted to know she was safe and well.

He walked through the park until he arrived at the swings. It was empty — no kids, no giggles of laughter. He walked up to the one empty swing, pushed it hard, turned his back, and left.

That night Mike ate alone in a local café and got to thinking how much he both loved and hated his job. He loved the idea of saving babies, but what he hated most was facing inhumane human suffering and desperation. His phone rang as he was paying for his meal.

"Mike? Mike, listen, it's Stella. We have three babies, but you must come now!" she whispered urgently into the phone.

"Stella, slow down. When are you getting them?"

"I've got them here. We've got them now."

"Are you saying you are already ready for a pickup?"

"Yes, yes, Mike. We have two girls, and we will also have a little boy early in the morning."

"Okay, Stella, listen, I can only get there when my staff arrives and that will be the day after tomorrow sometime. You must look after the babies until then. Is that possible?"

"Mike, we offered the people money for their babies. Come now, please."

"Stella, listen up. It is not possible. I can only pick them up when my staff arrives. They are in another country right now. I am sorry. Tell the people we will pay them extra if they hold onto the children a little longer. If you have to keep the babies now, go buy milk and whatever you need, and I will reimburse you, do you understand?"

"I suppose, but we have no cots — where will they sleep?" she said, sounding disappointed.

"Let their mothers take them back for a day or two longer if you can," Mike implored as he walked towards his hotel.

"Mike, it does not work like that," Stella hissed, frustrated.

"It does now," he insisted. "Do what you have to, and I will call you back within an hour." He hung up before she could respond.

Mike immediately phoned Fern. It was about lunchtime in Melbourne, he thought, as he glanced at his watch.

Fern didn't answer.

He called Oliver.

"I've got three parcels here in Bulgaria, with an urgent pickup deadline and another crucial collection outside Nairobi on the other side of the globe in fucking Africa. You need to fuel up and get your arse here now. Where's Fern? I can't reach her."

"Okay, Roger that. I'll call Morrie and get on it. I'll also make sure Fern calls you."

Mike glanced at his cell. There was a call waiting. It was Fern.

"Gotta go. Fern's on the other line. Talk later."

"Mike, you there?" Fern asked.

"Yep, listen up, Fern. I've secured three parcels outside Sofia. Oliver and Morrie must get cracking now and send Alice and Sheelah with them. Once they've dropped the parcels home, they'll be off to Kenya."

"Okay, let me get the ball rolling. I'll call you in five," she said, quickly adding, "Oh Mike, do you think you will need more helpers — should I send Maggie too?"

"Send her," came the short reply.

Oliver called Morrie—they were flying out that day.

Fern checked in with Danny. He assured her all the documents were in order and ready to deliver to Oliver. She then called Alice and Sheelah and told them to be ready in an hour and a car would pick them up from Alice's place. She called Mike back and gave him the news: the postal service was operating in full swing, and the couriers would be there to collect as arranged.

Fern rushed to find Megan, deciding literally on the run that she would go instead of Maggie, and her mother and Maggie could hold down the fort. It was time she got a feel for the business in the field.

Fern packed a small bag, grabbed her passport, and in minutes was on her way to Alice's place.

The girls were surprised when Fern showed up and joined the team and not Maggie. They left for the airport and rendezvoused in the VIP waiting lounge while Oliver and Morrie were doing last-minute flight checks and stocking up on food and snacks.

Oliver was surprised to see Fern and gave her a wink but didn't say anything.

He warned everyone to try to sleep as much as possible on the flight as a total of five stops in different time zones would make them more jet-lagged than going to the moon.

Before long, they were packed and had a full tank, and cleared for take-off. Destination Sofia, Bulgaria, via Darwin, Bangkok, and Oman.

Arriving in Sofia, Fern instructed Oliver to phone Mike to say they would reconvene at the hotel and not disclose she was on board. She wanted it to be a surprise. Mike asked Oliver to rent a car through the concierge for the next day for the *parcel* pick up. Oliver put the phone down before Mike got a chance to ask him how many people were in his party. He was hoping Fern had sent Maggie, along with Alice and Sheelah.

Mike phoned Peter and invited him to dinner. So far, Peter had been reliable, and he could use him in the future. He also confirmed he would need him to be on standby for tomorrow.

Mike called Stella back and told her he planned to be there around 10am for the pick-up. Stella sounded relieved. She had been juggling and holding off a few angry and hungry people.

Mike tried to call Fern, but there was no answer. He sent a text to everyone to meet in his hotel room at 6:15am for a briefing and update. It was agreed that the call time would be 7am and to make sure everyone had breakfast before they left for Stolipinovo. It would be a long day.

Later after dinner, Peter dropped Mike off at the hotel. He paused as he entered the lobby at reception, where there was a young woman on duty. Mike smiled while stopping at her desk. "I have not seen you here before, have I?" he asked, his smile making her feel she was the only woman in the world.

"It's my night shift week, sir. That's probably why."

"Do you work here full time, Violeta?" Mike read her name tag.

"No, sir, I'm studying at university."

"That's good to hear, Violeta. Education is important."

With another smile, he headed towards the stairs, and then a thought entered his mind and caused him to turn back. "Can you do me a favor, Violeta?" he asked.

"What is that, sir?" she said, eager to please this charming man.

"A few friends of mine have joined me. They only arrived today. I need to confirm they are here. Can I see the guest list?"

"I'm afraid I am not permitted to do that, sir," Violeta said with a regretful smile.

"It will only take a few seconds, Violeta. Please, I will make it worth your while." Mike removed his wallet, confident a student could not resist the chance of making a little extra.

He was right. With a slight blush staining her cheeks, she turned the computer screen around and Mike flicked through the visitors' names, looking for Maggie. He saw Alice Wilson and Sheelah Carrera but no Maggie Watson, and then he paled as he saw another name: Fern Jones, room forty-one.

Mike thanked Violeta and slipped her a generous tip.

He entered the elevator and got out on the fourth floor. He walked to number forty-one and stopped at the door. The light was on and he knocked hard.

"Who is it?" Fern called.

"Me, Fern, open up!"

Fern was caught off guard by the loud knock.

She opened the door with a big smile. "Hello, Mike, surprise, surprise!" she opened her arms wide in a big welcome gesture.

Mike stormed into her suite. Fern shut the door, confused and deflated.

"And now, what's the problem, Mike?"

"You are!"

"Eh? What do you mean?"

"You shouldn't be here! What are you thinking!" Mike was fuming. "Let me make myself very clear. For God's sake, Fern, this is a covert operation. What do you think that means? Business owners and leaders hire people on the ground to be their faces in the field. Why on earth did you come?"

Fern felt her blood pressure rise and her face go hot from a mixture of anger, disappointment, and embarrassment. "Mike, how dare you speak to me like that! As you point out, this is my business, my brainchild! If I want to experience the operational side and witness a collection myself, then that's my decision," she snapped, trying to regain her dignity.

"Not if it endangers the entire mission!" he spat back, and then, seeing she was close to tears, he added more quietly, "Look, I understand the desire to experience first-hand, but there is an element of danger in these pick-up locations. They are not pretty, and not only is the poverty ugly to witness, but the drugs and addicts and living conditions are very unhealthy. What happens if the jet goes down, or we have a serious car crash, or we are mugged or robbed? I tell you what happens. The Stork Center dies. Yes, no more Stork Center. Everyone, the pilot, the navigator, the head of operations, the nurses, and the owner, perish. Who else would be left to run this operation and keep it going into the future? No one, that's who," Mike had softened, feeling for his young charge." And for this reason, you can never do it again. Fern, please, I know these things. Please listen to me. If you had phoned from Australia, I would have explained then and there."

There was silence for a few seconds. Fern knew he was right, but she didn't want to admit it. "Fern, it's you I'm thinking of," Mike said, more friendly. "Come on, give me a hug and show me you're not about to give me the boot." He grinned kindly.

Fern gave a reluctant smile and then hugged him tightly. "You are right. It will not happen again. And the last person I'll be giving the boot to is you."

"Okay, what's done is done. Now that you're here, you might as well make yourself useful. We have a long day ahead of us tomorrow—get some sleep. The team meets at 6.15 am in my room."

Oliver arrived first, then Morrie, then Fern, and finally Alice arrived with Sheelah.

"Good morning!" Mike welcomed. "How is everyone doing? Nice to see you all." He smiled at Fern, looked back to the team, and continued.

Fern was grateful he didn't embarrass her in front of them but got straight down to business.

"Oliver and Morrie, we don't need you for the pick-up, so after breakfast, head back to the airport, fill up the jet and be on standby."

"Ladies, the place we are going to today is rough. It's very rough. It's a slum. We have a local driver. His name is Peter, and he has proven himself to be dependable. I am serious when I say make sure you stay close to me at all times. There are pick-pockets and beggars, so it is important you listen to me and do everything I tell you so everyone stays safe, and we get in and out without any trouble."

They all nodded in agreement, somewhat apprehensively.

'That's it for now. Alice, I take it you have all the supplies we need for the babies on board and also the essentials for the trip to pick them up and the car ride back to the airport?"

"We do," Alice assured him.

"Now remember we are not coming back here, so pack and take everything with you after breakfast. It is now 6.20 am. Let's go eat and at 6.55 am be ready outside. Oliver, will you take care of the hotel bill for everyone at the reception, and we will reimburse you? As you guys don't have to hurry, take all the overnight bags with you and make the jet ready for departure. We will see you at the airport, probably around lunchtime. Girls, you are responsible for the babies' bags. Now let us go — I can smell the bacon."

They all rolled out of Mike's room and headed for the dining room. Mike went outside to make sure Peter was in position.

After breakfast, they said goodbye to the pilots and climbed into Peter's car.

"Girls, meet Peter. Peter, meet Fern, Alice, and Sheelah. Now, let's move."

Mike sat in front, and soon, they were well on their way to Stolipinovo, the largest gypsy ghetto in Europe, for the rendezvous with Stella.

There was little discussion. It was still early, and a sense of trepidation hung in the air.

Fern was relaxed but alert and keen to get the babies. She saw it as a rescue operation.

Upfront, Mike chatted with ease with Peter, and eventually, they reached Stolipinovo.

As they approached the slew of shantytowns, Mike glanced at the girls in the mirror and observed their shocked, and sorrowful faces take in the squalor.

They drove deeper into the hell hole of humanity, and finally, Mike told Peter to stop.

"Okay, listen up. Girls, remember to stay close to me. Peter, you wait here until we come back. Keep your phone on."

"Yes, boss."

Alice looked at Mike and Fern, concerned. "I do not understand. Are we not picking the babies up from an orphanage?"

Fern turned to Alice, "Alice, I will explain more when we are on the way to the airport. Just know that we rescue discarded or neglected babies. We get them from the streets or from people who don't want them. We save them from mothers who might even abandon them or are in danger from family members. Trust me, we're not into exploitation, trafficking, or child labor. It's…"

"Enough—let's go," Mike interrupted. He felt this was not the time to be defending what they were doing. "Peter, see you soon."

They climbed out of Peter's car and followed Mike as he looked around. While walking, Mike phoned Stella to say they were approaching. They climbed the stairs to Stella's dark building and followed Mike to her door. They heard a baby crying, then a second. Mike knocked hard.

Stella heard them. She jumped up from her chair and opened the door.

"So glad you are here. We haven't slept well."

"Stella, good to see you. This is Fern, Alice, and Sheelah."

"Pleased to meet you, ladies. Come, come see."

Inside, Stella's grandmother greeted them all.

Fern, Alice, and Sheelah went straight to the babies while Mike chatted with Stella and her grandmother.

"Alice, Sheelah, come, let's check them out, change them and give them a fresh bottle," Fern said.

"Where's the third bambino?" Mike asked.

"I am going to fetch him now. It is just up the road. Mike, come with me."

He wasn't sure. It would split the team up, but it gave them time to organize the first two while he collected the third.

"Sure, let's first settle." Mike removed a small wad. He had the money ready, plus some extra. "You can count it; it is the amount we agreed upon plus some extra for your help."

Stella checked the money and smiled. "Thank you so much, Mike. Give me a second to put this out of sight, and then we go."

Mike spoke to Fern.

"You wait here until Stella and I return. We are going just a couple of blocks away to get the little boy. Stay put until we are back."

"Will do."

"Let's go, Mike," Stella said as she returned from her room. As they left the tiny flat, Stella handed Mike a little wrapped packet.

"What's this?" Mike asked as he took the small packet.

"A surprise snack, and believe me, it is. Have it later."

Mike knew he could not reject it. It was how the poor operated. Their kindness often surpassed the generosity of the wealthy, he thought.

He took the packet and placed it in the wide back pocket of his cargo pants.

Stella touched his arm every now and then on the way over, making him think perhaps she liked him. The feeling was kind of mutual.

While crossing a dirty path littered with empty beer bottles and plastic trash, something caught Mike's eye.

"Fuck!" he whispered loudly. "We've got trouble, Stella."

"Why, what do you mean?"

"When I was here before, two guys attacked me. Don't look now, but they are following us. They are after me, not you. I tell you what — when we get to those shacks ahead of us, you go grab the baby, and I'll lead them away. I'll meet you back at your place."

"Are you sure? I worry for you."

"Don't. Now go. Go!"

Stella glanced at him with concern and left, quickening her pace.

Mike glanced over his shoulder. They were half a minute behind. He noticed a semi-demolished building ahead. There were broken bricks all around and junk. The roof was gone, but many walls still stood erect. He ran to the building. He knew he had to lose them and return quickly to his team. The two thugs gave chase.

Mike entered the derelict building. He glanced left and right and turned sharp right, where there were more broken walls and rubble. Undaunted, he turned into an area where there was a high pile of junk, and amongst it, he could see a rusted metal fence post. Mike grabbed it quickly and soundlessly. He then crouched behind the junk pile and switched his cell phone onto silent.

Tense seconds later, via a gap in the pile, he saw one of the attackers enter the room with a knife in his hand; it was the big guy. The large thug looked around, then turned, and as he turned, Mike struck him full force across his head with the metal post.

He collapsed with a gaping, bleeding wound and was out for the count.

He knew the two had split up to look for him and the thin assailant concerned him more with his weapon. Mike left the big guy sprawled on the ground. He glanced at the knife that lay on the floor next to the attacker's hand but did not touch it as the metal post was a better weapon.

Mike clutched the short metal bar and stepped out into the passage, and as he did, he saw the thin assailant about fifty feet away to his left. The thin thug saw him at the same time and aimed and fired three quick shots with his pistol. Mike high-tailed it and ran, zig-zagging as he did. The attacker gave chase. Mike ducked into another broken-down area which was larger and resembled an old store room. Mike quickly hid behind a broken door. Suddenly, he felt dampness in his pants, and it was slimy. Was it blood, he thought? Had he been hit? There was no pain. It entered his mind that perhaps a nerve was severed, and that was why he felt nothing.

The thin attacker walked without a sound as he entered the room and approached the door with his gun ready to fire. Mike heard heavy breathing by the door. . Calmly, he slammed the door with all his might. It hit the attacker, and Mike followed it up with a punch that connected with the guy's head. A bullet went off from the attacker's gun but luckily went wide. He collapsed to the ground, still clutching his gun. Mike followed up again with a kick to his face. He knew he had to silence the thug. The last thing Mike wanted was to be chased with his team and the babies; he had to be silenced. Mike looked at him as he lay on the floor. The gun was inviting. The scumbag lay on the floor, moaning, and slowly started to get up. The metal bar came down, and the attacker was floored. Mike felt his pulse on the side of his neck; it was still beating.

He was relieved he hadn't killed him but also knew both men were concussed, if not worse.

In the confusion and chaos, Mike forgot about his pants and the dampness.

He dropped the iron bar to the floor and kicked the guy's gun away amongst some waterlogged empty carton boxes, and left.

As he was walking, he felt the slime in his pants and panicked for a second. He was highly concerned that if he was not wounded, he had soiled himself. He stopped and inserted his right hand down his underpants. He brought his hand out; there was no blood, but he was shocked to see brown goo on the tips of his fingers. "Fuck!" he yelled in embarrassment. He brought his fingers to his nose and then erupted in laughter. It wasn't crap; it was Nutella Chocolate Spread. A bullet must have nicked his pants, torn his pocket, and smashed its way through Stella's treat. A sandwich thickly spread with Nutella. Stella must have somehow obtained a jar of Nutella and thought he would enjoy it. She clearly didn't have much of an idea of the appropriate amount to use.

Still laughing in relief, he glanced at his cell phone and saw he had several missed calls from Fern and Stella. He took his phone off silent mode.

"Mike, what'd happened? We've been calling. Everything okay? We've been so worried. Stella's been back for a while."

"All good, Fern. I will see you shortly. Let me talk to her."

"Okay, hold on." Mike heard Fern call Stella to the phone.

"Mike, are you okay?"

"I've got something to ask you. The snack you gave me, it was Nutella, wasn't it?"

"Yes, I know you Australians are addicted to it. Why? Did I not put enough on?"

Mike laughed. "Aussies are addicted to Vegemite, although Nutella is also popular."

"What's so funny? Don't you like it? I went out of my way to get it for you."

"I'll tell you later," he chuckled.

He hung up and called Peter. He picked up the pace. Peter had heard the gunshots and asked Mike if he had heard them as well. "Of course! All good. Be ready within the hour. We will be leaving for the airport."

Mike walked through Stella's front door, and everyone stood up to greet him, showing off the three new little babies.

Stella was the first to speak, "What happened with those two guys? We thought we heard gunshots and were so worried," concern was written all over her face.

"All sorted, but I do need to get new pants on the way to the airport. Come, we must leave now."

Fern looked at Mike, "Your pants are torn and look dirty."

Mike immediately improvised, "Fell on the path and slipped. It was wet. Come, we must leave now."

"Wait,' Stella's grandmother interjected. She went off and returned with two pairs of men's pants. "I have these—they were my late husband's—try them on."

"Thank you, very thoughtful of you." Mike took the pants and went to another room. The style certainly belonged to an older person. He tried the grey pair on, and although a bit short in the leg, they were better; the only thing he needed but could not ask for were clean underpants.

"Stella," Mike called.

She came to see the new look. They chuckled, and then he explained what had actually happened; the chase, the attacks, and his pants ripped by a bullet shot that had grazed his backside and hit her sandwich!

As funny as the Nutella story was, she was concerned the two attackers might come looking for her. He reassured her they were not going anywhere in a hurry.

He kissed her goodbye, feeling a certain warmth between them, and said, "Stella, you'll see me soon. I promise."

Fifteen minutes later, they squeezed into Peter's car with the three babies and were on their way to Sofia International Airport, leaving behind the shantytowns of Stolipinovo and away from the Plovdiv district.

Oliver and Morrie were relieved to see them. The jet was fuelled up and ready to go.

Before flying out, Mike called a meeting in one of the departure lounge coffee shops. They all stood around him with the girls holding the babies. Both baby girls were quiet, but the boy was restless.

Mike addressed them. "Okay, listen up. Fern, Alice, and Sheelah, I suggest you visit the ladies and check out the baby-changing facilities. We will meet you back here at this coffee shop when you're finished. It is a long flight back home with the usual stops."

With the girls gone, the three men grabbed a large corner table.

"Nice pants you've got there, Mike," Oliver teased with a grin.

"Fucking hell, I was shot at, and a bullet grazed my arse. It sliced a neat path, cutting my pants. It was a very close shave."

"What? When, bro?" Oliver asked, alarmed.

"Jesus! What happened?" Morrie asked.

"I'll tell you when Fern gets back. I don't feel like repeating myself."

Mike suggested they order something to eat before their flight and handed Fern a menu as she sat down with a baby to join them.

She turned to Mike, "What do you mean, aren't you joining us?"

"Fern, think? Think…"

"Of course, you have got to get to Nairobi urgently."

"That's right." Okay, first things first. Do you want to know what happened to me in Stolipinovo?"

They all looked at him expectantly.

"Well, on my first foray into Stolipinovo, I ran into these guys and got involved in a fight. They attacked me, and I got the better of them. They didn't like that, and when I went with Stella to pick up the last little fella, we ran into those two scumbags. We had to split up so they would follow me. Long story short, we ended up in a broken-down building, and one by one, they found me. I took care of them, but one guy fired a few bullets at me while I was running for cover. A bullet slashed my cargo pants at the back and cut through my undies."

Mike paused for a second or two.

"What!" Fern uttered in disbelief.

"When we left Stella's place, she gave me a care package. She told me it was a snack for the road. What she didn't say was it was a Nutella sandwich spread so thickly you wouldn't believe it. I reckon she must have used half the jar. Later she told me she bought it at an international shop somewhere in Sofia. She was so proud of having found something special for me. But she sure didn't know how to spread it!" he grinned mischievously.

"She's got the hots for you, my boy," Oliver chuckled.

Mike ignored the comment and continued, "Well, when the second guy started shooting and shot my arse up, the Nutella sandwich exploded inside my undies. I could feel something sticky and put my hands down my pants, worried that I'd been shot. Well, my fingers came out dark brown. I panicked. I thought I'd shat my pants!"

Oliver started to laugh. "So, you're telling us you kept your cool when two blokes were trying to kill you and then went to pieces over a bit of shit?"

Morrie joined in, "Yeah, any normal person would be more afraid of being shot, but you, dude, you worry more about crapping your pants."

Everyone started laughing, including Mike. They laughed so hard that the people at the other tables turned to stare at them."

At that moment, Alice and Sheelah returned with the two other babies wondering what was so funny.

Mike finally called them to order.

"Okay, enough, guys. Do what you have to. I'm staying behind to grab a shower. But first I'm going to buy new undies and decent pants, then I'll book my flight to Nairobi. Fern, I will coordinate with you from Nairobi because Oliver and Morrie will have to pick me up. I'm not boarding any international flight back home with a baby. Send Alice or Sheelah to fly back with me, but this time, to make it easier, I will arrange to meet them at the airport with the baby. I do not want any of the girls to accompany me into Kibera. It's not safe. Kibera is the largest slum in Africa, outside Nairobi in Kenya. There are a quarter of a million people there. I do not want a repeat of Stolipinovo."

Fern added, "Mike's right. It will be much easier to touch down and take off instead of everyone running around in Nairobi and Kibera. You know the nickname for Nairobi is *Nairobbery*, so be careful, and no Nutella, please." That set everyone off laughing again until Mike once again called them to order.

"Enough! Let's get something to eat. I'm hungry. Then you guys must be off."

"I agree," Fern said and turned to Mike, "A quiet word, please." They stood up and stepped away from the others. "I need someone checked out, someone who wants to adopt a little boy. His name is Bill Pinkston, but he goes by the name Pinkie. There's something about him I do not like. He gives me the creeps. When you get back, I want him checked out."

"Will do."

"Lastly, some good news — we are getting a lot of hits on our website, and there are more inquiries to adopt."

"Wow, well done, Fern! It looks like we're in big business," he beamed.

Mike was lucky to get a seat to Nairobi via London with British Airways.

He needed a rest and knew the others did as well. Sofia to London was just over three hours and London to Nairobi eight hours and thirty minutes.

There was no time to shower before departure, but Mike bought a pair of pants and extra underwear at one of the airport shops, and by then, it was time for boarding.

He phoned Stella.

"Mike, Mike, are you alright?"

"Sure, Stella."

"Shortly after you left, there were police sirens going off everywhere, and it is now on the news. They found a dead man with a cracked skull, and the other one is in a coma fighting for his life."

"These things happen all the time and all over the world. It will look like a gang-related fight. Nothing to do with us at all."

"You sure?"

"We're good, Stella. I will be in touch."

"Mike, you sure you're coming back?"

"Of course, hang in there and say goodbye to your grandmamma from me."

He ended the call and threw the phone in the trash before boarding his flight to London.

Chapter Forty

Mike had always adored London, particularly the parks where he could sit and unwind and marvel at the city's history that engulfed him.

He walked towards Hyde Park and passed a group of young men near Piccadilly Circus who looked a bit rough. Mike told them he'd lost his cell phone and needed to buy one urgently. He asked if one of them would be interested in selling their phone, and Mike showed them a roll of cash. It didn't take long for Mike to own a new phone.

After all the excitement and action in Sofia, he felt lonely in the new city. It entered his mind to fly Stella over to join him for a couple of days. He thought she would be the perfect recruiter for babies not only in Sofia but elsewhere as well, including London. He was also feeling a little guilty about leaving her to deal with the fallout of his encounter with the thugs. He was not worried for her safety, but she might nonetheless be feeling anxious.

He was about to call her but decided against it. It would be better to do so after the Kenya collection.

The next morning, he enjoyed a full English breakfast and then took an express train to Heathrow and boarded his flight to Nairobi.

Halfway into the flight, they experienced severe turbulence. At times like these, Mike remained relaxed. He figured he couldn't do anything about it, so there was no point in fretting. He gazed at the different people, noting the fear and worry on their faces. He even saw a man in an aisle seat praying frantically as his thin lips moved up and down.

The turbulence eventually passed, and much later, the captain announced they would be landing soon.

Walking through arrivals, Mike looked for the tour guide he had hired. He quickly saw a pleasant-looking African man, neat and dressed in khaki shorts and a jacket with polished brown shoes holding up a sign that just said, *Mike.*

Mike approached him and saw his name tag; it was James.

"Hujambo, James," Mike greeted him.

"Hujambo, how are you, Mike? How was your flight?" They shook hands, and James took Mike's bag.

"Flight was long, a bit of turbulence, but I am used to it."

"You know some Swahili, I see, Bwana Mike."

"Not really, James. I googled a couple of words a short while ago." He grinned.

"So, we are going to Nairobi, Bwana Mike?"

"Yes, James, I'm booked in at the Radisson Blu."

"Okay, Bwana, that's just a minute from the center."

"Great. Tell me a bit about yourself, James, and what you do."

"Born and bred here, Bwana. I come from a poor family and lived in Kibera for many years, and thanks to Mungu, to God, I now live with my wife in a small place away from the slums. In fact, not far from your hotel. I love nature and people, and showing tourists around gives me great pleasure."

"So, you really know the area, eh? Have you had dinner?"

"Not yet, but my wife will have something for me after I have dropped you off."

"Would she be upset if I took you out for dinner? You see, there are some important things I need to discuss with you. You are welcome to ask her to join us."

"Bwana Mike, it would give me great pleasure. My wife and I have a young child. She will be looking after our little girl, so it would be just me. I know a good place to dine out."

"Splendid, it will not take long, our discussion. How old is your little girl?"

"My baby girl is four years young. English is a complex and strange language, Bwana, and that is why I say four years young, not old."

"You have a point, James. Right now, take me to my hotel, and after I check in, you can take us to the best restaurant Nairobi has to offer."

"Ndiyo, Bwana, yes."

The drive to the city took an hour, even though it was just sixteen kilometres away. The traffic was bumper to bumper, and they crawled along at a snail's pace. James told Mike he was lucky; during peak times, it could take two hours.

Check-in was quick. Mike put his bag in his room, washed quickly, and went downstairs to the lounge where James waited.

James opened his car door for Mike, and they drove off.

Gazing out his window, observing the scenery and foot traffic, Mike saw a group of African youths slouching about, smoking, and joking around on a corner of an intersection.

"Stop here for a second, James," Mike said casually.

"Why, Bwana?"

"I just want to ask those guys something."

"But what, Bwana Mike? Nairobi can be a dangerous place."

"Pull over, James," Mike said with more authority.

James obeyed, and Mike hopped out.

Mike walked toward the group, and they all turned to look at him.

James pulled up alongside and watched.

Mike looked at James. "Tell them I need a phone. I lost mine."

James hesitated but did as he was asked.

The group leader removed a new Samsung from his pocket.

"How much?" Mike asked.

There was a brief conversation in Swahili.

"He says he bought it for eight thousand Kenyan shillings and would take nine thousand for it," James translated.

Mike knew it was roughly eighty US dollars.

"Okay—deal."

The group stepped towards Mike.

"Stop," Mike ordered, raising his palm. "My deal is with your leader, not all of you. Stay where you are. I don't want trouble, but if you want it, you will get it," he threatened quietly.

They didn't argue. The leader came up to Mike and took the cash. Mike now had a local phone.

They immediately left.

"Bwana, why did you buy a phone from them when you could have bought one from the phone store, brand new?"

"Don't worry about it, James. I'm hungry. Let's eat."

They dined at a well-known place where different game meats were on the menu.

They both ordered a tasty Kenyan stew with vegetables and ugali, a staple cornmeal diet, washed down with Tusker lager, a popular local beer.

During the meal, Mike spoke about how they assisted charities worldwide and how they rescued babies from shocking conditions.

He explained they were looking for a baby from here for an Australian couple who originally came from Kenya. It was important, he said, to first do reconnaissance in Kibera and locate someone who could provide a baby or direct them to someone who could.

Mike stressed they were not into stealing children; it was important the parents or family didn't have the means to care for the baby, and they were prepared to relinquish it without fuss. He told him he would pay good money, but the baby had to be healthy. Ideally, the baby would be orphaned or possibly dumped with no hope of a good home.

James confirmed Mike's theory, Kibera was just the place, and he even knew some people there who might be able to help.

Mike told James to phone his contacts and to advise them they would be there tomorrow morning.

As soon as Mike paid for the meal, James put a call into a relative in Kibera.

The relative agreed to meet mid-morning.

James dropped Mike off at his hotel and told him to come back for him at 9.30 am.

Mike asked James what he would charge for driving him around for a couple of days or so. Again, like with Peter in Sofia, Mike offered to double his quote with an added bonus if everything worked out well in the end.

Back in his room, Mike found the internet speed slow. It was frustrating, however, there was nothing he could do about it but adapt. He took a shower while waiting for his emails to download.

He also checked in with headquarters.

"Howdy Fern, how is my boss today?" he asked jovially.

"Anxious, Mike. We've got a deadline for the parcel for our Kenyan couple."

"Relax, I am making headway this end. Tomorrow, get Oliver and his co-pilot to fly here with Alice on board. As soon as I get off the phone, call them. With all the flying and different time zones in the last week, they will be buggered, so it won't make a difference. I will book rooms for them at my hotel."

"Have you secured a parcel?"

"Not yet, Fern. Rome was not built in a day. I expect to have a little one tomorrow, I promise. But, here's the thing, AIDS is rife in Africa, and when we fish in slums, there are chances the little fish may have AIDS and even malaria. Tuberculosis is also prevalent here as well."

"What are you saying? Should I get Lance to join the crew as well?"

"No point, because from what I understand, an AIDS test needs to be done at birth, then at several intervals apart like six weeks, then twelve weeks, then eighteen months, and at twenty-four months before there is an all-clear."

"God! How do you know this? Did you talk to Lance?"

"Doctor Google," he smiled down the phone. "I checked it out on the internet, and besides, I've chatted to Lance in the past. When Alice arrives, she can listen to the little one's chest, and blood tests can be done immediately in Australia. The responsibility will be on the couple who adopts. You must make that clear to Mr. and Mrs. Mwangi. If all goes well with our first test showing negative, then the onus is on the guardians, on the adoptive parents. Let me go now so you can get on the phone."

"Okay, will do, but too much info on the phone is not good. You taught me that," Fern warned.

"I am using a burner phone, and so is yours. I gave it to you, particularly for these calls. You can chill. And tell Danny to send a few birth certificates as I do not know what the age of the baby will be; let him have one ready for a one-month baby, three months, six months, and a year just in case."

Fern smiled on the other side of the world, "Will do, and good luck! What would I do without you?"

In the morning, before James came to pick him up, Mike went to the Bureaux de Change and exchanged two thousand dollars into the local money.

The morning traffic was hectic, and they drove southwest towards Kibera, only six kilometres away.

"Bwana, you'll be pleased to hear we are meeting someone I know, and it looks promising."

"That's why I chose you, James!" Mike said, appreciating his new guide.

Soon they reached a gravel road. It was like Stolipinovo all over again, except they were in Africa. Tens of thousands of shacks with rusty tin roofs stood side-by-side like stacked sardine cans. There was pollution everywhere, garbage, plastics, filth, and kids played amongst it all, oblivious of the dangers. These children had never seen a green park in their lives. The only green around were the clumps of weeds growing between rusted cans, stones, open sewerage lines, and more plastics. The plastics, in different shades of green, brown and black, were covered in algae and slime.

Some skinny kids were running barefoot, pushing an old punctured and worn tire down a slight slope. Mike noticed they were smiling despite their surroundings. One kid was very thin. His scabby legs looked like two matches, and his knees like the match heads. Mike's stomach was still full from breakfast, and he felt guilty as he watched.

A few minutes later, they arrived at a shack that had a poorly painted hairdresser sign outside. It was leprous looking and blended in with all the others.

James parked his vehicle while Mike surveyed the area. James ran around the vehicle to open the door for Mike. As he did a few scrawny chickens ran for cover, clucking their displeasure at the disturbance. A flea-bitten looking dog watched them from a short distance away with all its visible ribs poking through.

"No, James, I appreciate your courtesy but let me open my door myself. Don't be offended, brother."

"No problem, bwana. Come inside. We are meeting with Goma. She is a distant, distant relative." As they arrived at the entrance, a lady opened the door before they knocked. She gazed at Mike. A sudden movement to Mike's side caused him to glance over but it was only a mangy-looking goat climbing up a swollen garbage heap outside.

"Good morning. Come, come inside," invited the lady happily.

Mike smiled without saying a word. She led them inside, and immediately, he saw out of a back corrugated tin door into a courtyard where two kids were jumping about. She gave them a stern warning, telling them to play elsewhere.

There were a few rickety wooden benches and a worn wooden box that served as a seat in the small but clean room.

She mumbled a few words to James in Swahili and then looked back at Mike.

"Sit, sit," she said, smiling frantically.

Mike and James sat.

"I am Goma. Pleased to meet you, Mike. James has told me about the purpose of your visit."

"Pleased to meet you too, Goma."

"Can I get you some tea or would you prefer something stronger like changaa?"

"May I ask what changaa is?" Mike asked cautiously.

She chuckled, "It is a home brew we make from millet, maize and sorghum with a few secret extra fermented ingredients."

"We will pass, auntie, thank you. Now down to business," James said.

They both looked at Mike waiting for him to open.

"Yes, I am sure James briefed you."

"Ndiyo, yes, but I want to hear it from your mouth, Mike."

"Well, we are an international team and we seek out unwanted babies for wealthy couples who cannot have children of their own. We check these people out thoroughly before placing a baby with them. I must stress we only work with the cream of the crop who can prove they will provide kind loving homes where the babies will be cherished. It certainly is not slavery or for any other illegal purposes. We are happy to pay the families to help them financially, or the mother, if we know who she is. We will also pay an agent fee to help locate the right child. That could be someone like yourself. Lastly, we plough a portion of the money back into the community to help the economy in the area."

For a few seconds there was silence. "Mister Mike, if I put the word out, there would be a line outside my house from here to the other end of the world," she said sardonically. "However, if you make it worthwhile to me, I will have a baby here, in an hour or so."

"What do you have in mind?"

"It is simple, wait and see." Then she shouted out a name. In seconds one of the children appeared. She whispered to him and he ran off.

"What's happening?" Mike asked.

"You will see, Bwana Mike. You are sure you do not want tea, coffee or changaa?"

"I'm good, thanks. What about you, James?"

"Tea for me, Goma, please."

Mike was reluctant to order anything, especially when he had no idea where the hell the water came from. He couldn't afford to chance it. Not with a long flight ahead of him.

Goma disappeared to make tea for herself and James.

"Bwana Mike, I know why you do not want tea. No worry, I understand."

"You guessed right, James! Do you know where she has sent the kid?"

"Not sure, Bwana."

"I think, James, she has sent for someone she knows and trusts. I think there is a chance someone will appear with a baby very shortly."

Goma appeared with the tea for James. She handed him a hot mug while sipping her own.

"You sure I cannot get you something, Bwana Mike?"

"I'm good, thank you."

"I heard what you said Bwana Mike. You are too clever." She shook her finger in mock jest.

"There is a baby on the way, Goma?"

"Yes, Bwana Mike."

"Who is the mother? Does she agree?"

"Wait and see, Bwana, and before the mother arrives, tell me exactly what is in it for us."

"One-thousand US dollars for you and for the mother or the guardian," Mike offered.

Suddenly there were loud voices outside.

Goma hurried to the front door.

There were greetings and more noise. A young girl appeared with a baby in her arms.

"Mike, meet my niece, Ducha," Goma said.

Mike stood up and greeted the girl.

"Where is the mother?" Mike asked.

"She is the mother, Bwana Mike."

"Hell! How old is she?"

"She just turned fourteen, Bwana Mike."

Mike looked at the girl, "Who is the father, Ducha?"

The girl remained silent.

"She cannot speak English at all," Goma explained, "but she will not say in any case. She was raped."

"This is a cruel world." Mike felt like smashing his fist into the wall. "And who looks after her and the baby, may I ask?"

"Her mother and drunkard father and I do when I can, Bwana Mike."

"Is it a boy or girl?"

"It is a boy. His name is Badru because he was born during the full moon."

"Goma, excuse us for a minute please. James, let's step outside."

He looked around and checked they were alone. They walked a short distance away, making sure no neighbors, including the hairdresser, would overhear them.

"Here's what I am thinking. Can you, me, Ducha and the baby go to Nairobi?"

James looked at him surprised.

"Confidentially, I need your help to open a bank account and deposit some money for Ducha. You can then drop me off at my hotel. Within a day or two the rest of my team will arrive and one is an experienced nurse. Let the girl and her baby sleep over at your place since you are close to my hotel. When my team arrive, they will need to time to rest, freshen up and eat before we turn around and go back home to Australia. I will phone you when we are ready to leave and you can bring the girl and baby to the hotel, and then drive us to the airport. Are you with me?"

"Yes, Bwana Mike, I do not think that will be a problem."

"Good, I will pay Goma now, I have money. I will pay you when I get to the bank, and when you drop us all off at the airport, I will have your bonus for you, understand? At the airport Ducha will part with her baby for good. Am I clear, James?"

"Loud and clear, Bwana Mike."

"Now let's go and pay Goma her cut and let's get the hell out of here. The people seem friendly but the poverty is hard....." And he could not finish his sentence. It was too painful.

As they were moving back inside, Mike heard a noise that sounded like a small rock rolling down a stony slope but as he turned, he saw it was just a few more scruffy, ravenous goats entering the fray on a high pile of junk and garbage.

"Goma, this is what we are going to do, but first things first." Mike took out the equivalent of fifteen hundred dollars in local currency and gave it to Goma.

"There is an extra five hundred dollars for you, Goma. We are leaving now, going into the city for a short while. I may or may not see you again, but, thank you and stay well. I will take the girl and the baby with us. James will accompany us to Nairobi and they will stay with James and his wife for a day or two. James will bring Ducha back to you after we leave. As for baby Badru, he will be well looked after and very much loved in his new life."

"Yes, I understand, Bwana, it is better, I think, for the baby and everyone."

"Can you explain to Ducha so she understands," Mike instructed.

Goma explained to the girl what was happening. She was quiet and merely nodded her head, saying nothing. She was so young and obviously still traumatized by the rape. She had little emotion about parting with the baby.

James drove them to the bank as agreed. Mike instructed the manager to open an account for the teenager and arranged for James to act as her guardian if there was any issue.

Mike deposited four-thousand dollars into her new account with a clause she could not draw more than two hundred dollars a month. Mike opened a second account with a five-thousand-dollar deposit, stipulating it was for educational purposes only and available when she turned eighteen.

Mike also settled his bill with James and reminded him that he would get his bonus when he dropped them off at the airport.

James was taken aback by his generosity and Ducha smiled for the first time.

Mike treated everyone to a meal and James brought along his family at the insistence of Mike. It was the first time in her life Ducha had eaten a meal in a restaurant.

Afterwards, Mike arranged for Ducha to buy herself some new clothes and, after more smiles of gratitude, they all went to a pharmacy where Mike purchased two milk bottles and milk formula for four-month-old Badru and disposable diapers. He knew all of this would be on the jet but, in the emotional excitement, he got carried away. He wanted to make sure Ducha and the baby would be comfortable for the next couple of nights before it was time to leave.

As Mike climbed out of James' car in front of his hotel, he turned towards him.

"My team will arrive soon but I've got time to kill. How about tomorrow, you take us all on a safari, somewhere close. I see Nairobi National Park isn't far from the city."

"Tomorrow morning good, Bwana?"

"Yes, let's take your family, Ducha and the baby and go beat around the bush for a while. I couldn't possibly come all this way to Africa and not see any wild animals."

James drove off while Mike sent a text message to Fern. "Parcel secured and ready for collection."

James turned up in the morning with just Ducha. His wife felt it would be better if she stayed at home and looked after their daughter and the baby.

Mike happily paid the entrance fee for the park, and soon, James was in his glory. He was now a true guide doing what he loved best.

Ducha never took her eyes off the animals and they experienced tremendous luck when a leopard crossed the road and disappeared in seconds.

"Bwana Mike, you just don't know how lucky you are to see *chui*, the secretive leopard."

"Not luck, James, you organized this, didn't you?" and James laughed.

Mike's phone pinged when they rounded a corner in the bush. He looked at the text, "Landing in Nairobi at 3 pm your time."

Mike responded confirming he would be at the airport to receive them.

"James, I have to be at the airport at 3pm. We still have a few hours to enjoy ourselves here. Then we'll drop Ducha off back at your place, and you and I will shoot through to the airport to fetch the team."

"How many are coming, Bwana?"

"Three of them, so we can all fit comfortably in your vehicle. What time does the gate shut?"

"7 pm, Bwana Mike."

"Okay, done and dusted. Let's drive for another hour, then we'll take Ducha to your place. I also want to get some of those Tusker beers and a few snacks on the way to the airport. "

"I understand, Bwana."

Ducha had not said a word the whole safari, but her happy face and the way she bowed shyly to Mike in farewell at James' home, told him she possibly had the best day of her short life.

Mike smiled back at her with satisfaction.

They bought a cooler bag and a dozen Tusker beers and some nuts and biltong, a beef jerky snack and headed to the airport.

At 3.45 pm the team arrived through an executive door near the arrival hall.

Mike saw them first.

"Come, James, let's grab their overnight bags."

"Good to see you, man," Oliver said patting Mike on the back.

"Always a pleasure," Morrie said.

"Welcome to Africa! How are you, Alice?"

"A long flight but very comfortable, Mike, thank you" Alice said.

"Good, lady and gentlemen. Meet James, our driver, and guide."

James smiled, extending his right hand and, according to African custom, touching his right elbow with his left hand each time he shook hands.

They walked to the parking lot and hopped in.

"I thought we'd have a picnic. We can also catch up at the same time. The baby is with James' wife and in the morning, he will pick us up with the little one. That's when you can check him out Alice. And then we can hit the road back to Down Under."

James was happy to chaperone these executives around. It made him feel important. The only thing that confused him was this *down under*. Where was that or what was it, he wondered.

Near the city, Alice noticed in awe many women carrying boxes and bags, even overloaded buckets, on their heads. She had often seen this in pictures but it was quite another thing to see it in real life.

A short while later James pulled over and told everyone this was a safe picnic spot to stretch their legs, right near the National Park. He carried the beers and snacks to a small and well-used wooden table.

Mike handed everyone a beer, "I propose a toast, to Fern, our lady General, our Queen, and also to Africa."

"Hear, hear," they all responded in unison.

Right on cue as though arranged, a lion roared. The mighty sound lasted for several seconds and was followed by several shorter, softer roars and grunts which echoed around the bush.

When it stopped, James noticed Alice was nowhere to be seen. She had jumped into the vehicle for safety.

James went to find her, laughing, "Do not worry," he reassured her, "the lion is a few kilometres away. He is not close. Did you know a lion's roar can be heard eight kilometres or more away?"

"Wow! It is so powerful—it reverberates right through you!" Alice said, still feeling a little shaky.

"You bet. Thanks for bringing us here, Mike. This is fantastic!" Morrie said raising his beer bottle in salute.

"Don't thank me, thank James."

"Strange tasting beer, but pleasant," Oliver said as he drained his bottle.

"Will we see any lions?" Alice asked James with a nervous look around.

"I am afraid not, ma'am. Come back one day and spend a few days in Kenya, and I will show you lions, many lions," he grinned.

The car ride back to the hotel was pretty quiet, since they were exhausted and lost in their own thoughts. Everyone thanked James as they got out of the car.

"I recommend we leave around 8am tomorrow for the airport," Mike told the group.

"James, bring Ducha and the little one and be ready outside."

"Ndiyo, Bwana, yes, and have a pleasant evening, everyone."

After the party checked in, Mike made a suggestion to his team, "It's nearly 7.30 pm folks. Let's meet in the lobby at 8.15 pm and eat here in the hotel restaurant. It's a good menu. We can then get an early night."

The four of them enjoyed a quiet dinner. Mike told them about Kibera and also discussed the possible health issues with the little boy but was hopeful. Next, he planned to target Europe and then the Far East. There were many Asian Australian citizens and was sure many longed for children.

Oliver and Morrie listened intently but in between spoke about flight paths, weather forecast and conditions and other aviation topics.

Alice said, as long as she lived, she would never forget the roar of that lion. The hair on her neck, she said, still felt electrified.

James arrived on schedule with Ducha and the baby. In Alice's room, she checked the baby, his large eyes looking from corner to corner. Ducha remained silent as she watched her baby being examined. It was hard to know what she was thinking.

Alice knew only in-depth checks could be done back home in Australia, but her examination revealed no obvious problems. This child, if originally unwanted, had nonetheless been well cared for.

Mike settled the hotel bill, and they all departed for the airport.

James and Ducha accompanied everyone into the departure area.

After check-in, Mike exchanged more cash from the Bureaux de Change and gave James his bonus, as promised.

James was over the moon but sad to see them go. He had enjoyed their company.

Alice gently took the baby from his teenage mother. Ducha showed no emotion, but Alice was compelled to say, "I am so sorry you will not see your little boy again. Please know he will be treated well and will have a kind, loving home and a bright future ahead of him," she said touching Ducha's arm.

James translated for Ducha and they all turned and walked towards the tarmac after exchanging farewells.

A second or two later, they heard Ducha shout out in Swahili, *Njia imendezayo Mungu.*

Mike looked at James.

"Bwana, she said *It is God's way. God has decided.*"

Chapter Forty-One

Fern was there to welcome them with her mother and staff. There were smiles and greetings all round and much admiration for baby Badru.

"Oh my God, look at the little one, he looks strong!" Fern gazed at him in delight. "Maggie please rustle up some sandwiches. We will have them in the boardroom. Alice, Lance is popping in to check the baby in a couple of hours."

"Little Bwana looks alert, doesn't he?" Mike said.

"Is that his name, Bwana?" Fern asked.

"No, it's Badru."

"So, what is *Bwana*?"

"That's like our *mister*," Mike said.

Fern smiled, she felt so happy to have Mike back on home soil.

Sheelah came and got the little one to take to the nursery and they all went to the boardroom for a debriefing. Maggie brought a large plate of sandwiches in and everyone helped themselves to coffee.

Fern stood up and pushed her chair in while the team stared in dead silence.

"Firstly, I thank you from the bottom of my heart for the last two successful missions, and also thank you for your great loyalty. It has not gone unnoticed and in due course I expect to express my deep gratitude with financial rewards for your dedication."

"I've already phoned our Kenyan client and told him his future son is on the way. He is very excited. Mr. Mwangi will collect baby Badru in a few days; the exact day will depend on the full check-up with Lance, who is coming here today."

"In the last few days, we have had dozens of more enquiries, some very serious. I also had a call from little Ivan's dad. Our first little boy and girl are doing extremely well and Ivan has adapted to his new family completely and is loving his new life."

"Yesterday I donated one-hundred-thousand dollars to a local orphanage and fifty-thousand to a local shelter for abused women. This is a direct result of everyone's hard work."

All of you get some rest and we will see you back here in three days."

"Thank you, Fern." Alice excused herself and left for the crèche.

"Mike, Oliver, thank you. You both mean the world to me. Oliver, go get some rest. You and Morrie will be back in the air within a week and I need you in peak form. We can talk later."

Oliver stood up. "No worries—actually, there is something I wanted to ask you. I will call you this evening, okay?"

"No problem."

Now that they were alone, Fern turned to Mike, "Remember the guy who gave me the shivers? Bill Pinkston, aka Pinkie. I want him checked out as a priority this week. His reaction was bizarre and disturbing. He stormed off after I indicated acquiring a baby wasn't as simple as he thought. The bastard's car key hooked my Fendi purse and he forcibly ripped it and damaged the corner. He was boorish and I suspect lied when he said he was about to be married. There is something about him that I do not like. He must be in his '60s and too old to adopt. I highly doubt he will be getting a baby from us."

"Leave it to me, Fern," he said confidently.

"And, Mike, we need to start planning the next collection. We are going to be under the gun, if the inquiries keep increasing as they are?"

"We sure are. I've been thinking, we should recruit Stella in Sofia long term. She's proved herself to be reliable and honest. If she's agreeable, I would like to appoint her my agent for Europe." Mike did not add that he found her attractive, but Fern felt a stab of jealousy anyway.

"By all means," she said, adding in a teasing tone to disguise her jealousy, "Sounds like there could be an attraction there." She grinned cheekily.

"No, she's cool and reliable and proven herself to be street savvy, which is what we need."

"Yes, I agree.!" Fern's feminine intuition kicking in.

"Come on, Fern, enough. Write down the number of that Pinkie dude and his full name. Wait, you met with him, didn't you? Did you get his business card?"

Fern handed him the card, which was on top of her notepad.

Mike hung around for a while. Neither seemed to want to leave. He was still there when Lance arrived.

Mike looked at his watch, "My, time flies. I need some rest. Fern, are you going to the crèche now?"

"Yes, absolutely. Uncle Lance, are you ready?"

"Sure, let's go."

Mike ordered a cab and made his way down to the gate, and opened it with his own remote.

A couple of minutes later the cab pulled up and Mike climbed in the back. He was drained and fell back into the seat for much needed silence. He looked at the business card which gave him an office address, cell phone number, and an email address for a Mr. William Bill Pinkston.

He was dropped off home about an hour later. He showered and slept and when he woke, he was starving. He looked at his watch; it was nearly 10 pm; he had slept for hours. He drove to his local hamburger joint where he ordered two hamburgers and a large portion of chips and went back home to guzzle it down with a coke. He went to the lounge and switched on the TV for company.

He turned on his laptop and opened up Google. He typed in the name William Pinkston without any luck. He also searched Pinkie and Bill Pinkston to no avail. He was not on Facebook nor on other social media sites. Mike typed in the business name in the search bar from the card and experienced some success. There were no photos of the so-called Pinkie but there were some pictures of sample linens and fabrics the company had been importing since 1980. He then searched the company address and tried out the new google map software was soon looking at a street view of the building.

He took a break. It was midnight and 5pm in Bulgaria. He picked up his phone and called Stella. She sounded elated at hearing his voice. He asked her if she would meet him in London. He would send her a ticket. Although excited at the prospect of an overseas trip, she asked why. He said it was twofold. First, he wanted to see her and show her London. Second, he had a job offer for her. Stella wanted to know more details, but Mike said he preferred to tell her in person. He told her he would arrange everything for next week. She had to shyly admit that she didn't think she had the right sort of clothes for London. He told her not to worry, they could shop in London too! He then said good night and hung up.

At 6 am the next morning he was on his way to St Kilda Road. He wanted to be there before Pinkston arrived at his office.

Mike arrived at 7 am and found the main door locked. Looking around, he saw a door leading to the garage and stairs, which brought him up one floor to ground level. He noted there were no security cameras. Then he took the elevator to the third floor and approached Pinkston's office door. Again, no CCTV, and the door was locked by an old keyless keypad lock. There was also an old mortise lock that required a key. Mike slipped on a pair of surgical gloves as he looked at the numbers from zero to ten. He looked closely and noted there were numbers that were more worn down than others: zero, five, six, and seven. Mike made an educated guess the code to enter would be a sequence of these numbers. They probably represented the fifth of June or July or a special date like a birthday. If not, Mike would play around with another order using only these worn digits. His only concern, once inside, was the possibility of an alarm. He examined the exterior and could not see an alarm light, which was a good indication there was none. He looked around to make sure no one was in sight. The door opened a quarter of an inch. Mike removed a key ring from his pocket, which housed some metal picks. Mike knew picking a lock was all about the amount of tension used. After playing around for a few seconds, the lock clicked, and the door opened fully. Once inside, his eyes darted to the top corners of the ceiling to verify there were no alarm detectors or CCTV. Nothing. He quietly entered and looked around.

No wonder the security was a bit lax. The office was empty, except for a desk with a landline phone and a desktop computer. The only other furniture was a single chair and an old two-door metal filing cabinet. Mike was super alert, listening for any noise. There were also a few curtain swatches on the desk, and that was all. He surmised Pinkston possibly had a storage facility elsewhere for his materials, or he had no materials, and this office was a front for something else. He opened the desk drawers and was shocked. There were numerous pictures of skimpily clad teenage boys in pornographic poses with naked older men. It sickened him. He went over to the filing cabinet and opened it. There were a few porno magazines, DVDs, and an address book with names and contact info. All men. He carefully closed the drawers and left the office, wondering why this pervert did not have better security on his front door.

He made a call as soon as he got back to his car.

"Len, you son of a gun, long time no see!" he said cheerily.

"Well, well, I know that voice. It belongs to Mike. How are you, man?"

"I'm good, Len. You busy this week?"

"So, so—what do you have in mind?"

"How about lunch today? Let's catch up."

"Sounds good. Let's meet at the usual place, even if it is only every five years or so," he chuckled.

"Sure thing—at the clocks—12.30 pm."

"Cool—see you there!"

Mike was still sick to his stomach, and the breakfast he had in mind was now just a cup of coffee back home.

He took a tram to Flinders and, at 12.30 sharp, viewed the steps just below the clocks and noticed Len. You could not miss him. He was average height but broad like a door and extremely well built.

"Hey, bud, good to see you," Mike said as they shook hands as they gave each other a vice-like grip.

"You haven't changed, Mike, still looking young and adventurous. You look good."

"Come, Len, let's go to Flinders Lane. There're some good cafes and good grub too." Mike's appetite was coming back.

They crossed the road and walked into the lane. The coffee shops and restaurants were busy but not packed.

They entered a small restaurant and were ushered to a table by a smiling waitress.

"Bring us two coffees while we check the menu out. What are you drinking, Len?"

"I'll have a cappuccino, thanks."

Mike looked at the waitress, "Make that two, please."

She left.

"Well, well, what have you been up to lately?" Len asked.

"Busy, a lot of overseas travel and so on."

"And the so on, what's that?"

"Ah, a bit of this and that, Len. And you?"

"Staying alive and surviving! A few small things on the go, nothing too exciting, though. So, what brings us together today?"

"I've got a job for you, and I will pay you well. If you refuse, it's simple, I'll fuck you up," Mike said and smiled.

Len also smiled. "Out with it then."

"Okay, all confidential, as usual. I work for a very wealthy young lady. She's a lovely person, and we are involved in providing homes for abandoned babies. We are terribly strict about the parents we select. These married couples are checked out like never before. If they shit, we know about it. Just a couple of weeks ago, this single guy tmet with my boss and expressed an interest in adopting a little boy. He says he is about to get married."

"Go on," Len was now very intrigued.

"Well, my boss met with him and became highly suspicious. There was something about this guy that didn't feel right. Today, I accessed his office without him knowing and rummaged through his desk and so on. He's a fucking pedophile! His office is full of pics, child pornography and adult men, etcetera. If I get involved, and if someone were to see me, it would jeopardize my operation with abandoned kids. I can't risk it."

He cleared his throat and lowered his voice. "I want him fucked over badly. Take a hammer. I mean it, dude. Break his knees and get a message to the cops and expose this pedophile ring he is operating. He deserves everything that is coming to him," Mike said disgustedly.

"What's his name?"

Just then, the waitress returned.

"You guys ready to order?"

"I'll have your soup of the day and for my main course, make it a spaghetti marinara," Mike ordered.

"I'll also have the soup and the spaghetti with meatballs, thanks."

The waitress smiled and departed.

"William Bill Pinkston, aka Pinkie."

Len's face darkened, "Fuck! I know that name. He's a well-known pedophile. Read about him in the papers a couple of years back. He is already on the cops' radar but somehow has managed to evade any arrest. Fucker belongs at the bottom of the Yarra River," he hissed under his breath.

"Okay, here's his business card. Do it and let me know when it's done."

" Consider it already done, Mike."

The plates arrived, and they ate in silence.

Mike noted Len had gone very quiet. "You all right, Len? Food no good?"

"All good, Mike, just savoring it."

They ordered more coffee, and Mike looked at his watch.

"I need to hit the road as soon as I finish this cup. What's your ride today?"

"My Harley, and you?"

"Public transport—the tram. I've gotta run and go talk to the boss."

"Thanks," Len said. "See you."

Len walked to his pride and joy. He revved the Harley engine and slowly drove to Pinkston's office. When he arrived at the old building, he parked the bike around the corner. He intended to do this smoothly and without being seen.

He walked up the stairs to Pinkston's floor. The door was closed. He put his ear to the door. There was no noise, no voices. He knew Pinkston would be at lunch and might soon return. Len looked up to the floors above him on the opposite side. He knocked on the door, but there was no answer. He glanced at his watch and left the building. He took up position across the street and waited. He would recognize Pinkston immediately.

Len remembered walking past the numerous shops on this street and stopping one day at the toy and hobby store. He had gazed into the window wistfully at a beautiful little army helicopter, and even though he had no money, he had gone into the shop to look around. After a while, he'd left, stopping outside the window again to admire the toy helicopter. It was then he felt a light tap on his shoulder and turned around. A man with a friendly face and a dark mustache was asking him what he liked so much in the window. Little Lennie pointed to the helicopter. The man said he was very rich and enjoyed buying things for children, especially toys. The man told him to wait and went inside and came out with the plastic helicopter for Lennie.

He also gave him a small paper bag with a few plastic soldiers he'd bought too. The man said he had more toys at home and, as his children had all grown up, they no longer needed them. He asked Lennie to accompany him; his home was close by. Lennie t thought the man was being nice. He naively went to his apartment, and the man told him to sit on the bed while he fetched the toys.

He came back with a toy car and sat next to little Len. Then the man put his hand on Lennie's pants and said he was going to do something he would enjoy.

The man opened his own fly and took out his penis. He also took out two dollars, which was a lot of money to young Lennie, and told him to do something terrible. Little Len refused. The man grabbed Lennie's head and pulled him closer. Eventually, Lennie managed to escape his grip and run to the door. The door was locked, but the key was still in the lock, and in a second, Lennie was running as fast as his small feet could carry him. He was too ashamed to tell anyone. He never forgot the number on the door -702.

A few days later, with his heart pounding, he went back to the block of apartments because he remembered all the residents' names were displayed on a board in the lobby. He quickly looked up 702, and next to the number was the name, *William Pinkston*. He read it to himself a few times until the elevator doors opened, and little Len nearly fainted from fright. Luckily, it was not Pinkston but a cleaner. He ran back home without looking back. He promised himself when he was big and strong, he would get him.

But when he returned years later and looked at the board, the name on number 702 had changed.

Now, he couldn't believe his luck. Here he was, an adult with many years of experience, standing across the road from William Pinkston's office.

"Karma is a bitch, best served cold," he sniggered menacingly to himself.

He waited and waited for nearly an hour, and then he saw him. He had aged, but he still had the same mustache, albeit now grey. Len watched him closely, then crossed the road. He watched him as he disappeared into the building.

Over the weeks, Len set up surveillance and followed him regularly from his office to his home to familiarize himself with his habits. He had a new flat in the Elwood area. Len now had his office address and home address.

He noted his patterns, and every Saturday morning, he went to the same coffee shop not far from where he lived. There he met another man, the same man every Saturday. They would sit for hours eating and drinking, but what caught Len's attention was, without fail, Pinkie would leave his friend and cross the road to a small shopping center where he would walk up one flight of stairs and go to the men's room. There was no restroom at the coffee shop, and going to the mall's restroom was a routine he never wavered from. He would then walk home.

There was not a resident listing board at his new complex, but he picked up the different Wi-Fi signals as he walked down the passage and passed Pinkie's apartment. Using his cell phone, he was able to pick up the Wi-Fi name *Pinkie One* outside Pinkie's front door. Len also checked the mailboxes and confirmed Mr. William B. Pinkston received mail at the address, including a bill from an optician addressed to Pinkie Pinkston. Len had him. After all these years, all the nightmares, he had the bastard.

Len wondered how many others had been molested over the years. He cringed at the thought. His mind was made up.

Chapter Forty-Two

Bruce Nash sipped a large glass of Merlot and, with a shaking hand, addressed the small padded envelope to Ms. Fern Jones. He inserted the ring and a note:

Dear Ms Jones,

Twenty-one years ago, when I was a detective inspector in the police force, the body of a woman was washed up on a beach in Victoria. She was the victim of a shark attack.

The poor woman was young, blonde, and probably once very beautiful. She had an unusual feature: one blue eye and one brown eye. The autopsy revealed that she had recently given birth. We tracked her down and found out she was a Russian immigrant who had fallen on bad times and had been working as a street walker. Her pimp had gotten her addicted to drugs. Her name was Sophia Semenov. She had no family in Australia, and our efforts to find family in Russia were not fruitful. Unfortunately, despite extensive efforts, we were never able to find her newborn baby, and the case was eventually closed.

As a token of goodwill, I am enclosing a gold ring, which was found on the young woman's finger and inscribed 'Sophia', because I believe this woman may have been your mother. You look just like her. It is uncanny. You have the same rare genetic feature, your

age is right, the area is right, and I recently found out from your
mother that you were adopted.

Should you wish to pursue this matter with a quick DNA test,
please do not hesitate to contact me, as I still have connections in
the police force. I clearly see you have a good life, and since so much
time has passed, there is no need for your adopted mother to fear
any consequences if your adoption was illegal.

Yours truly,
Bruce Nash
Detective Inspector (Retired)

Nash drove himself into the village, talking to himself every now
and then, and mailed the letter. He then drove home, continuing his
ramblings some more.

To calm himself down, he decided to enjoy his garden and put
food out for the birds to watch them. He walked to the bird feeder
and bird bath and broke up the bread into tiny pieces, and returned to
his veranda to sit and relax. He poured himself another glass of wine,
waiting and thinking about his late wife.

He wondered if he had made a huge mistake by mailing the letter to
Fern. He had no idea if she had been searching for her biological mother
and this would be closure, or would getting details about her mother's
life and how she had died upset her? Nash grimaced when he recalled
her muscleman Mike's threat to expose his wife's mercy killing should he
contact Fern again. He took a large gulp. Well, the hell with him, he thought.
He would not be blackmailed but rather take the consequences instead.

Two days later, the team met at the center.

Mike was the first to arrive, and when he stopped at the front gate,
he noticed some mail sticking out of the mailbox. While he opened

the gate with his remote, he jumped out to grab the mail for Fern and Megan Jones.

The small padded envelope caught his eye. The writing was messy and inconsistent, as if written by a shaking hand, but readable. Mike flipped it over. There was a return address from Bruce Nash. Mike took the padded envelope and shoved it into the glove box. He drove in and parked his car, and took the rest of the mail inside with him.

The whole team, including Lance and Danny, met for nearly two hours in the boardroom with Fern.

Everyone was given the opportunity to ask questions and share thoughts.

Interest in their service had soared. Fern had scheduled an average of twenty meetings a month with couples wishing to adopt in Australia alone. The Stork Center was even receiving requests from overseas. Among the hundreds of inquiries applications came in from the USA, Russia, Canada, England, Italy, Germany, New Zealand, Switzerland, France, Dubai, Holland, Greece, and even Mauritius.

Fern instructed Alice to find and interview more nurses. She wanted two more experienced neonatal nurses who could take care of newborns and teach new moms the ropes.

Fern said the policy for the center would continue to focus on fulfilling Australian couples' dreams from collections from abroad but if a particular opportunity arose from an ex-pat, the request might be considered.

Lance had examined baby Badru and was happy with his progress so far. He would continue taking further blood samples for testing to monitor his health. A date was set for Bayana and Dinka Mwangi to fly in from Sydney to take him home.

Fern thanked everyone and also told Alice she would soon be traveling again. The pilots were on standby, fuelled, and ready to fly as soon as they heard a word from Mike.

Alice smiled and cleared her throat. She stood up.

"Before everyone disappears, I would just like to say a few words. When we were in the National Park in Kenya with our guide, James, we stood under a beautiful African sunset and raised our glasses to you, Fern. We toasted and acknowledged the amazing person you are and what you do. Just then, a mighty lion roared in the distance. I'm sorry you were not with us because it was like the lion roared in acknowledgment of your successful leadership, dedication, and generosity. Thank you so much." She paused as she was getting choked up but managed to finish, "I am so appreciative being part of an incredible team."

"Why Alice, such kind words, thank you, my darling."

Alice blushed a little, but she meant every word.

Mike spoke to Danny on the side and gave him additional names, papers, and permits to create, and Danny left with a mountain of work.

Lance made a few important points, then he excused himself and went to spend time with his sister-in-law.

The pilots took off too, and Fern and Mike were alone to carry on going over other business matters for another few hours.

Mike did not mention Nash's letter.

Afterward, Fern went to join her mother and Uncle Lance, and Mike booked his flight and Stella's ticket to London. A little while later, he stopped by the kitchen to inform Fern he was leaving for London at the end of the week. He said goodbye to Lance, and Megan and Fern walked him to his car.

Fern touched Mike's elbow. "Mike, you haven't mentioned Pinkston? What have you found out?"

"Your gut feeling about him was spot on. He's a real bastard, a pedophile!"

"What!" Fern was shocked, despite her gut feeling. "So, what's being done about it?"

"It's being dealt with."

"Have you told the police?"

"When it's over, they will know."

"Over? What do you mean, Mike?"

"I've got someone watching him. He needs a lesson. The police will be involved soon."

" I trust you're being careful. The last thing we need is trouble, but I agree the bastard needs to pay…"

"Fern, it's being taken care of. Will talk later."

Mike hopped into his car, and smiled at Fern. She waved goodbye as he drove to the gate.

He drove around the corner and pulled up at the side of the road in a suburban street. After a momentary hesitation, he took the padded envelope out of the glove box, opened it, and read the letter. He inspected the ring and held it in his fingers. He placed the letter back in the envelope and put the ring in his pocket. Then he drove to Nash's house a few blocks away.

Mike parked his car and noticed the old guy sitting on his veranda. Mike approached.

Nash only noticed him when he was halfway up the path. He stood up.

"Mr. Nash, you remember me, don't you?"

"How could I forget? What do you want today?" Nash responded, holding his ground.

"It seems I need to reiterate something. I know what you did to your wife was more a mercy killing than a murder, but the law won't see it that way. You're familiar with the law," he sneered.

"I asked you very politely never to approach a member of the Jones family again, but now I see you've posted a letter to Fern, guaranteed to upset her. Just so you know, I intercepted it and destroyed it. There is no need to open old wounds just so you can feel good and close a case.

"Let me make myself perfectly clear for the last time. I will not file a report for what you did to your wife, but the Jones' residence is out of bounds to you. You are prohibited from approaching them or confronting them, whether on or outside of their property. If you do, I guarantee you will spend your last years in prison. I will make sure your name will be plastered over every newspaper in every state and more. Your reputation and legacy will be in shreds. Are we clear?"

"I meant well," Nash responded, "Fern has a right to know. You are too hard on her and on me. What gives you the right to decide what she should and shouldn't know? She is of legal age to make up her own mind and decisions."

"You think she'll be happy to find out that the woman who abandoned her was a drug-addicted prostitute who got herself eaten by a shark, and not a single member of her family came forward to claim her? Really?" he glared at him. "Mr. Nash, you have only seen the good side of me. You don't want to see the other side. Trust me! Goodbye, Mr. Nash. Goodbye for good."

Mike strode back to his car, where he left it. He felt slightly sorry for Nash, but he had to sock it to him hard. Not only did he want to spare Fern the knowledge of her past, but he also wanted to make sure once and for all this guy did not poke around and expose the business and jeopardize The Stork Center. He did not want Fern's well-intentioned hard work to be seen in the wrong light.

Mike drove home via St Kilda. He walked along the pier slowly and, at the end of the pier, paused to watch the seagulls in flight. His eye was fixed on the horizon, and the vast ocean sprawled in front of him. Mike was conflicted. He cared for Fern deeply and had seen how Chester's last act had torn her apart. He didn't want to see her suffer again by letting Nash dig up the horrors of the past for a second time. . He withdrew the ring from his pocket and, with all his strength, threw it as far out as he could back to where it came from.

Len sat by the window. He grabbed one of the café's newspapers for patron's use and opened it up to the sports section. He could not believe his favorite Australian football team, the Cats, had been beaten by the Crows. Not a good start to the day. He casually perused the rest of the paper while keeping one eye on the coffee shop across the street. He relaxed a bit when more customers arrived, making him less conspicuous.

He ordered a refill. Then he saw Pinkie. He was walking with a tall slim man with curly brown hair thinning on top. He was smartly dressed but obviously needed a shave. There was a small diamond stud earring in his left ear. They walked side by side as they entered their favorite place.

Len paid and sauntered along the street, appearing to window shop but he was actually watching the reflections.

Double checking there were no CCTV cameras, Len stood in a covered doorway. He could feel the paper notice through his pocket. He tapped his other pocket, satisfied he was ready.

Pinkie descended the few steps from the coffee shop and walked towards the small office buildings that also housed a few shops, which were closed for the weekend. Len quickened his pace. Pinkie entered the building and walked up the stairs to the public restrooms. Len was at the bottom of the steps when Pinkie reached the top. When Pinkie turned to walk toward the men's, Len hurried up the stairs. Len knew no CCTV existed from scouting out the joint earlier, and he was thankful for it.

Pinkie entered the men's bathroom, and as fast as lightning Len removed the notice from his pocket and, with one piece of Blu-Tac, quickly pasted it to the outside toilet door. It read, *Out of Order.*"

When Len entered, he saw Pinkston peeing in the urinal. Len walked up to use the urinal next to him.

While urinating, Len moved his penis to the side and pissed on Pinkie's pants and shoes.

"Fucking moron! Look what you've done!" Pinkie barked, jumping out of the way with his dick poking through his zipper.

"I know," Len sneered disgustedly. "But look what you've done."

"What shit are you talking about?"

"Don't you remember me, you fucking limp dick pervert?"

Pinkie looked at Len for a few seconds, his mind racing, hastily zipping his pants.

Len removed the automatic flick knife from his pocket. The cold blade sprung open, and in a second, Len struck with all his might, slicing Pinkie's throat wide open. Pinkie's eyes expanded in shock, fright, and burning pain. His eyes resembled a Pug's, bulging out of their sockets.

Pinkie's hands went up to his throat, clutching the gaping crevice of a hole. Just before he collapsed, Len sliced into Pinkie's inner thigh, severing his femoral artery for insurance using all the years of pent-up anger and shame in the one thrust. Pinkie's thigh burst into a fountain of blood and was partially absorbed by his pants. The white walls were splashed in blood, and the white floor tiles turned red. It was as if a river of blood had burst its banks, spraying and gushing torrents of blood everywhere.

Len glanced into the mirror. Miraculously, there was only a small spray of blood on his face and just a few spots on his gloves. With haste, he rinsed his face, washed his gloves in cold water, and left.

He jogged lightly down the stairs, his heart pounding but with a wicked smirk on his face. He took a slow walk towards his bike, withdrawing a cigarette from his top pocket and lighting it. He inhaled, deeply sucking the welcome smoke into his lungs.

The helmet was still there. He climbed onto his bike like a cowboy mounting his stallion.

He clipped his helmet into position and hit the ignition. When he was on his bike driving towards the Nepean Highway, he heard the sirens. There was definitely more than one. A moment later, he saw two police cars with flashing lights and screaming sirens heading towards Elwood. Len turned left onto the Nepean, and as he got closer to home, he threw the cheap, blood-splattered gloves into an industrial dumpster.

He demolished a cold beer in two gulps as soon as he got home. He lit another smoke, enjoying it more this time, and reached for his cell.

Mike looked at the caller ID on his phone; it was Len.

"All good, Mike, but I need to see you now."

"What's up?"

"Need to talk face to face."

"Sure, when?"

"Now."

"Okay, where?"

"My place."

"I'll be there within the hour."

Mike was confident Len had taken care of Pinkie and scared the tar out of him from a crushed kneecap and probably a bit more. Mike couldn't fathom what was so urgent, perhaps Len needed his payment.

Mike went to his hidden safe behind his shoe rack in his walk-in closet and counted out five-thousand dollars. He put it in a packet, folded it and placed in his pocket and headed over to Len's.

He pushed the bell and Len immediately opened the door.

"Come in," he nodded seriously.

"What's up, Len?"

"Join me in a drink?"

"Jesus, Len, it's a bit early. What gives? Suspense never agrees with me."

"Do you want the good news or the bad news first?"

"Whatever—spit it out."

"I took care of Pinkie," he gulped on his second beer. "But I took care of him for good."

"What! Fuck, don't tell me you cut his prick off?"

"I killed the cunt. I murdered him." He looked at Mike in disbelief.

"Jesus, Len, are you serious?"

"Mike, that fucker is a known pedophile, yet he has never been caught or put away by the police. I reckon he must be protected in some way."

Len flopped down on his couch, "There is something I have never told you before." He took another gulp. "That bastard molested me when I was just a kid. Now he can't touch or ruin any more kids' lives. I promise you no one saw me. Something inside me snapped, and I killed him with a knife. Cut his throat from ear to ear in a deserted dirty public men's room. Very fitting, I think."

Mike was silent for a few seconds in deep thought.

"Right, I see," he said at last. "Fingerprints at the scene?"

"No, of course not. No fingerprints. I wore gloves. I have no criminal record, so no problem."

"Len, this must stay between you and me. No one and I mean not a word to anyone else. Do you hear me?"

"Of course, I understand."

"Problem, my boss will see it in the news. I will deal with that. She does not know you, and she will keep silent. I know her too well."

Len looked at Mike without saying a word.

"Now, I've only got a few dollars for you. Remember I never ordered a hit, only to be roughed up and a broken knee as an incentive, and that's what I am paying you for, capiche?"

Mike chucked the packet at Len, and he opened it.

"There's five K there—don't spend it all at once."

"You know, Mike, I've waited a long time to do it, and the dream came true today. Death can be tragic, and death can also be beautiful. Today death was beautiful," he said, raising his beer.

Mike stayed for a beer, and Len unburdened himself some more. Mike tried hard to listen with a sympathetic ear, but his mind raced about the possible consequences.

He rang Fern the instant he got back into his car after leaving Len.

"I'm on my way over. Are you home?"

"You're always welcome, Mike."

"Good. I'll be there in time for the 6 O'clock News."

Fern greeted him outside when he pulled up.

"Hi, what's up? What's so important about the 6 O'clock News?"

"Let's go inside, somewhere where we will not get disturbed."

"Ok, let's go to the boardroom."

Fern shut the door.

"Fern, I admire you greatly. You are tough, dedicated, and beautiful, but you will need to be extra tough with what I have to tell you."

"Okay, go on," she said cautiously. "What's on your mind?"

"Your man, Pinkston, Pinkie, is dead."

"What? Mike, are you fucking mad? I never said kill him," she almost screamed in shock.

"I didn't. Of course, I didn't. I just spoke with a good reliable contact of mine. I only asked him to make sure he never bothered you again nor interfered with the Stork Center, but he got carried away. I've just found out that it is one hell of a coincidence; my contact told me Pinkie molested him and badly when he was just a kid. All his life, he wanted to find him and annihilate him, and I just gave him the push without realizing it."

"Shit! Mike, what do we do now?"

"Zilch! We do nothing. It does not concern us. This stays between you and me. Nobody else—understand?"

Fern nodded in shock, "As you say, Mike, not a word."

"Between you and me, kid." Mike looked at his watch. "Put the TV on. It's 6 o'clock."

Fern obeyed and they sat waiting.

After the headlines, the news presenter announced, "Breaking news, we are taking you straight to a small shopping center in Elwood, a suburb of Melbourne, where a horrific murder has taken place. Our reporter is on the scene. Jim, what can you tell us?"

"Thank you, Hazel. Well, a ghastly murder has taken place, possibly a professional hit. It is too soon to confirm. A man known to the police has been slaughtered in a violent killing spree. His name has not been released as yet, but police were alerted by a shopper who saw blood trickling from under a toilet door in the public restrooms. A crime scene has been set up on-site, and the area cornered off. Police are saying that it's one of the worst crimes they've ever seen. I must tell you, Hazel, that one officer said it was as if Jack the Ripper was now in Melbourne. Back to you in the studio."

Fern switched off the TV.

"So now you know."

"I don't know what to say, Mike, except fucking hell!"

"The bastard probably molested more than one child. If he did it to my friend years ago, he must have hurt dozens and damaged so many young lives. Too many to count. It's disgusting and he has paid the price!"

Fern shook her head in disbelief. "Here we are, saving babies and toddlers. Their lives matter to me. I am not a violent person and don't promote it, but in this case, my heart goes out to the kids he ruined. At least he can't hurt anyone anymore."

They looked at each other silently. A secret oath passed between them.

Fern eventually broke the connection and turned to the liquor cabinet. "Drink? I think I need one."

She poured a shot of whisky for both of them and took a sip.

"Let's move on. When do you fly abroad?"

Mike admired how calmly Fern was taking this latest development. She certainly wasn't the hysterical type.

"I leave in two days for London. Make sure Alice and Oliver are on standby."

"I will. In fact, I'm expecting a call from Oliver this evening. He said he was going to call. Are you meeting up with the lady from Bulgaria, Stella?"

"Yes, I'll recruit her if she's willing. If so, we will need to look after her salary-wise. Fern, are you sure you are alright? You're a bit pale."

"I suppose so. I have to be. Err, I leave it to you, Mike. Whatever you think about her salary. Do you want another?"

"No, you go ahead. If you will excuse me, I've got lots to organize before I fly."

"Of course."

As she walked him to the door, she said, "I don't know what to say or think about Pinkie. I'm still in shock, but I guess he deserved it." She said, trying to find comfort in the latest incident.

"You got that right," he said and kissed her on the cheek.

Chapter Forty-Three

Mike landed in London and checked into a hotel in the heart of bustling Oxford Street. He'd told Stella to just bring an overnight bag and gave her the address of the hotel.

When she arrived, she checked in at reception. There was a note from Mike to call when she got in. She took the small elevator to her floor.

She had never known extravagance like this before. Everything was new to her. She had never stepped inside a luxury hotel in her life. She had only seen them in the movies.

When she opened the door with the key card, she stood for a few seconds taking in the opulence, before going inside. She was not tired, the flight from Sofia to London was a mere three hours, and she was too excited about seeing Mike again to want to rest.

She saw the phone next to the bed, and it took a few minutes to figure out how to call his room.

Mike picked up immediately. "Why, Stella, so nice to hear your voice from near and not from afar. Did you just arrive?"

"Yes, I'm in my room. It is so beautiful, thank you."

"That's good. I tell you what, let's meet in the lobby in ten minutes."

"Okay, see you then."

Stella looked in the mirror and freshened her makeup. She was pleased with what she saw. Her only concern was her outfit. Although it was new, and she had bought it from the money Mike had sent, it was out of place here in a top five-star London hotel.

Downstairs, Mike quickened his pace when he saw her and smiled.

They hugged.

"Stella! Let me look at you," Mike said as they pulled apart. "You look great! I am so happy to see you again.

"Have you had anything to eat or drink?" Mike asked, still smiling.

"On the plane. I'm not hungry, but tea would be nice. How about you?"

"Come, there are many shops and restaurants as you probably saw on your way in. Let's find a place to sit and enjoy a cup. Besides, I've got a little surprise for you."

"You have surprised me enough. Now what?" She was a little overwhelmed by the attention and generosity.

Mike cupped her arm in his, and they sauntered outside to the shops until they came to a cozy-looking tea shop.

They found a table in a quiet area and ordered tea and homemade scones, and strawberry jam.

"I am so glad you agreed to come, Stella. As I said on the phone, I've got a job offer for you. We also have a few days here, and I want to spoil you a bit with a shopping spree. I want to treat you to some more new clothes."

"But, Mike, it too kind--" Stella interrupted.

"Please, Stella, please, I want to do it. I just want to spend time with you and be with you again."

Stella blushed. "I do not know what to say..."

The waitress brought the tea and scones and left.

"The first thing I'd like to do is get you and your grandmother out of Stolipinovo. I am happy to help you find a decent area where you would be comfortable renting an apartment. I don't mean to embarrass you, but I am in a position to help and want to. I know this might be unsettling at first, but we can take care of it this week. What do you think?"

Stella's face tightened, and she sucked in her lips with watered eyes. "Sorry, Mike, but it is just too good to be true. I am totally lost for words."

"Well, it comes from my heart."

"Thanks, Mike, thanks. All I can say is thank you from me and from Grandmamma."

"Regarding the job offer I mentioned before — and let me say first that the offer I've just made to you stands whether or not you choose to accept the job." He looked kindly into her eyes.

"I want you to be our manager in Europe. We are expanding our operation and need someone on the ground full-time to monitor and locate potential collection areas. We need someone to infiltrate communities where babies are abandoned or abused and desperately need a new home. Babies who would thrive with love and care where they have no hope in their biological family."

"Mike, that sounds meaningful and worthwhile work, but where would I begin, and where do I find them?"

"We will research together. There is poverty everywhere, and people live in slums all over Europe. Of course, as you know, not every child is ill-treated just because of their environment, just as not every wealthy person is a savior or knight in shining armor. It is imperative we keep our emotions separate and not get too sentimental. We must research each case individually and let the facts speak, so we do not deal in stereotypes."

Stella was listening intently.

"Of course, I do not expect you to go alone into these ghettos. It is too risky. We will either go together, or I will recruit a bodyguard to accompany you when I am not around. I promise I will keep watch over you. We will have weekly face-to-face meetings or Skype calls to stay in regular contact. Stella, you have to understand, it's dangerous work — there's danger from the bad guys and the good guys."

Mike looked at her. He was very serious.

"You know, like the thugs we ran into in your neighborhood, and then there are the cops and authorities. We are doing special humanitarian work, but if we're caught, we can't expect others to see it that way. We risk being found guilty of human trafficking, which comes with real jail time. So, you need to give this serious thought. If your answer is yes and you decide you can handle it, maybe down the line, we can fly you to Australia if you would like to visit. You can stay at our adoption center and see how it operates first-hand. You've already met the owner, Fern Jones, but it would give you a chance to get to know everyone else involved. Think about it and let me know. As I said, there are no strings. The new clothes, this trip, and your new apartment is all yours, whatever you decide."

"Mike, I do not need to think about it. I have one word to say, just one: yes, yes, yes!"

"But that's three words," Mike said, and they laughed.

"I should add that this comes with a substantial salary and compensation package."

"I'm still lost for words, Mike."

"Good, now that's settled, we can relax and spend some time together and enjoy London. You ready?"

"You are my guide."

"First things first. Let's go clothes shopping. I want you to take something back to your grandmother as well, a jersey or two for the Bulgarian winter. Look upon this as a new chapter in your life. Also, I don't think it is a good idea to take a lot of clothes back to Stolipinovo. I suggest when we get back to the hotel, we research apartments for you and your grandmother in Sofia. We will follow up with some calls to make a couple of appointments to view these places. We can look for a furnished place in a nice leafy suburb and fly over together to secure your new home. We will then go for the last time to Stolipinovo to pack up your personal belongings and move you and your grandmother into your new pad. What do you think?"

"Have I been struck by lightning? Although, it's good lightning.."

"Enough said, now let's get going. I hope you've got lots of energy as you are going to need it with all the purchases I am planning."

In the late afternoon, they returned to their hotel, tired and overloaded with bags from some of London's most exclusive stores.

Stella invited Mike back to her room, and they ordered room service.

They talked about her new role, and Mike reiterated he would not throw her into the deep end but work alongside her to do the groundwork.

Mike was attracted to Stella, with her flashing dark eyes and blonde hair, and Slavik face with her heart-shaped face, but refrained from any temptation and made no attempt to approach the subject. He did not want her to think she owed him anything. Stella was also attracted to him and wondered why he did not make a move.

Together they viewed advertised properties for rent, and after a couple of calls to an agent, they decided on one particular apartment that seemed ideal. As good as his word, Mike immediately transferred the security deposit to hold the place until they arrived.

Two days later, Mike flew to Bulgaria with Stella. He rented a car at the airport, and they drove straight to her new apartment. The agent was there to greet them and give Stella her new set of keys. Then they went to the local shopping center where Mike bought groceries and all the basic essentials and fresh produce to fill her new fridge as well as wine and champagne to celebrate. Stella was speechless and so grateful for her newly furnished home that was clean and modern.

As she put her new clothes away, she was conscious of Mike watching her. He walked towards her quietly while she was stretching an arm into the cupboard and placed both of his hands on her shoulders. She turned around and embraced him.

"Stella, are you sure? I do not want to spoil our relationship."

"Mike, the day I saw you, I was attracted to you." She kissed him on his neck and lips.

They kissed long and hard while he lifted off her top. He then unhooked her bra, and she ripped off her jeans. She stood there facing him in her red panties, breathing heavily.

She stepped forward and unbuttoned Mike's shirt, and he started to get an erection.

He removed his jeans and took her hand gently, and walked towards her new bedroom. On the bed, he removed her panties and slipped off his boxers.

He caressed her breasts and kissed her nipples, sucking the left one and then the right one. He rubbed her vagina gently on the sweet spot, and she took him in her mouth while his eyes rolled back. Their breathing grew faster and heavier.

"Get inside me, Mike," she whispered, and he did. While he pumped away, she also moved backward and forwards, her hips swaying while gripping his butt hard.

She moaned in ecstasy, and then he did, as he felt the pressure of his semen shooting like a powerful water pistol in spurts deep inside her.

They lay in each other's arms in silence, happy and contented.

"Stella, that was great. I mean it," he said, kissing her affectionately.

"Oh, Mike, I want to be with you forever."

"I tell you what, let's go get your grandmother tomorrow. I just want to be alone with you tonight."

She kissed him passionately in agreement.

The next day they drove to her old neighborhood for the last time. Stella climbed the stairs with a spring in her step to tell her grandmother she no longer had to live out the rest of her days in poverty.

Mr. and Mrs. Mwangi flew from Sydney to Melbourne to meet their new son for the first time, and it was love at first sight. The couple stayed overnight to learn all the dos and don'ts about their new baby before taking him home.

Fern sat in the warm kitchen on one particularly cold Dandenong morning talking to her mother when her phone rang. She smiled. It was Oliver.

"Hi, Fern, the name is Oliver. Maybe you remember me?" he joked.

"Hold on a sec." She excused herself and went to her bedroom.

Okay, that's better. I was with my mom in the kitchen. How are you? I didn't hear from you the other night. Everything all right? You said you had something to talk to me about."

Oliver had tried to ring her that night, but she had not answered.

"So, what can I do for you, Ollie?"

Oliver knew he had her as soon as she called him Ollie.

"Aha, this weekend, I've got the company of *Lady Lucy*, and I want you to join us."

Fern was confused. Surely the son of a bitch didn't mean a threesome. She certainly was not into that. "And why would I want to join you and this *Lady Lucy*, whoever she is?"

"My dear Fern, *Lady Lucy* is the name of a luxury forty-foot boat cruiser I have access to. She comes with twin V8 fuel-injected engines, a fully equipped kitchen, a luxury bedroom, and bathroom, spacious seating, and a barbecue on the deck. I'd be a sucker to take her out alone," he chuckled on the other end.

"*Lady Lucy* belongs to a friend of mine who is overseas for a month. Remember, I mentioned before that I can borrow it whenever I like.

He owns a yacht and this beauty. I thought we could cruise out for a night or two somewhere not too far, like on the waters by Lorne and up to Apollo Bay?" he teased seductively.

Fern surprised him. "So, when and what time, Skipper?"

"Friday morning—drive to my neck of the woods, leave your car in my garage, and we'll pick up *Lady Lucy* from the marina in Brighton and then bon voyage. It will be good to head out early, around 6 am?"

"Ollie, I'll be at your place just before your cock crows!" There was a second or two of embarrassed silence.

"I mean, I meant to say just before the cock crows, bloody hell, dammit!"

Oliver chuckled, and Fern giggled and went bright red. Thank God he couldn't see her.

"Excellent. See you at 5.30 am. *Lady Lucy* will be waiting for you."

"Aye, aye. See you then, Captain."

Fern smiled again to herself, and so did Oliver on the other end, but more so.

She knew she needed a break, and it was ages since she'd had any fun. It might also take her mind off Mike, and whatever it was he was doing with Stella.

Chapter Forty-Four

Oliver and Fern carried the two large cooler boxes filled with food, wine, and water aboard the boat, as well as their own two small overnight cases.

It didn't take them long to unload and put the supplies away. Oliver started the engines and untied the moorings, and soon *Lady Lucy* carried them smoothly into the deeper waters of Port Phillip Bay.

It was a sunny morning, and Oliver handled the boat like a jet. He let out the throttle, and she eased forward smoothly, gaining speed as they exited the bay at Queenscliff and Sorrento, heading southwest towards the world-renowned Great Ocean Road.

Motoring out, Oliver turned to look at Fern, who was admiring the sea and enjoying the breeze while holding her straw hat down over her blonde hair.

The sea changed color to a light blue turquoise. As it was early, the seagulls swooped and dived in the golden rays of the morning sun.

Towards lunchtime, they arrived within a mile of the lush coastline of Lorne.

Oliver stopped the engines, and the boat bobbed up and down with the waves.

"Are you alright, Fern?" he asked.

"A tad seasick but nothing serious."

Fern helped herself to a bottle of orange juice.

"What would my captain like to drink?"

"I'll join you with a juice, Lady Fern."

Fern passed him a bottle while smiling.

"Here—why is the boat called *Lady Lucy*, I meant to ask?"

Oliver chuckled. "*Lady Lucy* used to be *Lady Viv*, named after my friend's ex-wife Vivian. He's married to Lucy now, a gorgeous Chinese girl — gorgeous like you, Fern."

"Wow, very flattering, Captain."

"I tell you what, let's continue for a while, and we can spend the night nearby, then tomorrow we can head out to the Twelve Apostles."

"I'm easy, Captain."

They had drifted about five hundred feet from the shore. They sat on the deck with the sun beating down, admiring the green hills in the background. Oliver started the twin engines, and they followed the coastline until they came to a spot where the Cumberland river flowed into the sea. The vistas were gorgeous. Oliver steered the boat closer so they could both take in the magnificent shoreline. He killed the engines, and they stood on deck, his arm around her as they rhythmically rolled with the waves in unison. They stared at the incredible natural beauty of the bush, the craggy cliff, and lush vegetated hills further inland. A couple of fishermen stood on the rocks with their lines, and they watched cars traveling in the distance going to and from Australia's famous Twelve Apostles. The boat rocked more, bobbing up and down, and Fern paled.

"Come sit, Fern. There's a smoother patch of water up ahead," he indicated, pointing. He started the engines again, and in seconds he had maneuvered the boat to calmer waters.

Fern felt easier, and once again, he switched off the twin engines.

"I reckon we can spend the night here, then tomorrow we can head to the Apostles and play it by ear. We could take a slow cruise back to Melbourne or stay another night."

"Sounds like a great idea. I'm feeling a better but a bit peckish. Are you hungry?"

"Sure am," Oliver agreed as he glanced at his watch.

"Wow, it is 2 pm already. Let's rustle something up." He weighed anchor.

They took out some cold meat and ciabatta rolls, and Fern sliced a tomato and a fresh cucumber while Oliver put a bottle of olives out. He opened a cold bottle of beer and passed it to Fern. "Not for me, thanks. I feel like a Coke. Have you got one?"

"You don't look like one but sure," and he opened a can for her.

She smiled at the old joke. "You want a glass?" he asked.

"Ollie, I don't mean to be anti-social, but I am tired, and nothing would give me more pleasure now than taking a nap. I need my strength for later."

"Sure, I understand."

He folded the seats, which converted into a double bed. Fern lay down and fell asleep in seconds, lying there peacefully, fully dressed.

Oliver smiled to himself. He liked her comment about needing her strength for later.

He let her sleep and removed a powerful pair of Swarovski binoculars, and sat on the deck to survey the view around them. He saw a fisherman land a fish and observed the birds enjoying the sea air. An albatross flew close by, and he was in awe of its enormous wing span and a flock of terns cruising parallel to the shoreline. The sun burned, and he grew tired too and lay down next to Fern.

She woke up some two hours later, feeling awake and refreshed. Oliver stirred, opening his eyes and rubbing them.

"Come here," he said softly. She did and started to remove her clothes. He admired her beautiful body.

Then he undressed and walked naked to the small bathroom area to freshen up, returning with a partial erection.

"You have a beautiful body, Ollie. Such strong muscular legs."

"Yes, I need strong legs to support a heavy third leg," he chuckled.

She rolled her eyes at his corny joke. They tore into each other, kissing and rubbing up against one another. She moaned when he massaged her clitoris gently, and she came quickly. Then she took him in her mouth while gently jerking his penis up and down.

"Enough, stop Fern. I don't want to come so quickly."

He got up to fetch something and returned. She saw he had a plastic bottle of honey.

"It's my turn now. I owe you one."

He squeezed some honey on each nipple, and then he licked and sucked the erect nipples dry. She moved her head backward and moaned in delight.

He then squeezed a few small drops of honey on her vagina and clitoris and proceeded to gently lick and suck while rubbing her clitoris with his left middle fingers. She moaned some more. Then ever so gently, he opened her legs and entered her, up and down, down and up. More moaning. He withdrew his penis and sucked her more while licking her vagina as if it was his first ice cream. Then he entered her again, and he finished deep inside her while he groaned with pleasure. She then took him and sucked him clean, and in fifteen minutes, he was fully erect again. The boat seemed to rock from their movement and not only from the ocean swell. This time she licked his balls, and when he went down on her, they found themselves in the sixty-nine position, enjoying every second. From sixty-nine she moved and sat on him, up and down until they came some more. The boat rocked gently with the ocean. Somewhere overhead a few seagulls squawked. Spent, they lay quietly in each other's arms.

At sunset they went on deck, each with a glass of red wine. Fern was quiet.

Oliver looked at her. "You alright, my girl?"

"Yes, Ollie, just that I would give anything to know where my real mother is, and my father for that matter."

"Sorry, kitten. I wish I could help. I wish I knew."

Unknown to them and especially to Fern, they were in the very waters and almost the exact spot where poor Sophia Semenov, her real mother, had ended her life many, many years back.

The sun dropped below the horizon, and it was soon dark. They ate a meal of fresh fish and filet mignon and a pinot noir and the only witness to their sexual pleasure was the flickering stars up above.

As they lay in each other's arms, Oliver suddenly said to her in an uncharacteristically serious tone, "I think I could be falling in love with you. This isn't just a fling to me anymore, you know."

She sought a light response. "I dig you too, Ollie. But let's not rush anything. There's a lot of serious stuff we have to focus on. Let's keep what we have together as our escape, our relief valve."

Fern knewshe was not in love with Oliver, but she didn't want to hurt his feelings or lose him as her pilot. She also knew that she was not looking for a husband.

It occurred to her that she had no close friends outside of work and no blood relatives. Her friends were her staff, and her love was her business. She wondered again what Mike was doing.

In the morning, they sailed past the Twelve Apostles. The awe and wonder of nature's beauty were revitalizing for her. Even so, they decided to head back slowly to Melbourne as Fern was suffering from seasickness again.

The next day Fern was back at her desk and Mike called to say he would be staying in Europe to secure a constant supply of new babies for collection. He would be gone for several weeks.

He had been in touch with Danny, who was beavering away at his desk preparing certificates and various permits for the influx of deliveries. Oliver and Morrie were on standby, waiting for the green light. Fern briefed Lance and all the staff at the Stork Center.

Mike and Stella worked tirelessly, researching the best cities and communities that had the poorest families and were most known for unwanted pregnancies and births. They regularly flew to various places outside Bulgaria to different European countries, including Greece, Italy, Romania, Germany, France, Spain as well as England.

They also spent time hiring local informants and agents, and Mike used his connections to cement useful relationships with corrupt customs and border officials. And they also loved being together.

Chapter Forty-Five

The years passed. Oliver and Morrie clocked hundreds of thousands of kilometres with Alice and Sheelah on board to collect and deliver to the Stork Center.

Lance's schedule was packed with the Center's work, and Fern increased the staff roster. She even extended and enlarged the nursery to house up to thirty babies at a time up to the age of three years. .

Fern continued to make large donations to abused women shelters and orphanages all over Australia. Always anonymously to stay out of the media spotlight. The business flourished and the income piled up to the tune of over a billion dollars.

The orders flowed in and Fern was frequently shocked how much these wealthy clients were prepared to spend and how desperate they were to have a family.

She noticed her clients average age was between forty and fifty-five, simply because the adoption process denied them due to their age.

There were certain cases Fern had to sadly turn down because they were in their sixties despite meeting the Stork Center's rigorous criteria. She acknowledged that adopting a baby in their late forties/early fifties had worked out for Chester and Megan, but as a general rule, she felt it was better for the parents to be younger.

It was during this time, Mike met someone who was well connected in the USA and soon the American market opened up with sales and hundreds of requests.

The babies were flown from the US back to Melbourne and, after they were processed, flown back to the USA to new American parents and a new life.

Fern and Mike left no stone unturned and continued to vigorously complete background checks on new parents confirming their financial status and no criminal record or any sealed sex offence on file as well as making sure there was no hidden alcohol or drug addiction in their history.

Stella ran operations in Europe, proving her dedication and loyalty working around the clock.

Mike made regular international trips between Melbourne and abroad, always making sure he caught up with Stella whenever his schedule allowed. She had by now become not only his co-worker, but his steady girlfriend.

Chapter Forty-Six

Then came an incident that got Fern and Mike rethinking the entire operation.

At a family home in Florida in the United States, a babysitter was watching over a fifteen-month-old toddler, while the parents were at work.

It was a hot summer's day, and the babysitter was sitting in the shade on a garden bench while gently rocking the stroller.

The baby was sleeping quietly so she decided not to disturb her and quickly ran to the bathroom.

She was only gone a few minutes and returned to an empty stroller. Her high-pitched scream alerted a neighbor.

Minutes later, police sirens and flashing lights with officers combing the area disrupted the quiet suburb.

The sobbing babysitter called the parents and thirty minutes later they returned home. The mother had to receive medical attention for shock while the police questioned the distraught father as the echoing blades overhead from of a police helicopter intensified the search of the area.

The toddler had been taken from a good loving home and, as the senior detective was being interviewed on television, the little one was whisked to Australia.

Alice and Oliver, oblivious to the details of what had happened, brought the child home to Australia with all the necessary forged documentation. The baby came in on its own passport with the same last name as Alice's. Mike had set everything up through his American contact, relying on him to make all the arrangements. When they arrived home to the Center, Alice commented to Fern how this child was different to the norm. She was clean, well-dressed and well cared for.

Mike arrived as Oliver and Morrie left for a much-needed rest.

He immediately agreed with Alice. He looked at the toddler's top, then he checked the label.

"Christ! It is a Diesel, a well-known top designer. And, look at the shoes; they are Dolce and Gabbana. The shoes alone are worth $300 or more and the top is worth a lot as well!" he said incredulously. "This baby was not rescued from poverty nor monstrous parents. Shit! I think she has been kidnapped! There's no two ways about it."

Fern's face creased in concern, "What do you suggest? We've got to fix this now!"

"Let me check because our American could be involved in kidnapping. If so, he may demand a ransom; then when he has the money, he could point the authorities in our direction. I'm talking cops, CIA, FBI and our very own Australia Security Intelligence Organization (ASIO) and federal police on our case. You name it."

"Shit Mike! What do we do?" Fern said, fear written all over her face.

Mike looked at his watch. "I've gotta get hold of the American guy. He lives in Miami. It is 11 am here now so that means it is around 9 pm in Florida."

Mike started to walk to the boardroom. Fern followed while Alice took charge of the toddler and went to the nursery. Mike called his man in Miami as they entered the boardroom. Fern started to talk but Mike raised his index finger to his lips to indicate silence.

Fern observed Mike was using a different mobile.

"Hello."

The American replied. "Why, hello, Mike, what's up, buddy?"

"The little girl we just collected—we've got a problem, and I think you know about it."

"Mike, what are you talking about?"

"Don't act mister innocent with me, Barry! This little one was delivered to us wearing designer clothing worth hundreds of dollars. This is not a rescued toddler. This is a kidnapping! In my book someone will pay with their life and I fucking mean it, so tell me more, who snatched her?"

There was silence for a few seconds.

"I'm waiting, Barry, you sound guilty already."

"Mike, listen up, I recruited another guy a few months back. He is the one who provided the baby."

"Have you got his full name and address?"

"Mike, I can hear you are upset, yes, I know where he lives and his full name."

"Barry, you do not know what upset means? Let me tell you something, I have my own jet, and I have worldwide connections." He paused for effect. "All I have to do is click my fingers and the person responsible is history. And if you were involved you are a goner as well. Are we on the same page now, eh?"

"What do you want from me? I have nothing to hide."

"You phone your contact and ask him where he took the toddler from. Phone me back within an hour." Mike ended the call abruptly.

"Are we in trouble?" Fern whispered, getting scared. All she'd wanted to do was save babies who were in danger not kidnap them.

"Nothing that I can't sort out," he reassured her.

Fern exhaled deeply with a worried frown.

"Listen Fern, this is what is going to happen. I will fly out first thing tomorrow with Oliver and Morrie and get Alice to bring the toddler. I will see to it she is returned to her parents safely. I will then deal with the culprit and we will cut all ties."

He banged his fist on the table in frustration.

"Okay, change of plans. With our jet we get 5,600 kilometres but we have to stop to refuel three times. It's very long and tiring for our pilots, so let's leave them out of this equation. Alice and I will fly tomorrow with Qantas or another airline. We are looking at less than twenty-four hours if we take a non-stop commercial flight."

Fern nodded in agreement.

Mike continued his thought on the bigger picture, "We will sever all ties with the States for good. The risk is too great."

"We don't actually need them. We have enough supplies from other countries and we don't need to jeopardize everything we have worked for to fish in America."

Fern took out a packet of chewing gum and popped two into her mouth.

"You want some gum?"

"Yes, why not," he said absently.

Fern passed him the gum. Mike emptied two into the palm of his hand and tossed them quickly into his mouth.

They sat in silence for a few seconds chewing away. Fern chewed hard and quickly and she bit the side of her tongue hard.

"Fuck it, fuck, fuck it!" she said in pain inserting her finger over the bite.

Mike handed her a box of Kleenex. She grabbed a sheet and dabbed it on the bite area.

"What if someone notices the baby on the airline and identifies her as the kidnapped toddler. Maybe we should reconsider the Learjet," Fern suggested dabbing her tongue to stop the bleeding. "Well? What do you think?"

"Time is tight and I don't think it will be a problem. The news most likely hasn't become international news yet. If we fly in the Learjet, we still have to do stopovers at international airports. The layovers to refuel in the different countries will delay us too long and the news might travel and catch up with us by the time we land in Florida." Mike spoke while thinking out loud.

"Go online now and see if you can book the reservations. I am going to talk to Alice and explain. Also, make sure you book our return flights for a week later. I don't want to raise any suspicion."

Mike left for the nursery while Fern opened up the Qantas Airlines website. Mike also called Dr. Lance Jones. He leaned against the wall outside and asked Lance if he knew any American specialist doctors. He was particularly interested in paediatric heart surgeons.

He was in luck. Lance had met a paediatric surgeon at a conference a few years back.

Mike asked Lance to contact the surgeon immediately. He told him, Alice would be bringing a baby who had major heart problems and would more than likely need surgery. Aussie doctors were amongst the best in the world but he explained the baby had a rare heart deformity that only surgeons in the United States specialized in. Lance was unsure and didn't really buy the story. Mike said he would explain later, but there was no time now. He took down the name of the specialist and ended the call. He made another quick call to Danny and then went to talk to Alice who was rocking the little girl in her arms.

"Hi, how is she doing?" he asked quietly.

"She's fine, Mike, though a little restless. Where's Fern?"

"Booking airline tickets. I'm afraid we are off tomorrow, back to the US. I'm sure you've connected the dots. This baby was taken illegally—kidnapped. We have to get her back home pronto before we get implicated."

Alice looked up startled.

"Trust me, you will not be in any danger. Once we return the baby, we can relax for a few days."

"I knew it," she hissed. "I knew there was a problem!" He could see she was pissed.

"You are in good hands, please don't worry. I must get back to Fern. Now, go home and pack for a week. The other girls here will look after the other babies."

"A week, Mike, what do you mean? Why so long?" Alice said with a puzzled expression.

"I want to avoid any kind of suspicion when we go through customs at the airport in Miami. Let them think we are there for a vacation. Don't worry, you won't have to actually stay a week. We'll invent a story to get you back the next day. We will have our flight confirmation any minute now. Since I live far from you, we must meet at the airport check-in desk. You can grab a taxi with the little one and bring her with you, okay?"

"Yes, I'm just worried, I hope you don't blame me? And what about when we re-enter the States with a baby who was only in Australia for a day or two?" she asked thinking about the logistics.

"It will be alright, I promise. I'm taking care of that now organizing something to prove the little one needs heart surgery. Please, just trust me on this. Also, don't forget your passport and the baby's Australian passport too. I will call you later as soon as everything is confirmed."

Just then Fern entered. "You'll all set. You fly out tomorrow afternoon at 4 pm. Here are your tickets, I just printed your boarding passes."

Mike took both the tickets with a quick smile and put them in the inside pocket of his windbreaker.

"Good, I must go now. Alice, we need to meet at midday at the airport. Do me a favor and pack a big case. I do not want customs suspecting anything. I mean no one flies to the USA with an overnight bag."

Fern looked at Alice. "I'll take you to the airport. Leave now and pack and get a good night's sleep. Come here in the morning at around 10 am. We can prepare the baby and have breakfast together before we head to the airport."

"Thanks, Fern, I appreciate it."

"'Girls," Mike called taking off, "I have to go, lots to do."

He waved, climbed into his car, and disappeared.

As he accelerated onto the road he thought about Bruce Nash, the retired policeman. He wondered what the old bloke was up to. Loneliness must be one of the worst illnesses one can succumb to. He had no intention of being in that predicament.

Barry, the American agent, called, breaking into Mike's thoughts.

"Mike, you guessed right, my guy never took my call and it is all over TV. Someone is demanding a million dollars in ransom money for the kidnapped baby. I just saw the desperate parents being interviewed on TV."

"Okay, this is what you must do. Make contact again, and if necessary, go to his place. I know what he is doing—claiming the money but will give your details to the police. Now listen carefully. You tell him you want in on this and you have a plan and connections for an operation that will be worth a lot of money, millions and millions. Don't elaborate, just make it clear you want to meet. Tell him he will retire with a large fortune and you can pay him a chunk up front. If necessary, to entice him say we have a plan to snatch one of New York's wealthiest trust fund kids."

"And what about the little girl you have in Australia?"

"I will take care of that, Barry. Get onto your guy now. You need to buy some time, just a couple of days. Phone me back on this number as soon as you have made contact."

Mike ended the call.

When he arrived home, he phoned Danny to discuss the rush order on the medical referral, and the forged letter from the paediatric surgeon stating the baby needed urgent surgery. Then he changed his mind and told Danny an email would suffice. He would get Lance to email a referral to Alice's email address. Danny need not worry.

Mike quickly called Alice and brought her up to speed to print the email she will receive from Lance.

Lance was not happy but reluctantly agreed to the charade. However, he reiterated, he would never do it again. In his heart he was tired of the illegal operation. He was too old for these games and had no use for them.

The flight to Florida was long. Mike slept most of the time but poor Alice hardly slept looking after the little one. She was worried and concerned about the risk they were taking. She had given Mike the email when they had settled in their seats when they boarded.

Eventually after nearly twenty-one hours, they landed and stood in line at customs. Miraculously, the baby started to cry as they stood behind the red line in front of customs. Mike was pleased to see the customs officer hastily stamp their passports as her crying became a screech. Alice tried to soothe the little one, and Mike smiled.

"Long flight," he shrugged. "Our poor little angel needs attention. Thank God our doctor can see her tomorrow, she has severe ear problems and we think her tummy hurts too."

Right on cue, the baby wailed.

The official stamped their passports, one after the other, and they were clear. They made their way to baggage claim and then found their way to the rental car office.

"Mike, you were so relaxed. I don't know how you do it," Alice commented in awe as they drove to their hotel.

Mike used the GPS to find the fastest route and ignored the device when it said *Destination ahead one-hundred metres*. He passed it and explained to Alice best not to check-in with a baby as the hotel registration would make a note. It was important to drop the little one off first. Alice looked puzzled, completely confused.

He drove around and found a park and noticed a policeman patrolling the place. It was the perfect location. For her safety, it was necessary to find a public place so she would not be stranded for a long time.

Mike parked the car and made sure he found a space next to other cars. He looked around for security cameras. There was none. They walked to an area just minutes away from the rental. Mike saw a statue and about ten feet behind was a park bench in the shade. They sat on the bench like a picture-perfect family. There were no one around, no cameras; it was very peaceful. Mike placed the sleeping baby on a blanket under the bench on the well-kept lawn in the cool shade.

He then withdrew his US burner phone from his jacket and inserted the SIM card Danny had given to him that was untraceable.

"Let's go now," he said to Alice.

She silently obeyed.

They arrived back at the car a few minutes later. As they drove off, Mike called 911. In a perfect American accent, he told the operator there was a baby in the park near the statue. He named the park, but gave no other details and ended the call.

He assured Alice the baby would be just fine. The authorities and the whole police force were looking for her so she would be reunited with her parents very soon.

They checked in to their hotel and retired to their rooms to rest.

Mike was up and about well before Alice. He went downstairs and went for a walk outside and took a leisurely stroll around the neighborhood. He purchased a pair of scissors at the pharmacy and walked into another hotel where he used the men's room. He cut up the SIM into several tiny pieces and removed the battery from the phone and dumped it in the trash.

On his way back to his hotel, he casually dropped pieces of the SIM card on the pavement here and there and in different trash cans along the way. Three blocks from the hotel he trashed the cell phone in a restaurant dumpster.

That evening they watched the 7 O'clock News in Mike's hotel suite before heading down for dinner. It was good news for everyone as the presenter announced the missing toddler had been reunited with her grieving parents. The baby girl was in good health and the police were investigating.

The next morning after breakfast Alice changed her return flight and flew back to Melbourne without Mike.

Mike had prepared her in case she was questioned, so she was able to tell US passport control her sudden departure was due to her father having just suffered a massive stroke.

She didn't have any problems re-entering Australia using the same story and even went further to ask the official if a taxi was the quickest way out of the airport to the Alfred Hospital. Mike had taught her a lot, it turned out.

As she collected her luggage and walked towards the exit, she swallowed and breathed a huge sigh of relief. If the officer had suspected anything and taken her in for questioning, her story would have been checked.

Alice took a bus to Southern Cross station and from there a train home.

Mike spoke to Fern from Florida and advised her for their own best interest all their flights and their operation were on hold until further notice. He envisaged it would be for a few weeks, until things quieted down.

In her heart Fern shuddered. She feared by the tone of Mike's voice that things might come to an end. The Stork Center had saved hundreds of babies but there were still millions more in the world who needed rescuing.

Luckily, back home, their jet was housed in a semi-private hangar with a fixed-based operator who took care of general maintenance, refueling and storing the aircraft. Oliver had solid relations with a senior official in the flight tower and a colleague in customs and immigration. None of them came cheap.

He immediately arranged for their flight records to the USA over the past few months to be wiped clean. The history of their flights to the USA no longer existed.

After Alice flew home, Mike met with Barry, his agent in Florida, and told him the bad news. The operation was being shut down, effective immediately. Barry's contact who was responsible for the kidnapping had not returned any calls.

Mike stayed on in Florida for a few more days and then he flew to Sofia to join Stella.

The kidnapper was never heard from or seen again.

The designer-dressed baby fiasco was over. Australia was never considered in the FBI or CIA investigation, but it left a bitter taste in everyone's mouth. The team's morale took a hit and they seemed to lose their dedication and motivation.

Over the weeks that followed while Mike was abroad, Fern spent the time checking in and connecting with the couples who had been successful in becoming new parents. It gave her a feeling of purpose to hear how well the babies and children were doing.

She also spoke to the Harrises and learned that baby Nikol was now about to start school and that her brother, Ivan, was a good-looking lad who would soon be a teenager.

They were both doing well. Jack and Wendy Harris were changed people, happy to raise two beautiful kids, happy to give their attention and love, happy to educate them and mould them into a loving family.

Fern felt lonely at times. Her social life outside the Center was non-existent. She was often invited to the charities that she financed, to be a keynote speaker at their fundraising events or to receive an honorary award at their annual black-tie occasions. They even offered to name departments or new extension halls in her name and to cut the ribbon dedicated to her, but she always declined these invitations. Publicity was too dangerous.

After ten-years, all she had was an aging mother, an occasional lover, an illegal-business worth billions, which could not be sold and the danger might still land her in jail. Her thirtieth birthday wasn't far off and she thought about the future.

She walked around the garden to clear her mind. She left via the back door and walked through the parking lot towards the front garden, looking for Bonzo II. He always raised her spirits. She edged closer to the front garden and smiled when she saw him sleeping peacefully in the sun near the flower bed. She walked towards him and called his name, smacking her thigh. "Bonzo, come boy, come here boy." He was now ten years old and getting into his twilight years. She could not imagine ever being without him.

He did not respond. His hearing was going but, when Fern got closer, she knelt down in despair. He was still warm, but not breathing. He must have died in the last hour or so. She stroked his face lovingly and patted him in the warm sun, grateful that he had died painlessly. She put her face next to his and wept.

She pulled him out of the sun and into the shade and called her veterinarian. They would come by in an hour or so.

She was grateful her mother was out in the village and spared her the sight of Bonzo's lifeless body. Fern shared the sad news when she returned later that day. . A shadow seemed to have fallen over both of them. What with the uncertainty around the business and now the loss of second Bonzo, it seemed everything was coming to an end and another link to Chester and his legacy gone.

Mike and Stella were lying in bed in Mike's hotel room, her head on his shoulder and her hair splashed against his chest.

They both lay there thinking. She desperately wanted to marry him. He was thinking of Fern and wondering how she was holding up.

He was also thinking he had saved so much money from the operation over the years that perhaps he didn't need to be doing this sort of work anymore.

He opened his eyes and looked at her.

"What are you thinking, Stella?"

Stella sat up, "Mike, I will tell you. I'm tired of having to look over my shoulder. I'm tired of travelling and buying babies as if they were sacks of potatoes or loaves of bread. I'm tired of being separated from you for long periods, worrying if you are caught or harmed. I'm tired of it all." She sat still looking at him for a reaction. He just lay there, looking up at her, listening.

"Mike, it is time for you to stop being like a Bedouin or a Gypsy always on the move. It is time for you to stop wandering, don't you think?" she said more softly.

"Stella, you are one hundred per cent correct. It's been on my mind for some time too. Leave it with me, I plan to put this way of life behind me soon. But first I need to prepare Fern. I have to persuade her to call it a day as well."

He paused for a moment, "In fact, I think we should both try to persuade her. Remember I promised you a trip to Australia?"

She nodded. "Do you mean it, Mike? When can we go?"

"I'm thinking in a few months or so." Mike watched her face fall. "Or how about tomorrow?"

Stella jumped out of bed, naked, all excited.

"Seriously, Mike? Oh my God!"

"Why not? Australia is a huge country with so much to offer, so much to see — and wait until you taste the food there. Maybe we should not go. I'm worried about your gorgeous figure." Mike laughed when Stella hit him with the pillow. "I'm only kidding. Come, let's go down under! Let's go now."

"Wow! You mean it," Stella shouted incredulously.

"Tell your grandmamma we will be away for a few weeks. I'll book the tickets and then I'll meet you at your apartment."

"Done deal, Mike. Thank you for… who you are."

She sat back down on the bed and hugged him hard. He hugged her back but was the first to pull away.

True to his word, he booked two tickets. He was happy; and realized some of his happiness was the thought of seeing Fern again. He wondered how she would take his advice to close the business. It was her brainchild after all and had been her life for nearly a decade. He knew it would be tough on her. He wondered what she would do and whether he could give her another passion project to focus on. His mind drifted to the letter from Nash, and the ring. She had never mentioned her biological parents all the years he had worked for her. She never hinted if she was curious or pined for them. Was Fern strong enough to handle the news or would it have destroyed her? He didn't have the answer.

As he walked past a string of shops on the way to Stella's apartment, he watched the reflections in the windows from force of habit. It gave him visuals from across the street without turning his head.

He hailed a cab and in minutes was ringing the bell to Stella's front door.

She flung the door open full of jubilation and anticipation.

"Hi," she kissed him. "Come in, come," she said tugging his hand.

Mike entered and kissed Stella's grandmother on each cheek.

"Stella told me you are both going to Australia. Have you booked?"

"Yes, we leave tomorrow."

"Awesome," Stella said as she glanced at her grandmother.

"Grandmamma, why do you look so sad now? Minutes ago, you were full of smiles."

"I am just a little concerned you may not come back and end up living there."

Mike looked at the old lady. "If we end up living in Australia, I promise you I will bring you out as well."

Her face lit up and so did Stella's.

Grandmamma brought out a freshly made cake to celebrate. They stayed for a while before it was time to leave and pack.

They exchanged kisses. Stella hugged her grandmother once more.

"I will call you when we land. I promise you. Love you," she waved as she headed out.

As they walked outside the building, Stella stopped.

"Mike, did you really mean what you said about bringing grandmamma out if we stay in Australia?"

"You must know me by now. I make a promise, I keep it. But let's see what happens. I don't want to put the cart before the horse. Let's see if you like Australia first, then we take it from there."

Stella kissed Mike on the cheek. She had never in her entire life been so happy.

They packed, ate dinner, then Stella put on some soft music.

She showered and put on her favorite perfume and returned to the bedroom.

"Mmm, you smell good." Mike showered quickly and thinking of what lay ahead, and then returned to the bedroom. As always, they made love and then found themselves lying in

a comfortable silence together, the curtain by the window moving from a fresh breeze, and soon Stella fell asleep.

Mike lay awake thinking about all the little souls that had crossed his path over the years and the suffering he had witnessed. Deep down he hated the world for this. Disturbing images flashed through his mind of the tiny faces all sullen, some had wet tears, some had dry tears and snotty noses. There were white faces, black faces, brown faces and Asian faces. One face he could never forget was the little girl lost and alone in a dark and dirty alleyway next to a baker. Her clothes were filthy from sleeping rough and she was clutching a filthy doll and a torn old blanket She was about five years old and she was settling herself down for the night. There were other children milling about by the bakery door, as it provided warmth from the ovens that crept into the alley. He managed to shake the image and put it aside, and fall asleep.

On the way to the airport the next day, Mike phoned Fern and told her he was returning with Stella. It was time to discuss the future.

PART FOUR

PART FOUR

Chapter Forty-Seven

Mike took Stella to all the renowned Melbourne tourist spots after they recovered from jetlag. He showed her the overflowing and colorful Botanical Gardens and the popular Albert Park. They relaxed and enjoyed each other's company strolling hand-in-hand taking in the scenery as they took long walks to unwind. At Albert Park, Stella marvelled at the graceful black swans as they leisurely cruised the lake.

Mike took the occasional call but made sure his main attention was Stella and introducing her to his home town. Oliver was keen to know when they would be flying again and Fern was anxious to reconnect. Mike also let Danny know there would be a full team meeting soon. He planned to introduce Stella to everyone at the weekend and take her to the Stork Center on Saturday.

Saturday was good for Fern too. Her week was filled with appointments and the increased volume of calls and emails to current and new enquiries. She was also looking into assisted living accommodation in Brighton for her mother. Megan had started to slow down and become less active in the last year. Fern felt it might be time for her to be somewhere more relaxing where her every need would be catered for.

Saturday arrived and Mike drove Stella to the Dandenong to see Fern.

Stella was amazed how quickly the scenery changed from the sprawling flat built-up suburbs to the hilly lush forest of the Dandenong.

Mike used his remote to open the Stork Center gates and drove to the back of the house and parked. Fern watched them from the security monitors and went out to greet them. She approached them with a big welcoming smile. She was happy to see them, especially Mike.

"Mike! Mike, I've missed you."

"Me too, Fern." They hugged warmly and for a long time.

"You remember Stella, don't you?"

"Of course!" She immediately noticed how chic and poised she now was compared to the time she'd first met her in the slums of Stolipinovo. "Welcome to Australia, Stella, and to our place," Fern said as she hugged her. Stella started to feel more comfortable.

"Come say hi to Mom, you guys. She's in the kitchen, baking extra special cookies for you."

They entered via the back door. Megan was washing dishes in the sink.

"Mom, look who's here?"

Megan turned slowly and looked at them, particularly at Stella. "Why, Mike, it's you, so nice to see you again." Mike hurried forward and kissed Megan on the cheek. He quietly noticed how the last few years were wearing on her.

"Always a pleasure to see you, Mrs. Jones. Here, I want you to meet my girlfriend Stella."

Stella edged forward smiling and putting out her hand.

"Good day, Mrs. Jones, a pleasure to meet you."

They held hands briefly, then Megan looked at Stella.

"Mike has always had an eye for beauty and perfection, and I can see he has made a good choice."

"I'm honored to meet you. Thank you for those kind words, Mrs. Jones."

"Sit, everyone. Let's taste your cookies Mom, while I put the kettle on. If you prefer coffee anyone, help yourself. There's a George Clooney machine over there."

Mike chuckled as he gazed at the Nespresso next to the microwave. Over coffee they chatted briefly.

"Mom thanks, please excuse us now as we have business to discuss. Mike, Stella, come, let's go to the boardroom."

Mike thought a tour of the center would have been more appropriate before, but he knew Fern planned to convince them to continue with the business and a tour at the end would have more impact.

They thanked Megan and departed. Mike opened the door to the boardroom and gestured for the girls to enter first. Stella looked around as she entered while Fern sat at the head of the table. Mike and Stella opposite each other.

Fern's smile faded and got down to business.

"Firstly, let me say that it is great to see you guys. I've missed you, Mike, and I mean it, but you have nothing to worry about, Stella," she gave her best reassuring smile.

"I've just missed having my right-hand man at my side. Look after him, Stella, he's a good man." Fern paused a little while in deep thought looking at both of them and then continued.

"I am concerned, though, as I get the impression, Mike, you want us to throw in the towel. After all we've been through and what we've built from the ground up." Again, Fern paused and looked from one to the other.

"We've put smiling faces on hundreds of couples, who never dreamt it possible. We have saved hundreds of babies from dire circumstances and in some cases from certain death. I don't understand Mike, why you want to pack this all up and take away dreams for clients waiting in the wings. Mike?"

He stood up, his mind racing. He thought again about telling Fern about Nash's letter, and why he'd intercepted it. The shock might distract Fern momentarily from clinging onto the business, but it might also compel her to make it bigger and better and refuse to shut down. He decided now was not the time.

Instead he walked to the large mounted whiteboard on the wall. He picked up a black Sharpie marker and wrote 334. Then he selected a red Sharpie and circled the number. Then from the number he drew a few arrows. At the point of each arrow he wrote Bruce Nash, ASIO, Federal Police, CIA, Customs and Border Control and then for the last word he wrote *Other*. He then wrote out a list in red: kidnapping, murder, assault, bribery, fraud, forgery, extortion, blackmail, and smuggling.

He put the pen down and turned to face Fern as he stepped to the side so that she could clearly see what he had written.

There was dead silence.

"Did you know in some countries and certain states in America, these are capital punishment crimes which means execution or life in prison? Here in Australia we would be looking at somewhere between fifteen to twenty years behind bars, even with the best lawyer in the world." He looked at the deadpan expressions.

"Fern, behind the scenes I am convinced people are talking to authorities. We have penetrated so deep we have made a few waves. This would be viewed as an international syndicate and the authorities and Government would come down very hard on us. Yes, you have put smiles on three hundred and thirty-four babies and toddlers and three hundred and thirty-four childless couples. It is something to be most proud of. But now is the time to stop before our luck runs out. Compulsive gamblers can attest to this. Think about it, the recent Florida kidnapping was a very disquieting lesson for us. We need to take heed."

Mike walked back slowly to his chair and sat down.

Fern was silent and teared up. This was her home. Her mission. She was giving babies who had been abandoned like her a chance, just as she got.

Mike grabbed the Kleenex and passed it to her.

"Can I make you a cup of tea, Fern?" Stella asked kindly but Fern ignored her.

Fern cried silently staring straight ahead without looking at either one of them. So now more babies have to die, she thought. She dabbed her cheeks dry with a shaking hand.

Mike got up and stood next to her. He hated seeing her like this. He carefully pulled her up in his powerful hands and held her. He put his arms around her and gently pushed her head against his chest while patting and rubbing her back gently, soothing her.

She finally let go and sobbed.

"You're right. It's just so hard to throw in the towel after years of dedication and hard work. It's what has defined me. It's helped me cope with my own story."

"I understand. I truly do more than ever, and I'm proud of you, Fern, so proud." Mike was now convinced, he had done the right thing with Nash and throwing the ring back into the water.

"What's the *other* you wrote on the board?" Fern asked interrupting his thoughts.

"Other allegations the authorities would make against us. We could, for example, be accused of human trafficking and child stealing amongst everything else."

"Thank you, Mike. I'm all right now." She released herself and sat down, a little embarrassed in front of his girlfriend.

Mike nodded slightly in acceptance.

"Tell you what," he said, in a rallying tone to break the ice. "Why don't you show Stella your Stork Center and then she can spend some time with your mom, while you and I have a chat about the logistics of closing down the business."

"Good idea," Fern said wiping her face and grateful to refocus. "Come Stella, it will be a pleasure to show you what you have been part of."

"I'll wait for you here," Mike said, smiling.

The ladies departed while Mike considered a strategy and prioritized the necessary steps. He roughly calculated a profit and loss statement to give himself estimated figures. Each family had paid anything from two hundred thousand up to a million dollars. Less all overhead and operating expenses from wages to traveling and accommodation to incentive packages for key people and intel. He estimated the Stork center was sitting on about eighty-five million dollars plus.

This did not include the value of the property, which as a boutique hotel or a private resort, was worth a vast sum.

Fern returned twenty minutes later.

"Was Stella impressed?"

"Sure was. She's there now with Maggie and Alice. Mike, it is really hard for me to take in what you said, but I do reluctantly agree with you. What do you think we should do?"

"First of all, we still have three babies waiting to go home, don't we?"

"Yes, all three will be going within the next two weeks."

"The way I see it, I have briefly calculated where our profit stands which is around eighty million plus mark. That excludes the property and the jet. We need to call everyone in and tell them we are packing up and reassure them there is a generous retirement compensation package.

"I'm suggesting we give your uncle one million. Danny is worth two. For the two pilots, Oliver deserves the larger cut. I suggest three for Oliver and half a million for Morrie. I am thinking Maggie and Sheelah would be happy with two hundred thousand each, but suggest a little bit more for Alice as the head nurse. It is of course your call."

"Sounds good, I'll go with your suggestions. Alice I'd like to give a half a million. She's been here almost from the start and has been very dedicated. She has also put in a lot of travel time and has been privy to an awful lot. Danny, I suggest we cut it down to one million. What do you reckon we will get for the jet?"

"No idea, that's Oliver's call. Probably two or three million, maybe a bit more. But it does have high mileage which might knock the price down."

"Mike, what if we give the jet to Oliver and less cash? Maybe a million plus his bird."

"That's a bit too generous. Let's see when we meet one-on-one. Also, we must write up very airtight NDAs for everyone and swear them to secrecy. Of course, they would implicate themselves if they do talk. They are big boys and I can't foresee we will have a problem. I know them pretty well. It's the girls, Fern, that we need to convince. We will be diplomatic but firm."

Fern smiled, "And you, my right-hand man, what do I give you?"

"Your call Fern."

"No, Mike, give me a ballpark figure of what you want, or expect?"

"The figure I have in mind is a good few MMs," he grinned.

"Jeez, Mike, that's a bit vague. What is a good few?"

"Ten," he said without expression.

"For God's sake, how much? You don't play, do you? You expect ten million! That's disappointing, I'm not sure I am willing to pay you that much."

Mike's mind was racing. Fern had a serious look. Did she mean it? he thought.

"You asked for a ballpark figure. Ball is now in your court, Fern; you tell me."

"Undersold yourself, Mike. I was thinking more along the lines of fifteen, but hell no, my final non-negotiable figure is twenty, twenty million, my infallible Operations Manager." She grinned impishly.

"Is that all?" Mike questioned playfully. "Only kidding, my girl, you are one hell of a person with one hell of a big heart, thank you. And by the way, I will pay Stella out of my cut, not you, let me make that clear. She's assisted on many rescue missions and has been loyal and devoted to our humanitarian cause."

"Thanks Mike, I leave that up to you — and, you know, it goes without saying we would never have succeeded and at this level without you." Fern choked up knowing how true this was.

Mike smiled again.

"What's next on your to-do list?"

"We call the team in one-by-one and the sooner the better. Let's plan for Monday. You and I can tell them together. Then that's it—*finito*—the end of the road," he said solemnly.

"I suggest you also think about getting out of this neck of the woods and soon. The buildings and land are worth a lot. Sell it—sell it all. Also, just so you know, I intend to continue my relationship with Stella and see where it leads. She's good company and I enjoy being with her."

"You deserve a good lady and every happiness. I'm putting Mom into a top-class retirement home in Brighton. What do you intend to do with yourself?"

"Rest, that's all I'm looking forward to is a fucking long rest. Probably take Stella and tour Australia. I want to show her the Great Ocean Road, then fly to Sydney, rent a car and see the Blue Mountains. I also want to take her up to Port Douglas and, of course, to Queensland and see the Great Barrier Reef. Then, who knows, probably another break in Europe and sort out Stella's grandmother. We need to see where she would be happy to settle or maybe even bring her back to Australia but not sure yet."

Fern was distracted and not quite listening to Mike. "You wrote on the board murder, who was murdered?"

"Pinkie, remember? My cohort carved him up right here in Melbourne, and don't forget the thugs in Bulgaria who tried to kill me. I believe one never made it."

"What about the guy in Florida who tried to extort money from the kidnapping?"

"Enough. Fern, enough. Come, let's go and join the others. Stella and I have plans. I will give you a call later today or tomorrow and confirm the times for our meetings with everyone."

When Mike and Stella left, Fern was watching from her window upstairs.

She felt so alone. Mike was out of her reach and Oliver was not what she wanted.

Her mind drifted. She saw herself as a baby left to die in the Dandenong. . She realized, she did want to know who her mother was and, for the first time in ages, she felt fear. There was nothing that money could not buy, she thought, except perhaps this answer.

She stood up and went to her mirror and stared closely at her different colored eyes, intently turning slightly to the left and then the right. She realized what Mike had said was serious. She needed a complete change, and perhaps that included a new face, new identification papers and passport and a new name. Fern Jones needed to disappear.

Monday morning arrived and Mike was there early with Stella. Stella went to visit with the three young charges in the nursery while Mike and Fern ambled into the boardroom.

Lance was first on their list, then Danny, Morrie, and Oliver followed by Alice, Sheelah, and Maggie.

Fern and Mike sat chatting about the past years, the pain and the glory, the tough work and the smiles they had put on the faces of so many people.

Mike asked Fern to make sure she had a box of Kleenex on hand, as these types of meetings were bound to get emotional.

Lance's meeting was brief. He was pleased to hear the business was closing and he was out of the illegal syndicate. He had long been troubled by it, only sticking around to support his niece.

He went to visit with Megan before leaving.

Danny entered expressionless. He guessed what was coming since the orders for his work had dried up. Only a quick twitch of one cheek gave away his pleasure when he registered the generous severance package. Afterwards, Mike told Fern his twitchy smile was genuine happiness. Morrie was also pleased with his cut and happily offered his future services if they ever needed a pilot for any other reason.

Mike offered Oliver two million for his dedication and hard work. When asked what the Learjet was worth, he estimated around three-million, considering the excessive mileage. Mike instructed Oliver to sell it and whatever he got above the three million mark he could pocket. Oliver was happy. They parted promising to keep in close contact.

The Kleenex came in good use when it was time for the termination conversations with the ladies. There were tears of joy at the bonuses, but also tears of sadness at the closure of the Stork Center and job loss.

Fern assured them they would remain on payroll until the three babies went to their new homes, which would be within the next two weeks. Fern said if they were interested, she might want their help to assist with packing up the center and also help her mother move to the retirement home in Brighton.

Mike made it very clear to everyone they were sworn to confidentiality and got them to sign the NDAs.

The ladies returned to their respective chores and duties while Oliver, Morrie, Danny and Lance departed.

Fern turned to Mike. "Well, that went well. It wasn't as difficult as I thought, eh?"

"Nope, but you know what, Fern, Oliver has excelled and my gut feeling is that we give him one million instead of two, but we throw in the jet for him to keep. What do you think?"

Fern pondered for a short while. She thought about his dedication and then she thought about her occasional fling with him.

"I think you're right. Best to keep the jet in the family, Mike. You never know when we might need a ride," she said smiling.

"What's the smile for?" Mike asked.

"Well, I'd like to see his face when we give him the news."

"Yeah! Let's call him now."

Mike dialled Oliver's number.

"Hey, Mike," Oliver answered, "you sure meant it when you said we'd keep in close contact!"

"Oliver, my brother, I've got good and bad news."

"Shoot, I'm all ears. What's up?"

"The bad news is we have reviewed our figures and see we have over-estimated your bonus. We can only offer you one million."

"Mike, are we on the speaker at the moment?"

"Yes, Fern is beside me."

"Well, then I won't swear. What kind of f***ing game are you playing?" he hissed.

Fern and Mike laughed softly. "Oliver, bro', you didn't wait for the good news. You've been so faithful and dedicated that I talked it over with Fern and she agrees. She has decided to give you your bird as a going away present. The jet is all yours, dude."

There was a second or two of silence.

"You still there, Oliver, or do you need some smelling salts?"

"Wow, you guys are something. Hell, that is so generous of you. Christmas has definitely come early. I'm lost for words."

Fern chimed in, "Oliver, you deserve it. It couldn't have a better home. Thank you for everything."

"Always a pleasure, my dearest."

"Good, we will see you soon, I hope. Keep in touch, and don't do anything that I wouldn't do," Mike said and then he terminated the call.

"Fern, I am going to hit the road now with Stella. I need to get a thing or two in Chadstone, then plan our road trip. I will talk to you soon." He kissed her on the cheek.

"Sure! I'll walk with you."

They strolled along in silence. Fern felt a bit down and was quiet. She would be alone soon and no one to share all the news.

Mike and Stella said their goodbyes to all and to Mrs. Jones.

"Where to now, Mike? I'm hungry. Would be nice to grab a bite somewhere," Stella said.

"I thought we could go to the shopping center in Chadstone. I need to buy a couple of pairs of jeans, and we can eat there."

The parking lot was busy with end of season sales going on, drawing a lot of shoppers.

As they climbed out of the car Mike heard an argument. He turned to see a father slapping a young girl across her face; she was barely a teenager. Mike's eagle eyes noticed they were standing next to a new Mercedes Benz and there was a recent dent on one of the doors. The man, full of truculence, slammed the Merc's door and was now pointing his finger in the face of the girl.

"What the hell!" Stella gasped.

"Shhh," Mike whispered. "Just stay by me." Mike grabbed his cell from his pocket and made a quick call. He phoned a connection of his who managed a call center at a massive insurance company in the city.

"Good afternoon, this is Dale speaking."

"Dale, it's me, Mike. I need a quick favor. There's a Mercedes Benz here at the Chadstone center that has a bad dent. I am sure you guys must have the owner's details on file because it must have been phoned in. Wait, I'll give you the license number: It's Y for Yankee, B for Bravo, V for Victor 237. I need a name and an address quickly."

"Sure, Mike, let's see. Yes, it was in an accident just a week ago, belongs to a Patrick Rutlidge. Have you got a pen handy?"

Mike removed a pen from his pocket and Stella quickly handed him a leaflet she found on the floor. Mike told Dale to stay on the other line.

The man was still shouting at the girl, and in seconds, Mike arrived on the scene. Mike gently moved Stella behind him.

"Is this your Daddy, young girl?" Mike asked in a gentle but firm voice.

"Y-y-yes," she stuttered. She was in tears.

The man looked at Mike. His nose crinkled and he spoke out the corner of his mouth. He was in a foul mood. "Mind your own affairs, Mister, and stay out of mine," he yelled.

Mike stared back at the man, "Mister, if it's trouble you want you've come to the perfect place."

Then Mike spoke into his cell again, "Dale, you there?"

"Yes, Mike, I need to go soon."

"No problem, I gave you this bastard's license plate and you said his name is Patrick Rutlidge. What is his address?"

The cantankerous bully was shocked as his mouth gaped open at Mike.

"Thank you, Dale, I have his address in Camberwell. I'll talk to our men."

Mike took a step closer to the man and he was ready. "Now I tell you what, only a coward hits his daughter. We will have you under surveillance twenty-four seven. I am warning you we are watching and will investigate if you ever lift your hand again to your precious daughter or any family members. Now run along before it gets dangerous and the real thunder and lightning start."

The man was silent, shocked, and immediately hopped into his car and drove off with his daughter.

"Thank God you were here," he turned to Stella, "I would have lost it, but also I did not want to do anything in front of that poor little girl."

"What a horror," Stella said.

"Yes, let's go. Before we do anything, I need to go to information. It's just on the upper level."

Mike quickened his pace and put his mobile on silent.

"Wait here for me. I will be a few minutes only."

"Okay, Mike."

At the information desk the lady smiled at Mike, "How can we help you today, sir?"

Mike looked at her name badge. "Hi, Vivian, please, I need a favor. I left my cell phone at home and I need to use your phone to talk to the police. It's about an incident that just occurred in the parking area."

"Sir, we have security to deal with things like that."

"No, the guilty party has left. It is serious, please."

She handed the desk phone to him. Mike called 911.

He gave the police officer Patrick Rutlidge's name and license plate of the Mercedes and told him what happened. Mike was concerned the daughter was in danger and needed child protection services to get involved. He left a false name and rejoined Stella.

That night Mike tossed and turned in bed. He eventually fell asleep but then the nightmares started.. Then he heard a kid's voice behind him saying *Please, sir, I'm hungry and thirsty. Please sir, help me.* A girl was tapping him on his body, the tapping got harder, more kids surrounded him and their voices were pleading in unison. Mike sat bolt upright in bed in sweating. He felt his back while breathing heavily.

"Mike? Mike, you alright?" Stella asked sleepily as she switched the lamp on, "You must have been dreaming."

"Were you tapping me to wake up?"

"No," she said rubbing her face. "It must have been in your nightmare."

She kissed him on the shoulder and soothed him by rubbing his shoulder gently.

He fell asleep and the nightmare resumed. This time he was in a sports stadium playing soccer. The stadium was packed to capacity and all the spectators were starving, impoverished and neglected children. Every time a goal was scored the kids shouted, pleading for help.

Chapter Forty-Eight

F ern and her mother took a tour of the gated retirement community and thought it was wonderful, better than their expectations.

It boasted beautiful gardens, assisted living luxurious condos and single-family homes in a sprawling five-acre community. There was everything to make retirement living relaxing and lavish for the wealthy.

When they got home, Megan said, "I was thinking Fern, my new place has a guest room and it's really about time you met someone your own age. The bedroom could be for a future granddaughter or grandson to sleep over occasionally?" she looked at her daughter hopefully.

"Really Mom, enough! If the time is right it will happen. I'm just closing down a ten-year-old business."

"And Fern, you seem like you have something else to say, I know you."

"Yes, you're right! It appears I may have to go abroad for a while, just to tie up some loose ends from the business, you know."

"When, where, and for how long?"

"Not for a few months and I'll be gone for a few weeks at most. Of course, I'll always be available on my cell phone. I'll be in New York and the time difference is around fourteen hours behind us."

"Why New York?"

"Business, but I will talk to you regularly when I go. I promise."

"I see, dear. Maybe I should move before you go."

"Maybe but I don't have a firm date yet. First, we will put the center up for sale. My home will make a great private retreat center with the additional guest cottages outside. Spiritual retreats are very popular these days. I am sure we will attract a buyer with no problem."

She headed upstairs to her room. She picked up the old stuffed koala bear from her bookshelf, her only connection to her birth mother, and absentmindedly stroked it while wishing her phone would ring, just to hear someone's voice.

Mike dropped Stella off at the hair salon, a small boutique in the suburbs. He strolled along the street looking at the shops and watching the passers-by. After a short while, he was bored and headed back to meet Stella. She wasn't going to be ready for another twenty minutes. He was in no hurry. He sat down and glanced at the magazines and something caught his eye in the *Herald Sun* newspaper.

It was a short notice on page seven; an orphanage was in desperate need of a financial sponsor to survive another year, otherwise it would be forced to close. Mike tore the piece out and inserted it in his pocket. He told Stella he was popping out for some fresh air and would be right back.

Outside Mike phoned the orphanage. He spoke to the manager and established it was a small orphanage. The children ranged from five to twelve years old and the home was trying to raise a hundred and fifty thousand dollars. Mike happily told the manager it would be his privilege to donate the amount needed and asked for their bank details. The lady was flabbergasted and asked if this was a prank.

He reassured her he was a serious donor and would call back in a few days to confirm the funds had arrived.

True to his promise Mike phoned the orphanage a few days later. The manager was ecstatic and wanted to meet Mike. They planned to mount a plaque in his name and name one of the dormitories after him.

Mike made it v clear it was to be considered an *anonymous donation*. He was emphatic and wished them every success for their future before hanging up, leaving the manager puzzled but elated.

Bruce Nash had aged. His short-term memory was something of the past but he did remember the shark-eaten body washed up on the beach on the Great Ocean Road and the threat from Mike not to pursue or visit the house in the Dandenong. He was also haunted by the memory of taking his beloved wife's life.

Nash, now in his 80's, continued to mumble to himself, and his past as an army officer and policeman played heavy on his mind. He had developed a peculiar habit of saluting other drivers when stopped at traffic lights. He would also do the same to pedestrians when he was out walking.

He still kept in contact with old friends and colleagues from time to time and showed no signs of any abnormal behavior but when it came to saying goodbye, he would stand up, smile, come to attention and salute.

Fern had just completed showing the real estate agent around the Stork Center property and had agreed upon a reserve price. It was high, above market average especially with its potential to be easily turned into an elite guest house, or an exclusive country hotel or a private club.

Later that day Fern heard from Mike. She shared the news the Stork Center was going on the market and the nursery was now empty and officially closed. All the babies had gone home. Mike reminded Fern to dispose of anything resembling baby furniture and equipment, like cots, clothes and toys and not to leave them lying around. He would arrange for everything to be collected. He would donate it all to charity and worthwhile causes. Fern agreed.

Mike also let her know he had finalized his vacation plans with Stella and they would be leaving soon to head up north. Fern also casually divulged her own upcoming trip to New York and that she expected to be away for a few weeks.

"I need a complete break, away from everything," she explained. "Closing the Stork Center has been more traumatic than I thought. I need to go somewhere, where nobody knows me. I want to be alone and chill and think of nothing."

Mike just listened, saying nothing.

"I promise, when I do book my ticket, I will let you know. Of course, I will naturally keep in contact," she told him. They said goodnight.

Mike's alarm bells signalled, something in her voice, but then he told himself he was perhaps reading too much into it.

Oliver loved being the owner of a Learjet. He was so grateful to Fern for her graciousness and soon set up business flying high-profile business people around the country along with a few overseas trips too.

Yet he could not stop thinking about Fern. It was not about keeping in touch or the high-level risk they shared in the business. Of course, he longed for the fiery passionate sex they had experienced but there was more to it. He had always avoided matrimony and lavished in the bachelor exotic lifestyle, but for the first time he started thinking about what it would be like married to Fern. Would it be such a bad thing to settle down?

He finally swallowed his pride and found the courage to call her.

She answered, "Missing me already, Oliver?"

"How did you know?" he lied. "Fern, I need to speak to you."

"Sure, that's why you called, isn't it?" she teased playfully, grateful for a friendly call.

"It is not as simple as that. Can we meet?" he said somewhat seriously.

"You better be quick then."

Several thoughts flashed through his mind.

"Why?"

"I'm flying to New York next week on Tuesday."

"Eh… Why the Big Apple? What's there?"

"Oh Ollie, just a break and I've always wanted to go there."

"Okay, can we meet over the weekend? It's your call. We can meet for a meal somewhere or whatever you want."

"A meal would be nice. Any suggestions?"

"Let's do a BBQ at my place, where it is quiet—just the two of us."

Fern thought for a second or two, "Sure, sounds good. I'll come by Saturday around 5 pm."

"Cool, see you then."

Oliver smiled to himself. All good, so far.

Fern also smiled to herself. She knew he wanted to have a good time and she could do with a good time herself. Maybe it would help her get out of the blue funk that had descended on her ever since they decided to close the business.

While shopping for dinner provisions, Oliver thought about the secrets Fern knew nothing about. Her father's ruthless business dealings might surprise and dismay her. He remembered the time Chester took advantage of a widow who didn't know her peanut farm was sitting on priceless sapphires. He'd bought the farm for a song, and successfully mined hundreds of pounds of sapphire crystals. He then turned around and sold the land for a vast sum. Or, there was a time when Chester bought a massive black opal from a desperate soul for well below its real value. Compared to Chester, Oliver thought, Fern was a saint. She might be on the wrong side of the law but her heart was in the right place, trying to help people, and not take advantage of them.

Fern parked her car in Seacombe Grove, just outside Oliver's home, a much sought-after area in Brighton.

She gently pushed the doorbell, and Oliver immediately flung the door open, and the song *Never Tear Us Apart* by INXS came floating through to the front porch.

She smiled, then chuckled when he raised an index finger to his lips. Without a word he scooped her up in his powerful arms and carried her to his bedroom.

Fern did not resist, and he put her down gently.

They lay there hugging, kissing, and caressing each other, fully clothed.

Then the evening heated up as he kissed her neck, her mouth, and closed eyes.

Her breathing came in short deep breaths at first, then longer ones. His breathing increased as well and soon their arms blurred as they almost ripped each other's clothes off, scattering them on the wooden floor.

She sat on top of him at first with legs apart, up and down, while he reciprocated with his thrusts. Then he was on top of her, hips swaying.

The steam train hit full speed, and soon joyous groans of ecstasy echoed across the room from both their mouths.

Afterward, they lay quietly for a while until Fern looked at him.

"So?" she teased him coyly with her blue and brown eyes. "What is it you want to discuss, my big guy?"

"I'll cut to the chase, Fern." He sat up on one elbow, looking back at her. "A long time ago, I said I thought I could be falling in love with you, and you said not to hurry things. Remember?"

Fern said nothing.

"Well, it's been years since and years since we've been doing this — clandestine meetings behind everyone's back. Don't get me wrong, it's been a lot of fun. But, now, I don't just think I'm in love with you. I *am* in love with you. And time is getting away with both of us. I want you to be my wife, Fern. I want to marry you."

There was silence in the room before Fern gently said, "I love you too, Ollie, in my way. But, I, honestly don't think marriage is for me. Please, don't be offended. I enjoy your company and love being with you more than ever. I love making love with you and I want to see you more as well. But … well, I don't think either of us is cut out for marriage, do you?"

His eyes flickered up and down in thought between the ceiling and back to her. This was not what he expected to hear, and yet a part of him felt relief. Maybe she was right.

Fern kissed him on the forehead and jumped up. "Let's not spoil the evening. You promised me a delicious meal, eh?"

He grinned and gave her a spare gown. They both went into the kitchen. He'd already made a large salad and after firing up the BBQ, he placed kebabs on the hot grill.

They sat down to eat, and Oliver played soft music in the background to enhance the mood. After dinner, they made love again.

Fern phoned her mother to let her know she wouldn't be home and not to worry. She would drive home early the next day.

Megan put the phone down and shook her head. Fern was not deceiving her. She knew Fern was with Oliver. His fascination would wear off soon. His type always did once the chase was over.

After Oliver fell asleep, Fern lay next to him, admiring his handsome face, but there was something missing from her, and she felt sad she could not fulfill his expectations.

Detective Ashley Hughes had become a highly decorated and respected officer in the police force. He had earned a reputation in solving cold cases in Perth and other parts of Western Australia, and his standing in the force had spread across the country.

Ashley was deep in thought as he looked at the old folder again. The folder was marked Sophia Semenov. He remembered the case well: confirmed drug overdose and suicide by drowning. The body had been washed up on the beach and partially eaten by a Great White. The autopsy findings concluded she had recently given birth, but the baby nor its body had ever been found. It was assumed the baby had drowned with its mother. The conclusion: no crime involved — case closed.

His eyes darted through the copious notes sent to him by Bruce Nash. It seemed he was keen to have this case re-opened.

He read the notes and perused the facts closely, and he concluded that his old mentor was obsessed with this case. He must be about 78 years old, and it had taken over his life after the death of his wife. The poor old guy was losing it. Remembering how sharp his mind used to be, Ashley felt sad to see the shaky handwriting and to read the barely coherent words that seemed to bear little relationship to the Semenov case, except for the last line:

> *Took chances a few times, watched the house from a distance with my old binoculars lying on a rise in the Dandenong bush, have seen cars come and go. In the main luxury cars. Ash, I think I saw babies on a few occasions. Maybe they are trafficking babies. But don't worry, if the daughter ever leaves the country, CCTV and cameras will identify her at the airport, and our cops in the Border Force will contact you. I'm too old now, and it is not for me to get involved. Remember, I gave you her name — Fern Jones — stunning looker, but something about her, I can't pinpoint it exactly, but I reckon she's it. She's the baby we searched for all those years ago. She has the same different color eyes as Sophia Semenov.*

Hughes shook his head. To him, the speculation the baby had drowned along with the mother made much more sense than these ramblings. He closed the folder and then opened his drawer and removed a rubber stamp.

There was a sharp bang on his desk as the red ink bit into the folder's cover from the thrust: *REJECTED*. They would not be reopening the old shark case and, as for the rest, well, it just seemed like the ramblings of an old man.

Chapter Forty-Nine

Mike and Stella returned from their vacation happy and relaxed and sporting healthy tans.

Mike had a strong feeling that Fern was up to something, but he did not know what. The feeling had been nagging him on and off during their trip, and he dropped hints with Stella that he might possibly go away on business when they returned from Queensland.

Stella and he argued for the first time because Mike had promised her he had quit the business. When he told her Fern had put the property up for sale and had closed down the adoption center, she reluctantly agreed. She understood wrapping up a multiple million-dollar empire takes time, and Mike would need to tie up loose ends. Still, she longed for the day when Fern Jones would be out of their lives forever.

Fern, in the meantime, phoned Danny directly. She asked to see him the next day on a private matter that was strictly between the two of them. He was not to involve anyone else, including Mike. This was a completely separate arrangement outside of the Stork Center business, and he would be rewarded handsomely for his services.

That night she pondered in front of her mirror, knowing this would be one of the last times she would see this reflection looking back at her. It was a poignant moment saying goodbye to her past.

The morning arrived quickly, and Fern took a deep breath as she walked to her car. It was early, and the morning crisp was refreshing. Her breath hung in the Dandenong air.

She hit the road before all the long-distance truck drivers and construction workers jammed the lanes, and she enjoyed a pleasant drive to Danny's home.

It was a very inconspicuous home situated in a normal family housing estate hidden behind overgrown shrubbery to protect the privacy of its occupants.

She parked her car on the street and went up to the front door, and knocked.

Danny opened it immediately.

"Come in, Fern, long time no see."

"I've been busy. You know how it goes."

"Come sit," Danny said as he led the way to the living room.

"So, what's on your mind? Something important, no doubt."

"Danny, this meeting has to remain between just you and me, agreed?"

"Of course. All my work is strictly confidential," he said, nodding his head.

"I mean it, Danny, I'm frigging serious. Not even Mike must know." Now she really had his attention.

"I've decided to change my name and my whole identity. Since closing the adoption center and wrapping up the business, I cannot afford my face to be connected to the operation. I need a brand-new beginning and a fresh start to a new life."

"I understand. You have my word, Fern," he said sincerely.

"I'm leaving for New York tomorrow." Danny didn't even flinch at her news.

"I will need a complete set of documents and papers for my new identity, including a birth certificate, passport, driver's license, and anything else you can suggest. I will send by courier new passport photographs so you can finish and send them back. I will then be able to fly back to Melbourne on my new passport."

Danny nodded. "I have one question. Do you have a new name to give me?"

Fern swallowed. It was the first time she had said her new name out loud. "Mia Williams," she said confidently. It felt good and had a nice ring to it.

Danny got up. "Come, let's go to my office. I want to check something."

Fern followed, and they entered a large open space room. She looked around. It was the first time she had visited his den of iniquity.

There were scanners, two huge photocopiers, and several printers, all neatly organized. The shelves were efficiently arranged with different ink cartridges and bottles, along with various paper stock in multiple colors and styles packed in neat piles. There were several types of stamps, a high-end DSLR Nikon camera, and a separate desk with a huge microscope and a medical magnifying glass. There was an Apple and a PC desktop computer with large twenty-inch screens and two laptops. On another table, there was a Dell 27-inch monitor surrounded by hard disk drives and other solid-state drives. A large adjustable lamp towered above some other documents. In open plastic drawers, there were an assortment of computer chips and electronic components. In the corner were the tools of his trade: artist's pens, brushes and various miniature metal tools, and more inks and dyes. It was a real Aladdin's cave.

"Hell, this is impressive," Fern grinned. "No wonder you were the heart of our operation."

"Oh, this is nothing. You should see my other room. You'll get dizzy looking around, Fern — I mean, Mia!"

"Ha! Still Fern for now," she mockingly laughed.

"Sit for a few seconds," Danny requested.

Fern pulled up an office chair and sat opposite him.

Then he turned to face a computer that was on.

"I just want to see if you have chosen an appropriate name."

He googled the most popular last names in Australia.

"I see Williams is one of the most common ones here. That's good. The last thing you want is to take on an unusual name or a unique spelling."

"It's why I chose it. You and Mike taught me that—I learned from the best! It's the most common last name in most English-speaking countries," she grinned. "Okay, what will this cost me, Danny?"

"This one's on me. I mean it. Hell, you've been my best customer for over a decade and always paid promptly. I truly admire what you have accomplished for so many lives—I am a big fan, and this is the least I can do."

"Danny, that is so kind of you—thank you." She affectionately put her hand on his arm. "It's really generous of you Danny, but this is a lot of work."

He put his hand up to indicate not necessary.

"I still have your bank details…" Fern winked.

She looked at her watch, "I don't mean to be rude, but I fly tomorrow and still have lots to do. Remember it is Mia Williams, Williams with a double *l*," she said, walking to the door.

"Wrong door, Fern, that's my main office." He opened it to show her.

"Help yourself—have a quick look."

Fern realized she was being invited into sacred territory! She saw machinery, unknown to her, but she did recognize a hologram stamping machine that had a UV light in the background. There was another printer more high-tech than in his main office which was obviously greater resolution. She tried to read the wording on one monitor but it was too small.

"Don't worry about that one, that's my special baby. It has government fonts from most countries, the ones, you know, used for passports, ID documents, and so on."

Danny closed the door to his Alibaba room and walked her out.

"Wow, Danny, I guess with all this equipment you can print your own money. Maybe you have already!" she roguishly grinned. "Okay, mum's the word," she repeated, confidentiality zipping her lips with her thumb and index finger.

He gave her his most beguiling trademark slight smile.

Mike was deep in thought about Fern's upcoming New York trip.

It made no sense. She knew no one there, and she was going alone.

He decided to scribble some points down on paper to try to figure it out:

a) *Just to have a break, as she alleges.*

b) *To meet someone. If so, who?*

c) *A reconnaissance of the area to maybe move there.*

d) *A reconnaissance to open another baby rescue center and to scout out potential wealthy couples or launch another similar business.*

e) *To see a plastic surgeon—fear of being caught and therefore changing her looks.*

f) *Investment opportunities.*

g) *Other?*

At the airport Fern checked in her luggage, bought a magazine, and was making her way to the boarding gate when the real estate agent called. She had a very generous offer on her property—a whopping nineteen million dollars.

Everything was moving super-fast and Fern was happy to accept.

She called Mike with the good news and told him about Megan's new retirement home. She asked him if he would be around to check in on her mother and help her prepare for her upcoming move.

He was happy to be of assistance and wished her a safe flight, pleased to hear she sounded more like her usual self. He chided himself on his suspicions and asked her which hotel she had booked into. She said she couldn't remember but it was situated in the upper east side and promised to let him know.

Mike phoned Oliver and Danny to see if they had any thoughts about why Fern was flying to New York. Danny denied knowing anything and Oliver wasn't concerned. He thought it made perfect sense that she wanted a break from everything. Growing up, her parents had taken her abroad many times and maybe she just wanted to explore a new city she had never visited.

Mike wasn't convinced. He phoned Megan to see if he could fish anything out of her. He told her he was around to help and reassured her if she needed anything regarding her upcoming move while Fern was away not to hesitate to reach out to him. She was grateful for his concerns. She professed she planned to move as soon as possible as she wasn't keen to hang out in an empty home all by herself. He asked her about the purpose of Fern's trip.

Megan told him she too was surprised, but Fern never had been much of one for confidences. She sounded uncharacteristically irritable, Mike thought. He took it as a sign she was also worried.

Mike went back to his notes and crossed out all the points except one.

Fern stepped out of the cab and the bellhop took her luggage from the trunk. She gazed up at the hotel. A recently renovated brownstone with deep olive-green awnings nestled amongst rich foliage and discreetly blended in with the surrounding. Its gold plaque recognized it as a protected historical building from the 1920s.

An elegant gentrified lady walked by with her dog and it reminded her of Megan and poor old Bonzo.

"Lovely here, isn't it, madame? The area is near Central Park and there are restaurants, coffee bars, museums, and plenty of boutique stores," he said cheerfully in a deep voice and coughed politely. "This way, madame," the porter said and Fern followed him to reception.

She eyeballed the immediate surroundings and took in the style and the furnishings and was pleased with her choice. It was the perfect place for an extended stay.

She saw a grand piano in the lounge and admired it. She was told by the receptionist they had a regular pianist who showed up every Friday and Saturday evenings for cocktail hour to entertainment guests. Occasionally they would play during the week as well. It brought back memories of learning to play the piano her father bought for her 16th birthday and the soft piano notes from the music played in the nursery at the Stork Center.

She had booked in under the name of Fern Jones but knew that would soon change, she thought.

Fern tipped the hotel porter and closed the door to her suite. She sighed heavily, finally alone and quiet. She marvelled appreciatively at her accommodation. The living room was large and spacious and bright from the natural light pouring in from the balcony. It was carpeted throughout in a rich thick cream wool and stylish marble flooring in the bathroom. There was a separate bedroom with a Californian King bed and a study area off from the main room, which led onto another balcony that overlooked an intriguing courtyard.

The lighting was superb and all adjustable by a single remote control. There was also a refrigerator and a small mini bar filled with miniature liquor bottles and soft drinks. On the dresser was a coffee machine, and a glass kettle with an array of teas.

Fern unpacked and then she went down to reception and through the lounge area into the courtyard. She felt excited about her new adventure as she gazed at the refined landscape lawn and immaculate manicured flower beds and plants. The greenery was rich and perfectly trimmed and clung to the stone walls. A smooth tiled chiselled floor led to an ornate spotless fountain surrounded by a gorgeous millefleur of lush plants below an antique-looking, wall mounted metal clock.

By mid-morning Fern was hungry. She went to the dining room for a late breakfast and enjoyed the extravagant buffet laid out for guests. She helped herself to a typical American breakfast of crispy bacon and eggs with coffee.

She sent a text to her mother to let her know she had arrived safely. Danny had provided her with an American SIM card and a new number.

It was dark when she woke up. She thought she had just missed sunset, but she was wrong. Looking at her phone she saw it was 11 pm. She sat up quickly; she had slept nearly twelve hours!

She checked her emails and flicked through the magazines left by the hotel. She grabbed a snack from the mini-bar and climbed back into bed and absently watched TV until she fell back to sleep.

The weather was pleasant when she woke. Glancing at her watch she saw it was just after 7 am. She showered and dressed and then went to the dining room and served herself a second breakfast. This time she ate a healthy cereal, with fruit and a glass of fresh juice.

She spoke to concierge who organized a cab for her. She admired the clean streets and interesting building designs again, and noticed the different boutiques lined up on either side of the street.

The cab dropped her off just outside the practice of Dr. Scott Parker, and Fern found herself walking up the few steps to one of the best plastic surgeons in the world.

The rooms were his, the building was his, together with a state-of-the-art operating theater, recovery rooms and a lot, lot more.

Fern was greeted warmly by the receptionist and a nurse came to meet her to take all her details as she sat comfortably in the waiting room lounge.

Dr. Parker was punctual as he stepped into the reception area to greet Fern. He was wearing a spotless starched white coat over his blue scrubs. His name was embroidered in gold on his pocket. He looked to be in his fifties, was immaculately groomed and striking.

"A very good morning to you Ms. Jones, delighted to meet you," he said as he shook her hand.

"Likewise, Dr. Parker."

"Thank you, please follow me," he said. He led her to his consultation room, which was large, bright and modern, resembling a combination of a boardroom and a stylish lounge.

"Fern, what I see in front of me is a beautiful young woman. What brings you all the way from the land down under to see me?"

Fern took a deep breath, "Dr. Parker, very briefly I was adopted and after many years my foster father took me to the place where he found me. I had been left dehydrated and malnourished, just days old and dumped in the bushes like garbage by the side of the road. I re-live that day almost every day and I have despised him for taking me there and sharing his secret with me ever since."

"Fern," he said softly, shocked at hearing her story. "Did you seek help? Have you ever gone to a psychiatrist to talk about this?"

"I am strong and resilient and threw myself into my work. I worked with discarded and neglected children — I saw to their safety and happiness and made sure their new homes and adoptive parents were the best of the best." He rubbed his face listening to every word.

"Dr. Parker, you make people younger, more attractive but what I want is a new face. Money is no object. I want a fresh start, to begin again as a new me with a new face and a new name. I want to forget what I looked like and the scrap heap I was discarded in."

Dr. Parker scratched his chin. He was silent for a few seconds then he looked at her seriously, raising one eyebrow. "Fern, out there, people come to me, they want to look like Brad Pitt, Johnny Depp or Natalie Portman, or a young Elizabeth Taylor and I turn them all down." He paused politely to let what he said sink in.

"What I do—what my work is all about—is to help men and women as they age to look a little younger with dignity. I restore their self-esteem. What I also do is help heal patients who have been severely injured in car accidents, work accidents, or when they have suffered horrific burns and so on. What you are asking me to do is a very different proposition." He paused again, without scratching his chin but he looked away for a second or two and then he looked back at Fern with that one raised eyebrow.

"There are plastic surgeons out there who specialize in reconstructive surgery but this is based on major birth defects. Also, there is a huge industry for ethnic cultures who want to alter racial features to create a more westernized look. I get requests all the time, but I will not do it. Having said that, I am willing to listen more and perhaps you can explain exactly what you want done?"

Fern smiled slightly. There was an opening. She felt a lot more at ease. "Briefly I want my nose reduced in size by just three or four per cent. I want to create dimples and have more dominant cheekbones. I know my ears are not big, but I want them to look smoother; a bit rounder at the top, yes, that's it. I am going to cut my hair short and dye it dark brown. And, of course, is there anything you can do about my eyes? I want them both brown?"

"Fern, what you're asking isn't excessive. It is doable. Rhinoplasty is relatively easy and takes about six weeks to recover. I will make a small incision inside your nostrils here, mould and sculpture the cartilage with your skin and tissue. Dimpleplasty is a procedure where I create your dimples. Dimples are lovely and this will add beauty and charm to your smile. Creating dimples is easy and without any risk because I work inside your cheeks. There is no external incision at all for this as I work inside your mouth. Raised cheekbones involve implants and I usually use Medpor, which is one of many implants, but to me it is the best and most trusted because the results are always perfect. Changing the color of your eye to match your brown eye, I will not do. A couple of celebrities have had this done and there were complications. One, in fact, partially lost their eyesight, so I will not go down this path. I would highly recommend, which is a lot safer is to get yourself fitted with a brown contact lens over your blue eye. And, you only have to wear one. Last but not least is Otoplasty, which is an ear procedure to change the angle or shape of your ears and round off the folds. It is something I have done thousands of times. In fact, what you are requesting is a simple procedure and is without risk and not complicated."

Fern nodded her head just once in acknowledgement. "So when can you start, Doctor?"

"Where are you staying, Fern, with family or friends?"

"I'm in a hotel close by, about three blocks away. It's lovely and quiet. I don't have any family in the US."

"Come, we will take care of you. Let's go and get you booked in. You've come to the right place. I have performed thousands of surgeries and your new face will look like you were born with it. Just stay off aspirin if you get a headache until after surgery."

From his desk he removed a large sealed thick envelope and handed it to Fern.

She took it and saw her name was typed on the envelope.

"Inside is our full package and guidelines with all the do's and don'ts, as well as a whole bunch of valuable information. Please read it before your next appointment so we can go over any questions you may have."

"I certainly will."

He escorted Fern to reception and spoke with the clinic manager. Her second appointment was confirmed and surgery pencilled in for the following week.

Fern took his business card and left. She hailed a cab to take her back to the hotel. Later in the afternoon she took herself off and went for long walk, taking in the hustle and bustle of New York. She was going to be a new person.

Chapter Fifty

Three days had passed, and no one had heard from Fern. Even Oliver's usual bravado and sangfroid were starting to slip.

He phoned Mike but he had not heard from her and had no idea what Fern was up to. He reassured him he would call Oliver if he heard any news. Oliver was feeling uneasy about the secrecy of Fern's trip. He phoned Megan, and learned she hadn't been in touch either and he started to really worry.

Mike's worry was also mounting by the hour. He talked to Danny again and Danny again told him he had no idea where Fern was. Mike knew he was lying but realized Fern must have sworn him to secrecy.

Stella had moved in with Mike and they spent a lot of enjoyable time together, but she knew Mike was preoccupied with other things on his mind.

Megan was adapting very well during her first week at the new retirement community in Brighton. She was settling in and enjoyed meeting new people and being surrounded by folks her own age. She even had a secret admirer, Fred who had been living there for a couple of years. He would pop by a couple of times to visit and bring her flowers. If it weren't for her anxiety about her daughter, she would lavish the attention.

As promised, Dr. Parker went over all the details with Fern at her second appointment, patiently explaining the finer points to her.

"You are not a smoker, are you, Fern?"

"No, I detest the habit — and the smell."

"Good, because the healing process takes longer with smokers. Go and enjoy New York, relax and I will see you soon." He smiled as he shook her hand.

"Thank you, Dr. Parker. See you soon."

Fern's heart was beating a little stronger with excitement and anticipation.

Surprisingly later that evening, while listening to the piano player in the hotel lounge, the sense of excitement had waned and a deep sense of loneliness wafted over her. Here she was on the other side of the world, away from close friends and family and planning a major transformation behind their backs. She realized she needed to hear her mother's voice or Mike's strong and calming assurance, or even Oliver's boyish charm. She also knew they were probably worried by her radio silence.

What the hell, she thought, she had nothing to hide from them as far as her phone number was concerned. She didn't have to disclose anything about her surgery. She could surprise them with a grand entrance after she was one hundred per cent healed.

She sent texts to all three, explaining she was enjoying New York and her time alone to relax and explore the Big Apple. She felt better afterwards knowing they all had her new phone number but didn't let them know where she was staying.

She dined alone in the hotel's elegant restaurant and retired afterwards to the lounge to enjoy her tea.

After a while, she noticed a middle-aged lady staring at her who was the type of person who loved to talk and gossip with strangers. She asked Fern where she was from and Fern obliged telling her she was from Australia. That was all the opening she needed before she bombarded Fern with more questions: How long was she staying at the hotel? Did she have plans to tour? Did she have family in the States? Her prying made Fern uncomfortable. She was looking around to see if there was a vacant seat somewhere else or deciding whether to go up to her room, when an opportunity presented itself. The lady turned to engage Fern again.

"Do you have family? I mean, any children?" she nosily asked.

Fern smiled. "Oh, yes I do."

"Oh, how many children do you have?"

"I've got many. In fact, I've got hundreds."

The woman wasn't sure if she was joking but Fern gave her a very deadpan look. She didn't know what to say or how to respond so after a few seconds gawking, she gathered her things and left.

Fern chuckled to herself, briefly thinking there was some truth to her lie.

She finished her tea and took the elevator up to her suite. She looked again in the full-length mirror to stare at her reflection. She knew this was the *before* picture and soon it would be gone forever.

Over the next day and a half, Oliver phoned three times and told her how much he missed her and needed her.

Mike phoned once. He was brief and aloof and said he and Stella were trying to adapt to their new life together.

She had a long conversation with Megan who had lots to report about her new life. Her mother's constant chatter made it easier for Fern not to have to explain the real reason she was there.

Megan was just relieved to hear her daughter's voice and to know her little girl was safe. She could now relax and enjoy her new home.

Fern checked into the medical building of Dr. Scott Parker and was escorted up to her private ward. It was modern, spotless and bright. The room included a computer, a large screen TV and a small fridge.

A nurse helped her unpack and stored her suitcase.

After all the usual health and medical questions, they took Fern's temperature, blood pressure, a second blood test, and listened to her heart and lungs.

A short while later Dr. Parker visited and welcomed her. He told her he would mark her face in the morning at 7 am and surgery was scheduled for 8am.

As he was leaving, the anaesthetist, Dr. Jeffries, arrived. The two doctors chatted very briefly before Dr. Jeffries addressed Fern directly. She stood up against the measuring chart so he could confirm her height and stood on the scales to note her weight to calculate the right dosage for her meds.

He soon left and the nurse came in with dinner. "It's only a light meal tonight, Ms. Jones, but you have a lovely choice. Dr. Parker prefers no more food after 5:30 pm. You must finish your tea by 6 pm and then it's nil by mouth until after your surgery."

"Thank you, I'm all ready and prepared," Fern replied.

"And, Ms. Jones, there's a safe in your closet. Best you remove your earrings and any other jewellery and lock them away before you go to sleep tonight."

Fern glanced at her name badge, "Will do and thank you, Ava."

Fern ate, showered then struggled to sleep. She was excited as she thought about the future. She had dedicated nearly ten years of her life to saving babies but there had been almost no social life, and no friends outside of her team. She would be thirty next month. She had a very healthy bank account but little else to show for her years of devotion.

She thought about her real mother and father, and again wondered who they were and if they ever thought about her all these years, or if they were still alive. Eventually, after tossing and turning, running question after question over in her mind, she dozed off to sleep near midnight.

She was woken early by Ava.

"How did you sleep, Ms. Jones?"

"Not very well, Ava. I am too excited."

"I'm afraid I've got one of those delightful hospital gowns for you to slip into. I'll pop back in a few with one of our porters."

Dr. Parker came by shortly afterwards and marked up Fern's face with a black marker, "All set," he said cheerfully, and she held up a mirror to her face to agree to the changes. As he left, Ava came back with the pre-op meds for Fern to take. "This will relax you and I also need to insert an IV for the anaesthetist." As she felt herself becoming a little drowsy, Ava and a porter wheeled her into the operating theater.

Dr. Jeffries greeted Fern and attached her to the heart monitor and an IV. "How are you doing Fern? I am going to add Sodium Pentothal to your IV now and you are going to relax and go to sleep." A nurse in full scrubs and a mask stepped forward and sanitized her face and that was the last thing she remembered. The anesthesiologist carefully administered the Anectine through the IV tube. He cautiously inserted the endotracheal tube so his patient would be able to breathe safely throughout the surgery.

As Fern drifted off into deep anaesthesia state, she was hooked up to the nitrous oxide.

"Ms. Jones, how are you doing? Ms. Jones?" the charge nurse in the operating theater spoke. Fern moved her head a bit, she blinked and her eyes slowly opened groggily. She felt tired as she regained consciousness. Dr. Jeffries, the anesthesiologist, smiled and Dr. Parker came closer, "I'm very happy, Fern, everything went well. I will see you later."

After spending a short time in recovery, Fern was wheeled back to her private room.

She expected her head and face to look like a mummy but was amazed when she looked into the hand-held mirror the nurse passed her. She had small bandages on her ears, a tiny splint with a dressing over her nose, and something on her cheekbones.

Fern spent the next five days at the clinic. She slept a lot and was put on a liquid diet so as to not disturb the sutures. She had to lie very still with little movement and Ava came in regularly with ice packs to put around her face to help with the swelling. She watched a handful of movies and managed to visit the spa. Fern passed a few polite pleasantries with a couple of other clients recovering from surgery but spent much of her time on her own.

When she checked out, she still had the splint on her nose and some bandaging. There was some swelling and bruising around the eyes from the nose surgery but with makeup she would be able to cover up the small amount of discoloration. It was hardly noticeable.

Ava gave her a new pair of Tom Ford dark glasses as a parting gift from the clinic, and Dr. Parker came to say goodbye.

"I will see you in a week, Fern. We will remove the dressings then and the nose splint. Oh yes, one last thing, please take this card. It is a card of a close friend, a very well-known psychologist. I think you will like him. It can't hurt if you have time to see him while you are still in the States."

Fern took the card, "Thank you, Dr. Parker, see you next week."

Fern walked to the cab that they had ordered for her. In the hotel reception, she saw a trash can and disposed of the business card.

Day by day the swelling improved and the bruises disappeared. Fern followed the doctor's orders lying quietly surrounded by icepacks. She spoke with Megan more frequently and kept up on the gossip and goings on in the retirement community. She made sure she kept her side of the conversation to a minimum to allow her face to heal quicker. She answered one of Oliver's calls, so he wouldn't pester anyone else to track her down. Oliver wanted to know when she would be back, but she let the calls from Mike ring and go to voicemail. Fern knew the moment she spoke to Mike, he would figure out what was going on from her restricted movement of her mouth and lips. With the downtime, she realized she needed another vocation.

Would marriage to Oliver be so bad? No, she was not in love with him and she would not marry without love. For some reason, Mike popped into her head. She wondered about his relationship with Stella and why he had not proposed to her. It seemed Stella would love to be married.

When Dr. Parker removed the splint and dressings his smile was larger than before. He passed a mirror to Fern.

It was incredible. She smiled gently into the mirror and saw the sexy dimples were there. Her lovely nose was lovelier, the ears looked superb, the high cheekbones were well balanced and even, but nothing was excessive. She was amazed with such subtle changes she could look so different.

"Don't worry about the slight swelling around the sides of your nose. Keep using the icepacks and the anti-inflammatory medication, it will soon disappear. In another week or two your metamorphosis will be complete from a lovely butterfly to an even more gorgeous and radiant monarch," he said delighted with his work.

Fern also loved what she saw.

"In ten days, we will schedule your last visit. Come, I'll take you to reception."

As Fern climbed into the back of the cab that the doctor's office had arranged for her, she pulled a note out of her purse which the hotel concierge had given her.

"Where to, ma'am?"

Fern looked at her phone again, "Lavish Locks Hair Salon on Fifth Avenue."

"Do you have a number, where on Fifth is it?"

"Give me a second, mister."

He beat her to it. "Relax, I've got it," he said punching it into his GPS.

Fern took out her tiny lipstick case from her purse and looked again at her image in the tiny mirror. She sat back in the cab. It was now time for the final polish, the final touch she longed for.

The cab dropped her off outside the salon. She stood on the sidewalk for a moment and took a deep breath before opening the heavy glass door and walked in.

"Hi, I'm Fern, and the concierge from my hotel booked me an appointment a few days ago," she said, approaching the young lady sitting behind the receptionist's desk.

"How are you doing, honey?" she replied cheerfully as she looked below at the reservations in her book.

"Ah, I see you have a long appointment today with Georgie, our most popular stylist. Have a seat honey, Georgie will be with you in about ten minutes."

Georgie checked the booking order to confirm her name while Fern sat down.

He smiled as he came near, "Hi, Fern, how are you doing?" he said in a friendly manner. "I'm Georgie. Come this way, please." He extended his arm with an open hand as he gestured to his chair.

"I see you made a reservation for a cut and color today, is that right?"

"I'm looking for a complete change. I want my long blonde hair cut short, shoulder length, and the darkest color you've got."

"A change is always good honey and I think it will be very striking. I only use Matrix -all my celebrity clients love it."

"Good, I'm all yours. How often does it need coloring to maintain?"

"Every four-to-five weeks, the last thing you want is the zebra look with blonde and black stripes, dearie," he giggled.

After he showed her the different sample shades, Fern picked the jet-black and he gave her a magazine to browse through the various hairstyles as he went to prepare her color. He came back and cut several inches off before putting the color on. "You know honey, you have lovely features and I know the perfect cut to highlight your cheek bones. Wow!" he suddenly noticed Fern's unusual eye colors. "One is blue like the Hawaiian ocean and the other is a gorgeous warm fall color, I've ever seen. Wow!" He was genuinely blown away. "You're going to look stunning—trust me?" he winked.

Fern shrugged her shoulders, "What the heck, why not?" She buried herself in the latest *People Magazine*.

After nearly three hours, Fern stared into the mirror. She didn't recognize herself. Georgie had given her a chic modified pixie bob. It was short and feathered around the edges, and her thick blonde head was now jet-black.

"This is the latest New York look which is all the rage. A modern Aubrey Hepburn, very sophisticated."

She looked in the mirror and smiled at herself. She felt lighter and younger and cocked her head from side to side, grinning at her new reflection.

"There's a new lady on the block," Georgie gushed. "Heads are going to turn," he smiled, pleased with his work.

Georgie removed the cape off her gracefully as if lifting a cover off a bust and then, in one quick movement, revealed a new head. Fern stood up gazing into the mirror. She was mesmerized and hypnotized by her eyes. She locked eyes with herself in the mirror like a faultless guided missile.

Georgie the hairdresser gazed at her, the lady upfront stood and stared at Fern to see her reaction. Three other hairdressers turned their heads. For a moment the silence was overpowering.

"Everything in order, Ms. Fern?" Georgie asked. "It usually takes a while to get used to a new look."

"Wow! It looks amazing! Thanks Georgie, nice job!" Fern was genuinely ecstatic with the new cut and color.

She gave Georgie a generous tip and asked the receptionist to order a car.

"Take me to the nearest department store or shopping mall, please."

"Sure, lady." Macy's was within walking distance but the cab driver needed the fare and took advantage of the heavy traffic and at a snail's pace drove to Columbus Circle shopping mall.

Twenty minutes later, the cab finally dropped her off, and she went to the department store guide at the main entrance. There were a couple of opticians listed but Morgenthal Fredericks, a well-established eyewear designer caught her eye.

The optician explained that all new glasses and contact lenses had to be accompanied by a current prescription. It was a law.

Fern immediately called Dr. Parker, but he was with a patient. Fern explained her situation, and asked him to call her back. In the meantime, the optician had a cancellation, and an appointment had opened up at 2 pm if Fern wanted to take it. She took his card and went to find a place to eat. Still no call back from the plastic surgeon. It was nearly 1:30pm1:30 pm, and Fern was getting frustrated; she wanted the brown contacts now.

She tried to call the optician but the line was constantly busy. She put her phone on the table annoyed and it immediately rang with an incoming call.

She did not recognize the woman's voice.

"Who is this please?" Fern asked.

"This is Melissa. I'm calling from Frederic's."

"Oh yes. I was just trying to call you."

"We have received Dr. Parker's email and he gave us all your details. Our optometrist will need to check your eyes first, Ms. Jones. Are you available to come in for an eye exam tomorrow at noon?"

Fern's eyes lit up, happy.

"Ms. Jones, you there?"

"Yes, yes tomorrow is good. I am still here at the mall, Melissa so I'll pop in again in ten minutes to get all the details."

"Great, see you in a bit."

The next day, back in her hotel suite, she gazed in the bathroom mirror. She turned her head to the left and then to the right for a couple of minutes. Then she looked head-on at herself and smiled. Her eyes got a little teary. The new look was even better than she expected. It was a strange but exhilarating feeling.

She glowed with happiness and wanted to cry with joy but she didn't. She had to remain expressionless so she didn't have any setbacks to the healing process for her face.

The days went by and the slight swelling in the nose area disappeared completely.

She contacted Danny in Melbourne,

"Danny, I'm having the passport photos taken tomorrow and I'll send them by express so you'll have them this week."

Fern had the photographs taken wearing her new brown contacts.

Fern took a walk in Central Park. She couldn't spend all this time in New York and not experience the famous Manhattan urban park. As she enjoyed the scenery along with the joggers and cyclists, Fern decided to change hotels. She would book into a new one under her new identity: Mia Williams and relocate as soon as her new passport arrived.

She found a delightful hotel, listed amongst New York's top ten places to stay and called to find out if they had reservations available in the near future.

"Hello, my name is Mia and I am looking for a reservation in about two weeks. I'm looking for something comfortable and large, maybe a family suite of some sort?"

"We are almost full but I do have a large stunning suite available. We will need a credit card to hold it for you. Will it be Visa or Mastercard? We also take American Express?"

"Thank you, let me think about it. I'll call you back once I have can confirm my dates." Fern terminated the call quickly. The last thing she wanted was to make a payment in the name of Fern Jones.

It was now a waiting game until her new passport arrived and Mia Williams would be able to officially debut at the new hotel. She would invite Oliver to visit her and at some stage Megan. Then Mike entered her mind. What was he doing? she wondered.

Danny worked around the clock on Fern's new documents. Occasionally, he took a break from his delicate intricate work to give his eyes a rest. He took a short walk to get some fresh air into his lungs and pondered in deep thought. He was no longer a young man and had several million dollars in the bank. Why carry on doing what he did taking all these risks? Fern had set an example. Perhaps, it was time he did something major as well.

In the small hours of the morning, he finally finished Fern's package. It included a new Australian passport, birth certificate, and driver's license.

He placed the documents in a sealed envelope and called the courier. They would be delivered to Fern's hotel in a couple of days.

In the late afternoon after checking and double checking all was in order, Danny sat down in his swivel chair in this office and poured himself a double scotch. He rocked himself gently with his feet on his desk. He looked at all his equipment, studying each piece as if it were a person remembering the people he had helped and also those he had regretted. He went to his inner office, his Aladdin's cave, the room he had shown Fern. It was part office, part storeroom and now, he reflected, part of his life.

He returned to his chair to swivel some more.

He poured another scotch, and hit a button on his keyboard. It began to erase all the data and he watched the software he had designed some time ago destroy all the information stored and eradicate the history and all the archives. He also initiated the degausser on another machine that played havoc with the magnetic domains on the drivers. It rendered the drivers useless. He calmly and methodically took an electric drill and drilled through the hard drive over and over, penetrating the platter and demolishing it for good.

He called a trusted friend to collect all the damaged equipment and dispose of everything at the waste site, where he worked. He was happy to give him all the state-of-the-art monitors in exchange for taking care of this for him.

Then Danny swallowed the last dram of scotch, pulling a face like a child having to swallow medicine as it disappeared down his throat. There was no going back now.

Chapter Fifty-One

Mike hung up with Stella after saying goodbye and settled into his seat. The flight attendant came by with a cocktail for him to enjoy while the rest of the passengers boarded the Qantas flight to New York. Stella was perplexed by and upset at Mike's sudden decision to fly and just felt it must have something to do with Fern.

Unbeknown to Mike, Fern's package from Danny was on the same flight.

Mike had secured accommodation at a hotel in Midtown Manhattan.

On the flight he carried a shortlist of all the five-star hotels in New York where he thought Fern might be and boutique residential hotels. He had a lot of groundwork to cover.

The flight was long as usual and he was thankful he was in business class. He could sleep for a few hours in comfort and walk around to stretch his legs whenever he was restless.

The Boeing Aircraft landed at JFK early in the morning. Mike took a cab directly to his hotel and he went straight to his room, ordered a sandwich and slept for the rest of the morning.

In the afternoon, refreshed he went for a walk to do a reconnaissance of the immediate area. Several blocks away he found a pawn shop and purchased a used cell phone and inserted an old SIM card that could not be traced directly to him. Mike gave a false name and address to the manager and using his years of experience was able to leave without having to produce any identification.

He grabbed a burger and fries on his walk back to his hotel.

He looked at the numbered list and started to call the hotels for Fern Jones.

No one had any guest by that name. He even spoke to the concierge desks with the guise he was looking for his sister, who had arrived in New York for a wedding from Australia. None of the calls proved fruitful. Most answered that no such person had checked in and a few receptionists confirmed they were not authorized to disclose such information.

Mike decided to try the same tactic he had employed in Bulgaria searching in the Stolipinovo district. He found an Uber driver willing to work exclusively for him for a couple of days or more. Mike sweetened the deal with a generous fee and a fat bonus at the end and the driver was more than delighted to shut off his Uber app. Mike told him he was on vacation and had just found out an old school friend, whom he had not seen in two decades, was also visiting the city and he was trying to locate him. If he knew his buddy, it would be a five-star hotel.

The driver wasn't bothered if the story was true or not, he was just glad to make decent money. He knew his turf and suggested they dedicate days to different areas and Mike agreed with his suggestion.

At the end of each day, the driver dropped Mike back at his hotel and arranged to pick him up the next day and sometimes as early as 6 am some mornings.

The next day they drove and drove, Mike hopping in and out of the hotels. By one o'clock Mike needed a break from the intensity of the search and the humidity of the jammed-packed streets.

"Buddy, let's go and eat a decent lunch. It's on me, of course. I'm sure you are hungry as well."

"You bet, sir," Buddy replied, grateful for a rest.

"Well, I'm in your hands. How does the best steak in town sound like?"

"Know just the place."

"What are we waiting for?" he chuckled.

They drove for thirty more minutes; the traffic was intense until they arrived at The Old Homestead. Mike couldn't believe the size of the portions but heartily tucked into a mouth-watering ribeye steak with sautéed mushrooms and a side of fries. They casually chatted while Mike continued googling hotels.

He also took out his list and checked off every hotel he'd visited and put a ring around the ones that might be worth another visit.

"I don't think this strategy is working. I think the next step is to spend some time hanging out in the hotel lounge and bars and get a better feel for the place. I've circled the six hotels where I think my friend is most likely to stay. If you can drop me off at the first hotel on my list and come back and get me in an hour. I'll be waiting outside."

"This friend must be very important to you."

The first two hotels turned up nothing. Third time lucky never took place. There was also no success at the fourth and fifth hotel.

Mike was aggravated and emotionally drained, it was unlike him to draw a blank on a job. Buddy pulled up to the last hotel on Mike's shortlist. He had called this hotel before and was told staff were not permitted to give out any information pertaining to guests.

The hairs went up on the back of Mike's neck and his sixth sense kicked in. He suddenly had butterflies in his stomach. He felt he was at the end of a long journey. The reception was bright and welcoming with a white marble floor. The lounge area boasted luxurious décor with neutral colors, imposing paintings richly framed. The architecture had her name written all over it.

He texted Buddy and told him to come back in two hours, not one.

Mike asked the young lady at the front desk if Fern Jones was around.

"Why yes, she went out for the day. How can I help you, sir? Do you want to leave a message?"

Mike was sure his heart skipped a beat. He glanced at his watch it was just after 7 pm.

"What time does my sister normally eat?" he smiled.

"Around 7.30 pm sir." Mike had that affable charm that easily lulled women into a false sense of security. "She often listens to the guy playing the piano before dining," she gestured towards the direction of the lounge.

Mike looked at where she pointed.

"Is there anything else, I can help you with, sir?"

"No, my dear, you have been more than helpful."

Mike went through to the lounge, excited. He looked around and saw the grand piano in the far corner from the entrance. He purposely sat to the side of the entrance next to a table that housed a small lamp. There were a few people in the lounge; some were enjoying their cocktails, while others were relaxing reading a magazine or gazing at their cell phones. Confident that no one was paying him any attention, Mike unscrewed the light bulb a bit until it went out. He now waited in the dimly lit shadows.

More people entered the lounge after a long day and ordered their drinks of choice—no sign of Fern Jones.

The lounge began to fill up even more and still no Fern.

A gentleman walked in and sat at the piano after lifting the cover. He flexed his fingers and started playing. The keys generated soft, professional tones and a pretty lady entered the lounge. She was alone but a bit short to be Fern. Mike watched with eagle eyes as he sat taking in the gentle melodic sounds of the piano.

A few more people wandered into the lounge; a young attractive couple, an elderly couple and in the midst was a lovely-looking woman with blonde hair but it wasn't Fern. Mike gazed at the entrance and a striking young lady sauntered in. She wore a peach-colored dress with a lovely elegant figure, long legs, short, jet-black hair. She walked with a slight limp and made her way closer to the piano. Mike's view was compromised with the lounge's capacity filling up and folks blocked his sight line as they gazed in the direction of the piano player. He tried to inconspicuously lean to see if he could get a better angle but the lady sat with her back towards him.

He watched and waited. Then in dribs and drabs people started to make their way towards the dining room. The lady in the peach dress also joined the throng.

Mike continued to survey the woman intensely but she looked nothing like Fern. He scrutinized her gait, which seemed oddly familiar but the slight limping didn't fit. Then as the crowd parted another attractive lady caught his attention.

With his eyes on both women, he quickly texted Buddy his driver to dismiss him for the evening, letting him know he would touch base in the morning.

Mike was mesmerized by both young ladies and followed them into the dining room. Neither resembled Fern. Mike wondered if Fern had gone straight to dinner that evening without listening to the pianist.

The attractive blonde was soon joined by a handsome man wearing business attire. Mike overheard them speaking Spanish. As he waited behind them in line to check in with the maître d', he saw the young lady in the peach dress sitting at a window table overlooking the hotel's garden. She sat alone.

Mike asked to be seated near her and was given a place a couple of tables behind. He looked around and decided Fern was simply not in the restaurant tonight.

He accepted he had struck out and there was no point hanging around any longer. He excused himself and said his plans had changed and left. He sat down in reception and kept an eye on the entrance to the hotel. He had to find her and see her. The helpful receptionist was no longer on duty at the front desk, and Mike breathed a sigh of relief.

Fern didn't have much of an appetite as she was tired. She was eager to get to her room and change the shoes she'd bought earlier in the day. They looked classy but were not comfortable and she'd developed a blister on the small toe of each foot.

She came out of the dining room thirty-five minutes later. Mike was still lingering not sure whether to stay or call it a day. He was looking outside to gauge the traffic and see if it had died down. She did not see him behind the pillar. She walked into reception, limping a little. There were quite a few people around and a tour group had just arrived to check-in.

Fern zigzagged and dodged between them, taking short steps. Mike felt her presence before he saw her. He looked up and saw the young lady in the peach dress. It certainly didn't look like her but his sixth sense told him to continue hanging out and watch. He got up and stood behind a few of the tourists and edged closer.

Fern placed her tan purse on the counter as a young man on duty handed her a small parcel.

Mike went cold when he focused on the purse as he saw that near the buckle there was a small chip in the leather of the Fendi bag. This was the purse that Pinkie the paedophile had damaged as he stormed out of the coffee bar in Melbourne.

Mike Barzel's heart stopped as he gazed at this gorgeous lady. Was this his Fern Jones? He stepped closer and while she was gathering her bag and documents, he saw her eyes from the side; she was wearing contacts.

Mike knew immediately they were there to camouflage her different-colored eyes.

She grabbed her purse and put the strap over her shoulder and picked up the newly arrived documents and turned and walked straight into Mike.

She did not see him as she bumped into him but when she looked up to apologize, she trembled more from surprise than fear. Mike was just inches away.

"Jesus Christ!" were the only words that came out of her mouth as she stood frozen.

A few guests turned and looked at Fern; then they looked away.

"Hello, Fern," he smiled. "Wow you certainly have changed!" he stepped back to admire her new image.

Fern froze. "Shit, shit, shit!" she said going beetroot red in the face. A few people looked at her again and one mumbled some words of disapproval.

They looked at each other, not knowing what to say or do.

The awkward moment was broken when Fern finally said, "Mike, not here, no, no, come, let's talk where its quiet," she said eyeing him warily.

"You're staying here—you know the place so lead the way," he said while laughing a bit from a mixture of anger, surprise and relief.

"The only place is my room upstairs," she answered, still in shock as they walked to the elevator.

She pressed the button to her floor. They stood in uncomfortable silence as other guests joined them. Mike stared at her, taking in the short jet-black hair cut, her brown eyes, and new face that was different but nevertheless stunning. The elevator stopped and someone got out. It stopped again on the next floor and the rest of the occupants exited.

They were alone. "Jesus, Fern, look at you, for fuck's sake, why the hell did you do this? And not tell anyone?"

The elevator stopped and they both walked out, Fern still limping slightly.

"Have you been dancing on thorns? I saw you struggling. Those shoes look new?"

She ignored his comment.

"Come on Mike, you know me better. I swear to God I was going to contact you soon and show you my new look. You just beat me to it."

She opened the door to her suite.

Mike looked around at the interior, "Very nice," he said, nodding his head.

"Drink?" Fern asked kicking off her new shoes in relief.

"Sure, I think I need it for the shock," he teased and went to the mini-bar to help himself.

"So, how do I look?" she asked coquettishly with her arms out turning around for the full effect.

Mike wanted to say something else but refrained. "Fern you look sensational, but you were stunning before," he sat down on the couch with his whisky. "Now, let's have it. What's going on, I'm all ears."

"It is simple really. I need a new me. I want to forget about the baby ditched at the side of the roadside and escape from feeling like garbage. I tried to wipe that whole dirty feeling by saving other babies from feeling like this. I built an entire business on this premise, trying to atone for my mother. I mean how can a mother abandon her own flesh and blood?" Her eyes glazed over with tears.

She sat down on the couch opposite Mike.

"All my life I've never had one fucking friend; I've felt alone as long as I can remember and being brought to that spot where I was left only made it worse. The Stork Center was born out of my desertion and I have lived every second pouring my heart into discarded souls to help them have a better future." Tears were pouring down her face.

"You scared me. I don't want to be chased down by the law and confronted by the authorities. We were doing good in the world. Making the world a better place but you're right, other people won't see it that way. And then, what? What is to become of me?" She was visibly weeping, "Of course, I was going to let you know. Of course, I was going to show you." She sniffed, rubbing her nose.

Mike saw the Kleenex on the half-moon glass side table. He brought it to her and sat down next to her.

She half smiled, "I have a new name now; Mia Williams. Here, I've got nothing to hide. As of today, I've got new identification documents, a new future and a new zest for life."

She blew her nose.

Mike replied, "Yes I know, my dear Fern. I figured it all out and that's why I came. I asked Danny if he knew where you were and he said he had no idea. I knew he was bullshitting. I could have got the info out of him but even I have scruples. I realized he's part of our team and I guessed you'd sworn him to secrecy. But Fern, I'm Mike, your right hand, your business partner; I hope you haven't forgotten that."

Fern fell into Mike's arms, clutching him and hanging onto him as if she were drowning, clinging on to him for dear life. Mike reciprocated and held her tight. He realized what she said was the solemn truth, and his heart ached.

"It's okay Fern, it's okay, my Mia," he said soothingly in a gentle voice, rubbing her back as a parent would do to an infant who was fussing and upset.

"Mike, Mike, thank you for understanding, thank you so much. You mean the world to me, you know."

She repeated how hard it had been to give up the business and how it was like being abandoned all over again. She emptied her heart out to him about the pain of not knowing why her mother had abandoned her, and then she pulled away.

"Well, Mike," she sniffled. "I've talked enough. Have you got anything to say?"

Mike's mind was swirling. He knew who her mother was and he knew he had thrown her gold ring into the sea and was lost forever. He was no different than Chester. He was protecting her in his own way. He was at a loss what to say.

Fern broke the silence. "What are your plans now?"

Their eyes locked. Mike slowly stretched his two strong arms out and gripped her shoulders.

"I've never been to the Caribbean and I'd like to go."

Fern's eyebrows puckered as she screwed up her eyes, completely puzzled by this curve ball. "I've just poured my heart out to you and you're planning a holiday? You're not making sense!"

"Well," he smiled provocatively. "It would not be a holiday or business, for that matter."

"For God's sake, Mike, just talk some sense — not holiday, not business, then what for?"

She nudged away from him on the couch, putting more space between them.

"For a honeymoon, Fern. I never told you but a long time ago I met this lady and I've had had a crush on her ever since, even while dating Stella."

"Eh? I'm confused. Have I met her?"

"No, afraid not, but you do know her well."

He was talking in riddles.

"So, where did you meet her and what does she do? What's her name?"

He grinned. "I met her almost ten years ago in Australia, in the suburb of Toorak. She was my employer and very young. Her name is, or was, Fern Jones."

He looked her straight in the eyes. "Fern, come with me to the Caribbean. Let's go on a honeymoon. I want you to be my wife. I've hated being separated from you these past few weeks not knowing how you were doing. I realize I want to spend the rest of my life with you? Marry me, Fern, marry me, Mia Williams," he implored going down on one knee.

"Oh my God, Mike, do you mean it?" she gasped, her hand covering her mouth with shock and excitement. Her eyes teared up again.

"More than ever, Mia, more than ever," he laughed, growing more confident by the minute. "I know I'm a bit older than you, quite a bit actually, but I am healthy, wealthy — thanks to someone I love — and

I'm strong. I can take care of myself and I would like to look after you forever," he said with a big lump in his throat. He had so much love and gratitude for this young lady who had turned his life upside down.

"But what about you and Stella?"

He smiled, "That sounds like a yes."

She chuckled aloud. "Mike, I've had this secret passion for you since we met, and now we are both in a mess. Poor Oliver. He wants to marry me too, you know."

"He's not good enough for you... How does Mia Barzel sound? "

He finally kissed her. A long, tender, passionate kiss on her lips. He kissed her neck and her cheek and then her forehead. He released her and took her hands. "

"Mia, Oliver will recover. I know him; he'll get his playboy legs back. Stella is more difficult. I realized over the last year that I needed company. I liked her, but I also know I felt sorry for her. I pitied her because of where she came from."

Fern's heart softened and made her want to take care of Mike instead of him taking care of her.

He cleared his throat before he became too choked up to speak. "Leave it to me. It will not be easy, but I will leave her enough money and an apartment somewhere so she has a roof over her head for the rest of her life. Of course, I will take care of her grandmother too."

"What do I tell Oliver?"

"The truth, Mia."

He laughed with joy and Fern joined in. They laughed in unison with happiness.

"We could always disappear. You have a new face and look, maybe I could do the same," he said. "I'm only kidding. The ball is in your court, Mia. My suggestion is we spend a couple of weeks here in America, then we fly home to Australia and face the music and take care of our personal matters. What do you think?"

Fern nodded. It was so good to have Mike back in her corner to take care of plans.

Later, Mike called Stella and told her he would be back towards the end of January. He gave himself enough time to have a chance to see Megan first and pave the way for the shock and surprise of Fern's complete makeover. He also planned to meet with Oliver face-to-face and clear the air with him before dropping the bomb on Stella.

"In the meantime, you should call your mom and let her know you are returning to Melbourne and will see her soon. I believe Danny has sent you a new Australian passport. However, as you left on your Australian one, go back with it. We will arrange with the Australian embassy to send them a new passport or photo, and explain your new look is due to a horrific accident, or a faulty barbeque that ignited a ball of fire into your face here in the States. We will organize a letter from your surgeon."

There was a moment's silence. "So, I am asking you again, Mia, will you marry me?"

"Of course, I will marry you, Mike. I would love to be your wife! The Caribbean sounds heavenly," she said with a strong New York accent, and they both laughed.

It was a scorching hot day when Mike and Mia touched down at Melbourne International Airport, over 105°, on the thermometer on the 25th of January 2019.

They stood together in line for customs. Fern went first through the self-service kiosk desk at the Arrivals concourse. Mike followed. Their passports were stamped without incident.

They took an Uber into the city and booked into a hotel for their first night back. Stella was staying at Mike's place, and the Stork Center had been sold. They needed time to rest and catch their breath before they met with Megan and faced the music with their respective soon to be former partners.

Mia phoned her mother and told her she had arrived back safely and would see her tomorrow.

The next day the weather had cooled, thankfully. After breakfast, they climbed into Mike's car and headed to Brighton. They drove in silence, each preoccupied with their own thoughts.

They drove into the gated retirement community and saw Megan sitting outside under the covered porch of the main building of the complex sipping lemonade with a few of her new friends. Fern ambled down the street to take in the new neighborhood while Mike went to say hello and prepare her mother.

"Hello, Mrs J, nice to see you," he said cheerfully, approaching the group.

The ladies all looked up.

"Mike, what a surprise! You know, my Fern is back too and should be arriving here any second." Mike came over and kissed Megan on the cheek. He was the only person to give her the nickname Mrs J. She liked it. It made her feel special.

Mike grinned, then he glanced at a vacant table under a small glossy, green tree.

"There is something I need to discuss with you in private, Mrs. J. Let's go sit there for a few minutes," he said as he pointed to a shaded area. "Excuse us ladies."

Megan followed him curiously while Mike pulled a garden chair out for her.

"Heavens, you're worrying me. Is my daughter alright?"

"Yes, Mrs. J. She is fine.".

He took a deep breath, "You know Fern took the closure of the center pretty badly, and I must confess our business was not above board."

"Yes, I know," Megan said matter-of-factly, taking Mike by surprise. "I'm not stupid, you know. I've known for a long time — ever since that nice policeman came calling. And it has worried me every day since. I, for one, am happy the business is finished."

Mike started to laugh. As he'd said to Fern, life was full of surprises.

"And, Mike, I know my daughter has done a lot of good too. Why she's probably done more for mankind than most people. She's rescued babies and infants from appalling conditions."

Megan shifted in her chair, "And, on top of that, if that wasn't enough, I know she donated a lot of money to the homeless and abused children's charities. I'm proud of her. I'm proud of all of you. But don't you ever tell a soul about what you did."

Mike smiled and was touched by Megan's intuition. He then grew serious again. "Mrs. J, there is something else that I need to tell you."

"Now what? You're not going to jail, are you?" She covered her chest with one hand as it suddenly occurred to her.

Mike took another deep breath. "Nothing like that, Mrs. J, but I have to say Fern was scared that might happen. No, your gorgeous daughter has taken steps to avoid that possibility. She has had a complete makeover. In fact, she went as far as to have plastic surgery to totally change her look. She used to be gorgeous, and now she is stunning."

Megan was silent. She rubbed the corner of one eye with her finger, "I see, so where is she now, Mike?" she asked a little irritably.

"Oh, she is here, waiting to see you! I'll go and get her now. She's taken a stroll, so I could tell you first, so it isn't too much of a shock. Stay here, Mrs. J. I'll be right back."

Mike smiled happily. It had gone better than he had thought. He found Fern pacing.

"She's tougher than you think. Come."

They held hands as they entered the garden and approached Megan, who was now standing up and looking at them intently.

"Mrs. J, meet your new beautiful daughter."

"Fern? Oh dear," she sighed, "I can't even tell if it's you, although your walk is the same! Fern?"

"Hi, Mom! It's me!"

"Fern, is that really you? It sounds like you," Megan said in shock. Her legs felt wobbly, and she grabbed the back of her chair for support.

"Mom!" Fern ran to her. "Mom, I've missed you. It feels like years. Oh God, Mom, dad is gone, Bonzo is gone, the business is gone. I've lost everything but you. Thank God I still have you."

Megan did not utter a word as Fern fell into her mother's arms. They held onto each other tightly, rocking each other. After a few minutes, Megan was the first to let go and moved back to study Fern's face. Then she hugged her again, overjoyed.

"I know you have always been there for me when my own mother couldn't—you're my true mother."

Even Mike's eyes glistened as mother and daughter were reunited, tears of joy and tenderness trickling down their faces.

When they finally separated, Fern looked at her mother. "Mom, there is something else." But Mike managed to stop her. He knew she was going to tell her mother about her new name.

Mike put up his hand to her. "Mrs J, what Fern was going to tell you," he smiled, "is Fern is changing her last name to Barzel." He let the news sink in. "You see, Fern has agreed to be my wife."

This time Megan took a deep breath in and placed both her hands across her chest. "Wow. The surprises don't stop," she looked like she was going to sob for joy. "This is wonderful news, just wonderful! Mike, I had always hoped one day you would be part of the family. I am so blessed. Congratulations! Come here, both of you."

This time they included Mike in the family hug. "Now I've got you, mom and Mike as well," Fern said with a smile.

"Now it is my turn to share a secret," Megan said as they broke apart. She sat down, and they followed.

"Mike knows. On the day all the furniture was removed from the Stork Center, I told Mike about the safe in Chester's study. I showed it to him because I knew Chester trusted him. My husband was a devil at times, especially ruthless in business. When he died, I found a long letter he left me together with the combination for the safe. It was a love letter of sorts with regrets. I also found the false teeth, which made no sense. None of us had dentures, so I invited Mike to check it out."

Megan looked at Mike and nodded.

Mike smiled. "There had to be something in the teeth. I got a set of pliers and broke one with a light tap and guess what? A real fancy diamond popped out. I broke all the teeth — all 32 of them — and there were 32 genuine diamonds of the finest quality. Chester must have been smuggling them from somewhere to someone, and probably for many millions. The diamonds must be worth close to twenty-million dollars and are in a safety deposit box in Megan's bank."

Fern's jaw dropped.

"And you Fern, you Mike, must decide their fate."

"One day, Mom, nothing urgent."

"I agree, Mrs. J."

The three gathered for a cold lunch on that summer day in January 2019, sitting under the Ash tree. For the first time in thirty years, Megan did not worry about her daughter.

Mike met with Stella and after a lot of careful explaining and many tears, she had no choice. It was painful, and it hurt, but Mike's generosity in taking care of her and her grandmother helped lessen the rejection. At least he was considerate and not cruelly tossing her aside.

Fern met with Oliver on that same day. Mike said it was always better to discuss sensitive issues when it was cooler because tempers flared in hot weather and produced explosive outbursts.

Fern delivered the news as kindly and calmly as possible. Oliver was very quiet receiving the news, but inside he was injured and deeply disappointed. It hurt knowing she had chosen his friend and mentor over him. He also knew deep down that it wasn't the end of the world.

There were plenty of other girls who would fall for his charms, looking for a good time. Besides, he was still the owner of a Learjet.

Dr. Lance Jones, inspired by his work and years at the Stork Center, completed a residency at a local teaching hospital specializing in pediatrics and became one of the oldest pediatrician staff members to practice and the most celebrated pediatrician in Melbourne.

Danny Smyth, *Danny* to the team, disappeared and no one ever saw or heard from him again.

As for Detective Inspector Bruce Nash, he became more confused as he entered his twilight years. He never managed to solve the mystery of the house in the Dandenong Ranges, and no one ever learned about him ending his wife's suffering. Fern and Mike kept their word and his secret remained safe with them.

Eventually, Oliver and Mike made up, and Oliver was the best man at the wedding of Mike and Mia Barzel. It was an intimate wedding and took place on the Yarra River with only family members, a few close friends, and the odd business associate in attendance.

The guest list also included Stella. She had hesitated about accepting the invitation but was glad she went. Oliver made sure she was never alone.

As Mike danced closely with his new wife Mia, he maneuvered them towards Oliver and Stella, who were also on the dance floor. The newlyweds were near enough to overhear Oliver say, "I think we both could do with a break at this point in time, Stella. You see, as luck would have it, a close friend of mine has gone overseas for a couple of weeks, and he has left me his luxury boat. Let's take a comfortable cruise up the coast somewhere for a few days. What do you think?" Then they overheard Stella's response, "Sounds like just what we need, Olli."

Mike and Mia suppressed their laughter as they moved away.

"That's Oliver for you, Fern — I mean Mia. Hugh Hefner could have learned a thing or two from him. He never loved you, Mia. You know, he doesn't have a friend who owns a boat. He never did. It's his boat."

"That sly bastard, son of a bitch. I bet he has used that line a hundred times."

"Times that by ten," Mike grinned.

"Come, Mr. Barzel, let's mingle and thank everyone for being here. Then we must take Mom back home."

"Sure, Mrs. Barzel, my sweet, and then the Caribbean awaits us."

* * * * * * *